I'M NOT COMPLAINING

Other Virago Modern Classics published by The Dial Press

ANTONIA WHITE
Frost in May
The Lost Traveller
The Sugar House
Beyond the Glass
Strangers

RADCLYFFE HALL
The Unlit Lamp

REBECCA WEST
Harriet Hume
The Judge
The Return of the Soldier

F. TENNYSON JESSE
The Lacquer Lady

SARAH GRAND
The Beth Book

BARBARA COMYNS
The Vet's Daughter
Our Spoons Came
  from Woolworths

HENRY HANDEL
  RICHARDSON
The Getting of Wisdom
Maurice Guest

MARY WEBB
Gone to Earth
Precious Bane

EMILY EDEN
The Semi-Attached Couple
  & The Semi-Detached House

MARGARET KENNEDY
The Ladies of Lyndon
Together and Apart

MAY SINCLAIR
Mary Olivier: A Life

ADA LEVERSON
The Little Ottleys

E. ARNOT ROBERTSON
Ordinary Families

ELIZABETH TAYLOR
Mrs. Palfrey at the Claremont
The Sleeping Beauty
In a Summer Season
The Soul of Kindness

ROSE MACAULAY
Told by an Idiot

SHEILA KAYE-SMITH
Joanna Godden

MAUREEN DUFFY
That's How it Was

ELIZABETH JENKINS
The Tortoise and the Hare

Ruth Adam

I'M NOT COMPLAINING

With a new introduction by
Janet Morgan

The Dial Press
DOUBLEDAY AND COMPANY, INC.
GARDEN CITY, NEW YORK
1984

A moderate livelihood we're gaining,
In fact we rule,
A National School,
The duties are dull, but I'm not complaining.

Ruddigore.

Published by The Dial Press

First published in Great Britain by
Chapman & Hall, Ltd. 1938

Copyright © 1938 Ruth Adam

Introduction copyright © Janet Morgan 1983

Manufactured in the United States of America

First printing

Library of Congress Cataloging in Publication Data

Adam, Ruth.
    I'm not complaining.

    (A Virago modern classic)
    I. Title.   II. Series.
PR6001.D275I4   1984   823'.912   83-23978
ISBN 0-385-27961-2 (pbk.)

Introduction

"If the house burns down, save the books first," she called, as I made off with her mother's work done up in a bundle. It was an apt warning; Ruth Adam's books are hard to find now and that family collection is dilapidated and incomplete: *War On Saturday Week*, the first novel, published in 1937 and slightly spotted with damp; *There Needs No Ghost*, the third, which appeared in 1939; *Murder in the Home Guard* (1942); *Set To Partners* (1947); a proof copy of *Susan and the Wrong Baby* and a reprint of *A Stepmother for Susan of St Bride's*, two novels based on a series, first published as a script, in the weekly magazine *Girl*; another novel, *So Sweet a Changeling* (1954), about the extraordinary heroics in which two people are obliged to engage when they adopt a child; four non-fiction works, a history of women's preoccupations, opportunities and diffi-culties in the first seventy-five years of the twentieth century, *A Woman's Place*; a biography of Beatrice Webb, written with her niece Kitty Muggeridge; an account of the glorious but, for Ruth, taxing years when the Adam family and an assortment of friends rented a large and beautiful house in the country; and a short history of America, *They Built a Nation*, which Ruth and her sister wrote for children in 1943, to teach them something of the allies who were about to enter the war; and, last, a tattered book with its cover and penultimate section long gone, which turns out to be

v

Fetch Her Away, a novel about the entanglements into which a well-meaning child care officer is thrust when she finds herself restoring two vivid and forthright children, almost adults but in important ways naive, to their own mother and a man who may, or may not, be her husband and may, or may not, be their father. Missing from this hoard is Ruth Adam's second novel, *I'm Not Complaining*, published in 1938, the family copy having, presumably, been temporarily liberated by Virago.

Obviously a stranger entrusted with this treasure would expect to keep it safely — but not simply because copies of Ruth Adam's books are at the moment few and far between. It is as much because these are the sort of books that, after only a chapter or two, induce in the thoughtful reader a vague feeling of responsibility. It is difficult to understand why this should be so. It may be that we sense that Ruth Adam wrote her books at some cost — even if we are not aware that, in order to give undisturbed attention to her work, she would shut herself away for four hours after dinner, until midnight every evening, that she looked after four enquiring and energetic children, a husband with his own demanding line of work, in which his wife wanted to take an interest, and in the late 1940s and early 50s what would later be called "a commune" in that enormous country house. If we did not know, or had not guessed, at these distractions, Mrs Q. D. Leavis takes care to remind us, in the course of a waspish review in *Scrutiny* of Virginia Woolf's *Three Guineas*, that Mrs Adam, unlike Mrs Woolf, knew what she was talking about when she wrote of the way in which women managed to wrestle with complicated ideas while simultaneously rocking cradles, stirring pots, and so forth.

Ruth Adam herself keeps a running toll of the costs of battle on two fronts at once; her stories are full of rueful descriptions of once lissome women whose bodies have collapsed under the strain of childbearing and housework, of dashing girls forced to abandon a diet of cigarettes and cocktails for one of milk and children's leftovers, of women who on the one hand long to run away — if no further than to a quiet bedroom in the country — and on the other search for the promising but ominous bondage of "the marriage tie". A realist, Ruth Adam made the best of the mixture of security and captivity that her own marriage and family represented; she wrote her books and newspaper articles, kept house in a thorough but erratic fashion, cooked unsuccessful meals and stitched like an inspired angel — fancydress clothes and robes of marvellous theatricality — pushed her children rather too hard, thought and talked. She was practical, and so are her books. They remind us that domestic upheavals are not only as grave as international political and economic crises but also that their causes — human carelessness and awful, inevitable passions — are much the same. She makes the right connections and she is observant, taking her material wherever she can find it: in the outpatients' ward of a hospital, the fishmongers' queue, riots seen on newsreels, a milk bar, a bare and icy playground.

Firmly, but always unhysterically, Ruth Adam's novels ask for respect because they are so immediately convincing — in their characters, setting and argument. She is not glib or artificial: the picture of Bronton in *I'm Not Complaining* reproduces exactly the nature and appearance of a "company town" hit by the Depression, the lower part squalid and seething, the upper suburbs desperately maintaining careful respectability; the inhabitants of Lower Bronton living for the moment, brawling, breeding, drinking, thieving, marching; their counterparts in Upper Bronton scraping for the future, sparing, saving, moralising, fending off uncertainty and debt; the one with fixed beliefs and tenaciously-held codes lying beneath its disorder and dirt and the other with turbulent currents of fear, violence, greed and lust churning below its prim and hopeless surface. And between the two worlds go intermediaries — policemen, school teachers, nurses, minor government officials, clergymen — carefully trained but suddenly doubting the professional certainties with which they have been fortified. They are splendidly confident of their liberation from the prejudices of their class or sex until they realise that their dormant assumptions have plunged them, and their charges, into trouble and complication. They are sure of themselves up to the moment when, because they are introspective and critical, or blessed with a sharp eye or an acute ear, a sense of history or of humour, they recognise that the ideology they have fervently embraced — of freedom of expression in sexual behaviour, dress, literature, religious and political beliefs, of emancipation from current views of what is an appropriate way for women, or workers, or any group in any hierarchy to behave, or, indeed, of the need to sweep away all hierarchies whatsoever — that none of these philosophies provides the complete answer to the problems of survival and helping others to survive and that some of them are daft, and others downright dangerous.

Ruth Adam's novels convince because they do not expound one theory or another. The 1930s, about which she writes in her first half dozen books, were a time of intellectual hesitation as much as confidence; Ruth Adam's books do not have at their centre characters who believe wholeheartedly in pacifism or rearmament and conscription, Communism, Capitalism, Conservatism or Fascism, free love or restraint, but people who are unsure — not morally or intellectually weak but inclined to test theory against experience and practice. She writes about people who are not secure in their place in the society around them: the clergyman's daughters who do not go to the local board school but do not expect to go to university, the nurse whose father is the highly esteemed local doctor but who is herself in hospital terms a lowly apprentice, the teacher, like Madge Brigson in *I'm Not Complaining*, who is neither at home in the rarefied world of lawns, horses and ruffled cotton dresses of Marian in the country, nor the passionate, fevered, almost tawdry life of streets and lovers and pink satin camiknickers, as lived by her friend and colleague Jenny.

Madge, the narrator of this novel, has firm opinions but she is not opinionated. She is attracted and repelled by the violence of the crowd, frightened but intensely interested in the nature of sexual experience, aloof from but at the same time caught up in the lives of the repulsive but horribly fascinating Hunt family, aware of the gaps and inadequacies of her professional training but conscious that it is her most precious buttress, her guarantee against a barren old age and Jenny's insurance against slipping back down the slope into Lower Bronton.

There were, and are, towns like Bronton, and people like the Hunts, and the well-intentioned Mr McCarthy, confused and idealistic Gregory, lovely, natural, slatternly Jenny, the starry-eyed and stupid Freda, fearfully high-minded Judith and her feeble, priggish husband. Ruth Adam knew them; she was the daughter of a Nottingham vicar, whose father was also a clergyman. Her grandmother, whose family were landowners in County Durham, was thought by her relations to have married beneath her. Ruth was born in December 1907. Her parents were unconventional and Ruth and her sisters were close — *War on Saturday Week* gives some of the flavour of Ruth's childhood and *I'm Not Complaining* indicates, in the picture of Gregory, something of Ruth's father's spirit. The descriptions of the towns in these two novels and in *Set To Partners* are derived from the parishes in which Rupert Wearing King and Annie King, Ruth's parents, lived and worked in the North-East in the early 1920s and in which Ruth herself taught in Nottinghamshire in the later 20s and the beginning of the 30s. Like her sisters, she had been sent to Yorkshire to a boarding school, plain and severe, established for the education of clergymen's daughters (there are echoes of it in *Set To Partners*). But, unlike her sisters and to her lasting resentment, Ruth was not sent to college to train as a teacher but began her career with no professional qualifications.

In 1932 she married Kenneth Adam, the star among the schoolboys in Nottingham and the undergraduates at Cambridge (*Set To Partners*, again, describes the dizzy pride, awe and disdain felt by the clergyman's daughter among the apparently self-assured and beautifully dressed young women at a Cambridge ball.) They lived in Manchester, where Kenneth was a journalist on the *Manchester Guardian* and Ruth, who as a twelve-year-old had written essays sufficiently fluent for her father to send them for an opinion to the manager of the local bookshop, produced partly out of loyalty to her father a chatty and instructive family page for the local Church of England newspaper.

In 1935 the Adams moved to London. Kenneth had become Theatre Correspondent for the *Star* and he and Ruth took a flat in Hampstead on Rosslyn Hill. This period, before the war and at the time of the birth of her daughter, Corinna, in 1937, was that which Ruth believed to have been her happiest and most productive. During the war Kenneth, whose poor eyesight excluded him from the Army, did propaganda work for the Air Ministry, while Ruth worked in the Ministry of Information; two more children, Clive and Richard, were born during the war and Nicholas was born in 1947, two years after the family, with various friends and acquaintances, had set up the household at Harpenden described in *A House in the Country*. By this time Kenneth, who had joined the BBC towards the end of the war, had become Controller of the Light Programme (in several of Ruth's novels there is a joke about a "golden-voiced BBC announcer", who, publicly adored, generally turns out to be unreliable in private life) and he ended his BBC career in 1968 as Director of Television.

The Adams had a large and argumentative circle of friends — leftward-leaning, energetic, optimistic people of their own age, who had been in their late thirties and early forties at the end of the war, had watched and in many cases worked for a Labour victory in 1945, had welcomed and often helped to establish the transformation in housing, health and education that makes the accounts of the Hunts' stratagems to steal school milk in *I'm Not Complaining* and the disinfecting of the runaway in *Set To Partners* seem nowadays extraordinarily remote. Those descriptions are some antidote to complaints about the soullessness and corrupting paternalism of the Welfare State, although Ruth Adam, watching and listening, reflected in her later books — *Fetch Her Away*, for example, and the *Susan At St Brides* series — some of the problems that a different set of arrangements, designed to be more benevolent, democratic and efficient, can bring in their wake. As she had taken in what her father and uncle, an Education Officer, had to say about wretched, or incompetent, or ill-educated, or all-too-cunning, humanity in the 30s, so Ruth now paid attention to the information passed on by her contemporaries — Peggy Jay, for instance — who knew about the practical consequences as well as the theoretical aspects of social welfare policy in the 1960s.

Ruth Adam died in March 1977; her eyesight had failed after a minor stroke, diagnosed too late, and her health deteriorated rapidly. She would probably have expressed no surprise at the condition in which we find ourselves, our schools, hospitals and cities, in the 1980s, nor would she have found at all odd or unusual our moral muddleheadedness over the balance between freedom and control, the benefits and dangers of constantly accelerating scientific advance, our confusion about how open or how certain a society we want to be, about how much we wish to leave to private and how much to public intervention, our agonising about the amount of discipline or freedom children need.

Ruth Adam was not sure of herself either, and she was honest about it. Her books are full of people who change their opinions, or people with fixed opinions who cause chaos thereby; of conflicts between two courses of action that both seem just; of the damage the well-intentioned can do to the weak — especially children. Her spinsters wish they were married and, when invited to marry, refuse. Her orphans, reunited with their parents, run away again. Her clergyman founds a Christian social club and allows the red flag to be hoisted above the door. Sensible training and a carefully designed system are no security against the irruption of passion and disaster: all the card indexes and certificates in the hospital archives cannot prevent two mothers getting the wrong babies; traffic lights and teaching a code of care and responsibility cannot prevent children being squashed to pulp. Into each prudently ordered environment — the school, the village, the hospital, the small and snobbish country town — can always come a disruptive force that cannot be predicted or contained: lovely Jenny or jealous

Freda; the ex-actress from London who sets the clergyman's son head-over-ears and the famous air ace who causes havoc in the village; the beautiful, opportunistic Sister who leaves a trail of catastrophe at the hospital and in Susan's private life; Hazel, who runs away when the nursery-governess in the doctor's family insults her own sluttish mother and who, ever after, comes back on summer evenings to haunt the doctor's pretty, prosperous and conventional daughter. It is curious how, in all Ruth Adam's books, everything goes wrong, yet somehow rights itself. Expecting the worst, Ruth Adam always retains her common sense; "If the house burns down, save the books first", is exactly what a daughter of hers would say.

Janet Morgan, Elsfield, Oxon. 1983

CHAPTER I

ONE MONDAY morning a remarkable apparition turned up, with a complaint. She had a man's cloth cap on backwards, a very fancy sprigged smock over an ancient grey skirt and boy's football boots. I met her at the door and asked her what she wanted. She said that she wanted to take me by the hair of my head and drag me down to the canal and put me in it. I said she had better come in and talk it over.

There is no need to conclude from that that I am one of those debonair young people who belong spiritually to the cloak-and-sword era. It was simply that I had heard that kind of thing so often that I was able to translate it immediately into what it signified in polite English, which was, "I am afraid I have a complaint to make."

She stamped in, looking at the posters on the walls, "Beauty Spots of England," with the lively interest of a savage in a strange environment, and I left her standing in the hall while I went to find the Head. On my way I nearly fell over the caretaker, who was on his hands and knees scrubbing the patch where Teddie Hunt had been sick a few minutes before. I noticed that he was laying on the soap very thickly and the water scarcely at all. The soap was paid for by the Government and he had to fetch the water from an outside tap. I remember this so clearly because those two incidents were really responsible for changing

9

several lives. If they had not happened, I suppose we might all still have been in our nice comfortable little rut, as we were then.

I met Miss Harford in the cloakroom, where she was making sure that all the windows were open. She was very keen on fresh air. I said, "A parent to see you, Miss Harford," and went back to my own classroom. Little Miss Thornby, who had been watching the class for me, told me that the woman was the parent of the seven little Hunts, and that she used to do some scrubbing for her sister and had stolen the artistic overall from her.

A few minutes later Miss Harford called me out to ask me whether Georgie Hunt was in school. I said he had gone down to the clinic. This inspired Mrs. Hunt to a tremendous flow of eloquence. She said that education was one thing, though she herself couldn't see the sense of keeping great lads and girls in school, when they might be out at work and would rather be in the factory and bringing home a bit to help their poor parents who slaved for them night and day, but that dragging them down to the clinic and pulling them about and frightening the lives out of them was quite another, and a bloody scandal besides. Miss Harford said that if she was going to use bad language, she was afraid she would have to ask the corner policeman to see her off the premises. Mrs. Hunt replied that it was all very well for some as thought they had the law on their side to be so mealy-mouthed, but that a lot of old maids couldn't be expected to feel the same about children as them who had borne and brought up, not only Georgie, but six others besides, and who should know better what was good for a child but its own mother? And if there wasn't a stop put to this dragging children who had nothing the matter with them down to the clinic and pulling them about something disgraceful, she herself would have the law on someone, policemen or no policemen.

Miss Harford said that if Mrs. Hunt doubted the legality of Georgie's appointment down at the medical clinic, she had better come across to my room and have a look at the printed clinic card, all properly stamped and signed. I thought this was a good idea. Printed papers have a wonderfully convincing effect on parents of Mrs. Hunt's stamp.

As we were crossing the hall, Mrs. Hunt stepped on the patch, now left to dry by the caretaker, in her football boots. Immediately she slipped down, heels over head. The grey skirt flew up, exposing faded pink garters, and she looked exactly like a pantomime dame doing a knockabout act, and yet somehow oddly pathetic. She hurt herself, too. She went quite grey in the face, and sat there groaning and clutching her stomach. We helped her up and took her round the corner into the little staff-room, where we had lunch every day. There was a gas-ring and a fire, provided by the Education Committee. I suggested that I should make Mrs. Hunt a cup of tea since she was so shaken. I knew that her kind drinks tea in every crisis, and the stronger the better. Miss Harford agreed, and said that she would send Miss Thornby to help me to revive the sufferer.

We put Mrs. Hunt, still groaning and hugging her stomach, on to four chairs which stood in a row along the wall. I took down an old jersey coat from a peg and rolled it up into a pillow. Miss Thornby put the kettle on, and I went to borrow some milk from the container that was delivered every morning for those children who could afford it, to drink at playtime.

When I came back, Mrs. Hunt was in full swing again. She was giving character-sketches of us all, in vivid terms and colourful adjectives. I was nothing better than a great lad in skirts, and a soured old maid besides. Miss Harford was a dirty old cat. Miss Thornby, though the best of the bunch, was a little rat without the guts to stand up for herself. As for that Jenny Lambert, with her lipstick and her painted face, and her dresses showing off her behind something disgusting, she was no better than she should be, and not fit to be in charge of innocent children.

I suppose Mrs. Hunt included her own offspring in this description. But even allowing for a mother's natural bias, it could only be regarded as a flat misstatement of fact. How they had managed to become not only familiar with, but expert in, all the main vices to which humanity is prone in their short span of life, was a matter of astonishment even to us, who were in charge of three hundred below the age of eleven, without a trailing cloud of glory among them. I also wondered, as I wrestled with the sealed top of the milk bottle, how Mrs. Hunt had got hold of Miss Lambert's Christian name. Jenny was my best friend on the staff at this time. I liked her, but I appreciated the justice of Mrs. Hunt's description. She did have her dresses made to show off her figure, and she did use powder and lipstick. She always looked very smart and the parents did not like it. Or, at least, the mothers did not. The fathers liked it a bit too much.

"Getting off with honest women's husbands," added

Mrs. Hunt virtuously. "Little dressed-up tart. I know a thing or two about her, too."

Miss Thornby poured out a cup of tea and added sugar and milk. Mrs. Hunt held out her hand for it and took a great gulp which scalded her mouth. She spluttered most of it out and poured the rest into the saucer.

"There's some as might have to get something for a cold in their insides, and no wonder, with money as short as it is, and the Government so skinny with unemployment relief and the magistrates talking about self-control, but when a young lady, so-called, no better than a dirty little tart, goes sneaking down to the chemist's on a Saturday night and her with eight pounds a week from the Government for a soft job if ever there was one, it's a disgrace, that's what it is."

This brought Miss Thornby and me abruptly out of our genteel calm, which is the prescribed attitude for use on foul-mouthed parents and rude little boys who shout after one in the street. "Having a cold in your inside" is a password in the slums. It is used when parents, driven by poverty to commit a crime which merits one of the heaviest penalties in the law, go down to a certain little chemist's shop to buy forbidden goods. Often they end up in hospital, with their object gained at the cost of intense agony and permanent disablement. The hospital authorities in Bronton were as well aware as we were of what went on, but they used to let offenders off with a stern warning, and never informed the police that I know of. They knew, as we knew, that after a long spell of unemployment, a new child seems like the last straw—a thing to be avoided at any price. But the hint about Jenny shook us. We gaped at Mrs. Hunt, and she was pleased with the effect she had achieved and sipped her tea with quite an amiable smile.

Miss Thornby was the first to recover. She breathed fast, and said "Well!" and then changed the subject. She said, "Your Teddie was sick this morning. He must have been eating something that disagreed with him."

Mrs. Hunt affably called Teddie a name which he could not possibly have earned at his age, and held out her cup for more tea. She seemed to be feeling better, and when I said that I would speak to the schools doctor about Georgie when he next came round, and see if he could not be let off visiting the clinic for the time, she said she was ever so obliged to me.

She added that she felt well enough to go home and we sent a little girl for the caretaker, so that he could go along with her in case she felt faint. We were not allowed to go off the school premises during working hours.

Presently there was a shuffling noise in the passage and Cook, the caretaker, put his head in the door.

"Oh, Mr. Cook," said Miss Thornby fussily. Caretakers in elementary schools are always "Mr." to the staff. We do not rank as employing classes. "I'm sorry to bother you, but will you be kind enough to see Mrs. Hunt home?"

He nodded his head gloomily.

"I'm afraid it's interrupting your work," apologised Miss Thornby, who could not bear anyone to be in a bad temper.

"I can't get on with no work this morning," he muttered. "On account of *them*."

"Who's that?" asked Mrs. Hunt, who, having got into a company frame of mind, seemed determined to keep it up. Miss Thornby and I knew. .

"Screaming and shrieking and kicking up a row something awful. A man can't turn his back for a minute but one of them pops up. Scream. It's enough to turn your liver over."

"Go *on*?" said Mrs. Hunt, very much impressed. It was Lower Bronton for "No, you don't say so?"

"I think perhaps you ought to be leaving," put in Miss Thornby. Cook was apt to get long-winded upon the subject of his troubles. He was an excellent workman, clean, honest, punctual and reliable. He was a jewel among caretakers. But he had a firm conviction that he was the victim of persecution by some beings of another world. None of us knew how much he invented, for the sake of effect, and how much of it he really believed himself. When any official came round, or when he went down to the office, he never mentioned them. He was certainly not in the least mad. Miss Thornby said she had an idea that the creatures who screamed at him were female. Something he had once said had given her the idea. But we were all so tired of the subject that we scarcely ever gave it a thought after so many years.

Cook pulled his cloth cap further over the black hole where his right ear should have been and turned to Mrs. Hunt. He was a tall, haggard man, with the bones of his face showing uncomfortably through his parched skin. But he was always tidy, clean and well-shaven. When he and Mrs. Hunt marched out of the school door, she in her sprigged overall and he in his blue overalls and white apron, they looked like part of the chorus of an idealised comedy of life among the lower classes.

Miss Thornby and I looked at each other, and neither of us could think of anything to say. At last I said:

"I wonder where they get the idea from that we get eight pounds a week? I wish we did." Miss Thornby laughed and agreed and we went back to our classes.

I put the children through Arithmetic and Reading and took them out to drill in the yard. That was an ordeal to any new teacher, though we all got used to it after a time. Any mothers who happened to be out shopping, or big brothers who were out of work, or fathers waiting for opening hours, used to stand with their noses pressed to the fence and criticise the class. If we reproved any child whose relatives were present, the relatives always joined in, either improving upon what the teacher had said, and making it a great deal more forceful, or else taking the child's part against us. Either way it was embarrassing. To-day there was only one very ladylike mother, who clicked her teeth whenever I said anything to her little girl, and said, "Mary, *dear*." Mary was soon in tears and I sent her in, and then the mother became noticeably less lady-like.

It was playtime at last. I dismissed the class, greeted Miss Simpson, who came out to take playground duty, and drifted into Miss Lambert's classroom. I thought I had better tell her what Mrs. Hunt had said before she started spreading a lot of wild tales. I did not suspect Jenny of having been engaged in crime. I think, in real life, you do not jump to the worst conclusion about someone you have known for years, rather than assume that there must be a very simple explanation. That is why I keep away from theatres and cinemas. People always do it there, and it is irritating. So I just hung about waiting for Jenny, supposing that there must be a very unimportant reason why she should have come out of the district where she lived and shopped, down to a Lower Bronton chemist's on Saturday night.

Jenny was not in her classroom. The little girl who was class-monitor was giving out books and grumbling at the child who was helping her. She was the most efficient monitor in the school. Jenny used to say that she could not possibly have run the class without her. She was one of those children who know where everything is kept and who keep everything in its place. She tidied Jenny's desk out for her, from time to time, and had an unerring instinct for what Jenny would like kept, and what could be thrown away. When you get a child like that, you can trust it with all your possessions without a moment's uneasiness. Just once or twice, in ten years or so of teaching, you come across them. They are like faithful dogs. I was looking forward to the time when Moira came up into my class.

When she had delivered the forty exercise-books, each one symmetrically in the middle of the desk, Moira asked me politely if I would please mind moving my elbow off Miss Lambert's desk, because she was going to tidy it out. I moved, and watched her idly, as she divided its contents between the side-table and the waste-paper basket. Jenny was terribly untidy. Her desk was a mass of papers and letters and powder-puffs and library books and chalk. Moira took out a circular that had been torn half across and then put back in its wrapper, and hesitated, her hand poised over the basket. Then she put it on the table, ready to go back into the tidied desk.

The picture on it caught my eye. I picked it up. There was a pink drawing of a svelte young woman wheeling a pram, and a question written in white on a pink ground. "Are you afraid that motherhood will spoil your figure?" It was an advertisement for corsets. I looked at the wrapper. It was addressed to "Mrs. Lambert" at the school. I tore it up as small as I could and threw the pieces into the basket. Moira looked distressed. She was still staring after me as I went into the hall and the bell rang for the next lesson.

I could not concentrate at all. I let Georgie Hunt, who had come back from the clinic, have a regular field-day with a packet of cigarette cards under the desk. He effected at least half a dozen swaps, and got the best of them all, I should say, knowing Georgie, before I confiscated them. When midday came I had not decided whether to say anything to Jenny about Mrs. Hunt's aspersions or not. This made a difference. I wondered if Miss Thornby would tell her.

But it was decided for me. As soon as the school was deserted and there were only a few yells from the playground, as the children dawdled home to dinner, Jenny came across to my room. I could see, when she was halfway across the hall, that she was in a terrible rage. She looked pretty, with the flush right across her face. She was rather tall and slim and straight. She was proud of her figure and never wore corsets—rather obviously not. She had a smooth, oval face, usually sunburnt brown, very dark eyes and heavy black hair, which she wore in a roll on her neck. She was extremely good-looking. People used to ask if she was foreign. I don't know why they should always say that if anybody is dark and attractive. However, so far as I know, she was pure English. Now, however, she was almost copper-red with anger, and did look like one of those æsthetic Red Indians you see in pictures. She came across the hall and into my room very smoothly and fast, and like a cat that will not actually run across to its saucer of milk, but does not mean to waste any time. I admired Jenny. I always have. We had been in the same school for three years and agreed about most things.

Jenny said, "May I ask what you mean by spying on me?" I denied it. She replied that Moira had told her that I had torn up one of her printed papers—the one with a lady wearing stays inside—and she hoped that it did not matter. Jenny accused me of going into her room deliberately and searching through her desk to see what I could find. I said it was absurd.

"Then why were you in my room at all?"

"I just wanted to speak to you."

"What about?"

I had not a word to say.

Then Jenny let loose. I was having a bad morning. But Jenny was better at abuse than Mrs. Hunt, through having been better educated. I scarcely ever blush, but when Jenny described me as the kind of emotion-starved old maid who gets her only sex-satisfaction by poking her nose into the details of other women's affairs, I felt myself getting hot. I was only thirty, but Jenny was twenty-four. She had all the men friends she wanted, and I had very few, and those only the husbands of my women friends. So it did sting a little.

But I was determined not to let this business degenerate into one of those Othello-situations, in which a tedious trail of misunderstandings develops just because someone did not have the strength of mind to explain themselves in plain terms at the very beginning. So, since there was no help for it, I told Jenny briefly and without comment, what Mrs. Hunt had said.

She stood quite still, thinking, and then she asked, "Do you think she will spread it?"

"I expect so," I said.

"Then I'll lose my job."

"Don't be melodramatic," I said sharply. "There's all the difference in the world between Mrs. Hunt just spreading one more dirty story about you among her own particular circle of parents, and between somebody creditable reporting a proved scandal to the office, and them taking it up and sacking you. It's not possible."

"But supposing the dirty story could be proved?"

"It never would be."

I spoke firmly, but I was shaken.

"You're shocked!" Jenny said it irritatingly, implying that she was a woman of the world, and I was a sheltered virgin. I would not rise to it.

"I am," I admitted.

Jenny was snubbed. She shrugged her shoulders and went out of the room. I collected up my Composition-books and my case with my lunch in it and went into the staff-room. The others were there already. It was the first week of the autumn term and we all had a great deal to tell each other at lunch-time.

There were five of us on the staff and we had a class each. The school fluctuated at rather less than three hundred children, ranging from five to ten years old. It was the Junior and Infant School of Lower Bronton. The senior school, which the children went on to, was in Higher Bronton. By the time they reached eleven or so the State decreed that their legs were quite strong enough to climb the long hill twice a day. So we were alone among the slums that sprawled around the factories. We nearly all lived—in rooms or little houses—in Higher Bronton's only respectable suburb. It meant a long tram-journey every day, but one had to get out of the squalor at night.

In the little green-painted staff-room three of the five were sitting round the table having their lunch. At the end of the table, eating a watery boiled egg, was Miss Simpson. She had been at the same training college as I had, but two years later. That made her about twenty-eight. She was extremely earnest. She was given to causes. It seemed as if she could not accept the general wickedness and cruelty of the world, but had always to be putting her little bit of weight against its irresistible force. Of course, she never made any real headway. I used to think that was why she was afflicted with a perpetual melancholy. Jenny said that it was because she was repressed, and that she would throw all her societies over if she could only get married. Jenny thought of so many things in terms of sex.

Really, she was not at all bad-looking, unless you saw her next to Jenny's glowing reds and browns. She had rosy cheeks, untidy thick hair and blue-grey eyes. I used to tell Jenny that I did not approve of cosmetics, but nine times out of ten I seemed to come in contact the next minute with Freda Simpson, with her nose like a red cherry outshining her cheeks, and think that there was something to be said for them after all. Miss Thornby, on the other hand, never used them and seemed not to need them. She was small and compact and neat, with brown hair tidily coiled round her ears, and her face wrinkled up with smiling like a little old gnome. She was not so old though—perhaps thirty-five or forty. Miss Jones, who had come new at the beginning of term, I had disliked at sight, and so had we all. She was obviously one of the old school of teachers. To begin with, she called herself a "National School-teacher." None of us ever did that. The expression went out long before our time. It smacked of those dreary tall buildings, whose air is always mysteriously full of floating blackboard-chalk, and of the Gilbert and Sullivan attitude towards them. We called ourselves "Junior-trained" or whatever we happened to be. It was snobbishness, admittedly. But then "National school-teacher" does call up a picture of a shabby spinster with dyed black hair and yellowing cheeks, and an embroidered canvas bag bulging with possessions. Just like Miss Jones, in fact.

She was eating potted-meat sandwiches, and smiling nervously round her. All teachers are eagerly amiable for their first week in a new staff-room. Miss Thornby was carefully taking a cracked pie-dish out of the oven, with the meat-and-potato pie she brought every day from home, and heated up for lunch. It smelt good. Her lunches usually did.

Miss Simpson looked up as I came into the room and then went on with what she was saying. She was describing the tortures of vivisected dogs, with details. I wished she would stop. It was not a good accompaniment to which to eat one's lunch. As I unwrapped my cold beef sandwiches I broke into her description to ask Thornby whether she had brought the holiday snaps she had promised to show me. That stopped her, and we all crowded round while Thornby took them out of her handbag.

She had been to Denmark. There were pictures of herself on the boat, with some other school-teachers, herself on the ramparts at Elsinore, and one taken at Hans Andersen's birthplace which looked familiar. It was a little cobbled street which was used as an illustration to one of his stories in the Infants' Reader. There was Thornby, who had told the story to so many generations of children, transported into it at last. Miss Jones said it was quite romantic.

After we had all commented on Thornby's, I asked Miss Simpson if she had any. But she said she had been away with a college friend and they had not thought it worth while to take any. Freda had been addicted to violent friendships at college, we had gathered, because she always spoke of some woman she still kept on with, in a tone which implied that any friendships she made at Bronton were only a poor imitation of this, the passion of her life. I did not want to hear any more about it, so I produced my own collection of snaps. I had been staying in rooms on the Cornish coast and had made friends with some suburbanites on holiday, whom I had found quite congenial, except for the fact that their children were always on the spot. I seemed to be fated never to get away from children. There we all were, grinning in bathing-suits, facetiously eating large slices of cake at picnics and sitting, untidy-haired, on the shore. They had seemed funny then. Now, with term in its second week, they looked foolish and feeble. I examined them gloomily. I was too tall—as tall as the young husband. My colouring, which was quite brown-haired, brown-eyed and sunburned in the ordinary way, dwindled to un-interesting grey in the photos. My jaw was too heavy. My eyebrows were too thick. My nose was too large. Never—even with a surf-board in the waves—did I look like a girl. I was always a woman—a young woman, perhaps, but a generation away from Jenny. In an access of sudden pessimism I came to the conclu-sion that I looked exactly like a school-marm on holi-day, and put the snaps away in my bag, saying I had some work to do and no time to waste.

Jenny had her lunch in her own room. She told Miss Thornby, who took in her after-dinner cup of tea, that she was marking books and thought she would get more done by herself. I did not see her again till tea-time. We usually went some of the way home together because we lived in the same district. I waited for her, as usual, and she went with me without a word. When we came to her tram-stop she asked if I would go in and have tea with her.

She had just moved into two rooms of a little house above a grocery shop. It was one of those modern hygienic shops, with tiled counters and linoleum on the floor. The rooms were rather seedy, but she had decorated them with pierrot dolls and photographs of Robert Taylor. She went downstairs to ask the land-lady for an extra tea, and I looked at her books. They were all either about teaching, or else romances. I thought it was strange that there were none of those shabby story-books one preserves from one's childhood. My own bookcases had several. All her college-books were carefully arranged in the place of honour. She was a good teacher.

Jenny came in with an extra cup and plate, and we sat down to have tea. There was fried fish with it. Most of us had a high tea when we came in from school, and cocoa and biscuits for supper. We were hungry after our cold lunch.

I was afraid to ask Jenny any questions because she had called me a spying spinster. But Jenny never kept a quarrel up a minute longer than she could help, because it bored her after she had ceased to be angry, and as she handed me my plate she said:

"I'm sorry I was so abusive this morning. But I was worried to death, and wanted someone to vent it on."

"You've got a classful of children. Why did you have to pick on me?"

"Because they couldn't answer back. Besides, it's duty that makes me row them, and this was pleasure."

"Did you want me to reply by pointing out to you the error of your ways?"

"There's no need. I already hate and despise myself for getting into this mess."

This surprised and embarrassed me.

"I don't think you need blame yourself as much as all that," I murmured, for the sake of something to say. Really, I did think so.

Jenny laughed a little.

"I'm not sorry I did it. I'm only sorry I've been caught. You know I haven't any morals, and it would be silly to pretend to you that I have."

"Mrs. Hunt said you weren't fit to be in charge of innocent children."

"I don't suppose I could teach hers anything," she remarked absently.

"They're not very well brought up," I admitted.

"Nor was I," said Jenny. "I went to a council school and lived in a slum. I only got to college because I was top girl in the class and got a scholarship to the secondary school, and a Government loan to train as a teacher. If I hadn't—I should have been what my sister is now. You've never seen her, and you're not likely to, because I keep my family circle separate—but she works in a factory, six days a week, folding cardboard boxes into the same shape, and she drops her "h's" and reads *Peg's Paper* and picks up boys in the street."

"It must run in the family."

Jenny giggled again. It was the sort of remark that amused her.

"On the contrary, my Waterloo was a college professor who taught us English literature three times a week."

"Since my time," I remembered thoughtfully. I had been at the same college, but some years before Jenny, of course.

"It was a woman before. But he married her, and later on he got the job, by some graft. They don't like married women lecturers, though they prefer married men. Peculiar, the way their minds work."

"Oh, your man was married, was he?"

"Oh yes, he was married all right. I was just at the age when I thought married men were misunderstood by their wives, and wanted a fresh young girl's love that gave everything and asked nothing—too boringly high-minded for anything, you know."

"But have you only emerged from this adolescent adoration in the last few months. Because I thought you said——?"

"I mean, that was how I felt about him when it started. We used to sit bang on top of hills and discuss Life."

"One does at college," I remembered.

"Miss Simpson does still. Isn't she a bore? Thank heaven we exhausted the subject in time and got down to action."

"It's a bad moment to give thanks for that now," I could not help reminding her.

"I suppose so," sighed Jenny. "But I'm glad, in a way, that we came down to reality. You know, it's funny. When you're in your teens, you believe in free love and free verse, and you only practise the verse part. The conversations we used to have, out in the wind on the heath, brother, proving that we had a divine right to sleep with each other if we wanted to, and that it was only the blindness and wickedness and general mal-organisation of society—with a large 'S' that prevented us, and that one day everyone would be sleeping with everyone in quite the purest intellectual way—you wouldn't believe the bosh we talked!"

"Yes, I would. I don't know any subject on which people get sillier."

"Well, then, after I left college I could only see him occasionally and I grew out of the Great Clean Free Love business. It was then that I began to go away for week-ends with him, without benefit of D. H. Lawrence or anyone else. Just ordinary vice, signing a false name in the visitors' book and everything else that goes with it. No justification except that we wanted to."

I thought this was honest. It was one of the things that I liked best about Jenny—that she did not make up a hypocritical reason for the things she wanted to do. She was sensual and immoral and a law unto herself. But she was clear-minded. I think that was what made her a good teacher.

"So now you've slipped up," I mused.

"Certainly I have. And I'm rather alarmed."

"Then Mrs. Hunt really did see you in the chemist's, buying the same kind of goods as she was herself?"

"The chemist wouldn't let her have it," remarked Jenny abstractedly.

"Why—if he'd let you?"

"She wanted the stuff on tick."

"Jenny—what on earth made you think of such an idiotic scheme?"

"I'll tell you. On Friday I stayed late at school, pinning up some new history charts. And I came home just as the factories were coming out. Oh—those girls! Greasy hair—blackheads and boils all over their faces —screaming silly jokes at each other—and at those awful louts of youths at the other gate—all going home to a stinking kitchen with liver-and-chips perpetually sizzling over the fire. You can't see it so vividly as I can, because it's what I came from. I know it all so well, and I got myself out of it. When I came home to these rooms—the books, the privacy, someone to wait on me—it looked like heaven. You can't picture what it means to graduate up to this by your own efforts. And I realised that this—this sickening business of an illegitimate baby—would mean just one thing—that I should have to go back to what I came from, and never get out again. I was absolutely desperate. I began to think that I *would* find a way out of it, whatever happened. And I thought of what Thornby had told me once, about that chemist's in Lower Bronton, where you could get a drug that would do the trick, and I thought I'd risk it."

"It was absolutely crazy," I cried. "It was criminal."

"Oh, it was criminal all right. Seven years you can get for it, can't you? But the other thing meant a lifetime—back in my own environment. So on Saturday night, when I knew there would be crowds anyway— they all do their shopping then—and I was sure no one would notice me, I borrowed an old mackintosh from the landlady's daughter, and I bought an old hat from a second-hand stall in the Back Street. I expect it had nits in it. My head felt scratchy all the way, I can tell you, and I didn't half have a shampoo and a bath when I got home. But I pulled it right down over my eyes, and I looked just like all the other sluts of women with their Saturday night chips in a newspaper bag, and walked down all the way to Lower Bronton. I avoided children. I thought they might recognise me. And I went into the chemist's and kept my chin in the collar of the mackintosh so that he wouldn't know me again —though I knew that if he let me have it I could blackmail him as well as him me—and muttered, in my sister's best accent, that I had a friend who had a cold in her inside and had asked me to slip round and get something for it. He looked at me very hard, but he went away to the back of the shop and it seemed ages before he brought the parcel—it cost two shillings— and just as I was going out I bumped into Mrs. Hunt in the doorway. I couldn't remember who she was. But I waited outside just for a moment, because there were some children nearby. And I heard her ask—just what I'd asked—but she hadn't got the two shillings. Then I came home and disinfected myself. I thought I'd better wait till I had a clear week-end to take it, to give myself time to recover by Monday morning."

"Can I have a look at the stuff, Jenny?"

"Whatever for?"

"Just a sex-starved spinster's morbid curiosity. No, really, I know a bit about chemistry—I took it—and I think I could tell you what's in it—if it's any of the more obvious drugs. Then I could tell you whether it would be safe to take it or not."

"Where did you take chemistry?" asked Jenny suspiciously.

"At college. I had an idea about going in for secondary-school teaching."

"I didn't know one could take chemistry at college."

"Oh yes. We were allowed to go to lectures at the town university."

"But how can you tell?"

"I can tell one or two really unpleasant drugs by the smell."

Jenny went into the bedroom and rustled among tissue-papers in the dressing-table drawer. She came back with a little unlabelled medicine bottle. It had some brown liquid in it. I took it over to the window, holding it up to the light, uncorked it, and as quickly as I could poured it away, down the sloping roof below, until it trickled into the gutter at the bottom. Then I threw the bottle into the fireplace, and looked a little foolishly at Jenny. I felt as if I had been behaving dramatically. Jenny stood looking at me.

"Thank you for saving me from myself, Madge," she

said, in the low voice in which she usually began to work up to a temper. "And thank you for flinging away the result of a few hours of the most difficult and dangerous thing I ever did. And thank you for your moral attitude, which insists upon an unwanted bastard dragging me into the slums again, but doesn't prevent you from abusing my confidence, prying into my affairs, and playing a mean trick on me that is so cheap and obvious that I never thought you could descend to it."

"Sh. The landlady will hear you," I said. Her voice was getting shriller and louder.

"Oh, you're so damned ladylike. You're such good form. You've got the law on your side, and everything except common decency not to betray a friend's trust in you. Just because I'm down, you—you—— Get out of here!"

"Listen, Jenny," I said.

"Get out!" she shouted.

There was a knock at the door. The landlady came in, looking startled and horrified. I pulled myself together.

"Just like that," I said hurriedly. "She was so angry that her little boy had not been given a prize, and she kept on shouting and screaming 'Get out,' and the police came in finally and told her to be quiet."

The landlady stood staring from one to the other.

"Did we startle you?" I asked unconvincingly. "I was telling Jenny about a drunken wretch of a mother who attacked me in the street last week. We do get some funny parents, you know, in our job."

The landlady made a melancholy noise of agreement,

31

and began to clear the table. I went on enlarging upon the story to Jenny until she went out and shut the door after her. There was a silence while we heard her clumping downstairs. Then I looked at Jenny, and found her laughing.

"Do you really believe that convinced her?" she asked.

"No, but it prevented her from taking a part in the scene. It was quite difficult enough as it was. But, Jenny, just before I go, do let me tell you--the reason I did—that—was only because I know one of the nurses at the Bronton General—and she had a patient who had taken some of that stuff—and it took her three weeks to die, though she wanted to after the first three days—honestly—I'll introduce you to the nurse if you don't believe me."

"Oh, I believe you," said Jenny listlessly.

We sat there without a word. Jenny was looking out of the window. Her face was smooth and expressionless as a statue's. I had noticed before that it had remarkably few lines of any kind on it. It was only when she was animated that it lit up, and then I think it was mostly the colour one noticed. I sat still and stared at Jenny.

The autumn sun was shining in Jenny's clean window. The street outside was Bronton's only respectable shopping street. It had wide pavements, with trees planted on the edge, and the traffic that went up and down consisted mostly of bright-painted tradesmen's vans. I pictured her as the bright little girl she must have been at school, ragged, cheeky, probably with an eye for the man who sold ices at the school gate, even then. I thought of her curious progress, via scholar-

ships and Government grants—climbing up out of it
all into that rarefied atmosphere of Higher Education,
where all the values she had been brought up on
became mysteriously transformed, as though her back-
street home were seen under the deceptive glow of
artificial lighting. She had learned (I reflected) that
loose living was not an affair of holes and corners—
and finally of illegitimate children tumbling about the
doorstep where the young mother had tumbled about
not so long before—but of poetry and hilltops, and
being a modern girl. And I could not help wondering
whether this misfortune of Jenny's was not simply that
the wheel had come full circle. She had had her first
meeting with any kind of idealism when she went to
college, and found young men and maidens just shaking
off the trammels of a respectable middle-class home.
And that very idealism had dragged her back where she
belonged.

I cannot help being a bit pharisaical. I was brought
up so puritanically and it seems to have stuck to me.
Besides, I never had the chance to test these things—
like Jenny. Men did not fall in love with me. But I
came to myself with a jerk at this point, and was glad
that Jenny could not read my thoughts.

"Have you told him?" I asked her.

"Who? What?"

"Your professor."

"Certainly not."

"But why, Jenny?"

"Oh, I don't know. I can't go moaning and begging
him for help."

"That's a pose," I said firmly. "You've been reading
Tess of the D'Urbervilles. And look where it landed

33

her. On Salisbury Plain with the entire flying squad to take her down to the jail-house."

"Did it?" said Jenny, interested.

"For heaven's sake—didn't your professor teach you any literature?"

"Mostly D. H. Lawrence and people like that."

"Well, you must tell him. He may have any number of helpful suggestions to make. He may have left his wife by now and be willing to marry you."

"You are a little ray of sunshine, aren't you?"

"Well, will you tell him?"

"I might."

I had to be satisfied with that.

"And have you got any high-handed scheme for crushing the scandal as well?" she added, as I prepared to go.

I stopped short. I had forgotten that.

"I think Mrs. Hunt won't do any great damage," I said, trying to be comforting. "After all, you can do a bit of reciprocal blackmail, if she does."

"Mm. Very helpful. And what about the mysterious circular?"

"Where did it come from?"

"That corset-shop in High Bronton."

"You don't know why?"

"Obviously someone's written to them in my name and asked for it. They daren't send those out unless they're specially requested. I don't see Mrs. Hunt doing that. She's not the kind who goes in for corsetry. Besides, now I think of it, that must have come on Saturday, before Mrs. Hunt saw me, because I found it this morning before the ordinary post came."

"Who else knows about the fix you're in?"

"Not a soul, besides you and Mrs. Hunt."

"And Miss Thornby," I reminded her.

"She didn't know till this morning."

"Oh, heavens," I said despairingly. "This is like one of those awful mystery novels. I expect it will turn out that you sent it to yourself in the end."

Jenny laughed at that. She seemed to have thrown off her depression and was herself again. She came down to the door with me. She did not say a word of thanks. She and I hated sentimentality and never spoke to each other about our friendship.

I lay awake for a long time that night, but not planning for Jenny. Instead, I thought about myself, from my well-disciplined childhood as the daughter of the village schoolmaster, through the bewildering, over-enthusiastic friendships of college, through the ten years' teaching which had left me with a third share in a little bungalow in the suburbs, a hundred pounds in the bank, and an expert knowledge of how to teach Mental Arithmetic—nothing more. I was sorry for Jenny, and frightened for her, and terribly jealous of her. Hardworking, contented women like me get this longing, from time to time, for all the experiences that have passed us by. We do not go mad over it, as women do in psychological books, nor even get a little bit queer. It goes off after a few days and we are ourselves again.

CHAPTER II

Two days later Jenny came rushing into the staff-room at five to nine—five minutes late for the time we were supposed to arrive—flung her cap on the table and her coat on a chair, picked up a letter that was waiting for her, glanced through it, muttered, "Oh, my God," tossed it over to me, and ran out into the hall to play the march to which the children came in to prayers.

As *Men of Harlech* began and the whistle in the playground blew, I picked up the letter and went leisurely into the cloakroom. My duty this week was only to see that the children used their own pegs and did not jostle each other on the way in. With half an eye on them, I read Jenny's letter. It said, "Jenny Lambert, I know about your goings-on and soon you will be pushed out where you ought to be as your goings-on are known to me and feel it my duty to inform those you are deceiving and you ought to be ashamed of yourself." It was written in the script we teach the children before they learn copperplate. The notepaper was the kind you buy, complete with envelopes that it does not fit, in any cheap stationer's for a penny a packet. I looked at the post office and knew then that it must have been posted at Bronton General Post Office, because it was the only place where they had a midnight collection.

I roused myself to find the last-comer—a Hunt, of course—rushing in to catch the tail of the lines, and followed him into the hall. Miss Lambert finished up

36

her tune with the line of rising chords that was all that remained of the battle-cry that had once inspired a nation to incredible deeds of heroism, and there was comparative silence. Coughing and sniffing and shuffling of feet filled it for a few seconds, while Miss Harford mounted the raised platform and looked sternly round. She believed that most coughs and all sniffs could be controlled by the child with a full sense of responsibility towards the school and towards its fellow-scholars. In deference to her views, these sounds dwindled down to a minimum. She gave out the psalm, declaiming the first line for the benefit of such of the infant choir whose knowledge of the poetry of the ancient Hebrews was not all that it should be, and Miss Lambert played over the chant. Three hundred or so slightly hoarse voices took it up.

"Lord, who shall dwell in thy tabernacle, and who shall rest upon thy holy hill?"

Thin, fragile, yet extraordinarily sure were their voices, like their lanky bodies and their limited minds. Eyes fixed unwinkingly on the swaying baton of the headmistress, throats stretched upwards like birds waiting for food, they outlined the character of the perfect man—that the State pays out three and a half millions yearly in the hope that we shall succeed in reproducing.

Miss Harford rapped sharply on the desk.

"This will not do. You are not using your lungs. This is lazy singing. Those big boys at the back are not breathing properly. God gave you voices to sing His praises. He isn't pleased with lazy singing. Now we'll have the girls first, only the girls, and then the

37

boys alone. We shall see then where the lazy singers are."

Jenny struck a chord and the girls raised their voices, with that uncertain feminine quality manifested only in their singing, underlying the shrillness. But when it came to the boys' turn I could not help looking from face to face of the other teachers to see if I could find reflected there the faint discomfort the sound always aroused in me. There was something in that eager burst of hard, shrill trebles that gave me shivers down my spine. Jenny was looking down at her brown hands, with their painted nails, moving steadily over the notes. Freda Simpson stood leaning against the radiator, her hands in her old college blazer pockets, frowning at the floor. Miss Thornby was suspiciously watching the youngest Hunt, who was giving an unconvincing imitation of a chanting cherub. Old Miss Jones was smiling sentimentally. I could not tell whether they disliked and loved the sound, and were wholly relieved when it ceased, as I was.

"Better," announced the headmistress, as the boys, having finally announced that a man who kept these few simple rules would never come to a bad end, closed their mouths and looked up hopefully for approval.

Jenny rose to her feet with a little sigh as the prayer began. I felt her letter crackle in my pocket, and stared meditatively at Stanley, the eldest of the Hunts at school, trying to remember whether his script was anything like the letter.

"Well?" murmured Jenny, as I passed her by following my marching class into their room.

"Police," I said briefly, as the column separated us, and I handed back the letter to her over their heads.

I enlarged upon it at the eleven o'clock break.

"It's the obvious and sensible thing to do. You don't want to be like the nitwits in those cases in the papers who get into the clutches of blackmailers through not having gone to the police at once."

"Do you think I'm going to give the whole history of my first love to some oaf of a sergeant?"

"There's no need," I said impatiently. "All you've got to do is to show them the letter and say nothing about the circular. The letter might mean anything— any of your flirtations—and the police will just trace the writer—perhaps—and frighten him—her—into silence. They're absolutely bound not to spread anything they got to know. If you don't you may find yourself the victim of a persecution, like—well, like Cook."

I was rather pleased with myself. I thought I was managing this delicate business rather well, and it was very interesting. To my surprise, Jenny meekly agreed. It was unlike her to be so yielding and dependent. But I think, after the nervous strain of keeping it all to herself for so long, she was relieved to have me take charge of the situation.

So at dinner-time we put on our hats and coats and went along to the local police station. A bald-headed sergeant was in charge, and a handsome young constable stared silently at Jenny all through the interview. He looked at the letter piercingly, as if he expected to discover something sinister about it, and asked us if it might not be a joke on the part of one of the children. We explained that we thought they were too young to have arranged it all—even to posting it at the General —without the help of some grown-up person. Finally, after looking very thoughtful, he asked if Jenny suspected anyone, and I told him that Mrs. Hunt had hinted at some grudge she had against her when she came up to school.

He said he would see what could be done, and told Jenny affably that she was not to worry. We went back to eat a hurried lunch in the remaining fifteen minutes of the dinner-hour.

It was one morning at the end of the same week that we found a clergyman standing by Miss Harford's desk, talking to her, when we came into the Hall for prayers. We knew what that meant—a Scripture inspection. My heart sank. Usually I was very conscientious about using the Scripture period for its proper purpose. But just lately I had been trying to get the multiplication tables up to standard for an examination Miss Harford was threatening to give, and I had neglected the stormy history of the Jews in their favour. I looked the man over to see if he was the tiresome kind who insist on seeing the formality of a Scripture inspection through to the bitter end. I did not much like the look of him. He was of medium height, rather slightly built, but with a square head, like a typical bulldog Englishman. He looked what Jenny called "dumb." I guessed that he ran boys' clubs in the parish and gave sporting sermons. Miss Thornby told me in a whisper, as she marshalled the babies into their lines, that he was the new local curate, and that he was supposed to be peculiar.

When he took prayers—Miss Harford always resigned her post of honour if there was a man present—I was pleasantly surprised by his voice. It was strong and light and expressive. He read the prayers rather rapidly, and did not look benevolently at the children, which is an irritating habit that most visiting parsons have. But I saw him look at Jenny and wondered if she would make another conquest.

Afterwards, I hurriedly got the Bibles out and turned to the Sermon on the Mount. I had got fairly good at gauging Scripture inspectors. The old-fashioned ones concentrated on the Ten Commandments and the modern ones on that. And I was right. It was the first thing he asked about. After I had picked the best ones to recite the Beatitudes, he told them to write out what they thought they meant, in their own words, and came over to my desk.

"I wanted to speak to you," he said. He had a perpetual air of being in a hurry. "You reported the Hunt family to the police."

"Yes. Why?" I asked.

"They were very frightened about it. I think you were rather unjust."

I thought this was impudence.

"I'm afraid you don't know the facts of the case," I said frigidly.

"But I do. I know all about it. And I verified what I knew with Miss Lambert just now. She got an anonymous letter and on the strength of some chance remark of Mrs. Hunt's, mentioned her to the police. That settled the case as far as they were concerned. Without proof or law or justice on their side, they went round to the house and put the whole family in gibbering terror for something that was not their fault. I have taken a sample of the handwriting of every member of the family who can write, and compared it with the note, and there is no resemblance whatever."

41

"They wouldn't be likely to write in their usual handwriting."

"It takes a much cleverer forger than any of the Hunt family to alter their handwriting so that it is unrecognisable."

"Did you come up just to tell us this?" I asked impertinently. When anyone tries to browbeat me who is better educated than I am, I cannot help returning to the impudent schoolgirl I used to be.

"I did," he said, and laughed. He had rather a nice laugh—natural, and not too hearty. Then he asked me to send on the papers when the children had finished, and went on to the next class.

At dinner-time we all discussed him. Miss Thornby thought he was nice. She said that her sister had heard he was a good preacher. Miss Jones said he was a well-spoken young man. Miss Simpson said she hated all clergymen. They were the symbol of all the hypocrisy and corruption and cruelty of the man-made world. "Look at the priests in Spain," she added. I looked at Jenny instead, to see what she thought, and Jenny remarked shortly that she thought he was a tiresome busybody. I could tell she was seething with fury and could guess why. Miss Harford was going about looking like a thunder-cloud and Miss Thornby told me privately that the curate had told her that the children were no better than little heathens. I laughed at that. "He's the first Scripture inspector I ever knew who had the courage to state the fact," I said. Miss Thornby looked rather shocked and said, "Oh, Madge, you shouldn't talk like that." It was unusual for her to criticise any of us. We were all at loggerheads that day because the Scripture had been inspected. It

42

seemed silly, because the Scripture is the one inspection that does not matter at all from the point of view of one's career. It is the merest matter of form. If your Arithmetic is not up to standard, if your Composition is bad, even if your physical training is not all it should be, a very black mark goes down against you, and will be referred to when a question of promotion comes up. But if you care to teach the children that Jesus Christ lived in the Ark with Noah, the only thing that will happen to you is that some old parson, without any power at the Office at all, will gently remonstrate with you, and the next inspection will be by a member of some religious sect who probably believes something equally odd about Bible history himself.

So I did not worry. For one thing, I had too much work to do. I had decided that I ought to be saving a little more money each year. In thirty years I should be retired, on one-third pay, and I had seen so many teachers living out a bored and dismal old age, restricted by poverty, that I had determined to think of it early, and save so much every year, so that with freedom I might also have a little fun. Therefore I had applied, during the summer, for some work in the evening classes that were held each night after the factories had come out and the children had gone home, on the school premises.

I had been given a class of girls, who, I was told, ranged from fourteen to eighteen and might turn out "a little difficult." That phrase had struck on my ear with an ominous significance. It was seldom that the Education Office admitted the existence of human fallibility. The fact was, the lame old organiser had explained to me, as she sat in her little room in the

Town Hall buildings, and looked at me searchingly over her spectacles, that the local authorities had decided that no good would come of the unemployed girls—thrown out of work by the failure of two of the big factories—running wild in the streets. I could have told her just what would and had already come of it, but it was nothing to do with me, and we looked at each other silently, two virtuous virgins dedicated to the reclamation of those who were no longer either. So the Committee had decided to run a night-school class three evenings a week with the object of salvaging the girls' self-respect.

"But do you think they'll come?" I felt compelled to ask. It meant a good deal to me. The great difficulty of night-school teaching is that you are judged by your attendance figures. If they fall, you are told that you are not keeping the interest of your pupils. So you have to steer a dangerous course between indulgence and discipline. "If their attendance figures do not reach a certain percentage, the defaulters will be deprived of their unemployment relief," she said blandly.

When I had time to think this over, I began to realise that I had been let off one difficulty to be plunged into worse ones. I could very well picture the attitude of girls earning their money by coming to a class against their will. I was more than a little frightened as the first day of the night-school approached. Girls in their teens are a very different proposition from children under eleven. I prepared myself for the battle by getting an exhaustive syllabus of work ready.

The day of the Scripture inspection I stayed on at school to copy out my plan of work. Night-school was due to start next week. It seemed odd to be settling down to the winter's work while the weather was still so hot that in the asphalt playground one seemed to be suspended between burning floor and burning sky.

The rest of the staff went home one by one. The school gradually sank into quiet. Presently, even the playground was deserted. I sat at my desk with the papers in front of me. The silence was odd after all that noise. It was an oppressive day. Down in that valley, at the foot of the town, I felt as if the very air I breathed was the same air that all the swarming, sweating inhabitants had been using all summer, and that it was stale from a thousand stinking breaths. I looked up to find a dark yellow pall hanging over the sky. I hoped that it would thunder. I listened to the silence. It was almost frightening. I seemed to be alone in a strange world.

There was a slight scuffling sound in the hall. My heart stood still. It was silly to be nervous, but it was an ominous evening. I could not get up and go to the door. A pattering came across the hall, and then my door seemed to open of itself. Moira came in. She was too small to show above the glass panel, and I should have guessed that it was a child. I suppose I must have looked startled, for I saw it reflected in her face. She was an attractive child in a small, meek-looking way. But the meekness was only apparent, so Jenny said. She had straight fair hair, always tidy, light blue eyes, and faintly pink cheeks. She used to wear neat little cotton frocks with knickers to match. She was one of our very few respectable children. Her father was a warder in the local jail. She always spoke in a high, respectful voice, and had never been known to be impertinent.

"Please, Miss," she began, and then stopped.

"What is it?"

"Miss, I'm sorry I told of you about those stays."

"Moira, what are you talking about? And what are you doing here, anyway?"

"Miss, I've stayed to tidy out the cupboards and I've just finished. And it was that picture of ladies' stays and Miss Lambert was cross with me about it, and I told Mummie and she said gossiping was the same as telling tales and I was to say I was sorry."

She was on the verge of tears. I felt angry with Jenny. She was brutal when she was in a rage. Although one loses all sentimentality about children, seeing them day in and day out in such quantities, Moira was a nice child and I did not like to see her unhappy. So I told her it did not matter, and that she was to forget about it. Then, seeing she still looked disconsolate, I asked her if she would like to do something for me. She brightened up immediately. She was a real Martha.

"Moira, I've got to work late, and I'm so thirsty. Can you make me a cup of tea?"

She ran off joyfully. She knew how to light the gas-ring, and just where everything was kept. In a few minutes she brought me in a tray, complete with biscuits out of Miss Thornby's private tin. She had put a sheet of white paper on the tray, by way of traycloth. I sipped the tea gratefully, and told her that she had better go home or her mother would be worrying. I heard her go skipping across the hall, and then there was silence again.

46

It was not the first time I had been alone in a deserted school, but it was the first time I had felt as if there was some evil hanging over it. I tried to work. I told myself not to be nervy and foolish, but the sense persisted. Twice I got up and walked to the window. The sill was warm with the sunlight that had disappeared behind the dull yellowish cloud. The town was perfectly still. In the distance, the smoke of the large factory that was still working hung motionless in the air. There was not a footstep in the street.

The school stood a little way away from the rest of the houses. It had been built during a boom period, after the war, and was one of the standard buildings, with classrooms opening off a central hall and playgrounds all round. My room was on a corner, looking out on to the boys' playground, and with windows all along two walls, so that I could look two ways—up the long hill to High Bronton, or over a space of waste ground, with ashes and old tins, to the new road they were building beyond. This road had been designed so that the traffic from the south, which reached Lower Bronton first, could by-pass its narrow streets and slums, and join the main road just past the school. When it was finished, Furlong Street, on which the school stood, would have one end on the by-pass and one on the road where the trams ran, and which the by-pass would join a few hundred yards further up. We were in a triangle of roads. I looked out at the half-finished by-pass and found that the men had packed up their tools and gone home for the night. They were not local men, but a gang that the contractor had brought with him. There had been some ill-feeling about that in the district.

I turned away, and leaned out of the window that looked up to the town. I tried to distinguish my own street among the rows of blue roofs, wondering idly if there would be more air up there. Down here we seemed to be in a dying community. The factory wheels were stilled, the men lifeless with long unemployment. Their houses were never repaired. Nothing new was ever built. And now the traffic was to be diverted away from us, as if to cut us off finally from the world where life still moved and increased. High Bronton looked upon us as a poor relation to be kept out of sight. In our festering stillness we were no more than a slag-heap below the town. I began to think that I would apply for a job in another school.

I thought of going into the playground for a breath of air. I wish I had. But I had too much to do, and I went back to my desk.

There was a scream. The sweat broke out under my armpits and spread all over my face and body. I could not have moved. It came again, high, piercing, ending in a moaning wail. Then there were two or three, so that I sprang to my feet, urged by that instinct, stronger than fear, to answer a cry for help. It was a child's voice, but an unchildish scream. It sounded as if someone was being hurt as they had never imagined a human frame could be. I ran into the hall, trying to think which direction it had come from.

Then I heard running footsteps—light footsteps—and knew, with a rush of relief, that it had not been murder. I ran to the window. Someone was fleeing in terror across the girls' yard. I caught a glimpse of a pink frock disappearing through the gate. I turned from the window to run to the cloakroom door, caught my foot on the edge of Miss Harford's raised platform and fell heavily on the floor. As I lay there, shocked and bruised, I heard someone else running—a man this time—and shouting savagely, "Come back, you little bastard! I want you, I tell you, I want you."

I picked myself up and hurried to the cloakroom door. The playground was empty. I went to the gate. There was no one in the street. Down at the corner, outside the shop where we bought our tea and biscuits, a big dog was barking fiercely. I could not understand how the man could have disappeared. He had not had time to get out of the street. I walked all round the school to see if he was lurking round a corner of the building, but there was no one.

I decided that I would go home and take an aspirin. I went back to pack up my papers and take my case. Just as I was turning the key in my desk I heard footsteps. They were not children's footsteps this time. I looked round me for some sort of defence. I thought it was perhaps a burglar. Somehow that thought did not seem so terrible. I don't know exactly what I feared.

There was a map of Europe, with a stout wooden roller, lying on the shelf. I picked it up and waited.

The caretaker came in. He had a bucket and mop and was dressed for working.

"Good evening, Miss," he said civilly.

I gaped at him.

"Oh, good evening, Mr. Cook. I forgot you would be coming in. I thought it was a burglar."

"A burglar, Miss? You don't need to be afraid of no burglars while I'm here."

But there was something about him that was unusual. Instead of his usual steady gloom, he had a quick, nervous affability. As he put down the bucket of water it shook so that water spilled on the floor. I looked at his hands. He might have had an ague.

"Did you hear that screaming——?" I was just saying, when the storm broke.

The lightning played over my window. There was a fraction of a second's pause and then a clap of thunder which seemed to go on and on. Cook dropped his brush, but its little clatter was stillborn in the noise. He rushed up to me, and seized me by the arm. I wrenched it free, but he clutched me round the waist. He began to shout something about guns. When the thunder died away, he sat down at a desk and buried his face in his hands, with shaking shoulders.

There was a tremendous downpour of rain. The drops danced about the playground like the clattering of a hundred little feet, as though a troop of ghostly children had come to play there. I hurried round the school, closing the slanting windows. Some of the desks were already wet. Halfway round, I noticed that Cook had overcome his fit of nerves and was closing the hall windows.

I felt like myself again. My head seemed to be its ordinary weight. I got out my papers and set to work again, till the storm should finish. To my surprise Mr. Cook took the tray away and brought it back with some fresh tea.

"I know ladies always likes tea," he remarked with what was intended to be a coy smile, but was not a great success. "Twenty-five years I been caretaking, and I must 'a made a million cups in my life. It's the nerves, Miss. Lady teachers always has nerves, along of the way they live."

"I daresay," I said absently. I wanted to get on. And I thought that it was no time for him to sneer at anybody for having nerves. He regarded me with his head on one side and a facetious air.

"Be getting married one of these days, I expect, Miss?"

"Not me, Mr. Cook. My courting days are over."

He stared at me fixedly, so that I had a horrible idea he was going to start flirting with me. He had a kind of leer. I said sharply, "I must get on with my work now, if you wouldn't mind taking the tray away."

He went away whistling. I heard him singing and whistling to himself while he cleaned all the rooms. Before he finished I packed up and went home. There was a deep uneasiness in my mind. It was good to get out of the hollow of Lower Bronton back to the garden suburb where we had our bungalow.

I could not decide what steps I ought to take about this mysterious incident until next day, at playtime, when Jenny remarked that she could not get anything done, because her best monitor was away, and no one else knew where anything was kept, nor which lesson followed which.

"Moira?" I asked, suddenly startled. "What's the matter with her?"

Jenny answered indifferently. "Her mother sent a note. The child got caught in the thunderstorm last night and is in bed with a temperature. Her mother says she's worried to death in case I should appoint a new monitor in her absence. Funny how they like all that extra work for no reward.

I thought this over and it still alarmed me. At dinner-time I went to Miss Harford. She looked up from her work with an impatient smile. "Well, Miss Brigson?"

"Miss Harford, it's no business of mine exactly, but —do you think Mr. Cook is—is quite to be trusted?"

"You've got a complaint about him?" she asked sharply.

I hesitated. The subject was so unsavoury.

"Well, after school yesterday, I was alone here with one of the children, and after she went, I heard her screaming in the playground, and then running to the gate, and I heard a man calling threats after her, and then Cook came in just before it began to thunder, and he seemed very nervy, and broke down over it, clinging to me, and you know he always seems a little —unhinged."

She looked down at her fountain-pen and said very quietly, "You would like to have him dismissed?"

"Yes, I would." I was relieved at this plain speaking. Miss Harford wrote a word or two on the report she was making out, opened her mouth and then shut it again, and then said, in the loud, firm tone she used on persistently anti-social children:

"I cannot understand the attitude of women of your age towards the men who saved your lives. I suppose you were too young to understand then, but by the mere fact of living you accepted their sacrifice. And when they came back, disabled for life, to drag out the rest of their days in crippled misery, you—you grudge them their very livelihood. You ought to be supporting them by your own efforts—we all ought—and instead you come to me with a fanciful grievance, based on nothing more than having heard a child playing noisily in the playground—and that poor man shrinking from thunder because he was shell-shocked—and ask me—

me—to throw him out of his job because you have a personal spite against him. I can't understand it, Miss Brigson. I can't understand how you could sleep at night with such wicked—I mean wicked—ingratitude on your conscience. I did my poor bit towards compensating him for what he suffered by arranging for him to be employed here, and you will have to bring a great deal stronger case against him before I am instrumental in condemning him to the misery of being supported by an ungrateful State."

Halfway through this phenomenal outburst I discovered that I was sitting with my jaw dropped in astonishment. I had never heard Miss Harford so eloquent, nor her tone so cutting, even when she had discovered Jenny smoking in the staff-room. When at last she seemed to run down, so to speak, I had not a word to say. I felt absolutely stunned. I said feebly: "I'm sorry. Of course, if you feel—— I'll say no more," and backed out like a child who had been scolded. In the hall I met Miss Thornby. "Heavens," I said. "I have been put in my place." I told her what Miss Harford had said.

"Didn't you know?" asked Thornby. She was always surprised that other people were not in possession of her infallible information. "Miss Harford was engaged to a young man and he went for a soldier."

"Oh, I see," I said thoughtfully. "I suppose he was killed or something."

"He's in one of those homes. He had both his arms and both his legs shot off. I think she goes to see him sometimes. But it makes her touchy about wounded soldiers."

CHAPTER III

"I'VE HAD a letter," said Jenny to me one morning that week.

"Don't spring things on me like that," I answered irritably. "Your letters always turn out to be something melodramatic and to stop me getting any work done for days. What now?"

"Quite the opposite. But I needn't bother you if you're busy. I just thought you might like to know, since it's your fault."

"Oh, well." I knew she would tell me, whether I wanted her to or not.

"It's from my English professor. I wrote and told him what had happened, and asked if he was going to do the honourable thing by me, if he could decide what it was, or leave me in the lurch in the good old-fashioned style."

"So what has he done?"

"You'd never guess. He's told his wife."

"That should be a lot of help. What does she say?"

"She says will I go and stay for the week-end and talk it over."

"You won't go, will you? Talking's not much good. Anyway, she'd probably abuse you."

"Certainly I shall go. I love week-ends out of town."

"I'm not impressed," I said coldly. I thought it was affected to pretend to take it all so lightly—like a modern play.

"And what's more, I want you to come with me. Do

come, Madge. Honestly, it would be too awful not to have any moral support. She may try to scratch my eyes out or anything—and you're so good at bullying people. Please come with me. They can easily put you up—and it's only fair I should have someone on my side, or it will be two against one."

The end of it was that I did go. It was only about twenty-five per cent. really wanting to help Jenny, and the rest was just plain curiosity. I was not in the least afraid of emotional scenes. I had lived through too many, with parents and children, to mind them. And I did want to know what happened when the eternal triangle involved three people in real life. I could not imagine what it would be like, or how they would act. There are advantages in living life at second-hand. You get all the drama and none of the soreness.

I asked Jenny if they were smart people, and Jenny said they were the sort who wear hand-woven linen clothes. So I put away the semi-evening dress that I so seldom had a chance to wear, and put in an extra blouse for my grey flannel coat and skirt instead. I had rather hoped that they would turn out to be the kind who have dinner at night with a couple of foot-men. I was so tired of picnic meals. For the last year I had shared a bungalow with two teachers from the senior school. At first it had been wonderful not to be dependent on the moods of landladies. But lately the housework involved in having a place of our own had become every bit as tiresome. The other two—Enid and Daphne—were inseparable and shared the work of getting their own meals. But I used to come in at slightly different times from them, through working farther away, and I usually had to get my own. My chief meals consisted of boiled eggs, ready-cooked meat pies which I bought on the way up and then warmed in the gas-oven, or else beans out of a tin. At the end of a few weeks of this I would have sold my soul for an exquisitely cooked and served meal.

However, it seemed from what Jenny said that I was doomed to a week-end of plain living and high thinking. I was further dashed when I discovered how much the train-fare was. It was more than I should save on food and entertainment at the week-end, and so I should be out of pocket. I hoped it would be worth it.

I watched Jenny from behind my paper. She was looking at a paper full of bathing beauties. She had put on her best dress, a scarlet one with rows of little black buttons. It made her look like a stage gipsy. Sometimes I used to think critically that she looked common when she was prettiest—but in such a way that you wished you were common too, instead of respectable and shabby-genteel. I could not imagine what it must feel like to be going to confront a lover and his wife. I read "Appointments Vacant" in a teachers' paper, and pretended to myself that I was going to move. Really, I knew I never should, unless I was made to.

It was afternoon when we arrived at Earlham. I watched the familiar roofs and modern spires of the University buildings come into sight, and remembered the first time I had seen them. I seemed a long way now from that uncertain, frightened girl from the country, balancing on the uncertain border between childhood and maturity. I had thought I was grown-up. Now I might know that I had known nothing, felt nothing, had no experience then, but ten years from now should I have moved on again? I had a moment's dull fear that in the next ten years nothing—*nothing* would happen to me, except that my hair would slowly lose its colour and my step its spring. There was Jenny, with college only three years behind her, so satiated with experience that she could afford to go on turning the pages of her magazine as we steamed into the station where her lover waited.

"I could have gone to a gala night at Bronton Palais to-night if we hadn't come on this wild-goose chase," she remarked, as if in answer to my thoughts.

"It's only fair to give all your boy-friends a chance," I said sarcastically. I thought she was showing off.

"There they are," said Jenny. She took down her bag from the rack. I looked out. There was a couple looking up and down the train in the dazed, foolish way one does when meeting someone. He was as romantic-looking as any maiden's dream. He had fair hair, carefully ruffled, and a blue sports shirt carefully flung open at the neck. He was tall and sunburnt and like something out of the chorus of a musical comedy. She was tall and big-boned and older than me. I liked her at once. Her hair was very short and rather untidy and she had a blue linen frock and Grecian sandals. She looked older than him, too.

When we met, she kissed Jenny and said she had been longing to meet her. I thought this was silly. He kissed Jenny, too, and would have kissed me if I had not ducked. He laughed and told me that I should get used to him in time. His wife said: "You musn't mind us. We're very unconventional." He took our bags and we went out to the car.

It was a very old open car. They sat in front with

their hair blowing in the wind. I held my hat on. I hate my hair getting untidy. He was not a very careful driver, and he tried to carry on badinage with a policeman at the cross-roads like an undergraduate. His wife and I made conversation about the new buildings, and how the town had changed in the last ten years. Jenny was silent.

Their flat was three rooms on the top floor of a house in the suburbs. They were whitewashed, with bright-coloured paint and linen curtains. The effect was quite pretty. Jenny and I were to share their spare room. They had divans instead of beds.

They asked us if we drank tea and seemed gratified that we did. It gave them an opportunity to tell us that tea was a soporific needed by those who were living unnatural and over-civilised lives. They did not drink it, of course, but she went out to a shop and bought some for us. They drank tomato-juice.

After tea, I helped her to clear up and get supper ready. It was just like being at home. She made a French mayonnaise dish, with a lot of drops of different kinds of oil and pickled gherkins and things. I did not much like the look of it. Her husband—Ronnie, as we were told to call him—sat in the spare room and talked to Jenny as she unpacked. The wife shut the door on them to show how broad-minded she was. I thought it ridiculous. I asked where their child was, and she said he was at school. It was a very enlightened co-educational boarding-school, she hastened to add, where there was no nonsense about segregating the sexes and thus putting impure thoughts into the children's minds. I said that we didn't have any nonsense about segregating the sexes at our school either, but that, so far as we could judge, the impure thoughts were in their minds all ready-made. She started to explain to me, in a long harangue, how, in a state of society where children were not repressed at all, ante-natally onwards, the thing would work all right. I thought she would have got on with Miss Simpson.

It was not until after supper that we got down to the subject that we had come to discuss. The Ronnie person said:

"Well, Jenny, Judith and I have talked it over and decided what is the best thing to be done."

"If you agree. We never believe in coercing anybody," put in Judith anxiously. Underneath her boyishly-cropped hair and linen overall she looked old. There was a kind of strain in her face, and her body had an air of having been filleted—as if a slice had been taken off here and there. I reflected that she might have been a comfortable person with a middle-aged spread and a husband her own age.

"You see, Judith and I understand each other perfectly," went on Ronnie, turning to me. "We believe in perfect honesty with each other, and perfect mental, physical and sexual freedom."

"I thought that was out of date by now," I said.

That stung him. He was a silly man. He began to discourse upon the subject of how to keep a wife and mistress at once. To listen to him you would have thought there was something wrong about a man only having one woman. She kept putting in a word of agreement with him. Jenny did not seem to be listening. She was looking at a book of paintings.

When he seemed to be running down, I said, "I thought Jenny came here to see how she was going to get out of the mess she is in on account of everybody not being as liberally-minded as you."

"Oh—that," he said offhandedly and affectedly. He turned away from me and spoke to Jenny. I was glad I had annoyed him.

"I've got a medical friend who will put it all right for you," he told her. "You can come and stay here for two or three weeks, and Judith will nurse you. She's a fine woman," he added solemnly, looking at her. Judith looked shy and happy.

"It's very good of her," said Jenny sincerely. I could see that she was relieved.

"Oh, I knew that Judith and I would see eye to eye on the point," remarked Ronnie airily. "You see, we always tell each other about our love affairs—if there's anything worth telling. The only reason I didn't tell her all about Jenny and me long ago was that it wasn't particularly amusing, to anyone but ourselves that is. But as soon as I got Jenny's letter last week, I explained all about her, and Judith thought out this solution."

"Didn't you know before?" I asked Judith.

"No. But I wouldn't have minded, of course," she added hurriedly.

"But didn't you wonder where he was going for week-ends?" I persisted.

"I'm afraid you've got an incurably French-farcical outlook on marriage, Madge," Ronnie lectured me. "You see, we've got above all that petty spying on each other and trying to catch each other out in infidelity. You don't understand——"

"I don't understand how he can have gone away for days at a time without your even asking where to forward his letters to," I interrupted, addressing Judith.

"Oh, well, you see, it happens that he prefers the moors and I prefer the seaside—so we often separate for holidays."

"You knew he went to Wilton-on-the-Moors? He said you thought he was in London," broke in Jenny suddenly.

"I tell you I didn't know or care where he was as long as he was enjoying himself. He just happened to have told me since, when the subject came up. Forgive me if I say that I don't think you can comprehend how small and petty and unimportant all these things seem to a couple like us," said Judith, a little irritably.

"Judith's above that kind of thing," announced Ronnie loftily.

"Oh yes—I do appreciate the way she's rallied to my aid," Jenny hastened to agree. The two of them began to enlarge upon how fine and noble and broad-minded it was of Judith. It exasperated me. I could not help breaking into their duologue.

"I don't think it's very noble."

They stopped and looked at me for the first time in ten minutes.

"I daresay you think it's a terrible crime," suggested Ronnie sweetly.

"Yes, I do."

"Only a crime against society," he explained. "The present social system, with its consequent code of morality, is entirely based, not on the ethics of individual good or evil, but simply and solely on the ancient laws of property. It's not really immoral for a woman to have a lover, but the old lawgivers were afraid that it might mean family property going to some other man's child. You see that, don't you?

We're not injuring any individual, you see, and that's all that matters, isn't it?"

I said: "I should have thought that all crimes were crimes against society. But, anyway, I don't care. But Judith is only being so high-minded and broad-minded because she's got something to lose if she isn't. She's so afraid of losing you that she entertains your mistress for fear of annoying you by refusing, or for fear you'll go off with her altogether if she doesn't. She's buying security at the price of murder. If she wants it so badly as that, well and good. But it's ridiculous to go on as if she was a modern Madonna."

They sat smiling broad-minded tolerant smiles at me. Ronnie started to lead up to something about my never having experienced love. But I saw it coming, from long experience, and interrupted him. "You've settled you're going to adopt this furtive and extremely unpleasant way of avoiding trouble. But hadn't you better arrange times and seasons instead of trying to justify yourselves?"

"The first time I've met a real, red-hot pious moralist. It's interesting," said Ronnie scornfully.

"I'm sorry I brought her." But Jenny smiled at me.

"Oh, we quite understood, when you explained about her, why she had to come with you everywhere," remarked Judith. She said it very meaningly, and looked from me to Jenny and back again as if she knew something about us. I laughed at that. But I was sorry, in a way, if I had hurt her so badly that she had to hit back. I was sorry for her. I thought her life consisted of the most wearisome keeping up of appearances.

They arranged that Jenny should come down to stay

with them when the children had their week's holiday for Bronton Wakes. The medical friend would give Jenny a certificate to say that she had developed some slight affliction and could not go back to school for a fortnight. And it would all be over.

They stayed up discussing children and their up-bringing. I went to bed because I was tired. Besides, I had not come all that way for a busman's holiday.

Jenny was in an odd temper for the next fortnight. At times she would be herself, calm and cheerful and selfish. At other times she would work up into a fear-ful rage about nothing at all. She had a row with almost everybody on the staff. Even placid Miss Thornby told me that she thought Miss Lambert was getting a little bit difficult. Miss Simpson would not speak to her. Only Miss Jones remained detached and imperturbable and returned the soft answer which made Jenny more wrathful than ever.

"Does she learn this heavenly forgiveness from that curate's church that she goes to every Sunday?" Jenny growled to me one day, when Miss Jones, having been undeniably in the right about an entry in the register totals, had gone out of the room with conscious virtue and an assurance that she would keep Jenny's mistake from the annals of the powers that be.

"I expect so."

"Well, I wish she'd take up something else. I can't think why she persists in being so sweet and kind to me when she knows I hate her like poison."

Jenny was always rude to Miss Jones. It was silly of her. Miss Jones was the first assistant, through having had longer teaching experience than any of us, and had some influence with Miss Harford. She could have taken it out of Jenny if she had liked. But she was always sweet to us all. It is a mistake to assume that spinsters get soured. Some of them go in the other direction and become positively saccharine.

"If you don't mind my saying so, Miss Lambert, I think you're not looking so well," remarked Miss Thornby, suddenly appearing with the new registers for the quarter, which she was distributing. "Can't you get away for a little, dear, at the Wakes holiday?"

"I'm going away from this place, thank goodness," answered Jenny rudely.

"That's nice, dear. Going home?"

"No. Going to Brighton with a lover. That's the best change I could think of from this atmosphere."

Miss Thornby tittered good-naturedly, left Jenny's register and went on to the next room. I looked after her suspiciously.

"Does she know anything about your goings-on, besides what Mrs. Hunt let out?" I asked.

"I don't know and I don't care."

"You be careful," I said, and went away to copy out my register. It crossed my mind to wonder whether it was Miss Thornby who had been responsible for the anonymous letter to Jenny. But, since it would not matter after the Wakes holiday, I did not think it worth pursuing. Jenny had begged me to go with her to Earlham. But I would not have dreamed of spending my precious week's holiday with her tiresome friends. Besides, I did not want to get involved in a criminal offence meriting seven years in prison. I was going to spend the time with some old friends of my mother's, in the country, and was looking forward to it. Now that night-school had started I was feeling as worn out as though I were doing two people's work.

My class of unemployed girls turned out almost as difficult as I had feared. The first night, when they had drifted in, in twos and threes, looking for all the world like a beauty chorus seen away from the footlights, my heart sank. Fifteen to eighteen, school discipline far enough behind them to be forgotten, their childish irresponsibility and silliness replaced by the more complicated and irrepressible silliness of adolescence, they were a teacher's nightmare. Half of them were dressed in rags and had dirtier faces than the children would ever have dared to appear with at school. The other half were made up garishly, with dead-white noses and blood-red lips and cheeks, and had artificial satin blouses and tight skirts, slit up the sides to show their legs above the knee, which were certainly not bought out of the few shillings a week that the Government paid to keep them alive until they should be needed, either for industry again, or to produce half a dozen more like themselves.

The eldest Hunt girl, Maggie, was among them, and was the worst of them all. The first time she saw me she observed in audible tones: "Oh, Gawd, have they given us that old bitch? Don't think much to her looks, do you, Gertie? She's no Marlene Dietrich, is she? I'm not going to stand for no bossing about the way she does the kids, anyway." They were supposed to be studying Commercial English, in case of the unlikely event of their ever finding themselves in office posts. That was the sop the organiser had offered them. Really, she had told me privately that the best I could hope for was to raise them a little out of the dead level of practical illiteracy that prevailed among them. It was discouraging to find how little they did know. I used to have a disturbing fancy that they represented the result of the ten years hard work I had put in with the five or six hundred children who had passed through my class. When I started teaching, these girls must have been in the infant school. And now, all those hundreds of sums patiently explained, those hundreds of exercises corrected, day after day, with conscientious care, their writing was unreadable, their spelling barely phonetic and their general level of intelligence only the cunning of a hunted animal. They knew how to keep out of trouble with the minimum of effort—no more.

They used bad language as the ordinary currency of speech. Their continual unemployment inspired them, neither with determination to conquer it, nor with despair, but merely with a dead level of indifferent acquiescence. The only responsive ones were those who had taken up prostitution as a regular thing. And I was afraid of those. I used to have a lysol bath when I got home if I brushed by any of them in the course of the evening.

The only redress for downright defiance was to report them to the superintendent of the night-school. This made a bad impression if one did it frequently. He judged one's power of maintaining discipline oneself by the number of complaints made. Anyway, I hated to ask for help. It seemed so inefficient.

The night before the Wakes holiday began Maggie Hunt was at her worst. I suspected that she had been drinking. She sat with her paper in front of her, and her pencil on the desk, and did not stir when I gave out the exercise. I told her twice to get on. She took no notice. Then I went over to her, and spoke to her quietly, asking her if she did not understand what it was she had to do. Maggie said, "Oh, I understand all right."

"Then get on."

"I don't feel like letter-writing to-night."

"You won't go home till you've done it, Maggie."

"Then I'll stay the night."

The others giggled. Maggie looked round her. She loved applause.

"My dad 'ull say I've lost my character if you make me stay here the night. He knows all about that old Cook."

All the others had stopped writing and were listening delightedly. I was tired out with the day's teaching and felt almost in despair. I was helpless, faced with twenty great girls with nothing to lose, however badly they behaved, after their attendance mark had been entered, once for all, in the book which might not be altered. But I tried not to show it.

"You can go home when the letter is written and not before," I repeated, and turned my back on her. I went round looking at the other girls' letters, praising the ones I could and gently remonstrating with the others. I had to try and get them on my side. I could hear Maggie whispering and giggling, and I could not help glancing furtively at the clock to see how long it **was** until nine-thirty.

"Can I leave the room, Miss?" asked Maggie.

"When you've finished your letter."

She whispered a comment, the nature of which I could guess, to her neighbours and set them sniggering.

Then she sat grinning at me. She had a smooth blonde head and a lot of eye-shadow round her eyes. She looked what she was—a vicious, dressed-up little street-walker.

For the rest of the hour she sat staring at me, with eyes like saucers, giving a running commentary beneath her breath on my appearance, age and probable private life. When the bell rang, she seized her vanity-bag and leapt up.

"Stay where you are, Maggie," I said quietly.

It was all I could do not to shout. But I knew that, immediately I raised my voice among girls like these, I should be lost. They were so used to shouting and violence, and their parents did it so much more proficiently than anything I could hope to achieve. My only possible way of maintaining authority was by the novelty of a self-controlled reiteration.

She paused for a moment. Then she began to push between the desks towards the door. I walked across to where I could cut her off. The others edged to the door, giggling and extremely interested. Maggie went round another way. But I knew the classroom better than she did, and crossed over to her and took her gently by the arm. She began to snigger and say, "Oh, Miss, you're hurting me bloody awful."

Suddenly I began to feel that I could not bear the idiotic and meaningless snickering of those twenty hoarse young voices any more. I turned absolutely cold with the desire to beat my fist in her silly grinning face. I could have knocked her down. Instead, I merely lowered her into the seat of the desk, propelled the rest of the class out with the swing-door, and went back to my place. I was trembling and disgusted with myself.

Not at what I had done—I had done the least I could
to maintain discipline—but at my murderous impulse.
I had longed, for a few seconds, for the acute pleasure
of brutal violence. There was a creeping delight all up
my spine at the thought of it. Now it was over I felt
weak and sick.

I looked up ten minutes later. The superintendent
had evidently succeeded in clearing the girls out of the
hall. I was alone. He came to my door and asked me
if I was staying on. I said I was staying until Maggie
Hunt finished her work. He asked me to lock the
school door and gate and hand the key into the caretaker's cottage. He hesitated a moment, wondering if
he ought to stay on. But he was lazy and only ran
the night-school for the sake of the extra money, and
with the minimum of trouble to himself. And he
had a wife and supper waiting for him, I knew. He
went.

Maggie sat grinning. Presently she began to hum
under her breath. It was ten o'clock. I had not thought
she would stick it out for so long. I wished to goodness
I had never started it. But there was no retreat possible for me. I had been going to call in on Jenny for
coffee and sandwiches on my way home. Soon it would
be too late. I wondered whether any of Maggie's family
would come down to see what had become of her. I
did not think it likely. She was probably often out
later than this. I began to correct the papers of the
girls who had finished.

Suddenly Maggie turned her head and a triumphant
little smile broke out over her face. She looked at me
cunningly. I heard someone knocking at the outer
door and went to answer it, hoping that there was a

policeman about if it was one of the Hunts. It was a young man, not very tall and rather ragged.

"I've come to fetch Maggie Hunt," he said.

"She will be coming presently."

"She'll bloody well come out now, you old bitch."

"I should be sorry to have to call the police and have you sent off these premises. You're not allowed in here, you know."

"I'll leave with Maggie and not a bloody minute before." He hesitated, and then added for some unfathomable reason, "If you don't mind, Miss."

"Are you Maggie's young man?" I asked.

"Yus, I am, Nosey Parker."

"Well, I'll tell Maggie you're here, and then perhaps she'll hurry up and finish what she has to do. You can wait for her outside the yard."

I went in rather rapidly, closed the door and bolted it. I heard him thumping on it. I met Maggie just coming out and took her back again. She began to scream in the best manner of a cinema blonde being kidnapped by King Kong. As I propelled her back into the classroom, a shadow appeared at the window. There was a scrape as the bottom was pushed up, and then a wriggling body began to lurch through into the classroom. It was Maggie's young man come to rescue her.

I abandoned Maggie for the moment and ran across to the window. I seized his hands, which were gripping the inside of the sill, and tried to loosen them. He had long black nails and they scratched me. I changed my tactics slightly and gave him a sudden push. I had the force of gravity on my side and he slipped back, his grimacing face suddenly receding a foot or two from mine. I was just trying to push his hands off the ledge, so that I could slam the window down and lock it, when I felt a sudden acute pain in my behind. I was so startled that I dropped the youth's arms and swung round. There was Maggie with her brooch in her hand, with open pin. She tried to jab me with it again. I made a grab for it, and received it full in the palm of my hand. I had not thought that a pin could hurt so much. I could have screamed with agony.

I heard a whoop of joy behind me and there was the young man right in the room. He seized Maggie's hand and rushed her towards the door. But the door was just opening of its own accord. There was a policeman there, and behind him the open window of the hall.

It struck me all at once as a farcical situation—the escaping little hooligans and the large policeman. But suddenly, horribly, it ceased to be farce. The policeman was badly cast for it. He was not the genial "Now then, what's all this 'ere?" kind, so prevalent in fiction and drama. He was the same one that had stared at Jenny that day in the police station. He was very young, very well-set-up and muscular, very good-looking, and his expression was very unpleasant indeed.

He said to me, "Just hold the girl a minute," and while I went mechanically towards Maggie, he leaned over and seized the boy by both arms. Somehow he jerked him round so that his arms were twisted behind his back. I had no need to hold Maggie. We were both staring at the two of them, rooted to the ground. I saw the policeman's strong, neat hands close over one of the boy's ragged shirt-sleeves, one each way, like a gymnast grasping the parallel bar. Slowly they turned round, twisting it, and a shriek seemed to be jerked out of the boy without his volition. Slowly the policeman dropped the arm, which fell down limply, like the arm of a corpse, and took up the other one. I tried not to look. I looked at the policeman's handsome, brutal face instead, and found there something which struck a hideous chord in my own shivering body—the very delight and desire I had been so ashamed of half an hour before. The boy screamed again—a hoarse, piercing cry which broke into a groan and then began again in a low blubbering noise. The policeman pushed him contemptuously away and he lurched across towards the wall and collapsed in a heap at the foot of the blackboard. The policeman looked down at the thin, twisted body. He pulled him up by one arm, roughly, jerked him to his feet, and forced him to walk out. In a moment he came back and looked at Maggie.

I was mechanically trying to tie up my bleeding palm with my handkerchief. Maggie was edging towards the door. She looked thoroughly frightened. My feelings about her and her young man had turned right over in the last few minutes. From being two tiresome and alarming law-breakers, the policeman's bullying had transformed them into two frightened and maltreated children.

"You'd better go home," I said to Maggie, as the policeman came in again.

"Excuse me, Miss Brigson," said the policeman, standing between her and the door. He produced a notebook and asked me how the young man had got in. He informed me that I should probably be wanted in court to testify that he had broken into enclosed premises and that he had assaulted a policeman. I thought this was ironical. I hate to see a dog with a rat. Dogs are almost human, rats are vermin. But you cannot help being on the rat's side at the time.

He came across to me in the middle of the questioning, took my handkerchief from me, tore it into a strip and tied my hand up neatly. I did not like his touching me. It made me shiver to look down on his hands rolling the bandage.

Finally he shut his notebook, put it away, and said he would come back later to make sure that everything was locked up and no one about. Then he said to Maggie, "Come along with me."

"I've nothing against her," I said. "She'd better go home now. They'll be wondering where she is."

"I hardly think so." He looked her over. "I'll attend to this now, Miss Brigson." It annoyed me that he had got hold of my name so competently. Maggie was watching him with something between fear and fascination. He took her by the wrist and disappeared through the hall, down the passage and into the darkness beyond.

CHAPTER IV

I CAUGHT my tram at last, after I had tidied myself up. When we passed Jenny's rooms I saw that her light was still on and I ran down the stairs and jumped off at the next stop. I needed some coffee and thought that she might perhaps be waiting up for me. The landlady told me that she had a friend with her. But, having taken the trouble to get off the tram, I did not feel in the least like stealing tactfully away. So I went up.

Jenny was lolling on the sofa. On the other side of the room, facing her, as if he had just been interrupted in the middle of an oration, was the curate who had come to inspect the Scripture and had annoyed us all so much.

"Hullo. You are late," remarked Jenny casually.

"I'm afraid I've drunk your coffee. Perhaps I can make some more," suggested the young man. Jenny got up lazily and lit her spirit-stove.

"I'll make some more. Sit down, Madge."

I sat down. I was glad I had come in. It was so interesting to find that Jenny had apparently made a conquest of the tiresome young man. They certainly had not looked pleased to see me, so I supposed they must have been enjoying themselves. There was a silence, while the little stove sputtered and popped. Then Jenny remarked maliciously: "Mr. Gregory is well in with the local gossip. He ought to get to know

74

Miss Thornby. Between them they would be able to get out a complete history of the neighbourhood."

"It would be an interesting document," agreed the young man calmly. He was quite self-possessed. I liked him for that. I cannot bear shy young men.

"Have you been here long?" I asked him.

"Six months. And you?"

"Five years." I looked back on it. I had thought the place a nightmare world at first. Now I took it for granted and found it not so bad.

"I'm afraid I've just been the means of getting another Hunt into the hands of the police," I said to him.

I told them about the little scene after night-school. The disturbance it had made in my mind was calming down a little. That sort of thing often happens in our district. The rebellious ones get a week or so in jail, or else are bound over, and it all passes off with no one any the worse for it—and nobody any better either—certainly not the jailed one.

"Are you going away over the Wakes?" enquired the curate conversationally, as I sipped my coffee, and Jenny glowered at us both.

I told him I was going into the country.

"I've been trying to get Miss Lambert not to go," he said coolly.

"You seem to have collected gossip to some purpose," I remarked.

"I have. I know that Miss Lambert is afraid of having an illegitimate child and means to avoid it by the crudest method. So I came here to see if she really knew what she was doing and to find another way out."

This embarrassed me. I did not like discussing the

75

business so directly. I could not think of anything to say. But I was spared the trouble by Jenny. She had plenty to say, and proceeded to say it. "Talk about interfering parsons!" she cried. "What hell business had you to go snooping around collecting information about my private affairs? Scandal-mongering old women wouldn't have a chance against you. Who have you been cross-questioning about this? Miss Thornby, I suppose. Was it?"

"That I can't tell you," said the curate. "One of the conditions of my being told was that I should keep quiet about the source."

"How dare you come here, with all the dirt you've collected, and try and preach me out of what I've decided to do? A fat lot of chance you have of influencing me. I never did think anything at all of parsons anyway. But if I was the chief church-going tabby of the neighbourhood, I still wouldn't dream of taking the advice of a curate who descends to listening to the tittle-tattle of the district. That's what's the matter with you clergy. You're too damn fond of interfering in other people's business. No wonder you never get anyone to church! Why don't you stick to your own concerns?"

"You said all that before," said the curate. "I daresay you get into the habit of repeating yourself with the children. But you're wrong about the church failing because parsons interfere too much. It's because they don't interfere enough. We're apt to be too much occupied in keeping on the right side of everybody and being careful not to annoy possible church-goers. I can tell you, I left my last post because the work consisted of doing that. I decided that if that was all I could do, I'd better become secretary of a mutual benefit society, and earn my money honestly." He turned to me. "One day there was a very bitter scene about the order of speakers at the opening of the church bazaar. Imagine the scene for yourself, Miss Brigson. There we were, with a possibility of a hundred pounds for the heating of the parish hall dangling in jeopardy, because I, God's minister, had so far forgotten myself as to say that I thought the younger churchwarden ought to propose the vote of thanks instead of the senior one. The senior one stammered, you see, and it always made the choir-boys giggle. Anyway, we reached the point where, though no one was actually laying violent finger-nails on anyone else's face, the atmosphere was distinctly strained."

"We have that kind of staff-meeting," I agreed. "How did you solve the problem?"

"I rose to my feet and said portentously, in the most traditional blessed peace-maker manner, that I thought we ought all to go home and pray about it. The senior churchwarden, after considering the suggestion on its merits, said that anyway it c-couldn't do any harm. Somehow that made me wake up. I said in stronger language than he had expected that it certainly could do a lot of harm, and that I thought that our whole meeting, our church bazaar, our parish hall and its central heating were a studied insult to the men and women who had worked and suffered and died for hundreds of years for the sake of the Christian faith whose name we had blasphemously assumed as the title of our rotarian club. And I proposed that we changed the name of our church to St. Saviour's luncheon club, keeping the title in memory of a long-dead faith that had once flourished there. But it was wasted on them. They gathered that I was angry and they just murmured that perhaps I was over-wrought and ought to have a little holiday."

"What did you do?" asked Jenny, who had been amused at the story.

"I went home and read the Minor Prophets."

"Which are they?"

"Oh, I forgot. You don't know much about the Bible, do you? I gathered that when I came round to inspect the Scripture the other day. Well, to put it as briefly as I can, they did not spare the feelings of their parishioners, and they interfered most tactlessly when they found people doing the sort of thing Miss Lambert does. I decided I would model myself on them."

"That should make you into a kind of Victorian parson," I said, as I thought it over.

"That's what he's being now. I think they were worse than modern ones," remarked Jenny.

"Do you ask the children what sort of teachers they think you should be?" he asked.

"Don't be silly. Of course not."

"You expect me to do the same sort of thing. But see here. You admit that I draw my salary for spreading New Testament morality, don't you? Well, look at it simply from that point of view. Did Jesus Christ, or did He not, interfere when He saw people leading vicious and anti-social lives? Did He keep off contro-versial topics? Did He leave harlots in the lives they had chosen for themselves?"

"You mean me," said Jenny. She said it as if she had caught him out. He looked a little confused.

"But if I called you a fast little gold-digger, you

78

wouldn't be insulted. You only think it sounds worse in Biblical language."

"I don't run my love affairs on a financial basis."

"Only because you get a decent salary."

Jenny was lying on the sofa. Her hair was ruffled and her cheeks flushed in the warm room. Her dress was twisted round her, where she had turned over on her side and pulled it tightly over the curve of her hips. I tried to imagine what it must be like to be a man staring at her. I could not tell whether she was very angry with him or not. She was just looking at him meditatively.

"So when you think you can insult me by telling me I'm an interfering parson you're paying me the greatest compliment I could wish for. You'll have to think up something else if you want to make me really angry," he said after a silence.

"Are you coming down to inspect the Scripture again?" I had been thinking that it would mean a lot of extra work if we had anyone as enthusiastic as him regularly.

"Again and again and again," he replied firmly. "Some of the grown-up people need a Jonah or a Jeremiah or an Ezekiel and a few tons of fire and brimstone from the skies to convince them that their troubles are their own fault. But the children are only at the beginning of things, and more receptive ground for me. No kindly idea about saving you trouble is going to keep me away from that school of yours."

"Is this the kind of thing you were saying to Jenny before I came in?"

"Something of the sort."

I thought this over.

"Then I can't understand how it was that you both seemed as if you were getting on so well together when I arrived. I thought you had joined the list of her admirers."

He looked at Jenny. She would not look at him.

"I had just made a suggestion which was more the kind of thing she is interested in discussing."

"He proposed to me," said Jenny.

"You must be mad," I cried without thinking.

"She's an old friend," explained Jenny.

"Can I tell her about it?"

"If you like." Jenny shrugged her shoulders.

"Miss Lambert admitted to me that she is going away to have an illegal operation. I told her that she was proposing to take human life for the sake of her own convenience and to avoid having to face the consequences of her promiscuity. Then she told me about the difficulties in her way—material ones, not just a question of what people would think of her—but the question of losing her job. I suggested that she should marry me, and go back to teaching after a year, either in a private school or under some local committee that didn't object to employing married teachers."

"It's a crazy suggestion," I gasped.

"Why?"

"You're behaving like a knight out of a story-book. And you couldn't possibly keep it up."

"No, I'm not. You're looking at it from the wrong angle. I'm not offering to marry Miss Lambert to save her from worse than death, but to save a child's life. If there was a child in the canal and I jumped in to fetch it out, not only would you not call me crazy, but you'd call me an uncivilised brute to stand by and not jump in, wouldn't you? And marrying Miss Lambert isn't necessarily any more difficult and dangerous than diving into a canal."

"The emergency isn't the same," I objected.

"Will anything else stop her from what she means to do?"

"No—and that won't either," put in Jenny.

"But the flaw is this," I pointed out to him, ignoring Jenny for the moment. "If you did this canal-diving business, it would all be over in a moment. Anyone can be heroic for five minutes. But you'd be taking on something for life. How do you think you would feel bringing up another man's child?"

"If I'd rescued a baby from accidental death and taken it home and brought it up, do you think I should spend the rest of my life worrying because it wasn't my seed? It is possible to bring a little reason to aid one's human relationships—at least, I believe so, though in fiction we're all supposed to be governed by the most primitive fleshly impulses."

"If you flatter yourself that you're governing your human relationships by the light of reason, you must be as mad as a hatter. You don't know Jenny. How could you love her?"

"I see where you go instead of church, Miss Brigson. You go to the cinema. You've been drinking in the commercialised proposition that the sexual relationship is the only thing in life that matters at all and certainly the only relationship worth considering. You don't act on it yourself. You know very well that you have something else to do in the world besides spending your time waiting on some hairy-chested young man. Then why do you assume I must put this same emotional dope before doing something humane and useful? If I told you I had spent ten years lying awake at night because some blond charmer wouldn't share my bed and board, you'd accept that quite calmly and without too much astonishment. I believe you think that you're the only person in the world who doesn't run round in circles at the beck and call of their emotions."

"Whether you're making this extraordinary proposal out of reason, or out of a sudden impulse of generosity that you couldn't keep up, it's completely unreasonable, because you can't expect Jenny to accept anything so cold-blooded. To say that marrying her isn't as bad as jumping in a canal isn't exactly ardent, is it?"

"When you two have quite finished discussing me as if I wasn't here at all, I've got something to say," Jenny broke in. We both looked at her. "I haven't the slightest intention of marrying you. Madge is right. It's a crazy suggestion. If I was so frightened by the mess I've got into that I had to marry someone, it certainly wouldn't be you. For one thing I scarcely know you, and for another you talk too much. If you weren't in a lunatic asylum by the end of five years, I should be myself. I don't want a baby, even if I could have it under the auspices of the Church of England. I've seen too damn many children in the last few years. I want to go on as I am, and marry the man I choose, not one who happens to come along at the right moment to help me out of a mess. Don't think I'm not grateful for the suggestion. If I could believe that you really understood what you were taking on I'd be extremely grateful. But I'd like to know just one thing before you go. Would you have made your proposal if I'd been ugly and old?"

"If you'd been so ugly and so old that it would have meant certain unhappiness and friction for life, I don't know that I should have done," said the curate thoughtfully. "But I'd better add, to prevent your thoughts from racing up the obvious channel, that I certainly should not have asked *you* if it hadn't been that I had an idea about preventing you from spoiling your life."

"It won't spoil my life," persisted Jenny.

"You're doing something that is unnatural and inhuman and that can never be undone. You're taking a risk that you'll never be able to have children of your own. I say that you are spoiling your life."

There was a knock at the door. Jenny called, "Come in." The landlady came in, with a flowered dressing-gown draped round her. "Excuse *me*," she said, with the emphasis that has a flavour of sarcasm, "but was you aware, Miss Lambert, that it is twelve o'clock past, and this is a respectable house, always has been, and what the neighbours will think if they seen a young man slipping out of here at this time of night I don't know."

"I know," remarked Jenny. "They'll say that the sooner he makes an honest woman of me the better. Isn't that right, Mrs. Sainsbury?" The landlady drew herself up and swathed her draperies closer around her.

"That's no way to talk in a respectable house, Miss Lambert," she was beginning feebly, when the curate broke in.

"There are three of us here, Mrs. Sainsbury, and you can see just what we're doing—having a serious discussion about a personal matter that has got to be settled at once. Your neighbours, if they're still awake, will be able to see Miss Brigson and I depart together leaving your house in its pristine respectability. So there's no need to disturb yourself."

"That's as may be, sir," Mrs. Sainsbury answered haughtily. "But twelve o'clock is twelve o'clock and this house is my house and I'd think shame if I were you and a clergyman at that to be calling on a young woman at this time of night and if you can't see your way to going right away, out of this house Miss Lambert goes first thing to-morrow morning, school-teacher or no school-teacher."

"All right," Jenny broke in. "He'll go now."

"You can't just knuckle under to that kind of dirty-minded Grundyism, Miss Lambert," cried the curate. "You become a party to it if you give way like that. For heaven's sake have some self-respect and stand up to it." He looked as if he was working up into a rage. But Jenny got up from the sofa.

"All right. I'll send him away. You can go back to bed," she said to Mrs. Sainsbury, who marched out with a cutting stare at the young man.

"Sorry, Mr. Gregory," added Jenny. "But I can't possibly be bothered to move out of here now I've just got settled in. So you'll have to go."

"I couldn't have believed it," said the curate, staring at her. "But, of course, I ought to have known. If you don't stop at murder in order to save appearances, of course you must be logical and keep it up all along the line—even adopting your landlady's imitation morality. On second thoughts, I'm glad you turned my proposal down. I doubt if I could keep up with your ideal of respectability. Good-night."

He picked up his hat, pulled the door open and ran downstairs. We heard him slam the front door and go swinging along the pavement. I crossed over to the window and looked out. There was a row of heads at the window opposite, following his progress as a cat's head follows a clockwork mouse.

"Well, that's torn it anyway," remarked Jenny, looking out beside me. She chuckled to herself. "Funny if I get turned out now."

"I must go," I said. Jenny sat down slowly and watched me putting my gloves on.

"I wish I didn't have to go to-morrow," she murmured. "I wish to God it was all over. I am afraid it's dangerous. I'm afraid it will hurt. I'm afraid I shall never come back again."

"Don't be morbid." I was sorry for her. But I was impatient too. I hesitated with my bag in my hand.

"You must go," she said, rising. "I'm going to cry. It always makes me feel better and it would embarrass you horribly. Besides, you'd feel obliged to keep on telling me to stop, and that's so irritating when one's doing it deliberately, for the good of one's system. I'll be back in three weeks. Don't let whoever takes my class make an awful mess of the Drawing-books. They're my pride and joy and I'm keeping them for the next Government inspection."

"Well—so long. I'll let myself out."

"Don't listen at the window to see if I'm crying. I'm going to have a bath first and you'd have to wait too long."

"Give my love to Saint Judith," I said. "Good-bye."

I woke up two nights later in the small hours and

lay awake thinking how wonderful it was to be in the country. Outside my window, where the laurel-bushes crowded together in a black clump, there was complete stillness and silence. I thought of Bronton, with the Wakes on—the tinny music from the market-place, the drunken shouting that went on almost till morning afterwards. I had been born in the country. It held the happiest memories of my life. Whenever I was back there all the fretful longings for a life I could not have seemed to fall away from me. I ceased to be the plain teacher, advancing too fast towards middle age, with old age beyond it, which I must provide for, and changed miraculously into the little girl I used to be, grown-up as she expected to grow up, with nothing altered except that I had money to spend and no one to tell me when to go to bed.

I was staying with an old friend of my mother's. When my mother had been the young wife of the village schoolmaster she had made friends at some local festival with the squire's daughter. They were both lonely and bored and about the same age. When the squire's daughter married they had not forgotten each other. As a little girl I had come to stay here for all-too-brief visits, and played with Marian, the lucky little girl who had a pony of her own. And after my parents had died ten years ago, they had still invited me once a year. Once a year, for one week, I lived the kind of life I should have chosen for myself.

I did not day-dream about marriage. But I used to day-dream, in the worst of school winter mornings, about living in a house just like theirs with panelled walls and shining glass and silver on a dark oak table, and with a slow, full, separate life going on around the back door, where grooms and maids and milkmen lounged in the doorway of the red-tiled kitchen and silently watched the horses being led in and out of the yard. It was one of those rambling establishments that are half manor and half farm. They were not society people, but they believed in living well. So did I, after a few months in our bungalow, with boiled eggs for breakfast and supper and a charwoman three times a week to "do" for us.

Perhaps it was because I was not used to a large dinner at night that I was wakeful. I went through it again mentally and came to the conclusion that the roast pork was to blame. I thought I would go downstairs for some soda-water. I scrambled across the enormous double bed, opened the door quietly and went along the passage in my felt bedroom-slippers, putting my dressing-gown on as I went. It was a large square house, slightly shabby, from disregard of appearances rather than poverty. The stair carpets—once expensive—had been trodden on by too many muddy riding-boots to retain their softness and colour. The pictures on the walls were all of beautiful horses, long since dead. Only these stiff paintings, inscribed with their name and fame, and maybe some of their own hot blood still thudding down race-tracks, remained to prove that they had not lived in vain.

I could see my way after a moment or two. It must have been some way towards dawn. At the turn of the stairs was a large window. It was open. The Dermotts would not have insulted the retriever that slept in the yard by insinuating that they needed any guard besides her sterling watchfulness. I stopped at the window and looked out. The night was still, with a faint mist rising from the meadows. There was no sound. I could see no light. I leaned out, drinking in the peacefulness and freshness of the autumn dawn. I could hardly believe I was the same person who had struggled with a noisy night-school class only two nights before. I realised that there was a faint rhythmic sound, too low to be called moaning. I held my breath and listened. But it was only the tranquil breathing of the cows behind their wooden walls.

I turned away from the window and saw that Marian's bedroom door was open. I tiptoed up to it, meaning to shut it if she was still asleep, and saw in the dusk that her bed was tumbled and empty. I wondered where she might be. Then I noticed a light shining under the kitchen door. I hoped very much that she was not having an assignation with some young man. She was the age for it and her mother had hinted that there was someone. I did not want to have my quiet week of escape broken in upon by any more of the sex business. Anyway, I wanted my soda-water, so I knocked softly on the door and went in.

Marian was alone, kneeling by the fireplace. Her fair hair was tumbled into curls over her brown woollen dressing-gown. She always looked more like the English rose than I had ever believed a real girl could. I suppose I think too much about beauty in women, since I believe it can buy everything I have to work for, but she was beautiful then. Her teeth were her only fault. They were uneven. But it mattered very little because she did not often smile. She was a remote person, cool and self-controlled and unapproachable.

She looked up now and said, "Hullo." I went into

the room. A setter puppy lay in her arms, nestling forlornly against the woolly sleeves. I thought that I should not like a dog—even a clean puppy—on my dressing-gown. I said, "I just wanted a drink of soda-water."

She answered with absent politeness. "There is a syphon in the sideboard in the dining-room. I'll come and get it for you in a minute." She was feeding the puppy from a bottle.

"He isn't well," she said anxiously. "He's always been the weakest of the litter. I was worried about him last night and I came down to look at him. I'm so glad I did."

She bent over him, coaxing him to drink. I fetched my own soda-water and talked to Marian for a little while about the sick puppy. I was not really in the least interested whether it lived or died. The only thing that irritated me at all about the Dermotts was their incessant conversation about animals. They used to lavish sentimental endearments on them until I fairly blushed. However, Marian in the red-flagged kitchen, with the shining pans on the shelf and the shining golden-brown coat of the puppy in her arms, pleased me in spite of myself. I wondered if I had caught her in her most sincere and warm-blooded moment. She was friendlier than usual.

At last I went back to bed. Marian said she thought she would stay up until it was late enough to go riding. I asked rather tentatively if she would take me. I loved riding, but the only time I ever got any was when Marian consented to take me out with her and give me offhand instructions. She promised to wake me about six. Before I went to sleep I remembered that it was

Monday morning and that I was expecting a letter. But I did not want to think of Jenny and her troubles to-day. I put it out of my mind and went to sleep.

Marian woke me an hour or two later, looking very much scrubbed and groomed. I got up hastily, shamed by her energy, put on the old breeches she had lent me and went out with her to the stables. It was one of those autumn mornings whose frosty chilliness induces comfortable thoughts of the mellow hours of sunshine to come. A man was milking the cows as we passed by the open barn door. The horses were fidgeting a little in their boxes. We heard the faint chink of iron on cobbles as they moved about. I wished that time might stand still and leave me for ever in that quiet courtyard, with the everlasting promise of warm noonday before me. Marian picked a mild and inoffensive animal for me and told me that I need not be afraid. She helped me on, swung herself into the saddle, and we started off with the toss and swing that corresponds to letting the clutch of a car in.

I jogged along, absorbed in keeping my hands down and my toes up. I was not an accomplished rider. Marian, though, was graceful and competent and performed some acrobatic feats opening gates. It was one of the very few times one heard her laugh. Knockabout humour was the only kind that appealed to the Dermotts.

When we got into the woods there was a long straight gallop between the trees. Marian left me and swung away down the avenue while startled rabbits scurried into the bracken and I caught my breath to see the two of them, the chestnut horse and the fair-haired girl, galloping away into the white mist. She waited for me at the gate and said, "I've got to go over to a village near about a bitch. There's an old parson there who used to know you. He came to dinner with us once. We might call on him."

"I'd like to. What's his name?"

Marian thought it was Wolfe. I remembered him well. He had been perpetual curate at Lower Bronton church for a long time. Then he had retired to a country parish in the diocese. I had met him once or twice at the school. I hoped he would remember me. People often forgot me and it was humiliating.

We settled down to trot along the lanes. Sometimes we had to go out on to a main road and pick our way carefully along the tarmac, while Marian watched anxiously to see that I did not damage the horse. A car with some young hooligans swerved up close to us, to see the horses start, and Marian turned white with rage, took their number and swore she would report them to the local magistrate. By the time we reached the village the sun was high and the mist completely disappeared. Some children turned from dabbling in the duckpond to watch us pass by. The rectory was hidden away at the bottom of a lane long after you thought you had reached the end of the village. It was a derelict, untidy-looking place. An ancient pony coolly regarded its social superiors from over a swing-door in the yard as we dismounted and tied them up. Hens wandered over what had once been a tennis court. Three or four dogs looked up from the doorstep as we leaned over them to ring the bell.

An untidy old woman opened the door and showed us into the drawing-room. It had been a fine room once, but the wall-paper was stained and the carpet very soiled. Half a dozen cats occupied all the arm-chairs and the sofa. I pushed an enormously fat tabby off a chair so that I could sit down.

"Don't—you mustn't," said Marian softly. The tabby was looking at me as if it could not credit the evidence of its senses. Marian added: "I forgot to tell you. Mr. Wolfe won't have the animals touched. The cushions are for them. He's always sacking maids for not being kind enough to the cats and dogs."

"Do you mean to say that I can't use this chair because the cat wants it?"

"Mr. Wolfe will be awfully hurt if he sees you. He's a bit queer about it."

I got up reluctantly. The cushion had been pleasant after the saddle. Immediately the tabby leaped back and curled itself up after a great deal of haughty experimenting as to the best position, insinuating, as plainly as ever cat did, that the chair was ruined since I sat in it.

The old man came in slowly through the French window. He had aged a good deal since I knew him. He had had a very bad illness and a nervous break-down and had been given this living to recuperate. The last time I had seen him was when he came to the school Christmas party. He had acted a little oddly then, I remembered, not answering questions and breaking suddenly out into conversation about some irrelevant subject instead.

He said he remembered me, but I did not think it was true. He seemed very vague and helpless. He was white-haired, small and feeble. His black suit was very shabby and stained all down the front like a dirty child's. He asked us if we would like some coffee.

Marian said she would go over to the farm to deliver her message while we were waiting for it. I was left with the old man. We stood uncomfortably shifting from one foot to another, while the cats slept on as if we were not there. I pretended to admire the least repulsive of them, and he brightened up, and began to pour out a long list of the intelligent things it did. I thought they sounded like the ordinary cunning of an animal of limited intelligence and unpleasant nature, but I said it was wonderful. From that we went on to the dogs. It was wonderful, we all agreed, the things they *knew*. From them we passed to birds. There were evidences all over the window-sill that they also acted as if the place belonged to them. When I felt that I could not bear it any longer, I asked if I might see the church. It was a bare whitewashed little place, without a stained-glass window to its name. I rather liked it and asked the rector if he got good congregations. He looked bewildered and said he supposed so. I began to think he was crazy. I asked him if he had quite recovered from his illness.

A bird swooped in at the open door, circled round and went out again into the sunshine. He looked at it dreamily, and then said, "Oh yes, I am quite well again now."

His voice was cracked and faint. It barely retained the inflections and rounded notes of a lifetime's training. I remembered him as he was when I first took up my post at the school and wondered whether the young curate would end up as he had done.

"Do you know the young man who has taken your place at Bronton?" I asked him. I had to repeat it twice.

"Oh yes, I saw him," he answered at last.

"He seems very enthusiastic."

He laughed, and there was something jarring and out of harmony with his gentle senility in his laugh.

"It has taken me a lifetime to learn that I can't work miracles. He still has it to learn," he remarked.

I hate that kind of conversation, all full of symbolic references, like a Girls' Friendly Society play, so I changed the subject and suggested that we went back to the house to look for Marian. He became almost animated and asked me if I did not think her a most wonderful example of what a woman could be, gentle, useful and beautiful. I agreed, but could not help adding that I thought she had a kind of youthful coldness, which I supposed would wear off as she grew older.

"Miss Dermott cold!" he exclaimed. "Miss Dermott, whom every bird and beast comes to naturally, as if she was their mother! Miss Dermott, who treats a sick animal as gently as if it were a human being! How can you say such a thing? She is tender womanhood personified."

I was fairly blushing with embarrassment at this impossibly sentimental conversation, and led the way over to the Rectory as fast as I could. I was longing for coffee, too. I thought that if the old Rector married Marian it would serve them both right. But when we went back into the drawing-room, where Marian was waiting for us, I found that one of the unspeakable dogs had been licking my coffee-cup, and I did not fancy drinking it after that.

It was quite warm riding back. Marian said it was St. Luke's summer. I got quite bold with the horse on the way home and had a gallop in the woods.

When we got in there was a letter for me from Jenny. She wrote: "It's all safely over and I feel quite all right and as if I'd made a fearful fuss over nothing. See you in about a fortnight. Send me something to read, will you? All their books are too fearfully highbrow. How are all your swagger friends. If you meet a nice hard-drinkin', hard-ridin' man I should hook him without hesitation. Isn't the thought of school too awful?"

Marian called me in to an early lunch. I crammed the letter in my jersey pocket. At lunch I said to Marian:

"It's so lovely staying here, I'm simply dreading the school again."

She answered absently. "Yes, it must be a frightful bore. I couldn't bear to teach."

"You can't help getting a bit sick of children," I explained. She was a difficult person to make conversation with, but I dislike eating in silence.

"Yes. They must be a frightful bore," she agreed.

I gave it up at that and we finished lunch in silence. Afterwards we sat in the garden in deck-chairs. I was tired out with my ride and dozed in the warm sunlight. I dreamed that I had a class of cats and dogs to teach and had my salary raised by the Education Committee. I woke up abruptly and tried to tell Marian about it, but she was not amused. She went away to look at her puppy again, and I reflected that while she had been going to untold trouble to save its life, Jenny had been saving her child the trouble of being born. I thought that there ought to have been a moral to that if I could think of it, but I was too sleepy, and merely came to the conclusion that I had peculiar friends.

CHAPTER V

W H E N W E got back to school we found that a Supply
teacher had already arrived to replace Jenny until she
should be well enough to return. She was a gloomy-
looking object. She had greyish-brown hair in untidy
wisps round a thin, pale face. Her name was Mrs. Lee.
I guessed that she would ruin Jenny's class for her in
the minimum of time. "Supply" teachers are in the
reserve, so to speak, and have to go temporarily anywhere there is a gap. It is the worst job in teaching,
since one never has time to get any results, and so only
the teachers who are not much good at their job and
cannot get permanent posts do it. I offered to help her
with one or two things, not out of kind-heartedness to
her, but because I was sorry for Jenny having her work
undone, and, anyway, I hate to see a good class drift
into a state of anarchy. But it was not very much use.
In twenty-four hours Jenny's class changed from being
a disciplined assembly of well-behaved children into
a mob of infant revolutionaries who had suddenly
found themselves in power. I used to pass by the glass
panel and see them all talking and drawing on each
other's books, and Betty Hunt usually standing on the
seat of her desk and shying paper darts across the
room.

It was no wonder that Mrs. Lee was gloomy. But
Miss Thornby said she had heard that her gloom arose
from her private rather than her public life. Her hus-

band had deserted her, and she had had to go back to teaching.

"I can't imagine how you get hold of all this information, Thornby," I remarked. "Where, for instance, did you get this exclusive story from?"

"A friend of mine was in a school with her before she was married."

"But how did you know what happened afterwards?"

"Well, my sister has a friend who is a typist in the Education Office at Bronton and she saw her letter asking to be reinstated as a teacher, and you know they have to be very well convinced that your husband isn't supporting you before they'll take you back."

"One of these days you'll find yourself in the courts for libel, with hundreds of pounds to pay, Thornby," I said, picking up my books and preparing to go into school.

"They don't fine you like that for libel, do they?"

"They do for blackmail," I answered carelessly as I went out. I glanced in the mirror as I passed it and saw that Thornby behind my back was turning red and looking very disturbed. She was an imperturbable person usually and it surprised me. I remembered about Thornby being there when Mrs. Hunt had first made her accusation, and began to wonder afresh if she had been responsible for the threatening letter to Jenny. In that case she had probably told the curate as well. But I could not understand what she had hoped to get out of it, unless gossip was so much her hobby now that she looked upon it as art for art's sake. But in any case it did not matter much to Jenny now.

It was partly because Jenny was away, and I was

suspicious of Thornby, and because Mrs. Lee was such a dismal creature, that I began to be more friendly with Miss Jones. I had discovered, for one thing, that in spite of her old-fashioned methods, she was quite a good teacher. She kept order in a different way, but she did keep order. I had noticed, when I was going round the old schools in my last year at college, doing teaching practice, how old-fashioned teachers always trot. They were always hurrying after the children as if they were afraid the little wretches would be doing something wrong if they did not get close enough to them to seize their arms and poke them about. Whereas we rather sauntered across the hall to our classrooms and merely stood fixing the children with a threatening eye as they came in from the playground or marched out to prayers. It worked well so long as one had a good standard of discipline. But I discovered that Miss Jones' children behaved just as well under her trotting and poking, and I began to respect her a little more and to be more friendly to her.

For another thing, she was very unselfish and obliging about taking playground duty, and it is essential to the smooth running of any school that someone should be this. It is so dreary, standing about in the chilly playground, with nothing to do but have mental bets about which child will win whatever fight is in progress. But it is not a duty one can ignore, because if a child damages itself when there is no one on duty one is liable to be summoned for damages. Miss Jones knew this even better than we did, and if ever she saw the screaming three hundred unattended, she would slip out without a word and mount guard until one of us turned up.

One day Stanley Hunt knocked a smaller boy down and kicked him and broke two of his front teeth. It was the first cold day of the year, and I was hastily gulping down a cup of tea before I faced the icy wind when I heard a commotion at the end of the passage, and ran out to find Tommy Bellerby, with his chin and his jersey covered with blood, being escorted in by a crowd of sympathetic fans. I immediately had a nightmare vision of court proceedings and all the money I had saved for old age being handed over to his indignant parents. Miss Harford appeared at the same moment, like an avenging bloodhound on the track, and said to me, "I thought it was your playground duty this week, Miss Brigson." But Miss Jones suddenly materialised from behind the crowd of children, rushed up before I could reply and cried breathlessly, "Miss Brigson had arranged with me that I should take her duty to-day because she had a cold, and I was in the girls' half of the playground when it happened."

That satisfied the head, because so long as someone is about, even if they do not prevent the disaster, there is apparently no ground for a summons. So she disappeared again, while Tommy Bellerby began to rinse his mouth out and spit blood all over the wash-room until it looked like the Chamber of Horrors. I turned to Miss Jones and hardly knew how to thank her. She was pleased. Her beady little eyes twinkled and shone like prisms and she giggled and chattered breathlessly about telling a little white lie and she hoped it would not be brought up against her at the Judgment Day.

After this I got quite friendly with her, and she began to tell me about her home life. It consisted of sharing rooms with another maiden lady in a little house in the suburbs. The other maiden lady, of course, had a dog and I got a little bit tired of its doings, but I used to get quite good at heading her off it. I liked best to talk to her about her class. She had really succeeded in turning them into quite good, hard-working children. I know that conversation about teaching is supposed to bore outsiders, but I never can see why it should be so much more a matter of reproach to discuss it than for actors and actresses, for instance, to talk shop, which is supposed to be rather Bohemian and intriguing of them. Anyway, Miss Jones and I got very friendly over the progress of the Top Infants.

One day, when the children were having dental inspection, and we were keeping our classes in the playground, waiting their turn, Miss Jones said to me:

"I shall be having a little outing one evening next week."

"How dissipated," I said, pulling a small boy away from the entrance to the girls' lavatories, which he was haunting in the manner of a Victorian buck at stage doors.

"My friend's brother is coming home on leave. He's a sailor. Very romantic, isn't it? I always admire sailors. And when he comes home he always takes us both out for a little outing."

"Where does he take you?"

She said vaguely that he took them out to high tea and then to something suitable. His idea of suitable, I gathered, was either to a Gilbert and Sullivan opera or to a concert. Anyway, it was evidently a great occasion for the two old things—the sister and Miss Jones—and she was in a great fluster about getting off early from school. I offered to see her children out of the classroom at four o'clock, so as to give her an extra ten minutes. She was terribly grateful; though, considering all the times she had done the same thing for each of us in turn, she need not have been.

Jenny appeared at school the day she was going. I hardly saw her until lunch-time, when I only had time to ask her if she was all right again. She said "Yes," though she looked rather thin and pale, and then went back to her classroom to try to repair some of the havoc wrought by Mrs. Lee. I called in on my way to the staff-room for lunch and found her looking despairingly through the copy-writing books, most of which looked as if someone had been learning decoding by a long and painful process.

"Oh, my God," Jenny burst out, as I put my head in the door. "Why on earth did they have to pick someone like her to wreck my class?"

"Hush," I said. "She's in the staff-room. She's staying on a day or two to help Miss Harford with the transferring to the Senior school."

"I don't care if she hears," snapped Jenny. "I've a jolly good mind to asked her what the hell she thinks she's been doing."

"Did you have a bad time?" I asked.

"Oh, not bad. It was soon over. And I feel jolly relieved. But it's awful to come back to this. Look." She picked up Betty Hunt's book, whose carefully-chosen poetry Betty had enlivened with some of the expressions which were the more usual currency of speech at her home. "Wouldn't you wonder how they remember it all?" I remarked as I read the page.

"It reminds me of D. H. Lawrence," said Jenny.

"Didn't he believe that we'd all be frightfully pure in mind if we'd only call all the bodily functions by their dictionary names?"

"In that case Betty Hunt ought to have a mind like a clean white sheet."

"It's unfortunate for her that I'm no longer a disciple of Lawrence." Jenny grimly made a note on her blotting-pad, "Strap B. Hunt," picked up the book and marched into the staff-room.

"Mrs. Lee," she began aggressively. The gloomy one looked up from her place by the hearth. She always huddled over the fire. "Have you any idea how this came to be in Betty Hunt's copy-writing book?"

Mrs. Lee took it silently and the others crowded round to look.

They all made shocked noises.

"I don't know, I'm sure, Miss Lambert. The little girl is very wild and undisciplined and I suppose she did it when I wasn't looking."

"She was disciplined all right with me," said Jenny rudely. "I should like to know how I am to explain this to an inspector."

"I think the best thing would be to tear out the page——" Mrs. Lee was beginning when she was stopped by a chorus of loud protest from us all. Tearing a page out of a child's exercise-book is equal to forgery in our job and the kind of thing for which you can lose your certificate.

"Thank you. That's not my idea of teaching. I think you'd better write a note at the bottom in red ink and sign it so that I can show it to whoever comes round. I've no desire to be judged on what is apparently your standard of teaching."

"You've no business to speak to me like that." Mrs. Lee got up from her chair and began to bristle.

"Why not?" asked Jenny.

"I'm an older woman than you and more experienced. The fact that I found your class difficult, through not having proper discipline, made it impossible for me to get their books as nice as I should have liked in the short time I had."

Jenny, by way of answer, began to turn back through the book and ostentatiously examine the comparatively neat copies that Betty Hunt had done before Mrs. Lee came.

"Oh, it's easy enough to help a child and bully her, so that the work looks all right in the book, and still she may be able to do nothing at all without assistance. I must say I don't believe in so much eyewash, as we used to call it. I've been longer teaching than you have, Miss Lambert, and I think I may say I know more about real education if less about getting perfect copies up for inspectors to look at."

"I've been over twenty years. Doesn't it seem dreadful?" put in Miss Jones, anxiously amiable.

"Well, I can't compete with that, of course," said Mrs. Lee with a kind of ghastly coyness. "But I've been—let me see——"

"You had a gap, though, didn't you?" remarked Miss Thornby, warming the teapot.

"Yes. Before my husband had to take this job abroad he used to like to have me at home. But since I came back I've been——"

"I can't think how you got them to take you on again," interrupted Jenny.

"At heart, you know, I believe they like married

teachers." Mrs. Lee settled down again by the fire, apparently under the impression that Jenny had abandoned the battle. "You know, I've been reading so many articles in the papers lately about how wrong it is that women teachers have to leave their work when they're married. There was one in the *Daily Telegraph* only this morning, pointing out what an advantage a real experience of life is to a woman in charge of growing girls."

Miss Simpson gave a short laugh. Jenny looked sweet and enquiring.

"So as to teach them how to hook a man of their own?" she asked. "Is that what all this pornography in Betty Hunt's book signifies? Because if you've been trying to teach her the facts of life instead of copy-writing, you've been bringing coals to Newcastle."

"I think it's all nonsense about married women making better teachers," I said quickly, to avert the storm which I foresaw as soon as it dawned on Mrs. Lee what Jenny meant. "Nine times out of ten they're so occupied with the housekeeping and their own brats that their attention isn't half on their work. And as Jenny says, we're not teaching them about Life, we're teaching them to read and write and do sums."

"We can't help forming character. And a woman with wider sympathies is more fitted for that," Mrs. Lee stated heavily.

"Don't you think perhaps that a woman without family ties or children of her own can lavish the interest she would have had in them on her class?" suggested Miss Jones, timidly and sentimentally.

"I think you do," I couldn't help saying. I had got fond of old Jones, and her children did adore her, always bringing dirty twigs that they had stolen out of the park to put on her desk and draw for Nature Study. Jenny looked surprised, then returned to the attack on Mrs. Lee.

"Well, anyway, Miss—I mean Mrs. Lee—if you'd kindly support your own theories by putting a note on the bottom of this page that it was only you widening Betty Hunt's outlook, and not merely her taking advantage of a teacher's slackness, I'd very much appreciate it."

"Don't be ridiculous, Miss Lambert," said Mrs. Lee stiffly.

"Well, what am I to do about it then?"

"If you're so passionately keen on your own class that you find fault with everything a substitute teacher does, I can't understand how you could bring yourself to take a fortnight off," announced Mrs. Lee acidly.

"Oh—but—she had to. She couldn't help it," broke in Thornby, and stopped suddenly, looking at Jenny as if she feared she had been indiscreet.

"What do you mean?" But I thought I knew.

"I mean, she was ill, wasn't she? She had a doctor's certificate."

"I did." Jenny crossed over to Thornby with her tea-cup and took some tea. She closed the book then and dropped the subject, and began to tell Thornby about the handsome young doctor who had attended her for her attack of influenza. Miss Jones, who admired Jenny, listened with a kind of shocked enjoyment, remarking, "Really, though, doesn't it seem dreadful?" now and then, and giggling at Jenny's descriptions of his bedside manner. That afternoon, which was the afternoon I had promised to let Miss Jones get off early,

Jenny came into the infants' cloakroom and was surprised to find her with her coat and hat on all ready to go. She was the last of us all to leave usually. I explained how it was and Jenny said amiably: "Well, it all sounds very suspicious to me. I believe you've decided you'll never be a good teacher until you've got a young man, Miss Jones. We all know what it means when someone wants to get off early to prink themselves up for the evening." Miss Jones giggled and then looked so solemn that Jenny said to me, as she watched the old thing trotting out of the school gate, "I say—have I been unspeakably tactless?"

"Of course not. Why?" I asked, helping Billy Hutchinson on with his coat.

"Well, she looked so odd I wonder what it must be like at her age, with all hope buried in the past, when someone makes a joke about getting married?" Jenny fished a handkerchief out of Billy's pocket and scrubbed his nose with it while the infant looked stolidly on, so to speak.

"You're like Mrs. Lee—imagining that everyone wants to get married."

"Don't you?"

"No. I want to be a headmistress."

"Why not an inspector?"

"I haven't got the necessary spying nature."

"You do pretty well," said Jenny maliciously, and went off to tidy up her room. She had to do it herself nowadays, because Moira had been moved up into my class at the end of the quarter, and I had promptly sacked my original monitor and now had the nearest thing I could ever hope to have to a faithful maid-cum-private secretary of my own. On the evenings when I stayed on for night-school Moira had taken to making me a cup of tea after she had finished the prolonged spring-cleaning which she insisted upon performing every night.

"There aren't any more biscuits, Miss," announced Moira fussily, coming to meet me in the hall. "Shall I tell Miss Thornby that she's got to bring some more for you from home now that you're always staying to tea?"

"I think I'd better buy some for myself, Moira. Will you go down to the corner shop and buy some? You'll find a sixpence in my bag." She ran off, and I heard her running through the yard. That reminded me of the time I had heard her screaming and of something I meant to find out. When she came back with the biscuits I said:

"Aren't you lonely walking home all alone?"

"No, Miss."

"Nothing to be afraid of, is there?"

"No, Miss."

I looked at her for a moment. Then I said carelessly, "There is something, isn't there, Moira?"

"No, Miss Brigson." But she had hesitated for a fraction of a second.

"Tell me what it is."

"Miss," said Moira, after a long pause, "there's a big dog at the corner shop and he lies outside the door and they fetch him in when the children go past after school, because he snaps at their knees, Miss, but after the children have gone, before I go home, they let him go out again and he might snap at mine and I only wear socks, Miss."

I looked at the legs. They were brown and rounded

and smooth as an egg. They might well tempt a dog. And I pushed away another thought that came unbidden to my mind, and remembered something Jenny had told me about her own childhood.

"If I were you, Moira," I said, "I should stop going out of the girls' gate, but go out through the boys' yard and through the little gate at the end that leads on to the new by-pass road. You'll have to look carefully when you cross it, but that will mean you don't have to go round by the corner shop at all."

She listened with grave attention. I saw her, later on, going out through the little gate with an important official air. Satisfied, I went back to work. In going through the boys' yard she did not have to pass by the caretaker's stoke-hole. I left the rest to her methodical mind, which delighted in doing the same thing at the same time every day. I had a look at the corner dog when I went out for a stroll before night-school. He certainly was an ill-tempered animal.

On my way back I stopped at the entrance to the stoke-hole, where Cook was painstakingly sweeping the steps. I thought I might as well settle the matter if I could and set my mind at rest.

"Has the little girl gone?" I asked offhandedly.

"Which little girl is that, Miss?"

"The little girl Watson—the one that stayed late the day there was a thunderstorm and got caught in it."

"I haven't seen her, Miss."

"Oh—I just wanted to make sure she wasn't still here tidying up. Her father doesn't like her staying on late."

"I haven't seen her, Miss."

"I'm afraid her father was rather angry with us the day of the thunderstorm."

He looked up quickly. Such colour as there was drained slowly out of his cheeks. He said immediately, in a hoarse voice, "Has she been telling him about me?"

"She mentioned you."

He began to tremble violently, and went down the steps away from me. I followed him down. It seemed to me that now I might get some evidence upon which I could get him removed out of the children's lives for good. I did not like to see him frightened and caught out. But the choice was between an ageing, haggard, neurotic man and three hundred with their lives before them. Even if fifty had not been my responsibility, handed to me by the State, I think I must have done the same.

He was standing by the boiler in the tidy little furnace-room. It was warm and cosy down there. It was his little sanctum, and he had a tea-pot and cup and various small possessions of his own around him, although his cottage was so near. I looked round me and saw a little coloured box of sweets on the table. I was surprised to think that he should spend his wage on buying the kind of confectionery with which you pay extra for wrappings.

"What a nice little box of sweets," I said. There was a picture of Mickey Mouse on the cover. He snatched it away and put it in the pocket of his coat.

"I thought I'd better mention to you about Moira Watson's father," I remarked. He sat down on a pile of boxes and put his head in his hands.

"They can't leave me alone," he said piteously. "Always on to me—all of them—and then there's *them*. I can't help it, can I? I'm an honest man, aren't I? I keeps this school clean and tidy as it could be, don't I? It's persecution, that's what it is. And now I suppose I'll be being locked up, and when I'm in a cell then they'll be shrieking and screaming at me all day and all night." He rocked about like an old woman crying into her apron.

"Wouldn't you tell me all about it, Cook?" I asked him quietly. I wish I had had the moral courage to ask straight out what I wanted to know. But the words would not come. Perhaps there is something to be said for married teachers after all. Perhaps one of them would have been able to settle the whole sorry affair that minute. But I was frightened of the words and frightened of the thought.

He would not say any more. He picked up his broom and went away up the steps. I did not know what I should do. I had nothing new with which to persuade Miss Harford. I thought that perhaps if I saw that Moira was not left alone in the school building it would solve the problem until I found a better way out. Next morning I said to her:

"Moira, I've decided that it is too much work for you with being moved up into a higher class and being monitor as well. So, just for a little time, I'm going to have a new monitor and you can go home with the other children."

I had not seen such stunned grief on a child's face before. I could see that she was trying to say "Yes, Miss," but her quivering lips would not form the words. She tried pitifully all the morning to do her work as usual, but her writing was shaky, as if she was ill. She watched the new monitor going about her work with eyes wide with the shock of something too bad to be believed. After dinner she came in very shyly and looking very scared and laid a note on my desk. It was better written than most of the parents' communications and on the prison staff's notepaper. "Dear Miss Brigson, I do not wish to interfere with any school arrangements, but Moira is very grieved and upset that you have chosen a new monitor, and begs me to say that I do not think it is too much for her to manage with her school work. However, I daresay you are acting for some necessary reason, and have tried to explain this to her. Yours faithfully, C. B. Watson."

I looked up and found Moira watching me with shivering hope. They always have a pathetic belief that nothing will shake, that an actual letter, written by a parent's hand, has a world-compelling power over any dictum of authority from the laws of the Education Committee downwards. Sometimes they even infect parents with their dazzling faith. Often, between the lines of the ill-written and usually threatening scraps, you can see a mental picture of the unhappy child, creeping into the fancied security of its home, out of the merciless machine of the State, begging for help— so sure that Father or Mother has only to put stubby pencil to dirty paper for God himself to climb down off His perch and let Tommy or Betty go to the lavatory when they want, if you don't mind, teacher. . . .

"All right, Moira," I said. "If your father thinks it won't be too much for you, and doesn't mind your getting home late, you can go on being monitor."

She was radiant with sudden joy. I can think of that

moment without it hurting me now. It seems a long time ago.

But I made one more effort. I bought a packet of sweets, with a Mickey Mouse box, at the corner shop. It cost me two shillings and that aroused my suspicions again. You do not spend so much of a workman's salary without some good reason. I put it on my desk, and told Moira that I would give her the box when the sweets were finished. Her eyes sparkled.

"Miss, I've seen them in the shop window," she said.

"Mr. Cook buys them," I remarked.

"Yes, Miss."

"Did you know?"

"Yes, Miss. No, Miss Brigson."

She had gone a little bit pink. My heart sank.

"Your mother wouldn't like anybody to give you sweets but her or your father or your teacher, you know, Moira. They might give you stomach-ache if you had too many."

"Yes, Miss Brigson. I know."

"Do you always say 'No thank you'?"

"Yes, Miss Brigson."

"Sometimes the caretaker gives the children sweets."

"I told him I'd got some at home, Miss Brigson."

That settled the question in my mind. Somehow I must get Cook away from the school. It was no use being sentimental. His disabilities might entitle him to special consideration. But here the next generation was involved. He came second then. You do not need to have had children of your own to know that.

CHAPTER VI

AT THE beginning of the winter the last big factory had to close down. We received the news via Miss Thornby, as usual, one lunch-hour when we were all huddling round the fire and had the staff-room window closed and a nice stuffy atmosphere to counteract all the compulsory fresh air of the rest of the day.

"But why?" asked Jenny, as if she thought it had been done specially to annoy her.

"I suppose people don't want any more of what they make," I suggested, trying to correct my Compositions in the teeth of the conversation. It was too cold to sit in my room.

"What do they make?"

"Mowing-machines or something," I remembered.

"Then why shouldn't they want any more?"

"Oh, good heavens, I don't know. I suppose it's the depression."

"I thought there wasn't a depression any more now," remarked Miss Jones. "It always says in all the papers that prosperity has come back."

"Not to Bronton."

"Oh dear, I hate it when all the parents are unemployed," groaned Miss Simpson. "The fathers have too much time to grumble about the way their infants are being educated, and too much time to hang about street corners making remarks as you pass by, and too much time to knock the children about at home, poor devils."

For a few weeks we did not notice much difference.

The district had been looking so derelict and abandoned that one more smokeless chimney, like a gaunt tree prematurely struck dead by lightning, merely added a little to the general effect of devastation. I used to think, as the tram swayed down the long hill in the mornings, that the blackened towns of Spain could not look much more terrifying. I would look up from the pictures of Spain's ruined houses and streets with gaping wounds to find we had come opposite the long-condemned slums around the waste ground where old tins and rags were for ever being examined by optimistic dogs. I used to have day-dreams in which I was transformed into one of His Majesty's Inspectors and went around criticising the way the Government did their job. My sarcastic report on their activities always ended by picturing the plight of the nation's children if teachers took their work only as seriously as the rest of Government employees. But no one else seemed to take our work very seriously anyway.

The very morning I reached this disgruntled conclusion I found it contradicted from an unexpected direction. Miss Harford was away at a head teachers' meeting and had told me to see the children into school and take prayers. It should have been Miss Jones' job, but she hated doing it because it made her so shy to stand up on the platform in front of us all. I rather liked doing it. It induced in me pleasant dreams of the days when I should be a headmistress.

Just as I was watching the children marching into school in orderly lines I found the curate at my side.

"Good-morning," I said. "It's too soon to have another Scripture inspection."

"Oh, I don't think so," he answered, putting his hat

down on the desk and smiling at Jenny, who was thumping out "Glory and love to the men of old" for the children to march to.

"If you've come to see Jenny, why don't you just see her and then go quietly home?" I asked impatiently.

"I haven't. I've come to inspect the Scripture."

"See here," I remonstrated under cover of the noise. "What is the sense of all this Scripture inspection? Zeal is one thing, but what good do you think you're going to do anybody by coming down here and bothering us all just when we're starting the day's work? I appreciate that you think you've got a mission and you're in earnest about it, but this fussing and worrying as to whether ninety per cent. of these little heathens know the Beatitudes properly is just silly."

"No, it isn't. I want them to learn how to live better than their parents ever have done."

"The Beatitudes won't help them."

"There I disagree."

"Of course, you're paid for thinking that."

"Exactly," he said amiably.

"But you can't really believe that. I mean it isn't practicable."

"Why not?"

"Do you really think that your coming down here once or twice a term is going to make them start their lives on your moral basis?"

"If you teachers all took it as seriously as I do, it could be done."

"In that case you ought to reform the teachers first."

"Remember, if I do, that it was at your suggestion," he said, and began to take prayers. He was not one of those people who were a great success with children, but they were a little in awe of him, and there was no flagging of discipline. When they were marching out he said to me, "I'm going to go to the top class to-day," and followed Miss Simpson into her room. She had the top class. I went back into my own rather reluctantly because I should have loved to have been able to watch Miss Simpson being reformed after all the reforming of other people that she was so keen about. At break I asked her what sort of a time she had had.

"Oh—very comic," she said. "He started cross-questioning them about the psalm they'd been singing and asking them if they knew what usury was—you know, about the man who dwells on the holy hill because he doesn't lend his money on usury nor swears to deceive his neighbour."

"I know it all right," I groaned. "You needn't repeat it again."

"Well, he started having a long discussion about the wrongness of lending money on interest and just then Miss Thornby came in with the bank-books and interrupted the inspection to collect their sixpences to put in the bank. They saw the point all right. Muriel Beacon pointed it out, officious little creature. But you know how tiresomely literal-minded children are. I told him that if he knew a bit more about how literal they were he wouldn't try to teach them the Bible."

Jenny came up and joined the discussion.

"Last time we had an inspection, when that old dodderer Wolfe was here, he invited my children to ask questions about anything in the Bible they didn't understand, and one of them insisted on knowing what harlots and concubines were."

"I've always said it was the most unsuitable book

ever printed for children to read," I said, preparing to go into the playground and blow the whistle. "It's coarse and violent and full of words and expressions they shouldn't know. The only way to treat it is to keep the whole thing so vague and remote that they won't ask any questions."

"All the same, it's refreshing to find a parson who has got the guts to take it literally after all the plausible explaining away that most of them do," remarked Miss Simpson unexpectedly. I came back at that.

"Don't say you've fallen for such a cheap gag, Freda," I cried.

"What do you mean?"

"Don't you see that that maniac of a curate is trying to rake us all in for his hot-gospel campaign? He's completely unscrupulous. He's already tried to rake in Jenny and now he's concentrating on you. He's found out somehow that you're a Socialist or a Communist or an Anarchist or a Social-Creditist, or whatever it is you are, and he comes in and picks this bit about usury that he knows will go down with anyone as green as you, and you fall for it as if you were ten years old."

"Oh, nonsense, Madge," said Freda angrily. "I don't believe in the Bible any more than you do, probably not as much, because I'm an atheist, but I suppose I can say I respect a man who takes his job seriously, even if he is a fool of a parson, without you insinuating that I've fallen for him?"

"I think all parsons are dreary bores, and curates merely comic—an old joke," stated Jenny, tapping on the pane of her classroom to indicate to the monitor that she was to stop pulling the other monitor's hair.

"I suppose they are. Why does everyone always make fun of them so?" mused Freda.

"Anyone in deadly earnest is a bit comical," I suggested, and I went out to fetch the children in. But I had an idea that Gregory's particular type of earnestness was likely to prove more troublesome than the traditional stage curate's. It was at least a change, I reflected, to find someone being serious and dogmatic about anything besides the question of who should sleep with who, and how, and how often. I hate that kind of piety. I wondered if Jenny was still seeing her earnestly Bohemian professor.

A day or two afterwards Georgie Hunt came into school full of suppressed importance. I could see that he was longing to announce something to all his neighbours, and at last, after reproving him for whispering six or seven times, I asked him what it was he was trying to say.

"Miss, Mr. Gregory was in a fight in our street last night."

"Was he hurt?"

"He was bleeding and bleeding. He was all bloody."

"I'm sorry to hear that, Georgie. Now you see what happens if people fight the way you're always trying to in the playground."

"Yes, Miss. Miss, it was because our Stanley told Mr. Levy, what lends my dad half a crown till Tuesday, that the Lord would strike him dead and Mr. Gregory said so and Mr. Levy's son knocked Mr. Gregory out when he come along our street and made his nose bleed like anything and he borrowed a little girl's pinafore to wipe it and her mother was ever so mad, Miss."

I told Miss Simpson what had happened to her fellow-Red and that she might expect that kind of thing herself if she followed in his footsteps. She was furious first, and then sulky. She would not speak to me for several days. She was an odd person.

Jenny, too, was in an irritating mood. She was full of the suppressed exhilaration that came over her when she had made a new conquest, singing to herself and getting excited and happy over nothing and behaving generally like a child who is keeping a secret and means to make you curious. She and I sometimes went out into the country together, on winter Sundays, and took sandwiches with us. But this week she said she was going out with a man. It was an understood thing between us that a date with a man always superseded a date with me. She invited me to guess who it was.

"Is it anyone I know?"

Jenny giggled and said it was.

"It's that idiotic Mr. Gregory," I suggested scornfully.

"Oh no, it isn't. I don't go out with curates. Anyway, parsons always work on Sunday. Didn't you know?"

"Mr. Walker from the Boys' Senior?"

"No."

"The chinless young man from the bank?"

"No."

"Well, I'm not interested." I was not going to pander to her vanity, nor take part in a childish game of "Shan't-tell-you." I thought I would have a nice restful day at home by the fire with a library book. In fact, for once I took the Bible literally and had a day of rest.

I was not at all pleased, therefore, when there was a knock at the door about tea-time and I found Miss Thornby on the step. She lived fairly near me, but we were not in the habit of calling on each other at the week-ends.

"I'm sorry to disturb you, Madge," she said as she followed me in. "But I think I ought to go down to the Hunts to-night and I wondered if you'd come with me. It's such a rowdy district on Sunday nights that I don't like to go alone."

"Oh, bother you, Thornby," I snapped. "I'll give you some tea willingly, but I have quite enough of the Hunts in the week. Whatever it is can surely wait till to-morrow morning."

She sat down while I boiled a kettle on the fire.

"You see, Madge, my sister teaches in the Sunday school, and she has Teddie Hunt in her class, and this afternoon, when she was showing them a picture of Isaac bound to the altar, he insisted that it was like their baby."

"Oh, good heavens," I said impatiently. "You know what a vivid imagination the Hunts have got. When I had Stanley in my class and showed him a Renaissance picture of Jesus Christ, he said it was exactly like his Grandad. And it wasn't in the least."

"That's not what Teddie meant. He said their baby was tied on to the bed all day, like Isaac on the altar."

"Oh, well, you know the Hunts' peculiar household arrangements. It's probably to keep it out of mischief while the mother's working. It's nothing to do with us."

"Well—but Teddie said their mother and father had been away since Monday, and that they had to leave the baby there while they were in school. And he said that the baby wasn't crying to-day and wouldn't have its milk out of the tin, so he had drunk it instead. I wanted my sister to come down with me because it sounds as if it was probably dying of neglect, but she's simply terrified of Lower Bronton and she's not very strong, you know, so I wondered if you would come with me."

"Oh, all right. I suppose I'll have to come," I said crossly. "But you are a nuisance, Thornby, with your charities. I don't see why we should have to be plagued with the children's troubles on Sunday as well as every other day."

I put on my coat, stoked up the fire ready for my return, and we went out to the tram. On the way I idly asked Thornby why on earth her sister taught in the Sunday school. Thornby said it was because she felt she ought to do something for the Church and because she thought at lot of Mr. Gregory.

"I shall be absolutely wild if she's sent us on a wild-goose chase to-night, anyway."

Thornby knew the Hunt's address. It was wonderful how many addresses she had in her head. She had a gift for it. We went down a labyrinth of alleys behind the disused factories. The men and women and children who were standing about, either staring silently at each other, or else carrying on a shouted conversation with someone a few yards away, looked at us as if they thought we were up to no good. Some of the children recognised us and formed an impromptu procession, greeting us with the joyful recognition of a discovered Livingstone, though we had seen them all forty-eight hours before. At the end of a narrow alley was a square yard, surrounded on four sides by buildings six floors high. Stone steps shut in by iron gratings gave access to all the flats. I looked up. Even the sixth-floor windows would be darkened at midday by the flats opposite. The whole building smelt of food weeks old. But the flats were not bad, as Lower Bronton accommodation went. They had stone sinks, with a tap on each floor for the use of the various tenants. We climbed up in the block Thornby indicated. There seemed to be a remarkable number of potato-peelings all over the place. "They do seem keen on potatoes," I remarked to Thornby. Thornby was occupied in trying to persuade the procession to wait for us at the foot of the steps. It was encouraging to find how well school discipline survived the environment. They waited most obediently.

On the fourth floor we met an enormously fat woman with her hair done up in curlers. I should have thought she let them out on Sunday, but perhaps they were being saved up for some festival.

"Are any of the Hunts at home, above you?" Thornby asked her.

"I'm sure I don't know," she answered haughtily. "I don't have nothing to do with them."

"Don't you?" I was interested to discover that there. were apparently social distinctions here, the cause for which was not visible to the naked eye.

"No, I don't, Miss. I'm respectable and I don't have nothing to do with them Hunts and that dirty little cat what I know a thing or two about that I told the attendance man when he come round. No right to live in a decent house, she hasn't, with her goings-on."

We went up another flight and knocked at the door. There was a little scuffling inside and then the door opened an inch or two. I pushed it quickly and slipped inside.

There stood Maggie Hunt, dressed in an old check skirt and a silk blouse. With her little round, fair head and her pale, pointed face—innocent of make-up for the first time I had seen it—she looked like a bedraggled schoolgirl. She glared at us and said, "What do you want here?"

I pushed past her. There were two rooms, opening off each other. In the first one was a worm-eaten table, a three-legged horse-hair couch, a pile of sacks and the inevitable potato-peelings. In the second were one or two broken chairs, a pile of newspapers and a large mirror, hung near the window. The most remarkable thing about it all was that there was a large double bed with brass knobs and a mattress. Beside the rest of the furniture it looked positively handsome. On the bed lay a child of two or three fast asleep, fair, rosy and extremely pretty as children go. At the other end of the bed was a baby, looking rather blue and with eyes half-open. A heap of cords lay on the floor beside it. Thornby went up to it and felt its hands and feet.

At that moment Georgie came running up the stairs and into the room. When he saw us he came slowly up to us, staring as if he could not believe his eyes. Maggie snatched her handbag off the bed and ran out before we could stop her.

"Where are your mother and father, Georgie?"

"They've gone away for a bit, Miss."

"When did they go?"

Georgie meditated for a long time, staring at the ceiling, which was patterned all over with house-bugs. Then he said, "Monday, Miss."

"Who's been looking after you?"

He looked vague, and said he didn't know, Miss. It was his favourite rejoinder at school. Thornby said she was going to fetch the woman from next door to have a look at the baby. I stayed with Georgie and tried to cross-question him. He admitted, after a long time, that he thought their Maggie had been looking after them.

"Have you all kept on at school every day?"

"Yes, Miss," said Georgie dutifully.

"Why didn't you say anything about your parents being away?"

He looked absolutely astonished and answered, after a pause, that he didn't know, Miss. I asked him if it was true that they tied the baby up to the bed every day, and he said yes, Miss, his Mam had told them to in case it fell off while they were all out. I looked at the cords and at the baby's wrists and ankles. They did look sore.

"Our Stanley ties its hands behind its back," volunteered Georgie. I began to feel a little bit sick.

"It doesn't need to have its hands tied, though, to stop it falling off, does it?"

"No, Miss. But our Stanley likes doing it. He's got a book with a man in. Shall I show you the picture? The baby gets ever so cross, Miss."

Thornby came back, scarlet in the face.

"She won't come. She says she's too respectable. Nor will the one below her. It's because of Maggie." She stopped and glanced at Georgie. "Does your

Maggie bring some money home when your mum and dad are away?"

"Yes, Miss."

"I'd better go and telephone for an ambulance. That baby is as good as dead already," I said. I had been feeling its hands and they were very chilly. "I suppose I'd better try to warm it," said Thornby doubtfully. It was odd how helpless we both were before the odd little creature just because it had not reached the age at which the State puts its children into our charge. When I got to the foot of the stairs I found all the other children obediently waiting there, and asked them to take me to the nearest telephone-box. They swarmed around me and quarrelled as to who should have the privilege of escorting me. In the end they all did. I phoned the hospital and gave the Hunts' address.

When I got back to the Hunts' rooms Thornby was nursing the baby and Georgie sitting on the bed watching her as if he had paid for a seat at a show. The other child had wakened up and greeted me with a grin and by bouncing about on the bed with joy. I might have been its oldest friend, returning unexpectedly from a long absence.

The shining white ambulance glided through the dark archway, six floors down, and two bored men came up with a stretcher. They were highly amused when they found it was only a baby they were to carry, and joked about whether they should put it on the stretcher like an adult. I suppose I had not made myself clear enough when I rang up. Anyway, they covered it up and took it away. Then we went down and telephoned the police about the other children. We waited till the police-car arrived and left them trying to catch the other six Hunts, one and all of whom had gone into hiding as soon as they saw the dark-blue uniforms.

"It must be odd to have a perpetually guilty conscience like those Hunt children," I said to Thornby as we walked out of the alley. "They're in a permanent state of congratulating themselves that they're not getting their deserts at the moment. They're rather like earwigs and things, hurrying away as soon as they see you, perfectly convinced that they've got no right to exist."

"It seems rather as if they hadn't, doesn't it?" Thornby had been rather upset by the whole thing. Usually nothing moved her except children spending their bank-money on sweets on the way to school.

"There'll be one less Hunt, anyway, judging from the look of that baby. I feel as if someone ought to be flogged for that."

"Oh, I shouldn't be surprised if it got quite well again," said Thornby, cheering up. "You'd be surprised what they live through. And, anyway, who would you flog, if you think flogging would do any good?"

"The Hunt parents, I think."

"They've only gone out to walk to London because they think they might find work there. And then they're going to send for the children, Georgie said. I don't think they meant to be unkind. They're just stupid. It was really only their wanting the baby to be safe that made them tell the children to tie it on to the bed while they were at school."

"Well, then, Maggie. It would do her good."

"I think she's done her best for them, you know. She hasn't looked after them, but she has given them some money, and Georgie says she's brought a lot of men home. But that was why the neighbours wouldn't go in, you see. Some of them gave the children quite a lot to eat in their own kitchens, but they seem as if they have to keep up this business of not associating with—with women like her. It's a kind of code of honour with them."

I thought I could understand this very well. It was the same kind of thing, I thought, as the Englishman dressing for dinner in the jungle. I suppose there are times when, in the midst of inescapable squalor, one's only remnant of civilisation might be a grandiloquent though useless gesture belonging to a remote social code. I left Thornby at the tram-stop and walked up home, feeling unhappy and depressed. Squalor did not frighten me. When you live so close to it, and are paid to fight it, it is not terrifying—merely a tiresome and tireless adversary. But somewhere beneath it all was something which did frighten me. It was as if there was a live, burning thread that ran through these human miseries that was not just mismanagement, nor stupidity, nor a faulty social system, but something living, primitive, terrible—something I dare not look in the face. A hundred nauseating images seemed to rise up in my mind—all somehow connected. There was the policeman twisting the thin young man's arms and then bandaging my hand. There was Cook coming into school and trying to flirt with me after I had heard Moira scream. There was Stanley tying the baby's wrists behind its back with string because he liked doing it. And I felt that if I had been one of those ragged women who lived near the Hunts I might have done as they did—refused to go near a home supported by Maggie's money, earned from the pleasures of the flesh, that were connected, by ties of blood that could not be severed, with the brutality that rejoiced in its power over others' bodies. Perhaps it was only my repressed imagination which tried to blacken this experience that I had never known. I comforted myself with the thought. Perhaps there was a point at which the lusts of the flesh ceased to be this fierce delight that knew no law, and became gentle, friendly, considerate. I expect it's only because I'm an old maid that I imagine a connection between the two, I said to myself, as I came to our garden gate and began to search through my bag for a latch-key.

A figure rose up from the doorstep and came to meet me. It was a tall, thin man.

"Hullo—who are you?" I asked, very startled.

"Are you Miss Margery Brigson?"

"Yes, I am. Who are you?"

It appeared that he was a reporter from the local paper. Not the *Echo*, he hastened to add, but the *Ranklin and Bronton Journal*. I never read it, so it meant nothing to me. He wanted to know about my finding the abandoned children. One of the Hunts' neighbours had told him my name and he had looked me up in a directory. Before I realised it he was in the sitting-room of the bungalow with his notebook in his hand. Daphne and Enid had come in and were toasting biscuits by the fire. Between their excited cross-questionings and the young man's perspicacity, he soon had the whole story.

"I can work that up into a nice little story about the evils of unemployment," he remarked patronisingly, smiling at Enid, who was the prettier of the two.

"What's unemployment got to do with it?" asked Daphne.

"Why—don't you see—these two driven to despair by prolonged unemployment and by seeing their kiddies starving—go off to London in the despairing hope of finding work. Meanwhile, in the heart of the world's wealthiest empire, these kiddies are starving. Does the Capitalist State care?"

"I'll tell you what interested me," I said to Enid and Daphne, remembering what I had meant to tell them. "All the Hunt children who are on our registers turned up to school every day just as usual. Their parents had impressed on them that they must, or else they'd have the Attendance Officer round. It speaks well for his work, doesn't it?"

"I might add that as the tyranny of Government hirelings," said the young man, opening his book again.

"Don't you think children ought to have to go to school?" asked Enid.

"I think it ought to be such a happy place that they don't need any Attendance Officer to dragoon them into going."

"It's evident that you've never been a teacher," I remarked. I had talked that sort of stuff myself at college, but I thought he ought to have got over it at his age.

"Anyway," added Daphne, who obviously disliked him, "it's all very well for you to say the Government didn't do anything, but they had the baby fetched to hospital and the children put in charge of the police, and I don't see what more you want them to do."

"It could never have happened in an enlightened State," announced the youth heavily.

"In that case your enlightened State would have to have police or social workers or something snooping round the whole time to make sure that the Hunts weren't living in the shiftless way that's most natural to them," I pointed out.

"Yes, and what about the freedom of the individual then?" put in Daphne.

He answered feebly that the Hunts would not be as anti-social as they were in an enlightened State.

"Then you'd have to reform the individuals, not merely the machinery of government," I suggested, hoping that he would agree.

He did.

"Surely the only way to do that is by starting when they're young," I went on joyfully.

He supposed so.

"Well, you just try doing that without a Government hireling to make them come to school," cried Daphne, taking my argument out of my mouth.

He began to mumble about our only teaching them to read and write and not to be thinking citizens, but we were three against one and we soon disposed of him.

CHAPTER VII

THE HUNT children did not turn up at school for the next week. Miss Harford told us that they had been sent to a home until their parents should be found. The school seemed quite depleted without them. Thornby rang up the hospital to ask about the baby and was told that it was going on well. They thought they would be able to discharge it in a few weeks. Quite a lot of people had sent subscriptions for it to the paper that had published the story, and it was in clover. My friend the nurse told me, when I met her in a shop one day, that it was an irritating patient because it simply screamed with fury when any member of the human race approached it.

"It's terrible, being in a children's ward," she said. "Of course you're sorry for them, but you feel you could murder them when they go on and on screaming like that. Thank goodness I'm not there permanently. It's only part of my training."

"I expect that even when you're furious with it, it gets better treated than with its own parents," I suggested. She looked surprised.

"Oh no—they're awfully good to them usually, Madge. It's all nonsense what people say about them ill-treating them. They're unwise—cram them with sweets and stuff—but they mean it kindly. It's just incompetence."

I agreed with this when she said it, but I was

impatient when the same argument was brought up by one of the magistrates when Mr. and Mrs. Hunt were finally run to earth in London and brought back to Bronton police court. Thornby and I had to go as witnesses and missed a morning's school in consequence. We knew what we had got to say, and it was quite easy. Then, just when we were thinking that the Hunts would get a stiff sentence, this old magistrate started sentimentalising about their having been foolish rather than wicked, and just driven to despair by unemployment. The Hunts brightened up, and the magistrates had a long consultation, and the court missionary was sent for, and the end of it was that they all decided to restore the Hunt family to each other's bosoms on the understanding that the parental love they had both earnestly professed (in the dock) should be given free rein.

Thornby and I went back to school. We both said it was ridiculous.

"It was that hard-boiled looking old party with a dewlap and creases in his neck that got them off," I remarked. "I've never seen anyone who looked so like the brutal big business boss that's always chewing a cigar in films. I couldn't understand it. I thought he'd be the kind who would give them years and years of hard labour."

"I understood from my sister," began Thornby, settling down to it, "that he was rather that sort of man until just lately, when it seems that he got somehow converted, and wrote to the people he'd done down and told them how sorry he was, and that he'd give the money to a hospital to make up. So now he has had a direction from God, so he says, that he's got to do some good in Lower Bronton with his money. He's got himself elected one of the school managers, you know, besides being a magistrate, so he'll have plenty of opportunity."

"I suppose he's decided to start at the bottom, with the Hunts, and work his way up. I hope he reaches us before long."

All the Hunt children were back in school by the end of the week, wearing new suits and shoes and being so pleased with themselves that they were more impossible than usual. The sentimental old magistrate, whose name was Mr. McCarthy, sent a cheque to Miss Thornby, who kept all the milk accounts and had charge of the milk-money, to pay for the entire Hunt family to have a bottle of milk each every day. That saved the Hunt children the trouble of stealing it, but the net result was exactly the same. For months now they had been in the habit of lining up in the milk queue without a shadow of right. In our school all the children who could afford milk at lunch-time used to bring the week's money in advance on Mondays. Then, each playtime, they had to line up in the hall, take their bottle and straw, imbibe it there and then, and put the empty bottle in the case outside Miss Harford's door. Out of the hundred or so there was usually someone away, and therefore an extra milk, and besides this the milkman always left a few spare bottles for the staff, or in case a child should turn up for the first time in the middle of the week. The Hunts only had to line up in the queue, with a sufficient air of assurance—easy enough for them—to get a drink without much difficulty. One of the staff was always on duty and perfectly well aware that the transaction was not legal.

But however much you may believe in rules being kept, it is not possible to judge a child who is consistently hungry, while you are full, for stealing a drink of milk. So the thing had begun to acquire an air of permanence and respectability and the Hunts to stand on their rights and grumble if there was not an extra milk for whichever of them happened to require it that day. We were quite relieved, therefore, when Mr. McCarthy sent his money and made the whole thing legal. It really seemed as if the Hunts were reformed characters in spite of themselves.

"My dad goes down to the club every day now, Miss," Betty remarked to me in the playground.

"Which club is that?"

"The unemployed club what Mr. McCarthy's started, Miss. They makes shoes and stools and all sorts and my dad plays draughts, Miss."

It turned out that this unemployed club was part of Mr. McCarthy's idea for doing what God had directed him. He provided occupation for them in order to preserve their self-respect. It was a pity that most of the Lower Bronton men were conservative and believed in working for the sake of a weekly pay-envelope instead of their self-respect. Some of them went regularly for a while, especially in the cold weather, when the club was warm and attractive, but they were difficult to discipline and used to spend all their time playing dominoes and ignore the shoemaking and carpentering tools.

Meat became dearer, so did coal and bread. Every now and then another little shop would put up huge notices outside its windows, "Temporarily closed for redecoration." The notice was supposed to deceive creditors and give the owner time to abscond. After a while, however, it became a mere formality and deceived nobody.

The men used to grumble ceaselessly to each other at street-corners, since they could not go into the public-house and their wives got sick of having them at home. But they were all quiet and peaceable, apart from private fights, until the curate started his club.

It was a pity, from the point of view of law and order, that Mr. Gregory was his own master in the district. Lower Bronton church is only a curacy, but it is the kind where the curate is in charge, and the vicar, if any, at a parish some way away. Anyway, nobody appeared to be Mr. Gregory's spiritual father and he had everything his own way. He started an unemployed men's club in the church parish room, and got the local Member of Parliament, who was only a glorified factory worker, down to open it. The most dangerous political agitator in the district, Stanley Rivven by name, joined it in the first week.

We first became aware of its existence when we came down one Monday morning to find the red flag flapping dismally over the parish room door. Jenny and I strolled down there in the dinner-hour, out of curiosity, and found Gregory, surrounded by some extremely villainous-looking young men, nailing up notices on the board.

"Hullo. Are you going to join my club?" he called to us. The young men eyed Jenny sheepishly.

"What's the qualification?" I enquired.

"Just a determination to reform the sorry scheme of things entire and—I can't remember the rest, can you?"

"You'd better ask Miss Simpson. It sounds more in her line than ours."

"She's a foundation member," he answered, feeling in the pocket of his ancient mackintosh for more nails. "Did you know that they were proposing to cut down the unemployment relief for large families? If they do, this club is going to make its first object to get them put up again, higher than they were, if possible."

"One of these days your Bishop will get to hear about your goings-on and you'll get sacked with ignominy," I remarked.

"Will you join, Miss Lambert?" He turned to Jenny.

"Not me. I'm not interested in politics." She smiled carelessly at one of the young men. He murmured something about her bringing the custom in all right if she joined, and Gregory looked contemptuously, not at the man, but at her. She saw it and it stung. She said a little spitefully: "Well, you've got Miss Simpson. She'll do, won't she?"

"I thought she was an atheist," I remembered

"When you told me I ought to reform the staff you didn't tell me what varied creeds they had," said Mr. Gregory to me.

"I haven't one at all," put in Jenny.

"I thought you believed in respectability," he said carelessly, and went on hammering. On the way back to school Jenny said to me mournfully that it was depressing to be despised, even by someone whose opinion you didn't care about. I told her not to try to talk in paradoxes. She turned very sulky and I avoided her and walked home with Miss Jones instead. It did not worry me much. I knew she would forget about it by next morning. Besides, I had a private plan of my own, which was occupying my attention at the moment, to the exclusion of Jenny's affairs.

I had noticed, from the window of my classroom, that Cook seemed to cross and recross the playground several times in the course of his morning's work. It did not strike me at first, but gradually it began to impress itself on my mind. I was in a continual state of hostile suspicion towards him and was ready to put the worst construction upon anything he did. When I did notice this, and began to try to remember when he had started these pilgrimages, I came to the conclusion that it was only since the weather had got very cold. It might be that the furnace needed stoking up more often, as the school had to be kept warmer, but I knew enough about the working of the furnace to guess that, even at its highest, it would hardly need as much attention as he was apparently giving it. I took to observing him narrowly, and once sent a little girl over to his cottage on some pretext. When she came back, I said:

"Are you cold, Nellie?"

"No, thank you, Miss Brigson."

"Wasn't it cold in Mr. Cook's cottage?"

"No, Miss Brigson. There was a big fire."

I sent her back to her place and took up my post at the window. The pockets of Cook's old coat were certainly bulging. When he came back they were flat.

I was not going to go to Miss Harford again. Nor had I any very strong feelings about petty thieving from the Education Office. But I thought he was a dangerous man, and that I must get him sacked in spite of Miss Harford's predilection for returned heroes. I had been looking out for a chance. Now I thought I had it.

I began to jot down the approximate times he passed by on my blotting-pad. I did it for two mornings, and then I went to Miss Harford and asked her if I might slip out for a few minutes to make an important telephone call. She was very chilly about it, and I had to pretend it was to a dentist, and that I was in raging agony, before she would let me off. I settled the children down to a sum that would take a good ten minutes, left the classroom door open so that anybody passing through the hall would hear a whisper, slipped on a coat and went out.

I crossed the waste ground, from where I could see Cook's cottage door, and stepped behind a broken wooden fence. I had time to get chilled to the bone in the damp November fog before I saw the door open and Cook, with his jacket turned up over his neck and his shoulders hunched underneath it, go across the road to the playground. I gave him enough time to get into the furnace and then followed quietly. I stood pressed against the school wall, outside the spiked fence that guarded his little stairway, and listened. I heard him shovelling coke into the boiler fire, and then there was a pause and he came up the steps. I slipped round the corner of the school building so that he should not see me. When he had crossed the yard, I followed him to his cottage, knocked on the door, and walked straight in. He was just emptying his pockets on to the fire.

"Good-morning," I said, to make time. A few pieces of coke dropped from his hand on to the clean floor. I picked one or two up and put them into my pocket. The coal-scuttle was full of the "washed nuts" that were provided for the school furnace and the fire was glowing as only a coke fire glows, with a dead, steady heat and no flame. I was just turning to go, not considering it a suitable time to improve the occasion, when he picked up the poker and made a dash for me. I tried to catch his arm, but only succeeded in deflecting his aim so that the poker landed on my shoulder instead of my head. It hurt me acutely and it made me terribly angry. My anger seemed to give me extra strength, and I seized his wrist and twisted it so that he dropped the poker. I am strong and he had something the matter with his shoulder—a muscle damaged in the war, I think—and I snatched the poker and kept it in my own hand. I thought that if there was to be any murder done I was not going to be the victim, anyway.

He dropped into a chair and I was left with the poker in my hand, the fight abruptly at an anti-climax and a supreme thankfulness that nobody was watching the ridiculous scene.

"I never meant to hurt you, Miss, gawd help me I swear I didn't," he began to whine. "Only you give me such a start coming in like that and I thought it was a burglar, honest I did, Miss. My nerves aren't what they were, and if I didn't have a bit of a fire at night after I'm left alone, there's them comes screaming and shrieking at me something awful." He calmed down and added quietly: "If you could see your way to keeping quiet about it, Miss, I would promise on my sacred word of honour never to take another nut, starving cold though I may be. I'm getting on now, Miss, and you know what unemployment is here nowadays and if you get me sacked from this job I'll never get another and it'll be the workhouse for me till the day of my death, and I bet you'd have me on your conscience something awful, Miss."

"I certainly shouldn't," I said. "Of course I shall report you."

I put the poker down and went back to my class. When the children had gone home for their dinners I went to Miss Harford and told her that I had discovered that Cook was stealing the school coke regularly for his own fire. She went quite purple all round her neck with rage—not with him, but with me. She told me that I was officious and interfering and exceeded my authority. Although she did not actually add that I was a liar, she gave me to understand that she suspected that my toothache had been considerably exaggerated. She compared my deliberate spying and dishonesty with Cook's trivial and comprehensible offence and drew comparisons between us to his advantage. But I hinted pretty broadly that I was only hesitating between going to the Office and the police, and she ended up by saying that she would report the matter herself, asking them to make allowance for his previous good character, his physical disabilities and the excellence with which he did his work. I agreed readily enough to all this. I was quite sure that the Office would not keep on the Archangel Gabriel if they had found him stealing their coke. And I was right. He was given notice immediately. The day I heard about it I went about feeling as if some awful nightmare had been removed from my life. Now I could put my nameless fears away out of sight and never think of them again.

He came over to the furnace-room for the last time, to collect the old sacks that he used to sit on, and his odd tools and pipes and various other possessions, and went sulkily off. He did not even say good-bye to any of us, nor stay to instruct the temporary man who came up from the Office in his duties. But the children, who had been hanging over the stoke-hole fence watching him pack, said that he had been calling names.

"Calling who names?" I asked. The verb is intransitive in Lower Bronton.

"Miss, the teachers. He said Miss Lambert was a Jezebel and you were an interfering old b——."

"That will do, Molly," I broke in hastily. "Never repeat foolish things you have heard.

I promptly disregarded my own excellent advice by telling the others about Cook going off muttering revenge.

"I shouldn't worry," advised Miss Thornby. "He can only spread scandal in the neighbourhood and I don't suppose that will do any harm."

"I hope we get a decent, tidy, methodical man who doesn't have any visions next," I remarked.

"Hope we get a dashing young Adonis," murmured Jenny.

"There have been four hundred applications," Thornby told us.

"That shows you what the depression is," growled Miss Simpson from her corner.

"But I'll tell you what I heard," went on Thornby confidentially. "I heard that Mr. McCarthy, who's got a lot of pull with the managers, wants to appoint Hunt."

"Hunt!" we shrieked, like a women's chorus.

"Hunt," affirmed Miss Thornby, thoroughly enjoying the sensation she had provided. "You see, he has taken rather an interest in that family because they're always begging from him, and they're very plausible, you know, and since that business of deserting the children it seems that Hunt has got round him some way."

When the school came in I asked Georgie if it was true that his father had heard of a good job.

"Miss, yes, Miss," said Georgie.

"Does he think he'll get it, Georgie?"

"Miss, he's going to sweep the school instead of Mr. Cook and we've all got to help him keep the place clean and tidy, Miss."

"I think you'd better begin practising by keeping your own home clean and tidy first, Georgie." One gets into the way of improving the occasion.

Georgie looked doubtful, as Hercules might have done when the idea of the Augean stables was first mooted. We all persuaded Miss Thornby to hint to Miss Harford that we thought that we ought to be consulted before a man like Hunt was trusted with the task of safeguarding our possessions. She answered, quite kindly but firmly, that she did not think it was anything to do with us.

However, the idea evidently registered with her, because when Mr. McCarthy paid one of his managerial visits he came into the staff-room at break and said he wanted to enlist our co-operation. He said that he had been privileged by the Almighty to have some little influence over George Hunt senior, and that Hunt had told him frankly how difficult it was for an unemployed man to go straight.

"It's impossible for Hunt," I remarked.

"Exactly," agreed Mr. McCarthy, with a vague idea

that I was trying to help him out. "He told me how little he had to live on, and how much of it he had to pay out on necessities every week, and I realised, when we worked it out together, that it is quite impossible for him to support his family on the unemployment relief that he gets. He told me how he really wanted to make good now and to make up to his children for that unfortunate expedition of his recently, and admitted frankly that the hardships he had to witness his wife and children enduring had made him break the law more than once in the past."

"He was in prison for embezzling the funds of a Christmas club," I put in.

"He told me that," went on Mr. McCarthy crushingly. "It does no good to rake up old scores, Miss Brigson. We have all made mistakes in the past—even the best of us—and we shall all make mistakes in the future, too."

"That's what I say. Hunt will go on making the same mistakes about what is his own property and what is other people's."

He looked at me very sorrowfully.

"Will you forgive me if I remind you about the story of casting the first stone, Miss Brigson? I am afraid I have an incurable faith in human nature. I will guarantee that this man Hunt will live up to the trust I put in him. I am sure—" he turned to the others, "I am sure that you find that the same thing applies to the children. Show you trust them implicitly and they will justify your faith. Isn't that so?"

Miss Jones murmured that it was indeed. I said, as loudly as I dared, that I did not think the Hunts had ever heard of that theory. But he pretended not to hear. He disliked me all right. And I disliked him. I thought he was a sentimental old fool.

But he was chairman, besides being the only person in the district with two gilt-edged securities to rattle against each other. So Father Hunt duly turned up in a new suit—from its size I supposed it was a cast-off one of Mr. McCarthy's—and a clean white apron, and applied himself to caretaking. He was a broad, beefy-looking little man, and used to go round wearing a conscientious frown. He was painfully obliging. He was always hanging about looking helpful, if not actually doing anything. The first week he came he had a tremendous spring-cleaning of the place. He kept on telling us all what a disgraceful state the last man had left everything in and how things were going to be different in future.

He turned out the stoke-hole and had the girls' yard spread with coal and coke and wood and old exercise-books for about three days. The girls used the things for fighting and Mollie Hardy had a black eye from being hit in the face with a log. Then he had a great cleaning of the staff cloakroom and all our coats were splashed with soft soap, and we had to wash our hands in the children's lavatory. He used to turn the furnace switches up so that the boilers were at their highest temperature, which meant that we were sweating all day and the children were too sleepy to work. Then we would have a day when he had it so low that we were all shivering. If we pointed out anything that he had done wrong he was so grieved and apologetic that it was impossible to get away from him.

The worst of it all was that the Hunt children now had a right to be on the premises more or less when they liked. When I stayed on for tea before night-school, expecting an hour's quiet, they would be making soap slides in the hall and sliding up and down on them. We had to lock everything up even more carefully than usual, knowing the broadness of their social code. They all began to assume an official air and to order the other children about. This was not to be tolerated, and the popular feeling reached such a pitch that whenever there was a fight in the playground you might be sure of finding a crushed and wriggling Hunt at the bottom of the mêlée.

One morning when I passed by the Labour Exchange, and saw the dismal queue that lengthened every day outside it, I noticed Cook among them. He looked wilder and thinner than ever. Even among that ragged crew he stood out. I was afraid that his unstable mind was not the sort to stand up for long against the ordeal of becoming an enforced parasite, and thought I would ask someone about him, and perhaps suggest that Mr. McCarthy took up his case. When I got to school I found Hunt, with my classroom still only half-cleaned, as usual, arranging and re-arranging desks, and asked whether he knew what Cook had been doing since he had been dismissed.

He gratefully stopped pulling chairs about and settled down to conversation.

"You see, Miss, it's like this. That there Cook, he may not have been much of a caretaker, and God knows I found a hell of a mess here what I had to tidy up before I could bring myself to stay in the place—but then I'm like that, Miss—but he was a decent, quiet sort of a chap and on the right side of the police. But now, Miss, he's got in with that Mr. Gregory and we all know what that means, Miss, and I must say I thought parsons were paid to help keep working men out of trouble, not lead them into it, but that gang aren't fit to live in a decent district, Miss, and that Cook's the worst of the lot."

"Why—what does he do?"

"It's not so much what he does as what he says, Miss. I've heard him say that what this country wants is for all the rich to be rooted out of the land and hung up on the lamp-posts and that the Lord God had appointed him to root the rich out. That's what he said in the public-house the other night, ma'am, when I happened to be passing by the door and heard him."

"That sounds a harmless sort of hobby to me— rooting out the rich. Is that all he said?"

Mr. Hunt took a deep breath and was about to launch out again when he saw Miss Harford come into school and briskly settled down to work. I gave up the idea of mentioning Cook to Mr. McCarthy. For one thing I did not want to ask favours of him, and for another I did not see why Cook, who had no children, should be picked out for charity from among the hundreds of other men whom poverty and boredom were steadily driving towards violence. In any case, he had apparently joined Mr. Gregory's gang, and if he was making himself responsible for the afflictions of the men, I was only too thankful to stick to the job I was paid for—the upbringing of the children. No one at all seemed to be concerned about the women, I reflected, but I suppose that if you are a wife and mother your little world consists of those two others. I used to give thanks for my single state. One day I picked a few verses for the children to learn for Scripture and, only half intending it, came upon the bit about weeping for your children, and blessing the wombs that never bare and the paps that never gave suck. I had never known, I reflected, what it was like to have your suffering doubled and trebled by too close ties to another human being. Then I flicked the pages over and chose a bit of the Acts instead, because the passage was quite embarrassingly unsuitable, and I was not going to spend the whole of Scripture lesson explaining away physical terms to children who knew quite well what they meant, but liked to be difficult about them.

CHAPTER VIII

I AM afraid that I must have a spying nature, as
Jenny says, because soon after my successful bit of
detective work on poor old Cook, I began to do the
same kind of thing over again, and with no excuse
this time except my own curiosity. It happened that
Tommy Bellerby, who was in my class, developed a
mania for collecting foreign stamps. He was always
bringing the collection to school to show me, and I
used to bring him any I got from some relatives in
Canada from time to time. Sometimes the rest of the
staff used to bring him one too. We all took an interest
in his collection and helped him with it, because it
seemed rather distinguished to have a child with such
a middle-class hobby as a pupil. It made us feel almost
like secondary-school teachers. Most of our children's
hobbies were more in the line of chalking rude words
on the walls around the school.

It took some weeks for the significance to dawn on
me, but I noticed that Miss Jones used to give Tommy
a stamp regularly once a week, and nearly always from
a different place. I did think once that she must have
friends and relatives in the most scattered spots, but it
was not until she gave him one from Gibraltar, and
he asked me which page of his album it ought to go
on—he never could spell—that something began to
connect up in my mind. I was improving the occasion
by telling Tommy about how the English sailors
stopped at Gibraltar on the way home, when I sud-

denly remembered the only day Miss Jones had ever
left school early. So I told Tommy to ask Miss Jones
if he could have two copies of any of the stamps.
Because, if she was just getting her stamps from her
old landlady, the sailor's sister, then that was of no
interest at all. But if he was writing to both of them,
then it did look as if Miss Jones' little romance was
not merely a figment of my imagination. Tommy got
his two stamps that week, and a fortnight later as well,
and a fortnight after that. From this I deduced that
the sailor was writing to his sister once a week and
Miss Jones once a fortnight, or else the other way on.
Then Tommy got a stamp from the Irish Free State and
a day or two after that Miss Jones asked me if I would
see her children out of the cloakroom at tea-time.

I said: "I never knew such a gadabout as you. Are
you going out with your boy-friend again?"

She giggled rather girlishly at that, and I wished I
had not said it. It was cheap and silly and inquisitive,
and, besides that, the whole idea of anyone as old as
Miss Jones fancying herself in love seemed ludicrous
and completely indecent. I began to hope fervently
that the poor old thing was not going to make a complete fool of herself, as only a middle-aged old maid
with dyed black hair and frumpy clothes can, when
accident throws a prepossessing male across her path.

Next day she was in a state of fluttering excitement
about her little outing, and told us all about it in the
dinner-hour. They had had salmon and tinned fruit
and coffee at some restaurant with a band, and after
that they had gone to see *Victoria the Great* at the
pictures. She kept on telling us about it, and repeating
the jokes the sailor had made—very middle-aged ones,

incidentally, and exactly the same ones that he had made last time. He must have been an old bore.

However, he apparently went back to his ship, because the foreign stamps started again, and I thought we had heard the last of him for some time. Then one day, when Miss Jones had stayed on late to pin some nature-drawings up on her wall, she came in to the staff-room where I was having tea, and Moira hovering about brushing imaginary crumbs off the tablecloth, and began to talk to me about how she was thinking of buying a new dress. I was rather impatient, because I was looking over my lesson for night-school and stringing myself up for it. It was still an ordeal.

"Do you think a red velvet dress like that one Miss Lambert sometimes wears would look too chickenish on me?" she asked nervously.

I considered, and said that I did not think so. Moira brought a clean cup and plate and put them quietly on the table, seeing, as plainly as I did, that Miss Jones was there for half an hour at least. Sometimes Moira's helpfulness was a little exhausting, and I told her to go home, in case she should encourage Jones to stay still longer. I looked meaningly at my books and papers, but Miss Jones was fairly launched.

She said very seriously that now she went out so much she really thought she ought to have a new after-noon dress.

I suppose I looked perplexed, because she added, "You see, whenever my friend's brother comes home—four times a year at least—he takes us out, and I don't like to look dowdy."

"Do you think he notices?" I asked.

"Don't you think men always do?" she said wisely.

I felt uneasy, and as if I had been dragged into a foolish situation. If only anybody from the ordinary world had seen us—two plain old school-marms, sitting in our drab schoolroom discussing how to attract men. I wished I could conquer this ridiculous humiliation about my job. But there are so many jokes about it—and about being an old maid, too.

Miss Jones began to tell me what I knew already, about the sailor writing to her regularly. She said they had corresponded for some years now.

"Of course, I know there's nothing—nothing *in it*," she went on, solemnly and very earnestly. "But it makes a difference, don't you think, to a man so far away from home and friends to have chatty letters from England now and then?"

I escaped as soon as I could, though I wished I had the courage to ask her what sort of things her letters chatted about. There was the sailor—with his boat full of some interesting cargo and rough men with tattooed arms—anchored perhaps in the harbour of some far-away town, sitting in his cabin with the chatter of foreign voices beyond, and reading about our day's doings at school—how Miss Harford had been cross, or Teddie Hunt sick, or what little Alan Wheatley said about the baby robin outside the window. . . . I hastily pulled myself together and began making notes for my night-school class. Miss Jones was making me as sentimental and romantic as herself.

At the end of the month the register-clerk turned up on one of his unannounced visits. The idea is to catch us out with our registers either added up too soon—before nine-thirty or two-twenty—or too late—after those times, or else not added up at all, which rejoices their hearts and makes them feel they are earning their pay—or best of all, added up wrongly, which causes them such acute satisfaction that it seems a pity not to do it oftener. But one scarcely ever does, because a register is the most sacred object in the school calendar. It is on a par with birth-certificates and insurance cards—one of those State records of a human creature's existence which are the rock-bottom of civilisation. There is a legend in all schools that you can be sacked, deprived of your teacher's certificate, and struck off the rolls without any appeal for a fault in your register. Anyway, we are all desperately careful and conscientious about them. So it was astonishing to discover that a teacher as experienced as Miss Jones had been summoned into the hall and was being very severely talked to by Miss Harford and the register-clerk, who was waving his blue pencil above her register like a conjurer at a party.

Directly the ball rang I went into her classroom to condole with her. I was sure she would be dreadfully upset. But she did not seem at all perturbed. She merely said that she had forgotten to close the register at all, all day, and wasn't it dreadful of her, after all the years she had been marking registers, and then said she wanted to ask my opinion about something. She did not want to betray a confidence, she fluttered, digging in her handbag for a letter, but she would like—— She began to read me a sentence from a long screed on steamer notepaper. "You know I shall be retiring at the end of the year, and I have a plan very dear to me. I scarcely dare hope all will turn out as I want it to, but the good things in our family have always come late in life."

She looked at me with grim earnestness over the sheet of thin paper, all covered with a spidery, precise, middle-aged kind of handwriting. Did it mean anything, or didn't it, she wanted to know? I supposed it meant something, but I could hardly think it meant what she was dying for it to mean. Just then Jenny came in to tell Miss Jones to cheer up, because she did not believe that Miss Harford was really as cross as she appeared to be about the register. Miss Jones said to her feverishly:

"Miss Lambert—you know so much about—about men. Do you think—what do you think—I want to ask you something in the strictest confidence." Jenny listened very seriously, and I could not help thinking that she had got gentler in some ways lately. Then she said: "I think it means something very definite. Old-fashioned men always walk round and round the point like that before they ever reach it." Miss Jones said nothing more, but she put the letter away in the innermost pocket of her awful old school-marm bag, with her eyes positively gleaming.

I remember that it was one of those mild sunny winter afternoons that come so occasionally in Bronton, and that the children were unusually good. I let them have the reading-books they liked best and their favourite story about an old ball who married a faithful top after years and years of waiting. I opened the classroom window and stood looking out on to the faint gold afternoon sky. Someone was having a bonfire on the waste ground and the smell reminded me of the country. I was nearer to being perfectly happy than I ever remember being during term-time. Old age—my own old age—suddenly receded into the distance and lost its terrors for the moment. I thought of it with pleasant speculation, and decided that I would have a very small cottage in the country and keep a little maid to do the work.

It was the last mild day. At the end of that week the winter began in deadly earnest, as though the cold days before had been merely a temporary substitute for the real thing. I had a persistent sensation, as we plunged deeper into those short, icy days, with their lowering fogs, that the town was plunging down with us. It was frightening. We all seemed to be one—the huge husks of the great factory buildings whose heart-beats had stopped—the grey, stained houses round them, the tragic men who stood for ever at street-corners, and the children who came to school in fewer and fewer warm clothes, because as the weather got colder they were pawned for food. I would like to have been detached from it—a visitor, coming down to work and then going away. But I could not get the feeling of detachment. I was part of it, bound irrevocably to their miseries because my work was their children. I felt as if we were all hemmed in some remote dungeon, shut right away from the comfortable workaday world and from ordinary humanity.

As soon as I appeared in the playground with the whistle these days there was a rush for the lines. Their one idea was to get into the warm school as soon as possible. When they got in they would edge up to the hot pipes, with sidelong glances to see if we had noticed them moving out of their orderly ranks.

"You'll make your chilblains worse if you put your hands on the pipes," we used to say to them. "And

if you sit on the pipes you can guess what will happen."
They used to laugh delightedly at that. It was funny
how they would suddenly laugh in the middle of such
discomfort that a grown-up person would not have
smiled at the greatest humorist living.

One day Miss Jones was rather silent and absent-
minded. At afternoon recreation she confided to me
that she had been expecting a letter which had not
arrived. I said that I expected the mails were late,
because they often were when the winter storms began.
She agreed eagerly, but a sinking feeling seized me.
Next day she went down to the General Post Office
at midday and came back with a newspaper and a
white puffy face. The mail that she had been waiting
for had come in at the beginning of the week. And
her sailor's boat was two days overdue at Jamaica and
no one knew why, except that there had been gales.

The fogs set in. We used to get them badly around
the school, because of its being a low-lying district. The
sight of those thick grey wreaths floating about the hall,
or like blotting-paper outside the window, reduced us
all to a state of more complete wretchedness than we
had ever thought possible. And still day by day there
was no news of the boat, and presently it was a week
late and began to figure in the news columns, not just
the shipping ones. There were terrible gales at sea, but
not one of them came to disperse the fog that hung
over us week by week, so that when Alan Wheatley's
father hung himself from the rafters with his wife's
clothes-line we felt no surprise, nothing but a chilling
wonder as to how many more would follow his
example.

It was at this lowest ebb of the year that Mr.

McCarthy called at the school one morning. I looked out through the panel and saw him talking to Miss Harford. There was much less traffic through the hall than usual. During the cold weather no child went out to the lavatories in the yard unless they really had to. In fact, we were able to take an informal census for use during the rest of the year as to which children were usually in the habit of asking to go out unnecessarily for the sake of missing a few minutes of the class. Nothing, however, damped the roving spirit of the Hunts, and two or three of them passed and repassed Mr. McCarthy. I let Georgie go out twice, for the sake of seeing him cross the hall with his eyes fixed on Mr. McCarthy's dewlap, while his feet carried him slowly past. Mr. McCarthy patted his head each time, not realising that it was the same child four times over, twice going and twice coming. I reflected that if he had an opportunity to examine the state of George's hair, as I had last time the nurse came round, he would not be quite so free with his well-manicured hands.

At playtime Miss Harford sent a message round to say that we were wanted in her room. Her room was warm, and we all came willingly. Mr. McCarthy said that he wanted to provide a Christmas treat for the children this year.

"They always do have one," put in Miss Simpson rudely.

Miss Harford glared at her, and explained to Mr. McCarthy that the schools usually had a little party towards the end of the Christmas term. Each child brought threepence towards the cost of its tea, and they did plays and had games. But it was a very simple affair, and, in any case, this year most of the parents would not be able to afford the threepence, so that his generosity would indeed be a blessing.

Mr. McCarthy looked a little bit doubtful and said that he had thought of something a little more permanent, such as providing a set of very beautiful religious pictures for each classroom and the hall. But we anxiously headed him off that, and told him that the three hundred's one idea of a little sunshine in their clouded days was to be given the opportunity of eating themselves sick. So he agreed to hand out the money.

Of course Thornby was put in charge of all the arrangements. Anything of that kind always falls on the infant teacher. I don't know whether it is because they usually seem to be the kindly, fussing sort that takes on voluntary jobs, or whether it is just because they can be spared best, since the infants' class is the one that matters least from the point of view of inspection. For even inspectors, appointed for the purpose by His Majesty's Government, cannot do much with these five-year-old outlaws, without discipline, respect for the powers that be, or any principles or manners of any kind whatsoever. I suppose they have some method of discovering whether some veteran of five years and six months, who is spending the morning in fits of reasonless and purposeless weeping, like a character out of a Tchekov play, could arrange his string of beads in graduated colours if he felt like trying, or whether the hireling appointed by the State to instruct him has ever got him beyond the first bead. Anyway, I have never known an inspector complain about the infant class, so I suppose they are as much in the dark as the rest of us about it. But it leaves people like Thornby free to do all the little odd jobs about the school and make us all cups of tea.

Her five-year-olds of the moment were neither better nor worse than they usually are. That is to say, they cried and screamed, were sick at intervals, had to be taken out to the lavatories personally and then did not know how to undo their buttons, and had sudden primitive feuds in the middle of an apparently tranquil half-hour covering their blackboards with masses of blue chalk. They appeared to be vaguely conscious of Miss Thornby's authority, and drifted in and out of the cloakroom and classroom more or less as she directed them. They took not the smallest notice of anyone else. It did not seem to make much difference to the sum of their daily progress towards education when she took on the organisation of Mr. McCarthy's party, and spent the day coming round our classes taking down numbers and asking us all how much we should each require for her order.

When we had all given her our advice and the figures of our class, she made out a very impressive list, beginning:

"Five hundred cream horns at twopence each."

She was a little conscience-stricken about the cream horns. They were those indigestible-looking horns of puff pastry, with preserved cream oozing out of them, and correspondingly expensive. She was inclined to think that cream buns, made of sweetened dough with a dab of cream, would have done equally well, and reduced the expense by two pounds one and eightpence. Also she was certain that one cream horn per head would be enough. It was Miss Simpson's idea to double them. Her generally hostile attitude towards the wealthy prompted her to help to sting Mr. McCarthy for as much as possible. Miss Thornby demurred:

"We musn't take advantage of Mr. McCarthy's generosity, must we?"

Miss Simpson said that was exactly what we must do.

"But it doesn't seem right," complained Miss Thornby, with her blue pencil hovering over the "500," ready to make it into "250."

"He's filched it from the poor and will have it taken away from him again one day, so why not let him part willingly with as much of it as possible while he can? It gives him an undeserved glow of generosity and the starved victims of capitalism two cream horns apiece," added Miss Simpson, warming up.

Poor Miss Thornby looked more worried than ever. She was so conscientious, and she was torn between the claims of the children and Mr. McCarthy. I thought I would help her out.

"If you order five hundred you can bargain with the caterers for a reduction on quantity. Tell them that if they don't reduce it to three-halfpence each you will only have three hundred. That ought to fetch them."

She brightened up, made a note in the margin of her list, and went on reading it to us. It was afternoon break and the children were in the yard, while we crouched over a smoky little fire in the staff-room. "Three hundred Swiss buns, a dozen large loaves, ready cut, two hundred and fifty chocolate biscuits, fifteen two-pound jars of jam——"

"You're making me feel as if I never wanted to eat tea again," remarked Miss Simpson. "I pity you having to wade through all those masses of food."

Miss Thornby murmured that she was glad to do it

and hurried away to summon her fifty minimuses into the cloakroom in order to avoid their being trampled in the rush which followed the whistle being blown for the rest of the school.

"Isn't she a bore with her conscience?" mused Miss Simpson, as we watched her through the window folding up her list and shepherding her children.

"Not such a bore as you are with yours," I could not help replying.

"It isn't a question of conscience so much as standing up for my convictions," said Miss Simpson stiffly. "I believe the children have more moral right to the money than that fat old vampire."

"I don't know where you get your ideas from."

"If you and Miss Thornby didn't go through life completely enveloped in your own little affairs you wouldn't be able to avoid seeing what is obvious to the meanest intelligence."

"Miss Thornby isn't half so wrapped up in her own affairs as you are. She's a heap more unselfish and helpful than you could ever become in twenty years."

"She's entirely absorbed in the petty little round of other people's business because her own life is so empty."

"On the contrary, she gets more fun out of her gossip and her little deeds of kindness than you do out of all your tub-thumping theories."

The whistle blew and left me with the last word. That was a triumph. Miss Simpson always had something to say and nearly always got it in. But the list was added up as it stood, and it was arranged that Miss Thornby was to go and buy the things at the local shop two days before the party.

We had to deal locally, because feeling would have run so high if we had gone elsewhere. All the district knew about the party, and the chief baker in Lower Bronton, who had three children in the school, was expecting the order. Miss Thornby called to see him about it, and learned that cash down was his motto, and that he would like the money the day the order was delivered, if she pleased.

"I suppose he never has this kind of order and he doesn't know the right thing to do," lamented Miss Thornby when she came back from the shop to tell us about this.

"Oh, rot," said Miss Simpson. "It's simply that times are so bad the people he deals with won't let him have anything on credit and he simply hasn't got the cash."

"I daresay he wants to get some little things for his family for Christmas and needs the money," suggested Miss Jones, who was conscientiously trying to behave just as usual, and not to read and re-read the newspaper all lunch-time in the hope of discovering some shipping news she had missed.

"I expect he wants to have a good blind on Saturday night," was my idea.

"I hardly like to ask Mr. McCarthy for the cash," worried Miss Thornby. However, she had to, and he gave her a bank-note to help the baker out of whatever difficulties he was in with his dealers and said he would pay any extra she had to spend on the day after the party. She was quite overburdened by the note. "I shall be glad when it's paid and I've got the receipt. I hardly like the responsibility of so much money," she remarked, as she locked it away in the little cash-box she usually used for the children's bank-money. "Now where shall I put this money till I take it up to the bank?"

Miss Jones lent her a tin that had contained cough lozenges. She gave the last two to Stanley Hunt, as the Hunts always had coughs, and nothing—even the most linseedy-and-eucaliptised sweets—ever came amiss with them.

CHAPTER IX

THE PARTY was to be on Friday. By Wednesday we were all in a fever of preparation. We did not trouble to prepare any lessons, because the children all divided their day between practising the carols they would sing to Santa Claus (alias Mr. McCarthy), rehearsing their parts in the concert and making paper wreaths to decorate the school. In the morning, while my room was littered with snippings of coloured paper, I looked through the glass panel and saw something which made my heart stand still.

In the passage leading from the playground, outside Miss Harford's room, were two masculine figures in well-cut overcoats, felt hats, and carrying leather despatch-cases. I looked twice. I could scarcely believe my eyes. I found myself shaking all over.

I went back to my desk, told Moira to collect up the paper chains, scissors and coloured paper and to give out the readers. I told the children that anyone who moved or spoke would be given the strap without further warning. I sat down, tore a page out of an exercise-book, and wrote on it "H.M.I. here," folded it carefully, and gave it to Moira with instructions that she was to take it to each teacher, ask her to read it and give it back to her, and then bring it back to me. Then I hastily started the lesson that was on the official time table. All the while I cursed under my breath that those abominable inspectors, on whom our livelihoods depended, should choose to come at such a time.

I supposed they had done it deliberately to catch us out if they could. I hoped that the others would get my warning in time to pull themselves together.

Moira came back with my note.

"Did you give it to all the teachers?"

"Yes, Miss, all but Miss Thornby and she's away."

"Are you sure?"

"Yes, Miss."

"Who's taking her class?"

"Miss Jones is taking them all for some singing in her room, Miss."

A few minutes later Miss Harford came in, trying to look like a headmistress whose house is so well in order that she has no need to be disturbed by official inspections, and not succeeding at all. She said to me in a low voice:

"Miss Brigson, Miss Thornby is very late this morning, on account of the business with the party caterers, I suppose. She was going to call and pay them. I sent her little ones into Miss Jones' room just till she came, and their register has not been marked. Would you take them back and mark the attendance? Keep them as quiet as possible, will you? We don't want the rest of the school disturbed."

I understood perfectly. I left my class working, under the most alarming threats I could think of, and collected the fifty small creatures and took them back to their classroom. Some of them were noisy and I slapped them. It is not allowed, and I do not approve of it, but necessity, in the form of that threatening couple, drove me to drastic measures. The ones that I slapped set up a howl, and I slapped them again, but there was no silencing them. It is disconcerting, when you are accustomed to children who have learnt discipline, to be thrust into the middle of those to whom it means nothing. I kept on glancing fearfully at Miss Harford's door.

I guessed that she would take the H.M.I.'s right across the hall to Jenny's and Miss Simpson's rooms if she could, to give Miss Thornby a chance to get back before they reached her. She had no business to have allowed the school routine to get so disorganised that a teacher could turn up over half an hour late, on account of ordering cream horns for a school party, and she knew it. I made up my mind that I would back her up as well as I could, for Thornby's sake, and also because, whatever our usual differences, we were all united in instantaneous hostility towards the inspectors.

Just as I had got the babies all sitting in their seats I heard the click of the office door. The two Government inspectors went by the panel and crossed the hall. I hastily began to pull the most extraordinary faces I could think of. I drew my mouth down and waggled my tongue over my chin. Then I put my eyebrows up as high as they would go and turned my lips up to match. I had my back to the panel, of course, and my face to the children. I hoped that the proceeding would achieve an appearance of order as the H.M.I.'s passed by. It was most successful. The children all gazed at me solemnly, as if they were drinking in what I was saying in the most serious and dutiful manner possible. It must have been an edifying scene viewed from the back.

Then, when I was sure they had passed, I went over to the desk for the register, took it out and hastily marked and closed it. Miss Harford came in looking very worried, and saying that she was sending all the infants into the yard to have their drill lesson together, so that I could get back to my class. I thankfully left them to her.

It was just as I was starting my reading lesson, and straining my eyes to see if Miss Thornby was coming in, that something stirred in the back of my mind—something was queer that I vaguely recollected and yet I could not lay hold of it. It was an irritating feeling. I knew it was something about Miss Thornby, but I could not think what. I wondered if she would come in by the far door, nearest the staff cloakroom, and would see the inspectors as she went to get her keys off the board. Then I remembered. Miss Thornby's desk had not been locked.

Members of the staff with classes above the infant school had a trustworthy monitor to fetch their keys and unlock their desks before they arrived in the morning. But Miss Thornby, with her fifty still in the moron stage of infancy, had no one to do it for her. It was just possible, I reflected, that she might have left the desk unlocked when she went home last night. But it was extremely unlikely. She was the most methodical of us all.

I could not rest. As soon as the next bell rang, which was the signal for me to take my class to drill in the yard, I set them marking time in the corridor and slipped into the empty Babies' room. I raised the lid of the desk and looked inside. There were no keys. I glanced at the lock. It had been broken. I looked to see if the cupboards were unlocked. They were all firmly closed and fastened as they were every night.

My first idea was that there had been a burglary and

that I must report it at once. Then I realised that Miss Harford was tied up with the inspectors and that I should either have to interrupt them or else wait until she was free. If they were to learn that the burglary had only just been discovered, it would at once be apparent to them, if I knew anything about their prying habits, that one of the school registers had not been marked at all at the beginning of the morning. That might very well mean a dismissal. I wished with all my heart that Thornby would come back.

I did not see Miss Harford at break, and I was desperately engaged upon my own affairs. There was a History lesson on my time-table and no equivalent lesson prepared in my notebook. I had intended to spend the time in having the children repeat the carols they were learning by heart. Now I began to draw a hasty sketch of the map of the Mediterranean on my blackboard. I had only got it half-finished when the children came in from the playground and the inspectors from Miss Harford's study. My heart sank as they approached my classroom. There was no escape now.

They both stood looking enigmatically at the class, in the irritating manner common to stage detectives and His Majesty's Inspectors of schools, as if they had some incredibly clever trick up their sleeves that you did not know about. I fussed with my papers and pretended that there was something written in my notebook. I was very frightened indeed. It was the fourth inspection of my life, but I had never before been caught so ill-prepared, and with my thoughts unwillingly running on something else, so that I could not concentrate. I tried to tell myself that it all did not matter and that nobody had ever yet lost their job on one unsatisfactory inspection, but the feeling of trial by ordeal was too strong to be reasoned away. There is a device I have seen used in a cinema film, when the producers want to indicate that the story is going back to some years before, when they show you a calendar fluttering backwards with the dates they are passing by. Something like that seemed to happen to me. Back and back I went, like an irritating nightmare, through the four inspections I had known—one three years ago at this school when I had not yet learned how to keep the exercise-books tidy—one two years before that when I still had a gigantic fear of men, and thought they were superior beings—one two years before that when I was new to a large school and quite overawed by it—and the years stripped me and left me standing, a raw recruit from college, facing my first trial. How the children had turned into malicious little savages, keeping me on the rack—how the middle-aged inspector had treated me impatiently, as a tiresome schoolgirl—how I had endeavoured to give an idealistic twist to the lesson by illustrating it with an Elizabethan love lyric—and how he had stopped me, in front of all the children, and told me it was irrelevant and unsuitable. Even now I could hardly bear to think of the foolish humiliation of that moment. I had cried in the staff-room afterwards and said I would not be a teacher. And he had sent for me, and I had found him reading my teaching notebook with its romanticism, its tags of poetry and youthful, portentous comments in the margin—"Try to make children realise extraordinary eager and debonair quality of Elizabethan golden age, exemplified in love lyrics." He had given it back to me with a sarcastic, middle-aged smile and said that if I stuck to the point in my History lessons, and remembered I was there to teach the children facts, perhaps my class would show better results.

Even after all those years—nearly ten years now—the memory brought up a surging of hot, embarrassed anger. The children sensed a tension in the air, in the uncanny way that they have, and sat up straight and stiff, looking anxious. I determined that I would not be the eager, tremulous girl of twenty. I would be myself, thirty, and an experienced teacher who had long ago weighed middle-aged inspectors in the balance and decided that they could not rule a class if you set them down before one and told them to get on with it.

I went over to the two silent dummies and said kindly: "This morning I am revising the term's History syllabus on the history of Greece and Rome. Won't you sit down?"

Now this is a thing that is simply not done, and I knew it. The correct manner with inspectors is to act as if they were not in the room at all. They both looked extremely chilly at my unconventionality and declined the offer of a seat with a cold bow. Then one of them turned and walked out. I was left with the other.

He was a tall, lean man, with eyeglasses and a thin brown face. His name, as I remembered, was Mr. Vick. Thornby had once told me that she had heard that his wife had left him. I glanced down the passage. Miss Thornby's class was just trooping into the hall. Apparently they were going to have their second singing lesson of the morning with Miss Jones' class. I pitied Miss Harford. She must be desperate.

Mechanically I requested someone to point out

Greece on the map. I picked a boy I was sure of and
he did it. The inspector was registering complete indifference. He might have been deaf and blind.

I began to question them about the siege of Troy,
giving the children a lead whenever I could. Not that
I thought it would deceive him. Inspectors have heard
that trick played too many times. But I was not going
to get stuck and give him a chance to contemplate my
embarrassment in the grim silence they are addicted
to. Just as we got the avenging Greeks and their ships
fairly launched a little boy slipped into the room. I
recognised him as one of Jenny's class. He handed me
a note. Glancing at the inspector, and cursing Jenny
with all my heart for being so foolish as to risk it when
he was about, I opened it. It said: "Hunt's been up
to fetch T. and found empty house. Keep quiet about
her not being here."

"All right," I said to the little boy. But while I was
occupied Mr. Vick had seized his chance. He strode
into the middle of the floor and addressed Georgie
Hunt with the threatening mildness of a prosecuting
counsel.

"Will you go on with the story?"

Georgie looked bewildered. But his neighbours
prompted him and he stood up, glancing pathetically
at me, as if imploring my help. I gave him a sickly
smile, intended for encouragement.

"So they went," he said, and sat down again.

"Who went where?" asked the inspector.

Georgie stood up with the pained expression of a
Job.

"Miss—sir, the men what was friends of the man
who the lady had been stolen off." He paused, but

there was no help from earth or heaven. Tommy Bellerby whispered to Georgie and the inspector looked from him to me, insinuating plainly that it was obvious to him that I allowed that kind of thing regularly.

"In ships," added Georgie triumphantly, after leaning down to Tommy for him to repeat his information.

"What sort of ships?"

"Wooden ones," interrupted Tommy promptly.

"Suppose you wait till I ask you," said the inspector freezingly, and then to Georgie:

"How did they go?"

"Please, sir, they had an injun inside of them."

"An Indian?" said Mr. Vick affectedly. It was the sort of joke that inspectors make and that I never have considered amusing. The children laughed dutifully. Georgie, however, was open-minded and amenable to correction from a higher source.

"An In—di—an," he amended. "At least" (he brightened up as a vague memory stirred in his mind) "there was twelve In—di—ans inside of it and the others thought it was a present from the Greeks, and so they took it in the house, and when it was dark they all come out through a trap-door and they gave it the others and soon they was all dead and they set the place afire and there was a great big fire and they all run about in their night-shirts and so the others had won."

There was a long silence. I was a little taken aback, but I thought that if Mr. Vick did not realise that there was at least one of Georgie's sort in every class he knew nothing about districts where mothers had a child a year and the brains seemed to have to be divided among them as sparsely as all their other possessions.

But he meant to make me uncomfortable. I think even my small show of independence had annoyed him. The children sensed it too in the long silence that followed. I could see Moira watching me, and knew that she was suffering as children do when the particular grown-up they are attached to is getting the worst of it. She timidly put up her hand. She was a loyal child. Mr. Vick just looked at her and said nothing. But Moira chose to take his look as permission to speak.

"Please, sir, the Greeks had sails, but if the sails wouldn't go they made a lot of men sit in rows and push it along with flat sticks, and it was a horse they got inside and in the night they got out and opened the gates for their friends and Georgie Hunt was away when we did about it, sir, because he has to go down to the clinic every Monday and it's History on a Monday when he's away because he has to have sunlight out of a lamp because his knees knock together, sir, and he's the only one that doesn't know about it because Miss Brigson drew a picture of the horse on the blackboard when he was away, sir."

I thought that even Mr. Vick must have been moved by this naïve defence of my proficiency. I thought what a wife Moira would make someone one day. The clinic card was inside my register, if he cared to look at it, and prove her accurate as usual. But he simply turned and went out of the room. A few minutes later the bell rang.

As soon as I was free I went to Jenny.

"What on earth is all this about?"

"I don't know." Jenny spoke in an undertone, and looked cautiously into the now empty hall. "But that old snooper has been cross-questioning me and third-

degreeing me about poor old Thornby until I was perfectly sure that something was up, and then when
Hunt came back and told us that the house was locked
up I thought I'd warn you not to give anything away."

"But there's nothing to give away."

"Listen to me, Madge. When old Sherlock Vick
had finished asking me how long Miss Thornby had
been here, and whether I knew what school she had
been at before, and what made her take a job as baby-
teacher when she should have been in a senior position
at her age, I began to get a bit detective-minded myself,
and I asked Susie Hall, the baker's infant, whether
Miss Thornby had called in with the party-money yet,
and she said that she had promised to, but she hadn't,
and that her Dad was very angry about it."

"She couldn't have absconded with it. There wasn't
enough to have made it worth while."

"There was all the party-money and quite a lot of
the bank-money too. Neither is in her desk. I had a
look."

"Oh, don't be silly. Anyway, the H.M.I. must have
been asking about her because he suspected she wasn't
here and wanted to find out why he hadn't been
told."

"No, but that's the funny part. The inspectors didn't
know that she wasn't here. Miss Harford said so. They
said, as soon as they came in, that they didn't want to
see any of the infant-school this time, and just before
they went they discussed with each other as to whether
they had time just to speak to the infant-teachers, and
then decided that perhaps they ought to go straight
away. The infants always do have singing and drill
altogether, you see, so they didn't notice. Anyway,

they were in our classrooms the whole morning. I watched specially, and neither of them went near the girls' door. So, you see, it couldn't have been that. But Miss Harford sent Hunt up to Thornby's, and when I saw him coming back I slipped out and asked him, and decided that we'd better all keep quiet about her."

Miss Harford put her head in the door.

"Miss Brigson, it looks as if Miss Thornby wasn't coming back to-day. So will you take her class this afternoon, and, Miss Lambert, will you take Miss Brigson's and your own for carols? The inspectors will not be coming back."

We sighed with relief. The children were rushing about the playground with their spirits soaring after the strain of the morning. It was odd to think that the test by which we stand or fall was over for two or three years. I had put in three years of conscientious work, hour by hour, day by day, controlling my impatience, my weariness, swallowing enormous quantities of aspirins to quiet my nerves when they rebelled against the wear and tear of fifty-six restless minds and bodies. And now twenty minutes of nervous embarrassment and His Majesty's Government had passed judgment on all I had done. It seemed a peculiar arrangement to me. I would not judge a child so lightly.

"But if the alternative is having them in every week or so, heaven forbid," I remarked to Jenny.

"I don't know what you're talking about," said Jenny. "What are we going to do about Thornby?"

"I suppose we ought to tell the police that her desk was broken into. It's funny that Hunt didn't notice it when he did the rooms."

"Probably he did it himself," suggested Jenny. "Anyway, I don't think we should get the police."

"But our only reason for not doing it is that she isn't here to-day, and therefore you suspect her of absconding with the money. Why should she break the desk? Anyway, people just don't do wild things like that."

"On the contrary, of course they do," Jenny argued. "Teachers are always absconding with bank-money, just as the treasurers are always absconding with slate-club funds."

But Miss Harford had noticed the broken desk herself, and had called at the police station on her way home to lunch and given the police a hint that they had better keep a better watch on the building at night, since the district was getting more and more lawless.

That afternoon the young policeman came up to the school to have a look at the desk. He was the same one who had dealt with the upset at my night-school class. At tea-time, when he had gone, Jenny asked me if I thought him good-looking.

"I suppose so," I said. "Why? Do you want to collect him?"

"You're so vulgar, Madge. As a matter of fact I have one of those clean boy and girl friendships with him as it is."

"So that's your new young man, is it?"

"Purely Platonic."

"Not with that face. He's really vicious."

"He's been to a public school. Policemen do now, you know."

"You are a little snob," I said, and it was true that

Jenny had changed in that way, too, the last few months. It seemed almost as if her brief glimpse into social outlawry had frightened her into wanting to be safely out of the squalor she had been brought up in once and for all. Yet in other ways she had coarsened, I thought, looking at her critically. She did not look quite so bloomingly young as she had done, and her clothes were even tighter and her lipstick redder. I pointed this out to her as we walked up home, and she indifferently agreed with me. I walked round by Thornby's home, after I had parted with Jenny, just to make sure that she was not in.

There was a light in the front room and I rang the bell. Miss Thornby opened the door and asked me in.

"Wherever have you been?" I cried, as I went into the little sitting-room. Miss Thornby looked quite herself, bright and competent, fussing to make some tea as soon as I arrived.

"Oh, I just had such a bad head, and a bit of a temperature, and so I thought it wouldn't matter if I missed a day for the first time in three years."

I stared at her. "But Hunt came up to your house and rang the bell, and it was all shut up."

"Oh, was that Hunt? I heard the bell, but I was in bed and didn't feel like getting out and going to the door in my nightgown."

"Thornby, you're making it up."

She took off the kettle and stirred the fire a little, then put the kettle back. She gave me the impression that she was hovering between a choice of explanations.

"You gave yourself away, because Hunt didn't ring, he knocked," I invented, with a hazy recollection of a detective story I had read.

"I lent you that book. It was my library book and I had to pay a fine on it," remarked Miss Thornby.

"All right. But you weren't in really, were you?"

"Really, Madge, you accuse me of gossiping, and then you come up here snooping round to find out why I miss a day at school. You have no sugar, do you?" She poured out tea, and went on. "I always think you can tell people's characters by the way they have their tea."

"Thornby, if you'll tell me what all this mystery is, I'll tell you why Jenny's young man, who is a policeman, is on your track."

She gave me my cup and sat down with hers.

"Sometimes I think we drink too much tea. Tea and gossip about each other—we live on them. I suppose it's because we're all spinsters."

"We've had the H.M.I.'s," I broke in.

"Yes, I know."

"That wasn't why you stayed away?"

"In a way it was."

"Well, in what way?"

"Listen, Madge, I'd much rather not tell you. Do stop worrying me."

"Oh, all right, all right. But while you were away your desk was broken into. Did you have the money with you? Because there isn't any there now."

She looked very alarmed. Then she got up and went to the writing-desk in the corner of the room. She took a key out of her skirt-pocket and unlocked it. Inside the lid was the little cash-box she used for the bank-money. She went into the hall for her attaché-case, took a key out of there and unlocked the cash-box. She stood looking at it as if she was trying to find out something from its interior. I crossed the room and looked over her shoulder. The cash-box was empty.

"They must have robbed it before you left yesterday afternoon," I said.

"I locked up myself. I had the money then," she said absently. She had turned rather white. I had never seen her little brown, goblin face pale before.

"We'd better tell the police," I suggested briskly.

"No!" cried Thornby, suddenly galvanised into life. She stood thinking. "Listen, Madge, did you say the police are making enquiries already?"

"They've been up to the school."

"Then we must stop them. See here, Madge, I'll tell you all about it later, but now you must help me. You must ring up the police and tell them it was all a mistake—that I broke the desk myself, say, because I'd lost the key and was in a hurry. You *must*, Madge. It's terribly important to me. Don't ask me a lot of questions, for heaven's sake. I've got something to do, and you must do that."

I gaped at her. I had never seen her so brisk and overbearing, except when two of her babies were fighting, or making messes during prayers. She fairly pushed me out of the door, pointed to a telephone-box at the corner of the road, and ran back into the house. I went down to it in a dazed fashion. Then I thought I would get on to Jenny and get her to persuade her policeman that there was nothing the matter. I knew there was a telephone in her grocer's shop and I found the number in the trade directory.

"Could I have a word with Miss Lambert?"

The respectable landlady, whom I had seen several

times, asked who it was, and grudgingly agreed to fetch Jenny.

"What on earth?" said Jenny's voice over the wire. She had no business to have such a sweet voice, deep and smooth and slow, as though she had been born in Mayfair, not dragged up in a slum.

"I say, Jenny, could you see your young man the policeman and tell him that it was all a mistake about the desk, and that Thornby broke it open herself, and nothing was stolen?"

"What did she want to do that for?"

"She lost the key."

"Why doesn't she tell him herself?"

"She doesn't want a lot of enquiries about her missing school to-day. You know the H.M.I.'s think she was there, and we don't want them discovering what we were up to to-day, pretending we had a full staff."

"Oh, I see. All right. I'll tell him this evening."

"Do you think you'll be able to stop him following the thing up?"

"Oh, I can stop him all right. The question is if he can stop the sergeant, or whoever it is. But I daresay he can. He's quite a good liar. You ought to meet him sometime. You and he would have a lot in common."

"You do what I ask and don't be so perspicacious."

I rang off and went back to Thornby. I let myself in and found her in the sitting-room standing silently by the writing-desk. In an armchair by the fireplace was an odd little second edition of her, older, with a more wizened look and without Thornby's genial, elfish expression. I guessed at once that it must be the sister, who had always been resting in her room at whatever time I had called at the house. She was supposed to be practically an invalid and did nothing much except a few good works and, I supposed, the housekeeping for Thornby. They had always lived together since their parents died. Thornby did not introduce me, and the sister merely looked at me silently. I said, "How do you do?" but neither of them answered. I began to feel uncomfortable. It was a stupid situation.

"It's all right about Jenny," I said at last.

Thornby said vaguely, "Oh, thank you," and the sister gave a short laugh.

"Well, I'll be going," I said feebly.

"I'm not good enough for you?" enquired the sister.

"Not at all. I mean, I didn't mean that at all." I was taken aback.

"None of Harriet's friends are good enough for me. She keeps her own little circle."

"That's not true, Miriam, and you know it," said Thornby quickly.

"Really. I know it, do I? You must pardon me if I venture to remind you of all the times this lady has been to the house and I have been sent away and shut in my own room in case I should disgrace you by my vulgar presence. You must pardon me if I remind you that your social life is entirely divorced from my little round of keeping this house and working my fingers to the bone for you."

"Would you rather I went?" I said to Thornby.

"No, it's all right, Madge. Now you've met Miriam you may as well stay. You can see why I haven't introduced you before."

The sister got up at that and began to hiss.

"She—she—she—oh, it's intolerable!" she cried.

"You see me, Miss—Miss—well, you may as well know now. You see how I'm worn out with scrubbing and washing and cooking and keeping the home together for her. And what do I get for it? I'm grudged the very roof over my head. I wear her old clothes. I get paid nothing at all. And she's ashamed of me, ashamed of me. Never a word have I said about the injury she did me, taking me away from my old home and all my friends, uprooting me, making an exile of me, because of her lying ways. I might have been a happily married woman by now if it hadn't been for her deceitfulness and trickery——"

"What nonsense," said Thornby sharply. "You never had a chance to get married."

"Nor did you."

Thornby turned to me despairingly.

"You see how it is, Madge. This is what I have to put up with all the time."

"But I've taught you a lesson this time," added the sister quietly and in a normal tone. "This time you've got what you deserved. You can't get off scot-free for ever. Man may not see, but God sees, and in His own good time He strikes."

Thornby looked worried.

"Miriam, what have you done? You haven't——?"

"I was God's humble instrument," remarked Miriam, who appeared to think that she had found a good line to follow up. "His hand guided me. I did what I was inspired to do."

Thornby suddenly crossed the room and seized Miriam by the shoulders. "Did you go down to the school?" she cried, shaking her fiercely. "Did you? Tell me the truth."

The sister began to go red in the face. Then she turned purple and a few bubbles of foam appeared between her teeth, which gripped together like a snarling dog. I began to be frightened and went over to pull Thornby off. But before I reached her the sister suddenly collapsed. She seemed to go limp, and slipped back in the chair, then suddenly began to slide off it and slowly descended to the floor. Her legs gave one or two feeble kicks in the air. Thornby leaned over and gripped her jaw in a business-like fashion, opened it, and released her tongue.

"Shall I fetch a doctor?" I asked, trying to be helpful. Thornby looked surprised.

"Oh no," she said. "If you'd just help me to carry her into her room."

We lifted the lifeless creature between us, manipulated her through the narrow doorway and up the short stair to her room. Thornby put her feet down while she opened the door. Inside was a narrow iron bed, dead-white walls, a jug and ewer, and a table with a crucifix and candles on it. We put her down on the bed.

"Will you go downstairs and make a cup of tea, Madge?" asked Thornby in her usual tones. "I'll attend to Miriam and I'll be down in a few minutes."

I went downstairs and boiled the kettle. I had an irritatingly bewildered feeling, as if I had come into a cinema halfway through a comic film and could not make out what it was about. By the time I had made the tea I heard the door upstairs open. For a moment a sound of sobbing broke the silence of the little house, and then the door closed again. Thornby came down.

"Oh, thank you," she said briskly, and began to drink her tea.

"I hope your sister's all right now?" I asked rather nervously.

"Oh yes, thank you. It often happens that she has these turns. I know what to do for them, and it's soon over."

"Thornby, if you don't mind, I'm going now. There's nothing more I can do, is there?"

"Nothing—except keep quiet about this business. Naturally I don't want people gossiping about it."

"Really, Thornby, you don't need to ask me that."

"Oh, well, I know you're to be trusted, but what about Jenny? Do you think she'll say anything? And will she be able to keep her policeman quiet?"

"She thought so."

"You see, Madge, my sister took the money. It was silly to mention to her about it. I always have to keep my desk locked when I'm out. But she must have taken it in the night."

"Can't you get it back from her?"

"She's given it away. She just told me."

"Given it? But why?"

"You see, Madge, she's a little bit odd. And sometimes she gets a grievance against me because I go out and earn money and she has to stay at home. And I can't afford to give her much."

"But what does she live on?"

"We both live on what I get."

I looked round the room. All the furniture was comparatively new. It was a mahogany suite, with an Indian carpet. There was a radio standing in front of a patch on the wall that was a slightly deeper colour than the rest of the paper.

I said: "Three of us share our bungalow expenses

and we can only just do it. You must be a good manager."

She looked frightened.

"It's all on the hire purchase. We had a piano, but they took it away because we owed so many instalments. We'd paid twenty pounds."

"But the rent?"

"I pay it when I can. Once I was nearly summoned for it. I had to sell some bookcases, and they weren't really ours till the end of the year. I'm so afraid of the people coming up and finding they're gone—the hire purchase people, you know. Ycu have to sign a paper promising not to move it."

"Then has your sister been paying bills with the party-money?"

"Oh no," said Thornby, looking very amused at the idea.

Then what did she do with it?"

"She's given it to Mr. Gregory."

There was a ring at the bell. Thornby mechanically got up and went to open the door. I heard a familiar voice wishing her good-evening, and His Majesty's Inspector of Schools, Mr. Vick, came blandly into the little room.

CHAPTER X

MR. VICK looked at me without a sign of recognition. Thornby, who had turned poppy-red, murmured, "You know Miss Brigson." He stared at me closely, said heartily but unconvincingly, "Yes, of course," and looked round for somewhere to put his hat. I said:

"You came down to our school to-day."

"Oh yes." His face cleared. "I'm so sorry, but we see so many new faces, and it's difficult to recognise them in different surroundings." Thornby took his hat away from him and laid it on the writing-desk. He looked relieved and sat down, then got up again as he noticed we were still standing. We hurriedly sat down and so did he.

"It's nice and high up on this hill, isn't it?" he observed, after a few minutes of painful silence. We agreed simultaneously and apologised to each other simultaneously. There was another long silence and then I said feebly that it was nice to get out of the hollow at night. This was carried unanimously, and then I gave it up, and decided that if he had got anything to say he had better say it, and that I was not going to try to put him at his ease. But I was not going to go either. It was far too interesting.

At last he said to Thornby:

"This is an unofficial call, of course," and laughed as if he had made a very funny remark.

"It's very kind of you," murmured Thornby. He looked at me, plainly longing for me to leave. I looked

back at him blandly. It was delightful to have the
tables turned like this.

"How are you getting on nowadays?" he asked her.
She thanked him and answered that she was getting
on all right.

"I missed you to-day," he said quietly. Thornby
looked thoroughly alarmed, and he glanced at me
again.

"Madge is a great friend of mine," put in Thornby,
following his eyes.

He regarded me doubtfully, but went on:

"I wanted to see you because I was afraid, from
what one of the other teachers told me, that you must
have stayed away to-day on purpose to avoid me."

Thornby was silent.

"Did you?" he asked gently.

"I suppose so."

"You needn't have done, you know." He was speaking to her now as if I had not been there. "That's what
I came up to tell you. It's—unnecessary to act as if
the past was always with us. You mind too much, I
think. You're inclined to act as if you were the only
person who had ever done anything they'd rather forget. Really, everybody does. And it needn't affect your
work unless you make it."

"Don't you think—what you've done makes you into
a different person, and so it can't help influencing everything you do?" Thornby spoke carefully, with knitted
brows, as though it were a tremendous effort for her to
follow the argument.

"Different, yes. But not necessarily a less efficient
teacher. It's only your feeling about it that you are
allowing to influence your career."

186

Thornby shook her head. He leaned towards her and said, quietly and earnestly:

"You see I know how you feel because I was silly, too, in the same sort of way. I married a girl out of my own office—a pretty, attractive girl younger than myself. I wanted—if you can understand me—I wanted a wife whom other people would envy me for having and wish they were in my shoes. And you know how that ended. But I made up my mind that I would not let it affect me—the rest of my life. Only part of me was that longing for admiration. There was all the rest left—the things I could really do—organising school work, making better what had been good before, and changing what was bad. The people who I wanted to admire me thought that was so dull and tiresome as to be almost comic. But I have had the satisfaction in myself. And in the end I came to be quite sure that what I knew about myself mattered more than what people thought."

He was staring at Thornby as if she had been a child to whom he was trying to make something clear. He seemed to have forgotten that I was there. She looked back at him with a puzzled expression. Just then the sitting-room door was thrown open and Thornby's sister appeared, her face quite swollen up with weeping. She was wearing a navy-blue dressing-gown and felt slippers. She gave one horrified look at Mr. Vick, then shrieked and ran upstairs again. Thornby ran after her. Mr. Vick and I were left gazing after them.

"I think I'd better go," he said nervously. "I remember now she had an invalid sister. I suppose she's——?"

"She seems to be having a bad turn. I think she was alarmed to find a man here," I explained.

He picked up his hat.

"Well, I've got a train to catch, and, anyway, my presence seems to be disorganising things a little."

"Aren't you used to that?" I asked. I was beginning to think he was quite human. He laughed at that, and asked me to convey his apologies to Thornby. "Tell her I never gossip, and she's to remember that next time there's an inspection," he added, as I showed him to the door. I directed him as to the quickest way to the railway station. Just as he was going he said to me: "I must say I thought all your efforts to pretend you had a full staff to-day were nothing short of magnificent. Only the fact that it might have damped your enthusiasm prevented me from congratulating you personally."

He waved his hat to me from the gate. I went back into the house, weaving a day-dream in which this friendly encounter with him resulted in my being given the headmistress-ship of a large city school at an incredibly early age. I was just being reported in the local papers as the youngest head in the country when Thornby came hurrying down the stairs.

"Oh—has he gone?"

I gave her his messages.

"You'd better stay to supper, Madge. I'm just going to get my sister some bread and milk."

I followed her into the kitchen and began to cut bread while she boiled milk.

"I didn't know you were on calling terms with the H.M.I.," I said.

"I used to know him."

"So I gathered."

"I used to be in a big school at Eastshields, where he came a lot. It was a Central school."

"You threw up a job at Eastshields Central School?"

"I had to. That's enough bread. Would you like to scramble some eggs?"

"Embezzling party-money again?"

"Oh no. Really, you do say the most dreadful things, Madge. There are some eggs in the frigidaire."

"How on earth do you afford——" I began, and then stopped. I began to beat the eggs.

"It was such a silly thing really, not half as bad as you think. You see, I was in a school where there was a large woman staff, very smart girls, some of them, with fathers who could afford to keep them so that they had all they earned as pocket-money. One of them had her own car, quite a big one. Then, besides that, there were three or four quite old teachers, of quite a different type, who had been transferred when the school was rebuilt. The young ones had a very gay time—lots of men friends and dancing and pretty clothes. And the old ones, of course, were—well, just old school-marms. I was stupid about it. I felt as if I had to belong to one circle. But my father and mother were dead, and I had to support my sister, so I hadn't much money, and I couldn't seem to be like the younger ones." She looked at herself wistfully in the kitchen mirror opposite. "And I thought they despised me because I wasn't like them. And the older ones despised me because I soon would be like them. And they all resented the fact that I'd been educated at a boarding-school. My father used to be a solicitor, you know, and I never expected to be a board-school teacher. But

189

when he died there wasn't any money, and it's the only thing a person like me can get a living wage at. All those other jobs are meant for people who've got some man behind them, aren't they?"

"Stop talking about men, Thornby. It makes me sick. You're as bad as that woman who came on Supply. I don't see why supporting oneself should have to be a second-best always."

"Well, I thought it was. There's a saucepan hanging on the nail, Madge, and butter in the cupboard. Anyway, I used to wish and wish that I was one of the young gang. But I couldn't seem to be able to meet any young men. And I couldn't bring myself to pick one up in the street. At least, I did once—a commercial traveller. And he called for me at school. But the others made fun of me because he was rather old and fat. So I saved up, keeping it a secret from my sister, though it was very awkward, and one summer I went to an expensive hotel for a week. I thought I might meet a nice young man there. It said in the prospectus 'All Social Amenities.' "

"You silly old thing, Thornby," I said. "I suppose it was an awful flop."

"Oh no." She took the saucepan from me and began to light the gas-cooker. "There were a lot of young men there, but most of them had their own girls. I used to stand in the bar in my best cotton frock—I knew it was wrong to dress up on holidays, so I'd bought myself an expensive cotton frock. I can't think how it came to cost so much. But none of them took any notice of me. Then, finally, when my time was nearly up, I got absolutely desperate and asked one young man, who didn't seem to have a special girl of his own, but only joined up with one party or another, whether he would take me out in a boat. He was awfully nice, and he did. After that he used to smile at me when he saw me. Of course I never said anything about being a school-teacher. When I had to leave I insisted on lending him a book, and kept out of his way so that he couldn't give it back to me, so that I should have an excuse to write to him and give him my address. I thought it might come to something if I tried hard enough."

"And did it?"

"Oh no. When I wrote to him about the book he wrote me a very nice note of apology and sent me a snap of the boat we'd gone out in. But I used to tell all the staff about it and talk about 'Ralph.' They had to believe me. There was the snap, and I made an excuse to read them a bit out of the letter, and I used to take the same letter to school every week and read it to myself very obviously when I was on playground duty. They all quite believed I had a love-affair. They used to tease me about it. When they began to ask me when I was going to be married I bought a ring at a second-hand shop and wore it. Sometimes I almost believed it myself."

There was a silence, broken only by the sputtering of the gas-ring. I waited for a few minutes, then remarked, "Still, I don't see why you had to throw up a good job like that."

"Oh, it was because things finally got to the point where I had to say when I was going to be married. In the end I left, saying I was going away to London for the wedding. They gave me a present of some transparent nighties. I've still got them." She paused, meditating. "And I applied for this job in Bronton, and got it quite easily, through having been at the Central school. My references were all right, and I asked the head at Eastshields not to say anything about my taking a new job, because there had been a scandal about my fiancé and I didn't want it spread. She was quite intrigued and promised not to say a word. I don't think she did, either. But I didn't want Mr. Vick to find me here. He knows so many teachers at East-shields. He might tell them. I've always avoided an inspection before, because I have a friend in the senior school who tells me when they go there, and I make an excuse to stay away. The last head got suspicious, but Miss Harford hasn't been here for an inspection before and so I don't suppose she thought anything about it. But to-day I had a quarrel with my sister and I was awfully afraid she'd gone down to the school to tell of me—I went after her, but I couldn't find her. I didn't know then that she'd taken the money and gone to give it to Mr. Gregory."

She was silent, and then added:

"You see, Madge, Miriam has always been angry with me about leaving Eastshields because there was a high-church parson there that she thought a lot of, and it meant leaving his church."

"And now she's transferred her affections to Gregory?"

"Oh, I don't think so. But she said he was a good preacher. And she teaches in his Sunday-school. It makes her very tired."

"Thornby, is she often as difficult as she was this afternoon?"

"Nearly all the time," said Thornby simply. She

picked up the basin of bread and milk and took it upstairs. I set the kitchen table, and when she came
down we had our scrambled eggs. I promised that I
would go down and see Gregory the next day and try
to get the money back from him. Thornby said she
could not face explaining her sister's peculiarities to a
strange man.

Just before I went home an idea struck me.

"How did the inspector find out?"

Thornby said vaguely that she supposed they got
so much into the way of finding out things they weren't
supposed to know that it got to be a profession with
them. I walked down the tidy little streets of the
garden suburb. There were lights behind all the orange
and green and flowered curtains. I wondered how
many of these identical, respectable houses held silly
little secrets like hers, and had all their mahogany and
limed oak furniture taken away in a plain van from
time to time.

Next morning I left home early and called for Jenny.
I told her about Thornby's sister having given the
party-money to Gregory and how Thornby wanted to
get it back and I was going down for it. To my surprise Jenny said:

"I'll go if you like."

"Why?"

"I don't mind having a walk at dinner-time. And
since I've headed that policeman off the trail I may as
well finish the good work."

I knew this was not the reason. But I thought that
if I suggested that it was because Jenny wanted to see
her one-time admirer she would be angry and refuse to
go. I was glad enough to get out of the job.

At two o'clock Jenny came hurriedly in and handed an envelope to Thornby. She said: "It's all right. He quite understood. He hadn't done anything with it yet, fortunately. She'd given it as a subscription to his unemployed club."

Thornby thanked her most gratefully. Then Jenny said: "Listen, Thornby, now you're feeling grateful to me, tell me one thing I've been wanting to know. Did you write me an anonymous letter just before the Wakes holiday?"

Thornby looked absolutely blank. "No," she said, shaking her head violently, as she put the money away in her bag. "No. I never wrote one at all. Why should I? Did you get one? What about?"

"I don't think I'll tell you," replied Jenny sweetly, powdering her nose in front of the mirror. "You're such an old gossip. I never know when I have you. But I've got a threat to hold over your head now, don't forget."

Thornby looked perplexed and went out to fetch her babies in from the playground.

It was the day before the party. We all rehearsed carols instead of doing any work that afternoon. At tea-time, when the children had gone home, we stayed late to hang the decorations. It was very exhausting, climbing about on ladders and hammering nails in. At one point I hit my thumb with a smart blow that I had intended for a refractory nail. It began to swell up and to feel very sore, and I went into the staff cloakroom to hold it under the cold tap. There I found Miss Jones. I think she had crept away to hide herself. She was leaning on the window-ledge and there was the day's paper on the floor.

"What's the matter. Can I do anything?" I asked her, feeling all kinds of a fool for having come in at the wrong moment.

She tried to pull herself together and said:

"It's only that—that Lloyds have written off my friend's boat."

She began to cry then, and I don't think I ever knew before just how dreadful the tears of an old person could be. Her face looked crumpled and wrinkled and terribly faded. Her hair was quite white at the roots because she had not had the heart to keep her usual appointment to have it re-dyed. She did not sob, but she whimpered, almost like a dog. It was terrible. I fetched aspirins and made a cup of strong tea, and finished her decorations for her. And I made up a lot of stories, pretending they were true, about boats that had turned up after being lost for months, and I don't think any of it was any use at all. I suppose it must hurt to have the golden hours, that you have hoped for all your life, miraculously offered to you during the last twenty years of your mortal span and then snatched finally and irretrievably away.

Next day it was the party. The bill was paid and an appalling number of those sickly cream horns were strewn all over the staff-room, bursting out of their boxes and bags. Some of the mothers came in to help us to spread sandwiches. It hurt me to see their delight and excitement in the tiresome task. The children who had taken their youth from them and condemned them to a life of endless drudgery, whose being had wrecked most of their physique for life, were screaming and shouting with joy in the playground. Now these same hard-voiced, red-handed women were transformed into light-hearted girls for the day simply because their disgusting offspring had a chance to overeat themselves for once. Everything hurt me that day. I sent Moira down for some aspirins and had three.

The children came in at three-thirty, jostling for places and with their faces washed ready to smear with cream. They ate everything there was and drank a remarkable amount of tea. After that they spent most of the evening running out to the lavatories. Mr. McCarthy, disguised as Santa Claus, gave them all a packet of sweets. They were not deceived, but they soon put the sweets away.

They were just singing *Good King Wenceslaus*, and I was thinking that my headache was the worst one of the year, when Hunt appeared at the end of the passage. I was standing nearest to him and he beckoned to me mysteriously. I stared at him for a minute, but he went on, so I slipped out.

"Someone to see you, Miss," he whispered hoarsely. Outside the cloakroom door I found Mr. Gregory. He said, "I just wanted to give one of you this." He thrust an evening paper into my hand and went away. I looked at it in the dim light of the cloakroom. He had underlined the Stop Press news. There, beneath the latest football scores, was an announcement that the cargo-boat *Bluebell* had arrived safely, though damaged, in Jamaica. All hands were alive and well.

I slipped into the hall and pushed the paper into Miss Jones' hand just as the children were announcing that the night was darker now and the wind grown stronger. She looked at it twice and then had hysterics. We had to hustle her out and dash water on her face. The children all stopped singing to stare and giggle.

Miss Harford sent them all home early, and most of the parents came up to school the next day to make a row about it, because they had all come to meet them with coats and umbrellas, and did not like them going home alone in the dark.

One more thing happened before the term finished. Thornby came to me, looking as if all her troubles had started over again, and asked:

"Madge, do you know anything about the bank-money?"

"What about it?"

"Well, you know I had it the day before I was away."

"But your sister took it and you got it back."

"No, no. The party-money was separate and she took that. The bank-money wasn't in the cash-box, because I was going to take it up to the bank, and so I'd left it in my desk."

I thought for a minute.

"It must have been taken when your desk was broken into. We must tell the police."

"We've already told them that I broke into the desk myself."

"My God," I said, quite stunned, or I would not have used the expression. "So we did. Why on earth didn't you think of it before?"

"Well, I was so worried about my sister taking the party-money and I only just remembered that the money was in two separate lots."

"We can't do anything at all," I decided at last. "If you tell the police you'll have to explain everything, including how you fooled them before, and, anyway, it's probably too late for them to get it back now. You know they never do. And it would mean Miss Harford knowing everything—about the H.M.I.'s day as well, probably. Oh, Thornby, you are a nit-wit."

"I shall just have to replace it," said Thornby.

"But how?"

"I suppose I shall have to sell something."

"You'd better sell those nighties that you've kept. That would be poetic justice."

I wished I had not said it. She looked so hurt and grieved.

"Don't sell anything," I said. "The bank can wait. You can say, after we're paid, that you forgot to take it up."

"Madge!" cried Thornby, thoroughly shocked. "Do you really think I would do a thing like that with the children's bank-money? I should never, never forgive myself. Of course I shall get hold of the money somehow and take it up to-night."

I don't understand how Thornby's conscience works. She brought the money to school next day and went up to the bank in the dinner-hour. After what I knew of her finances it seemed queer to have such passionate scruples about the children's little bank-accounts. Perhaps, after all, there was something in what the inspector said about one's private life not being one's complete self at all. I don't know. But I looked at her with new interest when she came round for the last bank-day of the term, next Monday. She had just finished collecting the sixpences, and carefully entering them up, when Georgie Hunt put up his hand.

"Miss, I want to have a bank-book, please."

"Have you got a sixpence?" Thornby asked cautiously.

"Miss, I've got a shilling, Miss."

There was a stir of surprise among the rest of the class. It was the first occasion on which a Hunt had ever been known to be in possession of the currency of the realm. Thornby called him up, looked the shilling over carefully to make sure that it was not merely covered with silver-paper, and then produced a clean bank-book. Georgie went back to his seat covered with glory and radiating the pride of being the latest addition to the capitalists of the greatest empire in history.

At twelve o'clock that day Miss Harford asked me to dress the children who had been in the Nativity play at the school concert in their costumes, so that she could take a snapshot of them for the collection she kept of school festivals. I dressed Georgie in his butter-muslin robe, and Miss Jones, who was in the most cheerful and happy frame of mind I had ever seen her, helped me. Miss Jones kept on telling Georgie how nice he looked. As a matter of fact he looked absolutely repulsive. He was impersonating the angel Gabriel, and the white muslin and silver stars went very ill with his little rat-face and shaved hair. Miss Thornby came in and pounced on him.

"I was just looking for one of you. Has someone given your mother a present?"

"No, Miss."

"Well, then, how is it that all of you—Betty and Teddie as well—have started bank-accounts to-day?"

"I don't know, Miss."

"Has Mr. McCarthy been to your house lately?"

"No, Miss."

"I can't understand it," said Thornby to me.

"Perhaps they saved it up," suggested Miss Jones.

"The Hunts don't even know the meaning of the expression," I remarked.

"Where did the money come from, then?" Thornby asked Georgie.

"I don't know, Miss," said Georgie patiently.

Miss Harford came in with the rest of the children dressed up ready for the photograph.

"Is your cough better, dear?" Miss Jones enquired kindly of Stanley Hunt, who was one of the shepherds, in a moustache and a white beard.

I stopped pinning Georgie's wings on. There flashed into my mind the picture of Miss Jones giving Miss Thornby the little tin for a temporary cash-box. Stanley had had the last two lozenges and had been told to throw away the sticky paper.

"Did Stanley open a bank-account too?" I asked Thornby.

"No. He was the only one that didn't."

"Come here, Stanley," I called after him. He came back, looking apprehensive. I pulled up his shepherd's robe and felt his pockets. One of them bulged. I put my hand in and pulled out a large bag of striped peppermint sweets in a filthy state.

"You spent your bank-money on these," I stated.

"No, Miss."

"I shall have to ask your father."

"Yes, Miss."

"Come straight back to me after the photograph, Stanley," instructed Miss Thornby grimly.

"It's simply disgraceful," she added warmly, as Stanley ran off again.

"You can't get the money back," I pointed out. She looked bewildered, and I explained to her that it was obviously Stanley who had broken into her desk and that the Hunts were now laying out the unlawful proceeds.

"I daresay you're right, Madge. But it doesn't alter the fact that Stanley's spent the money he was given for bank on the way to school. And that is a thing I will not allow."

"Are you going to punish him for wrongful disposal of stolen goods?"

"I'm going to punish him for not bringing his shilling. We must keep some sort of discipline about the way they use their pocket-money. What they're given for the bank they must not spend. If we let them get away with it, think what they'll grow up like. Why, it's—it's downright dishonesty in a most dangerous form. Stanley! Come into the staff-room with me."

Stanley went with drooping head and came out rubbing his hand. I went across for lunch. Thornby had settled down to making up the bank accounts for the term in alternating red and blue ink. She signed to me not to interrupt her, and went on moving her lips silently, as if she was praying.

CHAPTER XI

THE SPRING term began with frosts and fogs and occasional indeterminate snow. The first day it was so dark and cold that it was even harder than usual to get out of bed in the chilly dawn after ten days of blissful lying in. Bronton looked more dismal than usual. As I went down the hill on the swaying tram, almost ready to cry from the pain of my cold feet, I noticed that the by-pass road, that now segregated the school into a little triangle of roads, was open for traffic at last. Its long, straight sweep was an incitement to speeding. A car shot along it and side-slipped on the icy surface. Somehow the driver recovered himself. I thanked heaven for the grooved lines that kept the trams steady. When I got off it was difficult to walk along the street without slipping. The children were screaming with delight at the sight of passers-by sitting down unexpectedly. It only remained for me to make an undignified descent into the gutter and their cup of joy was full.

But when I got into school it was all put out of my head by the appearance of Miss Jones in the staff cloakroom as I was brushing myself down. She was seething with excitement, and as soon as I saw her I knew what it was. On the third finger of her left hand was a huge old-fashioned ring of opals, flickering with blue and green and flame. It had been his mother's, Miss Jones gasped, between our exclamations and her own panting and giggling. She thought sailors were usually superstitious, but he said this particular opal worked the other way, and it had been a lucky ring for him and his family. They were going to be married quite soon and we must all go to the wedding. We all congratulated her so heartily that the children started their year badly by being five minutes late into school.

At lunch-time that day all the talk was about her trousseau and where she was going to live. It would have been a marvellous opportunity for one of those people who say that working women like us think, in our heart of hearts, of nothing but marriage. She had got to get everything quite quickly, and it was funny that she, the oldest and least attractive of us all, should be the one to realise the stock day-dream of having to give in one's notice and get a whole new outfit suddenly for wedding and honeymoon.

For the next week or two the trousseau excitement still occupied our spare moments. Poor old Miss Jones was divided between passionate longing for the frilliest and flimsiest of garments and a haunting fear lest she should make a fool of herself by being turned out too youthfully. The old maid that she lived with—her sister-in-law that was to be—knew another old maid who did dressmaking and ladies' tailoring and could not make much out of it, and a wedding order—even a modest one like Miss Jones'—would be a windfall to her. So nothing would do for Miss Jones but that she must have everything made by this old party. And, naturally, they did not turn out well in the least. The tailored coat and skirt did not fit, and it wasn't tailored, anyway, but just cobbled together, and the afternoon-plus-semi-evening gown, with lace sleeves and a draped skirt, was just a plain failure. We were all in despair because, by the time the things were sent home, the money had been spent, and Miss Jones could not afford any more. Anyway, she would not send them back for fear of hurting the old dressmaker-cum-ladies'-tailor's feelings. Jenny made gigantic efforts, with much fitting and pinning, to make the clothes look more as if they belonged to their owner. We all subscribed to give her a present of a coffee-set, black with gold insides to the cups. Jenny chose it. I thought it was vulgar.

This event happens in every school from time to time. It disturbs all the rest of the staff much as prisoners finishing their sentence and going out into the world must disturb a jail. One shares the bride's excitement for a few hectic weeks, divided between real pleasure in their happiness and a disturbing, un-settled feeling that must be smothered in oneself. Any-way, there is the festivity of the actual wedding-day to look forward to. Afterwards we all return to school flat and bored and unhappy, hating the newcomer with a deadly hatred. We were dismayed to learn that Mrs. Lee was to take Miss Jones' place till the end of the year.

Miss Jones was married one Saturday at the end of January. I had my first opportunity of seeing Gregory at his proper job at the wedding. He looked attractive, I suppose, in his robes, taller than he seemed in ordi-nary life, and with that remote dignity that envelops anyone who is framed in the ceremonial of some ancient and immense institution. He seemed young, too, and eager, almost boyish. I think he thought that a suppressed exhilaration was the correct manner for conducting a wedding service. His voice wandered melodiously through the cadences of the ceremony and lulled me into a pleasant vagueness, like the voice of the B.B.C.'s star announcer heard from a distance making poetry of the fat stock prices. I saw Thornby's sister at the back of the church watching him with a kind of smouldering expression.

The blue tailor-made looked quite nice, after Jenny's efforts, and Miss Jones had a bouquet of pink roses, supposed to come from the children, though really they had only been able to subscribe a few halfpennies and we had added the rest. Her sailor looked grim and martial and weather-beaten, and I was glad it was her and not me marrying him. On the way back to the house from church Jenny began speculating as to what he would be like in bed, but I snubbed her into silence.

The wedding reception was crowded and full of a loud, unreal gaiety. There were toasts, and the sailor made a speech in reply and made all the same jokes he had made each time he had taken Miss Jones and his sister out when he was on leave. That amused us, though the jokes did not. But our appreciative giggles sounded all right and everyone was pleased. Then they got into their taxi for the station, and we were left with the dirty plates and cake-crumbs and a general feeling of depression.

Monday morning was greyer and colder than ever. I went down to school wrapped in black gloom. I have a superstition—my only one, I think—that when you allow yourself to become low and miserable for insufficient reason, Providence provides you with a real cause for misery, just to teach you not to give way about nothing.

The tram was emptying by the time I came to Lower Bronton, and as it passed by the end of Furlong Street, before drawing up on the other side, I came slowly downstairs, bracing myself against the swaying motion.

Up the street I saw a child running along the by-pass. Then the tram passed by. I got off, crossed the road and turned up the street. There was a little group at the top. I wondered idly what they were doing, then saw that a motor-lorry was halfway across the pavement, oddly out of place. Something chilled in my mind then, and yet I did not take it in.

I walked up briskly, vaguely regarding the lorry, and was just crossing towards the school gate when I stopped, hardly knowing why, and drifted up toward the little group. Something in their half-bowed backs, their air of immobility and the way they glanced toward me and not at me, struck me as queer. Then I knew. A child had been run over.

It is odd how you cannot keep away from a scene of violence, though you know it will frighten and sicken you. I went up to that little crowd and looked. I should like to forget what I saw. . . . There was a poem that I read once in the college library, but I am bad at remembering verse. I don't often read it. I only came across this one by mistake. I think it was called *Poem on a Dead Child*. It began, "Perfect little body without a fault or stain on thee." Some devilish trick of memory brought it into my mind when I saw that broken, crushed, red mass at the feet of the crowd. I turned away, with an irrelevant remnant of mechanical politeness, and was very sick by the roadside.

Then I pulled myself together, though everything seemed far away and had a nightmare quality. The mess must be cleared up before the rest of the children came along to the gates. I asked whether the police had been told, and saw a young policeman, who seemed to be vaguely familiar, running up. I think he took some notes and asked some questions. I was trying to keep the ground firm under me, and the buildings by their place in the roadside, by saying to myself, "It must be cleared up before the others come." I elbowed through the group of people till I found the policeman, and said, "It must be cleared up before the others come."

He was capable and efficient. He told me to go to one end of the street and sent someone else to the other to stop the children entering. He said the ambulance would be here shortly. I remember what trouble I had to keep some of the little ones down at the bottom of the street and along the wall where they could not look up the road. I do not remember which children they were.

There was a sharp ringing sound, like the alarm-clock which displeases you in your sleep, and the white shape of an ambulance flashed by. After a long, long time, during which I shouted and pulled half a dozen children about to keep their insatiable curiosity under discipline, it came back. Still I would not let them move. At last the policeman came round the corner and said it was all right.

They ran then, and I automatically called to them, "Look for motors," which is what we try to instil into their minds as a slogan, and then stopped dead, thinking how silly it was to say that now. I followed them up the street.

There was a strength and a consolation in knowing that I must do my day's work just as if nothing had happened. I took off my coat, tidied my hair, had a drink of water, hoping that I should not be sick again, and went into the classroom. Something was wrong there. My desk was not unlocked, nor were cupboards, and no books were given out. There was a thought that came back into my mind again and again, but I denied it, pushed it angrily away. Then it came back again and I surrendered and accepted it. Moira was dead.

I accepted it and then refused to believe it again. The whistle blew and I went out to marshal the children through the cloakrooms. They were excited and whispering. I reprimanded one or two. I thought that it was Monday, and I must start a new column in my register. Then I thought that I must look up the list of instructions at the beginning in order to find out what I had to do with the name and attendance marks up to date of a child who was dead. But I could not believe that Moira was dead.

We had prayers, but no singing. We went back to our rooms and called the names. I skipped Moira's. They all pointed it out to each other in a whisper. Some other child clumsily unlocked the cupboards and gave out books.

Miss Harford sent round a cup of tea to all the staff. That amused me a little. I felt rather sarcastic about it. But I drank it and was glad of it.

I gave Georgie a scolding about his Arithmetic. I was not going to let him think that, because there had been an accident, he was going to get away with a multiplication sum added up and the answer perfectly correct through having been copied from the next child. I said coldly, as we closed the Arithmetic-books, that Nellie would be monitor in future. She looked absolutely overjoyed. I understood very well that she was glad that Moira was dead so that she could have her privileges. It did not shock me. Children, when you come to know them as we do, are clear-minded and unsentimental. They do not know how to feel the things that civilised ruling tells them they ought to feel. Moira's presence and Moira's friendship meant less to Nellie than the inheriting of Moira's enviable position. I know that out of her three hundred school-mates, and perhaps twenty friends and special play-mates, there was not a tear shed that day for her. I should have despised a child who simulated sorrow for effect. I respected them for their inability to manage it. It stimulated me, and the nightmare feeling began to wear off a little as the day advanced.

I began to try to take a reasoned view of what had happened. It was a great pity, I told myself, that a good, hard-working, affectionate little girl should have been the one to cross the road in front of a careless driver. But my personal loss would wear off and dis-appear as another class came up and her playmates drifted out of my life. By lunch-time I felt much better, only very cold. I could not get near enough to the staff-room fire to stop shivering, and I sent out for coffee and made some for us all.

I corrected my Compositions and was halfway through Moira's before I realised that I was wasting my time. Then all my helpless, futile rage came tearing back at me. I thought of all the time I had already wasted in teaching her to spell and write. I threw her book angrily on to the fire before I remembered that her parents might have liked to have it to keep. I wondered who had had the task of telling her parents.

None of us talked about it. We talked quietly about

our work. We had not time to get up an atmosphere of bereavement. Afternoon school began before I had finished what I had to do. Just before the end of the afternoon Miss Harford had all the children out in the hall. She told them, briefly and calmly, that they must not think about what had happened, that it had all been over quickly, so that Moira had not had time to feel much hurt, and that now she was in heaven and they must always look both ways before crossing the road. They looked very much impressed and came back into the classroom completely subdued.

I was sorry for them then, for one foolish moment, and wondered if they were suffering more than I knew. One little boy put up his hand timidly to ask me something, and I steeled myself to answer coolly.

"What is it, Jimmie?"

"Miss, do we have a holiday for Shrove Tuesday like we did last year?"

"Yes, of course."

He sat down looking gratified. One or two began to talk to each other in a whisper about whips and tops and pancakes. I listened without appearing to for a moment, and then sent them home.

I packed up my things and went home to tea. There was sawdust scattered on the road, and the top class boys were looking for bloodstains. When I got home I did not tell the others what had happened. We had our tea and they went out to the pictures.

I was very tired and I thought I would go to bed. But it was a mistake. As soon as I had put out the light and got between the sheets I was very wide awake. It was as though all the thoughts that had been pushed out of the way during the day came back and wandered round and round my mind now that it was empty of immediate occupation. It was like the story of the man who swept and garnished his soul and his devil came back into it with seven other devils. Moira used to love that story. The sweeping and garnishing appealed to her domesticated soul.

Presently I got up, dressed myself and went out for a walk. A car passed me, travelling fast on the half-empty road. A young man cut a corner, and a fat, middle-aged one with a girl beside him overtook a line of inferior cars in front of him. "Show off," I found myself murmuring under my breath. "Go faster. Go faster than Nature ever intended you to. Be a daring fellow. Get a thrill of being the dominant male over the admiring woman beside you. Tell your friends when you meet them at the bar about how fast your car will go so that they will give you a second's faint congratulatory admiration."

I passed a butcher's shop with red meat displayed all over the counter, and ran into an alley to be sick again. I walked round the market-place, trying to recover, and read the advertisements. They all seemed to me to be saying the same thing. "Safeguard your children's health with our antiseptic." "Glaxo builds bonnie babies." "Children love choc-lax." You might have thought that the English were, above all, passionately careful of their children. Before they were born you must take patent foods to build up strong bones for them and wear a surgical belt lest they should perish before they flowered. From the time they entered the world there were hundreds of wealthy manufacturers panting to make them strong and healthy with patent foods, to see that their bowels worked daily, to clothe them in garments which eliminated all danger of a chill, to give them shoes which would prevent them from becoming flat-footed and to give them toys which would wash and thus prevent germs. As they grew older hundreds of insurance companies would safeguard them from being left penniless, from lacking money for their education. Hundreds of writers wasted miles of paper and gallons of ink on telling you how to bring them up without fear or repressions or unhealthy curiosity about sex. And fools like me wasted the best years of our lives in college learning how best to impress upon them that twice one are two. My college syllabus scampered through my mind, like a book read in a dream, with its modern methods, its psychology, its teaching practice. I saw the lecture-room again and myself taking conscientious notes. I thought of the years I had spent on teaching, never grudging the continual, drudging effort which no one but a teacher knows—until now. I grudged it now. A comical history of wasted effort—my life. For it took only one moment's miscalculation on the part of a workman in the routine of his day's driving and a child ceased to be the complicated mechanism that required so much time and trouble and became just an unpleasant mess to be cleared off the road so as not to offend the eyes of the neighbourhood.

How dare you talk about the birth-rate, I cried silently, as the front page of a weekly political journal caught my eye. How dare you ask mothers to bear more children when you can't even keep safe the ones struggling on the uphill road to maturity. How dare you penalise me if I lose a name from my register? For I lose only an abstract symbol, which can be recaptured and replaced. But you lose a living, breathing child that can never come back again, though centuries pass and mechanical engines learn to travel faster than light.

If Moira had left to go to another school I should scarcely have missed her. But I, I had told her to go round by the other gate. For my sake she had come to school earlier in the mornings than the others. And so she lay, broken bones, torn skin, flesh smashed to pulp, on a hospital shelf now, and her possessions would be tidied away and locked up because she would never need them again.

I stopped on the canal bridge and looked down into the water, with its muddy reflected lights. I thought that if I just straddled the parapet and then quietly dropped there would be a minute or two's struggling horror and then nothing more. I should be released, and the fact that this thing that was tearing at my mind was being repeated a thousand times all over the world would not exist any more. I tried to look at it reasonably. My work was all that I had. No personal ties counted with me. And now I felt I would never care to work again. For if my work led to this, then children would be better leading their uncertain lives in happy anarchy, untroubled by weary preparation for the future. I wondered how Moira's mother was spending this black night. Was her husband helping her to face its blank tragedy? I had no one, and no one knew that I had a right to feel it at all. Was she suffering so much more? Then I knew that of course she was. Where I had given months, she had given years. Where I had given only an eternal weariness of mind and spirit to the discipline of my work, she had given her body as well. Outcast and barren virgin that I was, even my sorrow did not belong to me. I was only her school-teacher, and my loss, in the calculation of the world, was nothing at all.

I felt too humiliated, too broken, to take any action at all. I turned away from the bridge and trudged on. Hardly intending to, I found myself at our bungalow door. In the row of bungalows, all along the road, lights were shining in the upper windows. There they were, the families that made up the world and would carry it on to countless generations, absorbed in the little round of daily routine that, repeated a million times, made up the sum of human endeavour. I stood outside, belonging nowhere. All I could do would die with me. I was one single spark of life that would be snuffed out finally, like a candle, in half a century, so that there would be no proof that I had ever lived. Standing on the doorstep, fumbling for my key, I reached the pitch of misery which mercifully wears out the body so that one sinks into a kind of stupor. Without ties of love one might also expect to be immune from the worst agony of mind. But if there is worse unhappiness than mine that night I cannot understand how man can experience it and live. I had never known such agony before. I never have since. I think that I never shall again.

It had been proved, as we thought, that the by-pass road was dangerous. Miss Harford wrote to the Chief Constable to ask if we could not have a policeman always on duty at the end of the street nearest to it, to see the children safely across four times a day. But we already had one at the other end of Furlong Street, where the trams ran and the greater number of the children had to cross, and so nothing came of her request. Some of the more respectable parents complained to the Education Office. Most of the poorer ones were too much afraid of official authority to obtrude themselves unnecessarily upon its notice.

We gave the children lectures in school about looking both ways and always reminded them when they went home. One of us usually hung about the gate to look out for the careless ones as they came up the street. It was difficult for us, because the times they were coming and going were the very times when we were most engaged in getting ready for a lesson or dismissing our own classes and clearing up work. Also we had no official authority over the children once they were outside the school gate, and no power to punish them for anything that happened out of school. They were careful for a while, but their memories were short, and within the next few weeks a little boy was knocked down and had his leg broken. He was taken to hospital. The young man who had been driving the car, a commercial traveller, behaved very properly. He came into the school while we were at lunch, with Jenny's policeman, to ask for the parents' name and address. I met them and they asked me to find the child's class-teacher.

I left them standing in the hall and went in to Miss Simpson, who was scrubbing ink off her hands.

"Your Bobbie Millson has been hurt by a motorist— not very badly—and they want his name and address."

Miss Simpson look startled, dried her hands with the red ink still on them, and followed me into the hall.

"What's happened?" she asked, frowning at the two young men.

"There's been a slight accident," explained the policeman. "A little boy has been knocked down and taken to hospital."

I saw him look Freda over contemptuously, from her untidy bobbed hair to her cotton stockings and brogues. Her nose was shiny. She had an old navy-blue skirt and a college blazer. I also saw Freda take in the look and bristle with resentment.

"On the by-pass road that you won't look after properly, I suppose," she said. "Did you do it?" she asked the young man.

The young man looked anxious and apologetic. He had a chinless pink face, with an enormous Adam's apple quivering below it, and a smart blue suit. He fidgeted with his bowler hat and told her that it had really not been his fault.

"The kiddie ran out before I could pull up. I did all I could. He's only hurt—leg broken, I think—anyway, nothing worse. But I feel very cut up about it—I just can't bear to hurt a little kiddie—and I wanted to see his parents and—reassure them, and perhaps give them a little something towards getting him quite well again, just to show my regret that the whole thing happened."

"I see. Five guineas will buy you the right to break a child's leg since his parents are quite insignificant and living on unemployment relief. A very nice idea," remarked Freda, with her passionate resentment of men and money trembling behind her voice.

"I don't think I should do that if I were you, sir," said the young policeman, smoothly, to the commercial traveller, ignoring Freda as if she had not been there.

"No, officer? Why not?" asked the unhappy young man.

"You put yourself in the wrong by doing it," explained the policeman.

I stared at him. I had not yet got used to policemen having educated voices. It still seemed unnatural to me. He looked back at me with his expressionless stare. It did not affect me as it did Freda. Neither his good looks, nor his arrogance, nor the uniform that made him more than his six-foot-two, moved me to admiration or anger. So we looked silently at each other, until the young man said worriedly:

"Just as you say, officer. But I'd better get the kiddie's address, hadn't I?"

"I'll give it to you," volunteered Freda icily. We followed her into the classroom and she took out her register and looked it up.

"I suppose you're prosecuting him?" she said loudly to the policeman, as the young man took out a red leather notebook and a silver pencil to copy them down.

"We shall do our duty." He did not add "Miss."

"If you'd done your duty the boy wouldn't have been in hospital."

He looked her over and smiled in a way that scarcely moved his lips from their habitual expression. I laughed a little. I thought Freda was being silly and emotional, but I was on her side all right.

The young traveller lingered to stammer about how worried and unhappy he was about the whole thing, and the policeman, after writing the name and address down, moved out into the hall. He looked through the panel opposite to where Jenny was rummaging in her desk, and Jenny saw him and came out.

"Hullo, Dick," she called to him, as he came through the door. "What are you doing up here?"

"Just business." I did not like him much better when he smiled properly.

She walked out into the playground with him and I heard her laugh. They leaned against the fence talking, until the young man, still offering pathetic explanations to the frigid Miss Simpson, finally got himself and his notebook and his bowler hat out of the school. Jenny did not reappear for ten minutes and then came into the staff-room singing to herself and looking flushed and pretty. Freda was fairly bristling. I could almost feel the hairs rising on her neck as she sat next to me savagely masticating a ham sandwich.

"You pick your time tastefully to flaunt your conquests, don't you?" she blurted out. Jenny looked surprised.

"I'm not flaunting, it's not a conquest, and though I didn't pick the time I don't know what's the matter with it," she answered lightly. "You seem all het up about something, Freda? What is it? Do you suspect poor dutiful Dick of being a Fascist?"

"I suspect him of being a coarse brute and you of being so absorbed in your man-hunting that you'd do it at your mother's funeral."

"Good God," cried Jenny. "What's bitten the girl?"

"He comes here straight from sending a child to hospital, and on his way to tell its parents, and you celebrate the occasion by having a bit of slap and tickle at the gate. I call it a little undiscriminating, not to say vulgar."

"Oh—pooh," said Jenny, sitting down to have her lunch. "Of course we're all sorry that another of the little idiots has got itself hit by traffic, but what's the use pretending it will disturb any of our sleep to-night? I wouldn't be such a hypocrite, Freda."

"I don't need to be a hypocrite to be upset that another moneyed young fool has broken Bobbie Millson's leg. We're not all as hard as nails and as self-centred as a prima-donna."

"Leave the sob-stuff to the child's parents who can feel it sincerely."

"How upset they must be, poor things," murmured Thornby, with a vague idea of averting the storm by a little good feeling.

"Freda's starved maternal instincts are all up in arms," mocked Jenny.

Freda got up and struck her across the face. I was so astonished that I could hardly believe my eyes. I always knew that Freda was a suppressed volcano, but I thought she had been too well brought up to behave so naturally. Jenny, on the other hand, was in her element immediately. She leaped on to her chair as lightly as a dancer, leaned across the table and seized a register that was lying there and brought it down as hard as she could on Freda's head. It sounded worse that it felt, probably. They are made of stiff cardboard. Then she turned it sideways and hit Freda first on one cheek and then on the other, shrieking: "Vicious old cat! How dare you hit me, how dare you!" Thornby turned quite pink with the excitement. I could not help laughing a little, but I wrested the register away from Jenny and said: "Do shut up. The children will hear you."

That sobered them both. They sat down, looking foolish. Jenny said, "Oh dear, I haven't enjoyed anything so much for ages." She looked at me and saw me laughing and after a moment she began to giggle too. She always recovered her temper quickly. She turned to Freda and said:

"I'm sorry, old thing, but it's a tradition in our family that you must always return sock for sock."

But Freda did not respond. She got up without a word and walked out. I heard her sobbing in the lavatory. There was a most uncomfortable silence. Presently Thornby got up, tucked the register—which was hers—safely under her arm, and went out murmuring something about putting it out of harm's way. Jenny said:

"What a field-day a Freudian psycho-analyst could have probing into Freda's mind."

"I daresay," I answered, pushing away my empty plate and reaching over for my exercise-books. "But I'm not sure I wouldn't rather have a few repressions than be quite as promiscuous as you."

"You don't fancy Police Constable Dick Hannaford?"

"I think he's a particularly unpleasant piece of work. Your English lecturer was a noble triumph of civilisation beside him."

"What do you carry on with him for, Jenny?" I asked, after waiting for a few minutes for her to make some comment.

"He's attractive, Madge."

"He's coarse."

"I daresay. But after that insultingly cold and righteous curate I need someone who's natural and passionate, even if his finer feelings are a bit difficult to decipher."

I turned round to look at her. She was staring at me defiantly, as if she needed to convince me of something.

"Jenny, you're more impressed than you know by the Reverend Gregory if you trouble to get an antidote to him."

"You've been reading *Peg's Paper*," said Jenny. "Ordinary people's minds don't work to schedule like that."

It was no wonder that the whistle blew before I had half-finished all that I meant to. But I had to stay late after school in any case. When I went for a stroll, before night-school, I noticed a little group of people standing on the edge of the by-pass earnestly discussing something. I thought I recognised Freda among them, but I could not be sure. I thought it would be interesting to see what happened to the young commercial traveller when his case came up and whether the local feeling about the by-pass would influence it.

It did not, apparently. I saw in the local paper next week that he had been completely exonerated. It had been the child's fault, the magistrates agreed. I showed Freda the paper, and said that I thought it was disgraceful the way everybody refused to take any responsibility for the silliness of children when anyone who had ever had anything to do with them knew that they had to be protected against themselves, but she scarcely answered. I had only approached her in the hope of making friends, because I was tired of her going about glowering silently at everyone, and at this I abandoned the attempt. But later on in the day she came up to me and observed abruptly:

"Madge, there's a meeting to-night in the church hall to protest against the negligence of the police and the magistrates about children on the by-pass. Will you come?"

"Not me," I said. "I never interfere in local politics."

"It's important," she urged me. "It may have some good effect. And we all ought to do what we can."

"Who's running the meeting?" I asked.

"Mr. Gregory."

"Then I certainly shan't come. He talks too much."

"Moira's mother is speaking."

"Is she?" I said, with assumed indifference. But it aroused in my mind things that I did not care to remember. I was not going to sit in the parish hall and have my secret feelings lacerated in the glaring light of a public meeting. That finally decided me not to go.

I heard that the meeting had composed letters of protest to be sent to the Chief Constable and the Urban District Council, and that they had passed a resolution that motoring offences ought not to be tried by magistrates, of whom the majority were car owners.

"I suppose that was your suggestion," I commented to Miss Simpson.

"It was my idea, and Mr. Gregory approved of it and took it up."

I thought to myself that I should not be at all surprised if she fell for the curate, but I kept my reflections to myself. I did not want to be involved in a free fight. I heard from one of the parents, via Miss Thornby, that there had been a threatening temper at the meeting.

But it was kept in check for a week or two. It was beginning to be a little warmer and we were all thinking longingly of spring. The roads were no longer so dangerous now that the frosts had gone, and there were fewer skids along the by-pass altogether. The policeman still appeared on duty regularly at the far end of the street.

Then one of the Hunt children, who had no business at the wrong end of the street anyway, was chased off the pavement—probably with good reason—by one of the big girls, and ran out into the road straight in front of a limousine. Stanley never even saw it coming, but the chauffeur saw him, and pulled up with great presence of mind within a yard or two. Stanley was knocked down, but very gently, and not touched again. He was a little bit shaken, and was taken home by the car owner, a rich old lady who was coming in from the country to do some shopping. The neighbours all collected in the street to watch Stanley's triumphal home-coming, and I expect that Father Hunt stung the old lady for a handsome sum. Anyway, the Hunt bank accounts, which, since Christmas, had all stuck at their first shilling, suddenly went up by fifty per cent. We prepared a stern reprimand for Stanley and thought that the matter was finished with.

But that night the attendance at night-school was unusually low. The superintendent could not understand it, but concluded that there must be some local entertainment that he had not heard about. We all got off early because the classes were so small. It would cost some of my girls their week's income.

As I came out of the school gate I became aware of a murmuring sound in the distance. I thought that perhaps some minor edition of the Wakes people had brought a caravan or two, and a roundabout, to cheer up the off-season. They sometimes did. I walked down towards the church, thinking that I would see whether any of my missing night-school girls were spending their evening there, so that I could check up next time on the excuses they gave for their absence.

The lights were on in the parish hall, and a crowd was flowing out of it, breaking up into little groups to discuss something. I passed by the open door and went back to look in again. The place seemed to be festooned with banners. "Stop the Massacre of our Children!" and "Make the By-pass Safe!" and "What are the Police paid for?" Evidently they had been having another meeting. Sure enough there was Freda Simpson, beside the table on the platform, discussing something vigorously with Mr. Gregory. There was an air of angry excitement about everyone. I waited for a moment to speak to Freda and ask her how the meeting had gone. Several of the little groups were drifting homewards, some of them across the very road in question. As usual, a flock of children wandered along beside them with that determination not to miss anything of interest, which is the strongest characteristic of the children of the proletariat at the tender age of ours. A streamlined sports car came along the road. There were people scattered all over it, and the car drew aside to avoid them. Some of the children who were tagging along the roadside had to leap out of the way. It was not the motorist's fault, but to all of us, I think, in the light of recent happenings, it looked ugly. Even I, who had not had my feelings worked up in the mass meeting, went hot with anger. And it was all that the crowd needed. There was a moment's pause, it seemed to me, with a murmur of voices and the hooting of the car, and then suddenly all the voices rose in a high, confused hubbub. I saw them surround the car and swarm on to it. They were like a crowd of angry flies, who have been disturbed from their carcase, going back to it with buzzing and humming. The driver leapt out. He gesticulated, but two or three people grabbed hold of him and dragged him out of the way. I was frightened, but I was exhilarated too. I half-wished that I was one of that crowd, drunk with the sense of their own unity and the comfortable anger of emotions shared. I think that I shouted and cheered as they dragged the car off the road, and pushed it and pulled it, laughing now, and shouting and jostling each other, towards the piece of waste ground.

From the parish hall all the rest of the meeting began to flow down towards the waste ground. I skipped out of their way and went back to the safety of the school fence.

But I was happy and excited. This violence was like wine rushing to one's head. I laughed to see the harmless young man in a checked motoring cap, held in the brutal grasp of two local fathers, making feeble and helpless gestures towards his property.

Everything happened in dreamlike succession—without plan, and yet as swiftly and surely as if it had happened many times before. There was a shout of "Stand back!" and there were a hundred elbows in my ribs and my feet were sharply conscious of other feet bruising them, and we were all pushing, struggling and cheering at the tops of our voices. Then a single flame shot into the night sky. Terrifyingly, the elemental force that we had aroused swelled, like the genie that came out of a jar in the fairy story. Great flaring, leaping flames filled the open space. There was a smell like pear-drops, only fifty times stronger and more pungent. The intense heat scorced our faces, and I was really frightened then, thinking that I was going to be burned alive, and shrieking them to let me out of the crowd. Someone fell, and I stepped on flesh. The whole night became alive with flame, and I struggled out of the thinning mass of people and staggered down the street. Near by me someone was crying in deep hysterical sobs. I caught a glimpse of a checked cap tipped rakishly over one ear and saw that it was the owner of what had been a streamlined car and was now a mass of hot, white fire.

I began to run down the street, realising that I had dropped my books in the crowd, but too panic-stricken to go back for them. There was hopeless confusion at the cross-roads. Some were running away and some running up to see the show. I heard the long, threatening hooter of a police-car. A tram had stopped opposite the end of the street and the driver and conductor were leaning out of its upper deck watching the burning.

I climbed on to the tram and sank into a seat. My legs felt as if they would never bear me again. I felt like bursting into tears and crying until I had drained all the seething, unaccustomed feelings away. But I sat huddled up, shutting my ears to the shouts and screams and my eyes to the glare. After a time I felt the tram begin to move. The conductor came for my fare and I was annoyed with myself that I could not keep my voice from trembling. When I got off I could scarcely walk up home. Daphne let me in, and I told her that I had seen a car on fire and was too upset to talk about it. She helped me to undress and gave me some aspirin tablets in a glass of hot water.

I slept badly and dreamed too much. Next morning I was reluctant to go to school. But I found that the wreck of the car had been already moved from the waste ground, and that the neighbourhood was merely assembled in quiet little groups gossiping about the excitement. Miss Simpson was not at school.

The children all tried to tell me what had happened, but I told them firmly that I knew and was not going to listen to any talk about it. Miss Harford came in to ask me whether I had heard anything about Miss Simpson being mixed up in the rioting of the night before, but I said I knew nothing about her.

She came back at lunch-time with her arm in a sling. She said that she had sprained her wrist, but she would not talk about it. Dennis Millson said that his father was in prison, and two of the other children, not to be outdone, chirped up that their fathers were in prison too. Miss Thornby told me that four of the men whom the police had caught had been given heavy sentences and the rest had been set free. The curate had spent the day at the police court, pleading with such magistrates as would listen to him, on the men's behalf.

At tea-time, when I was putting my books together in the staff-room, Freda came in. She looked very white and had black rings beneath her eyes, but she seemed calm and with a fire burning under her quietness. Jenny came in and began to comb her hair in front of the mirror. I liked to watch her at the mirror. She was as unselfconscious as a baby filling its stomach. She hummed to herself and remarked: "Hope that policeman of mine hasn't been so involved in the aftermath of the car-burning that he keeps me waiting. I feel such a fool standing outside the cinema as if I wanted to be picked up."

Freda was fumbling with her coat. Jenny turned round and helped her to put it on over the sling.

"Is it sore?" she asked. "How did you do it? Blacking someone's eye?"

"No," said Freda coldly.

"Was P.C. Hannaford in good form?"

"He made some of the arrests."

"Not you?"

"I wasn't arrested—only cautioned."

She looked steadily at Jenny, challenging her to ask for details. Then she picked up her books and bag in her free hand and went out.

"Good God, isn't the boy rough?" said Jenny, turning back to the mirror. "I'll tell him in no uncertain terms to keep his hairy hands off my friends in future, great clumsy brute that he is." She meditated silently for some moments, and then remarked: "All the same, it's my idea that Freda rather enjoyed it. Even the most ladylike of us have a secret liking for a he-man."

"You can except me," I said frigidly. Sometimes Jenny was disgusting. "But then I wasn't brought up among that style of love-making, though I daresay it's a charming way of showing your affection to those who are used to it."

I knew how to sting her, and I was glad to see the glowing red spring up to her cheeks.

CHAPTER XII

O N E N I G H T I was walking home from night-school because the room had been so hot and stuffy. It had been one of Hunt's "Heat on" days and I wanted some air. It was late, and most of the district was abed, with darkened houses. My footsteps echoed on the frosty pavement, and I began to listen for the echo, absently, while I went over the lesson I had given in my mind. It occurred to me that there was something unusual about the sound, and then I realised that there was another lot of footsteps following mine. I glanced round, wondering if the Superintendent was walking home too, but could not see anybody. This happened two or three times, and then I knew that the footsteps stopped when I did. I experimented, to make sure, and knew that I was being followed.

Even on a well-populated road in the daytime it is an unpleasant feeling. I suppose all sorts of buried memories of ancestors of jungle days rise up and take possession of one. But at night, on a long, lonely hill leading up out of a district where the crime record is high, and pickpocketing one of the least sinister of the prevailing offences, it was alarming in the extreme.

I wished I had gone on a tram. But I had deliberately let the last one of the night go on without me. I tried to remember whether any parent had a grievance against me at the moment I crossed over the road. For a few minutes the footsteps ceased and then they started on my side. It would be easy enough, I

considered, for whoever was following me to dodge
from yard to yard and to slip out of sight when I turned
round. The shadows of the tall, closely-built houses
lay across the pavement, and the occasional patch of
faint lamplight was only a few yards wide. The hill
loomed up endlessly before me. I thought I would
make a last experiment to make sure that I was not
imagining it, and ran a few yards. The footsteps ran
then, too, and I caught sight of a figure slipping into
a shop doorway as I stopped and turned round.

Having established the fact that it was a real pursuer,
I thought I would do the obvious and sensible thing
and get hold of a policeman, who was, after all, paid
to prevent my being robbed or attacked, and not merely
to avenge it afterwards. I remembered that there was
a telephone-booth down one of the side-streets, and I
walked back, a little way down the hill, towards it. I
crossed over, as I did not want to pass too close to
whichever doorway the man was lurking in. Now I
had decided what to do I did not feel panic-stricken
any more, but still I was a little frightened. The footsteps followed me down the hill. I found the booth.
It was one of those whose light switches on when you
close the door and stand on the floor of the box. It
was tempting Providence to have it in a district with
unruly children like ours, and I expect they ran the
Post Office's electricity bill up to a handsome sum. But
I was glad of the bright light, and rang the local station,
whose number was written up, instead of merely calling
Police. While I was waiting to get through a most
startling thing happened. A whitish face appeared out
of the darkness, beyond my brightly-lighted box, and
pressed against the window, so close that it would have

touched me but for the glass wall. I could not help giving a little cry—it was so sudden—and the face disappeared into the blackness again. I became aware that a voice was speaking at the other end of the line.

"Well?"

"Is that the police?"

"Rester Street police station. What is it?"

"I'm in the telephone-booth on Acacia Street. I'm —er—being followed."

It did sound silly, put into words.

"What d'you mean, you're being followed?"

"I was walking up the Bronton Hill and there has been a man following me, and he hid whenever I looked round."

"Wait a minute," said the voice.

I could hear him speaking to someone in the room. He evidently forgot to put his hand over the receiver. "There's a woman says a man is following her up the Bronton Hill."

"Doesn't she want him to?" asked someone else.

"I should think her complaint is that he won't catch her up."

I knew that voice. It was Jenny's policeman. It was the sort of joke he would make. Then the first man spoke into the telephone again.

"Madam, you're quite sure he is following you and not perhaps just walking in the same direction, like?"

"I shouldn't have rung you if I hadn't been sure."

"Well, ma'am, I'll send a man up to see you out of the district if you wish. Would you give me your name?"

I told him, and heard Jenny's policeman say: "Oh,

one of those old school-marms. They would think they were being followed."

"I'll wait here," I said, and hung up.

It was rather unpleasant waiting there and scanning the dark windows for the face. After some time I heard a bicycle bell and opened the door. The light went out and in a moment I saw a policeman come cycling up. It was Jenny's young man, and I wished it had been anyone else.

"Was it you rang us, Miss Brigson?"

"It was."

He looked amused. I could see that in the faint lamplight.

"Well—where is the fellow who was following you?"

"He didn't wait for you."

"No? Well, I'll see you home."

He arranged himself so that he could push his bicycle and walk beside me. There was a silence, and then I weakly felt that I must try to justify myself. His manner said so plainly that I had imagined it all.

"I wouldn't have troubled you except that it is such a lonely road at this time of night and this man had been following me for such a long way."

"It's a pleasure," he said impudently.

"If you'd been a bit sooner you could have gone home with him instead and that would have been only the same trouble for more result."

"It's difficult to arrest a man merely for walking up the hill, Miss Brigson."

"He came up to the booth while I was 'phoning you and looked in."

"Oh—we heard you screaming. But even that isn't

a criminal offence, you know, to look at a lady through a telephone-box window."

"You think I imagined the whole thing, don't you?"

"Oh no, Miss Brigson. But, you see, in our job we find that maiden ladies are a bit apt to think that quite inoffensive men mean to do them some injury."

He looked me over and he got the best of it. Though I had a job requiring more brains than his, though the State paid me more for my public value than it did him, though he was only doing the work for which my tax-money paid, I could not get even with him. The whole weight of public opinion which believes that there is something comical and humiliating in being an un-married woman, and something rather dashing and enviable in being an unmarried young man, left me without an answer to crush him. His tone said never so plainly that my own repressed longing for a man of my own made me into a nervy old maid. I felt a hot rush of anger, which mounted up my neck and over my face, and which he could see under the light of the "daylight" lamps we had just reached. He smiled and looked closely at me, and I would willingly have struck him if I had not been brought up to believe that the tongue is the only legitimate weapon of anger.

"There's an old lady up the Crescent who telephones us regularly to say that there is a man under her bed," he remarked.

"Really? Well, I can get a tram here—they run later on this line—so I needn't trouble you any more," I said, and wished him good-night. But all the way home my face burned and I could not sleep for the hot, humiliated anger that stupid and boorish young man had the power to arouse in me. And the humiliation was as much in that he had this power to sting me, and that I could not ignore it, as in the fact itself. I thought I would wait long enough before I ever asked for police protection again.

In the morning light it looked a silly story. I thought I would not say anything about it at school. But a day or two later Jenny remarked:

"Why didn't you tell me about Dick seeing you home?"

"Oh, he told you, did he? Chiefly because I wished to spare your tender feelings from hearing my comments on his way of doing it."

"He has a filthy mind," observed Jenny imperturbably. "He seemed to think that you rang up the police station because you were short of a man. I told him that if you did want one you'd stipulate for one with brains and not merely for a moron in uniform."

"What did he say to that?"

"Oh—something very personal, but no more references to you."

"I don't know what you see in him, Jenny."

"My dear, practically all I see in him is visible to the naked eye. He's large, good-looking, ornamental, and believes in actions rather than words."

"Oh, well, I expect you'd make quite a good combination if you got married."

"And live on a policeman's salary? Not me. Besides, he's probably one of those who believes that a woman's sphere is kitchen, kids and kirk, or whatever the saying is. Do you know what he told me? He thinks that the top class boys are too old to be in charge of a lot of women and that they ought to have a schoolmaster for them. I said if once we had a schoolmaster in the place he could consider himself jilted, because it was only the fact of his being handy in a manless spot that made me go out with him at all."

In a way it was some consolation to me to think of the constable being snubbed by Jenny, even as light-heartedly as that. And yet I knew that what I really wanted was to be able to humiliate him myself, and that proxy was a poor satisfaction. Then I was angry with myself for thinking any more about it, and dismissed it from my mind. I would not go home early from night-school, nor go on a tram if it was a fine night, because I wanted to believe that I had forgotten all about it.

But I was still nervous. Once or twice at night I was again sure that I was being followed. And one evening, before any of the night-school staff or students arrived, I thought I saw somebody peering in at my classroom window. I began to think that I should be glad when the term was over and there was no more night-school.

During February the night-school had an exhibition of work. All the handwork and dressmaking and drawing was laid out on tables in the hall and visitors came and looked at them. The cookery class sold sweets and cakes and the elocution class recited Shakespeare. It was very exhausting having critical parents and friends all over the school and trying to keep order as well. After all, we had to stay late, when the visitors and students had gone, to clear away the work and get the rooms tidy enough for school in the morning. I was so tired that when I saw from the clock that the last tram would have gone I felt that I could not possibly face the long walk home. I asked the superintendent how he was going to get home, hoping that he had got a car and would offer me a lift. He suggested that we should share a taxi, and went out to telephone one. I arranged to meet him at the bottom of the street in ten minutes' time, to save the few extra pence it would run up turning round at the school gate. Left alone, I piled the plates in the children's wash-room for someone to wash up in the morning, pushed the few remaining drawings and exercise-books in the cupboard, and turned the lights out. I went round to the boys' cloakroom, made sure it was locked, and came back through the hall, putting out lights all the way. I let myself out, locking the girls' door by sense of touch in the dark, and went slowly across the yard, fumbling to get the school keys in my bag.

Suddenly there was a sound from beneath my feet. I went numb with fright. My mind seemed to gallop wildly through possible explanations, trying to find one that would bring me back to reasoned everyday. But there was none. The sound came from directly beneath me. I was standing on the asphalt playground. And the sound had been a child's scream.

Everything seemed to become remote and muddled. For a moment I was not standing there any longer in the dark schoolyard on a winter's night. I was sitting in my classroom on a hot, thundery afternoon, with a storm threatening overhead. There was the sound of a child's footsteps in the yard—a child's scream—and then the thunder and Cook coming in, white-faced and trembling. I think that, somewhere buried in the minds of the most material of us, there is a firm belief, cowering away from our reason, in spirits and the ghosts of the dead. At that moment I not only firmly believed in ghosts, but I was positive that I was in the presence of one.

I do not know how long I stood there shaking. I seemed to have become miraculously changed from myself, Madge Brigson, who was beginning to get a hold on the world and be able to cope with it, into the frightened, credulous little creature of twenty years ago, surrounded by bogies and strange bad men. Then, with a tremendous effort of will, I shook myself mentally, laid a hand on the flying coat-tails of the sensible, grown-up Madge, and brought her back to take charge of the situation.

My eyes were becoming accustomed to the darkness, and I looked around and saw the enormous shape of the school building looming up closer to me than I had expected. I must have lost my way crossing the girls' yard, through putting the keys away as I walked. Now I was on the edge of the stoke-hole. The stoke-hole— the very place where Moira—— But I would not think of ghosts again. It was ridiculous. There was obviously someone in the stoke-hole, I decided, since the sound had come from beneath my feet. Probably a child, from the sound. I ought to go straight down and look at once, since the screaming indicated some sort of distress, not wait ten minutes and then go down to the end of the road for the superintendent. Or I could call the police, I thought, and then, No! in case it turned out only to be a cat shut in and mewing to be let out. The thought of that other night lent me courage. I suppose it is always some sort of vanity that prompts it.

I went down, feeling my way by the fence down the steps, until I came to the door, which was open. I felt inside for the electric switch and turned it on. A man was sitting on an upturned box, with his arms sprawling over the table and his face buried in them. I recognised him by his one ear.

"Cook," I said, in a small, shaky voice.

He did not move. I had a horrible idea that he might be dead. But that would not explain the sound. I thought I ought to go across and feel him, to see if he was warm or cold. But I decided to get help first. With my foot on the bottom step I turned back. Why should I always have to get a man's help when there was anything disagreeable to do? I went up to him and shook him by the shoulder. It was quite warm, though the coat-sleeve was damp.

He slowly raised his head from his arms and looked at me through bleary eyes.

"Wass mar?"

"What are you doing here, Cook? You've no business here, you know."

He looked at me with swaying head and a ridiculous attempt at dignity.

"Thass just exactly where you're wrong. This is my job, a returned hero's job."

"It isn't your job any more, and you've no business to be here. You must get out and go home." I was almost enjoying myself now that I had overcome my fears and taken charge of a dangerous situation. It was like suddenly finding oneself realising one of those schoolgirl dreams in which one behaves with magnificent coolness and courage, startling any number of distinguished phantom men by one's gallant behaviour. And assuming authority—or browbeating, if you like— is one of the things I have learnt to do, and it is not so easy as outsiders imagine. But I was rudely jerked out of my self-confidence. He sprang to his feet suddenly, as if his head had cleared, and shouted:

"No, it's not my job and whose bloody fault is that but yours, you interfering old bitch, sneaking round and getting an honest man thrown out on his beam, when he's been through hell for you while you were asleep in your bed and all the gratitude you show is to rob me of my livelihood and put me out of work with all the rest that you women steal jobs from, thieving cats that you are. But I've got you now, and I'll show you, by Christ I will."

He leapt towards me, and I stepped back into a pile of coke and fell over. He came down on top of me, and I felt his hands pressing my neck and thought that at last my worst fears had materialised and I was being murdered. I screamed for help at the top of my voice. I tried to push him off, but he was strong and heavy. I grabbed blindly for his ears, thinking that I would force his head back, but my right hand encountered only a hole and it sickened me so that I snatched my hand away and spent all my strength trying to get away from him. Suddenly there was the sound of footsteps, and then a voice called, "Hullo, hullo, who's there?"

It was the superintendent. He hurried down the stairs, tripping over one in his excitement, and stumbling into the little room with his arms out to save himself. When he saw what was happening he flung himself on top of Cook, which meant so much extra weight on me, and I screamed out to him to get off. Somehow he got up and dragged Cook away, with me pushing behind for all I was worth. As soon as I had

clambered up from the heap of coke I said, "Quick—
come out and lock him in!"

We staggered across the room and slammed the door.
There was a bolt on the outside and we locked it, and
then ran hurriedly up the steps, elbowing each other
aside, and across the playground. At the gate we
paused, and he said, "You go for the police and I'll
stay here."

"I'm too exhausted to run. You go," I panted.

He looked at me doubtfully, then started off down
the street. I leaned against the gate, trying to press
my head against the cool metal, but it was not tall
enough for me. There was complete silence from the
playground, but I turned round and kept my eyes fixed
in the direction of the stoke-hole. I had no mind to
be taken unawares.

Just as the siren of a police car sounded round the
corner of the road there was a tremendous howling
from the other direction. Cook was screaming and
shouting and beating on the door, and every now and
then he set up a weird howl, as though he was imitating
the siren. It was the same howl that I had heard twice
before—a long, uprising shriek, lengthening out into
a wail. It chilled me to hear it again. I thought that
the sooner he was locked up in a lunatic asylum the
better.

There were two very nice policemen, one middle-
aged and one only a boy. They went down the steps
with flashlights, and in a moment or two brought Cook
up again, quite calm, and apparently in a stupor. They
asked if I would mind going along to the station with
them, and promised that they would call a taxi to take
me home from there. I sat with the boy in the front,

while the other policeman and the superintendent kept hold of Cook's arms in the back seat. He was quite quiet, but muttered to himself about shells bursting most of the way to the police station. I hoped that Jenny's policeman would be there so that I could score him off, but he was not on duty. But I did point out to the sergeant in charge that I had complained of being followed some weeks ago, and that nothing had been done about it, though this man, who was obviously a public danger, might have been sitting in the stoke-hole every night.

He admitted the next day, in one of his lucid moments, that that was what he had been doing. Since he had been thrown out of work he had had to move out of his cottage and take one miserable little back room with no heating and no light in it. In the cold, endless winter darkness I think that the memory of the warm furnace that had once been his own had been too much for him. He knew well enough which nights the furnace was on and at what times the caretaker came in to stoke it. I thought pitifully of the dull, desperate misery in which his sudden unemployment had drowned him in that unhappy town where it was the common lot. Once he had been one of the privileged few who had this irreplaceable gift denied to so many of our generation—a job, a position in the community, a reason for living. How should I feel, I wondered with a cold chill of fear, if my work was taken from me? I think I should come back too, an unhappy revenant, and haunt the place where I had once belonged. In a community of social outcasts—enforced parasites—the tragedy comes sharply home to you.

During the afternoon, next day, a little boy came in

with a message from Miss Harford that I was wanted in her room. There I found a slight, fair young man, with horn-rimmed glasses, and a shy manner that struck me as being assumed for the sake of encouraging others to talk. I was suspicious of him. He asked me mildly if I would mind giving him some information that might help him in the case of Cook. He was a mental doctor, I gathered.

"He admits that he has been following you about for months. Do you know any reason why he should?"

I told him that I had been instrumental in Cook losing his job, since I had caught him stealing coke. The young man played with his pencil and murmured that it was a pity.

"I have seen him once or twice in the last few years and I was quite sure that his trouble was over. You know that he was shell-shocked?"

"I understood so."

"When he got this job I thought he could hope for a complete cure, so far as they're ever cured. But since last summer there seems to have been some worry on his mind. It's a help in these cases if we know what— and I wondered, since he seems to have a grudge against you, if you could help me——?"

"He hasn't any family, so I suppose it couldn't be anything like that?"

"I know. No. He seems to think someone's been persecuting him."

"The only thing I ever did to hurt him was to get him dismissed."

He looked at me contemptuously, and I could not help saying, "Don't think I take that lightly. But there were reasons why we couldn't have him about."

"Reasons?"

"He was stealing, as you know."

He rearranged the blotting-papers on the table. "We shall be lucky if we don't have our asylum filled in the next few years from this district," he remarked irrelevantly. "But you can't help me? Remember anything that happened in the last six months or so that might be the key of his trouble?" I hesitated for the fraction of a second and found him looking at me.

"Nothing. I'm sorry," I said.

"Oh, well, thank you for seeing me. I musn't keep you from your class."

"I hope he'll get better." I got up to go.

He shook his head absently and I went back to my room. After the "home-time" bell, as the children call it, had rung, and when Nellie was left alone in the classroom collecting up the books, I called her to me.

"Nellie, you know that poor old Mr. Cook, who used to be the caretaker, has gone to the hospital, don't you?"

"Yes, Miss Brigson."

"I want you to try to remember the beginning of last autumn term, Nellie, just after the summer holidays. When Moira was here you were a friend of hers, weren't you?"

"Yes, Miss Brigson."

"Well, do you remember if Moira was frightened of Mr. Cook, because he was ill then, you know, and he used to—to act a bit silly sometimes, and I think Moira used to talk to him sometimes when she stayed late to do the monitor's work. Did she ever say she was frightened of him, Nellie?"

"No, Miss Brigson."

"Did she ever say anything about him to you?"

"No, Miss Brigson."

"All right, Nellie. You can finish the books."

She went on with her work. But when she brought the pile up to my desk she hesitated and looked timidly at me.

"Yes?" I said encouragingly.

"Miss Brigson, is it because of the Minnies Mr. Cook has gone into the hospital?"

"What Minnies?"

"Miss Brigson, the Minnies that scream, and they took his ear off."

"Oh no, Nellie, it was in the war that his ear was taken off." Then a light dawned on me. "Oh, I see, you mean the shells—yes, Minnies it might have been. But how did you know?"

"Miss Brigson, it was Minnies he says he heard screaming at him all the time, and he said that was what made his head bad, and he used to ask us not to scream if we were playing slides outside the stoke-hole."

"Oh—I see. Did he say they made him ill?"

"Miss Brigson, once when his head was very bad he told us how they sounded, like a scream, and he said when he heard one it made him scream too, and made his head hurt something awful. And Moira could do it ever so good, and it made him cry."

"I don't think it really made him cry, did it, Nellie?" But I knew she was truthful and unimaginative.

"Miss Brigson, when he was in the stoke-hole and sitting quiet, Moira used to lean over the fence and scream like a Minnie and he used to jump right out of his chair and sometimes the chair fell over and sometimes she made him cry and he didn't have a handker-chief and he had to use his apron. And he used to ask her and ask her not to do it and he said he'd bring her some sweets if she'd promise not to, but Moira said she had got some sweets at home and he said he'd tell of her, and Moira said she'd tell her daddie about him crying and then her daddie would lock him up in the loonies place at the prison because her daddie said that was where he ought to be anyway. And it used to be ever so funny to see him jump out of the chair and sometimes he used to chase Moira, but only to the gate."

"Nellie—wasn't it rather unkind of you all?"

"Yes, Miss."

"Wasn't Moira sorry for him?"

"No, Miss Brigson. She liked to see him jump."

"Didn't she like him, Nellie?"

"No, Miss Brigson."

"Why not, I wonder?"

"Miss Brigson, it's because he only had one ear, and Moira didn't like it."

She lingered a little and then went home to dinner. I took my fountain-pen out of its case, slowly, and sat down to write to the doctor. For a long time I sat there, till I noticed that the pen was dripping its un-used contents over my papers. Then I screwed it up and put it away again. I could not dig up the past. It would mean so much extra suffering, as Moira's parents realised painfully what I had known for years, though it had not shocked me so sharply till now—what strangers and traitors children are to the civilisation that now and then takes violent toll of them.

245

CHAPTER XIII

I T W A S a drizzling, chilly day in February. As soon as the bell rang and I had seen my children out I made a dash for the staff-room fire to warm my hands before going back to the classroom to clear up. Miss Simpson ran in, seized her coat from the peg, and ran out again, leaving me with my comment on the weather only half spoken. I wondered what on earth had bitten her now.

She came back a few minutes later, scarlet in the face and trembling.

"Madge—they've done it at last."

"Who's done what?"

"They've cut the unemployment allowances by one and sixpence."

"Oh dear. But I suppose they had to. They must be laying out an awful lot of money on relief in this town."

She looked at me with a kind of fiery hatred. Thornby came in carrying a saucepan. I told her the news. She looked perplexed.

"What a pity they couldn't have waited till the weather got warmer. Coal and light and things cost them so much—the parents, I mean. However, I suppose it can't be helped."

"Oh yes it can," broke in Simpson fiercely. We looked at her.

"They're going to march," she said. "We've been expecting it for a long time."

"Where to?"

"Why?" asked Thornby, knitting her brows.

"To the Town Hall, to demand a restoration of the cut."

"They won't be allowed to."

"They're going to take the right into their own hands. They've been played about with too long. In any case, the police don't know. It's being kept a dead secret. Promise you won't say anything."

We promised, but next day Jenny told me that her policeman had been dropping hints about a "pretty scrap" on Friday, and I gathered that the meeting was not going to be quite the surprise that the organisers thought. There was a threatening undercurrent of feeling in the town that week. It had been growing for months, but so gradually that it had not frightened us. But when I went home from night-school one evening, down the dark street, I passed by a row of glowing cigarette-stubs along the wall, and knew that there was a row of ominously silent men there, unspeaking, watchful. They were like the eyes of a crouching wild beast.

The police these days were going about in twos, swinging their truncheons. We told the children, each time the bell rang, that they were to go straight home and stay in their own yards. Each night when I got safely home to my own suburb I felt as if I had come along a jungle path, with immensely powerful savage creatures lurking mysteriously in the undergrowth.

On Friday, when the night-school bell rang, it was met by no response. No one in the playground, no one in the classrooms, no one lingering in Furlong Street. It was like being a teacher in a city of ghosts. The superintendent, after a few minutes, came into my room and told me that he was taking the responsibility of closing the school for the night.

"If I were you I should go straight home," he added. I had every intention of doing so. There was a pricking up my spine. The very air in the street seemed heavy with an unknown menace.

I waited for a tram, but no tram came. I thought I would go down to the terminus and sit in one of the ones that were always waiting there for their turn to start. I had an idea that it would be comforting to be in the proximity of the uniformed conductor and driver.

The terminus was in Stocks Square. In the old days people used to gather there to jeer at their fellows in misfortune, and from that it had become a local forum, where all the cranks and faddists, from the Catholic Evidence Society to the white-haired old gentlemen who pulled out teeth, gathered on Sunday evenings to shout each other down from rival platforms.

When I turned into the square I found it more than half-full of people. The tram-drivers were keeping up a continuous clanging with their feet to try to clear a passage for their vehicles. I hesitated, and one passed me by. I pushed my way over to the other side of the square, where two or three empty ones were waiting. This end of the quadrangle, usually the platform of the speakers, with its gloomy warehouse walls, was jammed tightly with an impassive crowd. They were all turned one way, and for the most part seemed to be men in caps. A few women were sprinkled among them, with shawls drawn over their heads. They were facing a rostrum of soap-boxes, behind which two men held a red banner. A young man was balanced precariously on the boxes. I recognised him as Stanley

Rivven, a well-known local agitator who had been in prison more than once for letting his tongue run away with him. He was hardly more than a boy. His little brother was in my class, and was in the habit of declaiming such poems as "Up into the cherry-tree, who should climb but little me?" in the very accents that Stanley employed to harangue his Sunday night audiences. The times when Stanley was in jail this child was so puffed up with pride that he was completely impossible.

I tried to get up to my tram, which stood among the jostling bodies like a shining lighthouse of safety in a perilous sea, but I found that it took all my energies to keep my feet on firm ground as the growing crowd around me swayed to and fro. The alternative was being lifted bodily and jostled backwards and forwards. I had not known before what is the mute strength of a crowd and how helpless one is when really hemmed in on all sides. My hat got tipped over my eyes, and the stink of unwashed bodies filled my nose.

All this time, from the half-dozen streets opening into the square, more people were arriving and drifting, with the slow relentlessness of a glacier, towards that corner where the young man's face was etched in the flare. I looked round helplessly to see if the police were about. But all I could see were one or two constables, rather bewildered, repeating, parrot-like, and without much hope of being obeyed:

"Out of the way of the tram."

"You must keep moving."

"On your way, there."

But we were getting jammed so tightly that all we could do was to make a pretence of moving. I had a sense that we were all waiting—though for what I did not know. I glanced at the faces of my immediate neighbours. They were blank, expressionless masks. Their mouths hung slightly open and they breathed hard. When the clangour of the trams ceased for a moment I could hear odd phrases of the young man's speech, but the people near his stand seemed not to be listening. They were growing impatient. "Where's Willy?" I heard someone shout. And then, like a pack of wolves, everybody took up the cry. It began as a mutter and swelled: "We want Willy. We want Willy." Rivven stopped short and bent down to confer with a little group that stood behind the platform. There was a moment's conference and then he turned to face the crowd again and held up his hand.

"Comrades," he shouted, "you want to hear Willy Stanford? You shall. Willy is here, and he's going to address you now on our plan of campaign."

There was a roar of approval. The temper of the gathering was changing. They took their lead from those immediately below the platform, and the emotions which seemed most highly charged there were reproduced in varying degrees through the ranks, like ripples in a pond. From being passive, they were growing restless, partly, it seemed to me, from the sheer physical torture of being unable to move either forward or back.

"Here he is!" yelled Rivven, and climbed down.

A short, stocky figure clambered up on to the boxes. So this was Stanford, I thought, interested in him in spite of myself. The papers had been full of him lately. Freda Simpson always spoke of him with a touch of awe, as though he were scarcely human. Sometimes in

Bronton children were told, "Stanford will get you if you don't behave." He was an ex-soldier with the Military Medal. It was part of his power, and he always wore the ribbon. I could see it dimly now on his coat. At one time he had been a disturbing fire-brand in the House of Commons. Later he had been sent to prison for his part in a naval mutiny. He had led hunger-marchers, scuffled with officials during deputations to Whitehall and had pleaded his own case in police court proceedings in such a way that even *The Times* had reported him.

He seemed a disappointing figure to me when he got up there in the wild light of the flare, bulky, squat, with clothes that hung about him like a sack, bulging at the waist, his hair brushed straight up into a fuzz. But when he began to speak it was impossible to remember what he looked like.

There was magic in his voiçe. It was full and rounded, and sometimes he almost sang the end of his sentence in a rich baritone key. He never seemed to be straining himself, but he reached the fringes of the mob without any apparent effort. At one moment he would be slow and caressing, at another urgent and explosive. It was a firework display among speeches.

"Comrades," he began, "we are met here on this Friday night to make history. If you respond, as I believe you must, to the lead given you by the movement, you will light this night a blaze which not all the capitalist forces, not all the money in the Bank of England, not all the powers of darkness which walk abroad in this land of ours, crushing, blinding, starving the workers, which none of these will put out."

He thrust out a hand, jabbed his finger at faces in

the crowd, swinging his body slowly round in a full
half-circle. "You men with wives—have they got plenty
of money in their bags for the week-end shopping?
Have they got fine clothes to wear? You men with
children—are they pampered? Are they petted? Have
they got money for a cinema to-morrow afternoon?
Pennies for sweets and new toys? You yourselves, have
you come here with full stomachs? I suppose I could
ask any of you for a fill of tobacco? You've enough
and to spare, I suppose? And what about a drink?
What about a pint or two before we go home? Plenty
of loose change, of course? What's that? No, you
say, no?"

They had said nothing, made no sign as yet. They
were open-mouthed, hypnotised by the richness of his
scorn. I doubted if some of the ones round me understood what he was getting at, but the flow of his eloquence held them quite silent. He swept on.

"These things are not true, you say. Not true?
Then why should the authorities behave as though they
were?"

He paused to let the enormity of this sink in. The
first murmur of interest and acquiescence rose from the
crowd. Stanton was working himself into a frenzy
now, swinging his arms up and down like flails, and
banging the strip of wood that served as a bar in front
of him till I thought it would break under his blows.
Slowly but surely he began to communicate his mood
to the crowd.

"I tell you," he roared, "this reduction in relief is
nothing less than a deliberate and immoral attempt to
depress the workers in the hour of their greatest need."
There were angry cries, and the man next to me, who

had a stubble of grey beard all round his chin, and smelled as if he had not touched water for a fortnight, suddenly lifted his head out of the muffler, said, "The bloody swine," loudly and savagely, and then relapsed into impassivity.

"Slaves! That's what they want to make you!" shouted Stanford, but I was beginning to thread my way under elbows and between close-packed shoulders in a last effort to get out of the crowd. The cheers were getting louder now, and there was a continual undercurrent of growling, and epithets were being flung about freely. Some of them meant nothing to me, though I had heard so many in the last ten years on the lips of children. Vaguely I heard that roaring, frenzied voice behind me as I searched for a way out of the labyrinth in which I had been caught unawares.

"Men of Bronton!" he was crying, as I began to push vainly against the solid wall of a stout woman. "Show you are still men! Take your courage in both hands, if you've got any guts left! Let them hear your voices and tremble!"

This time there was an angry shout. "Who does he think he is?" "We'll show 'em." "Yes, and him." And then, out of the hubbub, one or two voices— "What shall we do?" "What do you want us to do, Stanford?"

This, apparently, was what Stanford had wanted. I turned round painfully and saw that he was looking pleased and holding up both hands for silence.

"I'll tell you, comrades. If you are agreed that we should act, the committee suggest that we take our case to the Town Hall and lay it before the Mayor. We understand the Council is still sitting. We propose that this magnificent mass meeting of the workers of Bronton should show those in authority the strength of our cause before they go home to their comfortable suppers. A march, comrades, to the Town Hall to get our eighteenpence back. There are plenty of old soldiers here, like myself, who did enough marching in the last war not to have forgotten how. What do you say, comrades? Shall we go?"

They seemed to be rather undecided. There were some who bawled "Ay," but the shouting was rather ragged and this time most of the people seemed to be shouting different things.

"What about the police?" cried one woman near me, and another:

"The rossers'll stop us. We'll only get our heads broken."

Stanford stooped and I saw him beckon to someone at the back of the group round him. This someone was hidden from me, partly by the banner and partly by the darkness, for the flare was burning down. But I did see Stanford gesturing with his arms, obviously arguing, and then he nodded several times vigorously, and got up from his squatting position to face the crowd again. It seemed to me that this was rather a critical moment, and I wished more than ever that the crowd would disintegrate enough for me to escape. The mob was angry, I thought, but not worked up enough to make the definite move he wanted. Stanford, however, had a trump card. He leaned forward in a confidential way, and when he had got something like silence he said:

"Comrades, I want you to hear another speaker who has come here specially to-night, defying the conventions of his class and regardless of what the bosses will say of him, to join with us in this mass demonstration of protest. He didn't want to speak, but I persuaded him to get up here beside me and say a few words to you. We may not all agree with the things he stands for, but you all know him, and you all know he is a good friend of ours. Workers of Bronton, I ask you to give a welcome to the Reverend Mr. Gregory."

To my astonishment up clambered the curate. He had a long black robe caught in at the waist by a broad belt with gleaming silver buckle. A crucifix hung from his neck. He was bareheaded. He stood, rather nervously, I thought, fingering his chain and looking out over the square towards the far end where the trams were still vainly trying to enter. There was no doubt that they liked him. They jeered a little, but it was good-natured jeering, and there were shouts of "Good old padre" and "Come on, Rev," among which I distinguished, for the first time, women's voices. A little runt of a man, with foxy eyes and a battered bowler hat just in front of me hissed, "We don't want no —— God-peddlars here." Several of those round about turned on to the critic and bade him shut his bloody trap.

Gregory looked down in silence on the upturned faces. The shouts gradually subsided, and then he raised both arms, so that his wide sleeves fell back to the elbows, in a gesture half benedictory, half arresting. He began to speak. He had nothing like the powerful organ-like voice of Stanford. His voice seemed to belong, not to the raw rowdiness of the market-place, but to the stilled reverence of the cloisters. Yet it was high-pitched and penetrating and he used simple sentences that were free of Stanford's catch-phrases. He looked very different from the amiable young man who had sparred with us over the Scripture inspection.

"My friends," he began. "You all know me here, and I most of you. Some people in this town will think it odd that I, a priest of the Established Church, should appear on this platform. It is incongruous, they will say. I can only reply to that, very humbly, by saying that I follow a man who was God, and nineteen hundred years ago suffered because they said it was unthinkable that the Messiah should consort with the poor and lowly. I know that to some of you Christ is no more than an oath. I know that some of you will say that if there were a God he would not have allowed you to endure so much. But those arguments give me fresh courage, because I know that men who make them have not seen the light of the kingdom, though they are very near it. I tell you, men of Bronton, Christ was our example in this very hour. He rebelled against the corrupt and wicked society of his day. He fought, and he expects us to fight. Unless we make our own salvation, not only for ourselves, but for the children who suffer for the evils of this present age, we may fall back into slavery and barbarism. I say to you that I believe with all my heart that we should march upon the Town Hall to-night. Think of it, not as being for yourselves, or for the sake of hate you bear any living person, but for your comrades, your wives, your hungry children. We must go to the Town Hall. We must get that one shilling and sixpence back. We are the eighteenpenny men. It is important that we present our petition in an orderly way, for we must give the police no provocation, but it is equally important that we go.

What do you say, men of Bronton? Will you follow me?"

"Yes," shouted Stanford, jumping up again. "What d'ye say? Do we march?"

This time there was no mistaking the answer. Indeed, before Mr. Gregory had finished the crowd seemed to have changed into gear, as it were, and to be pressing slowly but irresistibly towards the outlet that led in the direction of the Town Hall.

Now was my time to escape. But I did not escape. It was as if some germ of desperate excitement had infected me and was burning me up in a fever. I had a blind sensation that I must know what was going to happen. I seemed to have lost my identity. I could not remember how I was supposed to be spending that evening. But I knew, and it was the only thing I did know, how I was going to spend it. I was going along with this angry, exhilarated crowd wherever they went. It was madness.

I was quite near the head of the procession which had already formed behind the flags and banners torn down hastily from the platform and borne aloft. I could see Stanford's thick frame and the thinner shoulders of Gregory in his gown. As we skirted by the platform where they had been talking, already half dismantled by the abrupt passage of the crowd, I caught my dress on a piece of sticking-out wood and it tore, making a penetrating sound in the sullen shuffling which had succeeded the initial wave of cheers. Some men close by me turned and laughed. It was not a pleasant laugh. But I was too busy pulling myself free to shudder.

We must have covered several hundred yards, and

were near to the edge of the square, when I heard a rattle and a sudden peremptory shout. The big folding doors of the warehouse to our right were swinging open. A squad of police ran out. At their head was a superintendent. He looked frightened, I thought, though it may only have been a trick of the uncertain light. He behaved like a scared man. He tried to rush Stanford, who stood, surrounded by a group of the leaders, passively watching this eruption of blue figures from the dark building. Stanford stood his ground and the superintendent shouted:

"Hi, you, are you in charge of this mob? Where the blazes do you think you're going?"

"No," said Stanford. "The people of Bronton have taken command. I am in their hands. So are you."

"Nonsense," retorted the superintendent, who was obviously taken aback by the grins on the faces of the crowd at this remark. "I saw you speechifying to them just now. I was watching them all. And you, sir," he turned to Gregory. "I'm surprised at you. If any of you think you're going to march out of this square you're mistaken. I've got men posted at every entrance. I've only to blow this whistle three times and they'll draw their batons. I don't want trouble, but by God you'll wish you hadn't started it if you don't go your ways and leave well alone."

Stanford was laughing now.

"O.K., super, blow your whistle and be damned to you."

The policeman hesitated and began to temporise. He turned to the curate. "Now, sir, I'm sure you'll listen to reason. I tell you, you'd better give up the idea of this march. It's not legal and you know it. Tell 'em to go home, and I'll see what I can do at the Town Hall to get them to receive one or two of you."

The crowd began to jeer at him. All of a sudden he lost his temper, blew his whistle fiercely, and made a grab at Stanford, who warded him off. At the same moment one of the men near Stanford aimed a blow at the superintendent's head. He ducked, but someone else made a pass at him, and in trying to slip this one too he skidded on his heel and fell on his face in the glistening wet roadway.

The warehouse doors seemed all at once to be alive with men. Out they rushed, brandishing their truncheons, driving a wedge into the midst of the marchers, standing in a square back to back, raining blows indiscriminately on any heads or bodies they could reach.

The crowd was wary, stood back on its heels, dodged and scattered as best it could. Only one or two men were caught and half-nelsoned by the police. But that was enough to let loose the full fury of the crowd. In three minutes they had stormed the police squad with their bare fists, set free their comrades, and plunged forward again. I stepped on something soft and squelchy that groaned.

A police sergeant on the steps blew another whistle, and the police turned and ran for shelter. I jabbed my toe against a truncheon. It rolled away from me. I had just time to pick it up. I felt happier with it. Nobody followed the police. That dark hulk of a warehouse, with its broken windows and its blackened bricks might have been a medieval sanctuary.

This easy triumph put the marchers in great good humour. One frightful creature, who clearly had not shaved for a fortnight, put his arms round my shoulder and tried to kiss me.

"Come on, comrade," he urged. "Just a little one to celebrate our luck." I felt his rough, dirty face brush my cheek. But I pushed him off and managed to dodge into another part of the crowd by dipping under several linked arms. We were marching down a narrow street now, and there was some instinctive attempt at order. Now was my time to go. The kiss episode had decided me. But at that moment one of the female comrades, walking arm-in-arm with the second or third row at the front of the procession, turned round to look at someone behind, and I saw it was Freda. She was hatless, and her old mackintosh, with flaming red scarf tucked into its neck, hardly distinguished her from the rest of the rabble. It was strange to see one of my own circle in that alien community, and I had an unreasoning instinct that I must catch up with her. For a minute or two I hurried along, half-walking, half-running, by the side of the procession, absurdly like the children who were trotting by our side and being told fiercely by their various parents and relatives to go home to bed.

By the time we reached the long hill most of the children had been discouraged into lingering wistfully on the pavements, and I had slipped into the procession again, thinking that I would wait for an opportunity to get close to Freda. It was my one idea now. She might have been my dearest friend.

Someone began to sing. It was an unaccustomed sound in those streets. It was a miserable, dirge-like chant. I recognised it as the "Red Flag," and thought grimly that any movement which had this as its anthem deserved to be suppressed.

The shops were still open, throwing their light hopefully on to the pavements. The tradespeople stood at their doors staring at us. There was one girl I remember distinctly. She had a blood-red jumper drawn tightly across her full breasts. She stood at the door of a "cut-price store," which, I had been told, was accustomed to sell something to men besides sweets and cigarettes, very cheaply, in the back room. Her attitude, hands on hips, head slightly on one side, was deliberately provocative. But I think I was the only one to notice her silhouetted there. The men, as they plodded along, had their eyes grimly fixed ahead, as they wailed:

> "Tho' cow-herds fa-il and tra-ay-tors sneer,
> We'll keep the red flag fly-ing-gere."

We pushed forward blindly. The people at the back were urging us on. Sometimes the leaders stopped and turned to shout a few words of encouragement, and beckoned to those behind with great sweeping gestures. I could see Gregory striding out, his robe flapping round his ankles. It was odd to see a man garbed as he was in the van of such a mob. His big, sprawling stride was unrelenting. Every now and then he too would turn round and wave us on, and as his eyes roamed unseeingly over our faces I thought of friars who wore a sword, and priests in Spain who put their hand to a machine-gun. There was something fanatic about him, something unmodern. The whole scene, with its rabble of self-appointed militia, its variety of leaders and its vague, hypnotic enthusiasm might have been that of a medieval print of crusaders off for the Holy Land.

They had only one idea in their heads now, to get to the Town Hall. They kept muttering to each other about it. "We'll show those lousy ———." "This time will be different, by Christ," and some men kept on shoving their way backwards and forwards by the wall, shouting: "Get in line, comrades." "Get in line, there!" "Let's see how well you march, comrades."

Every now and then we came to a street-corner and the leaders would stop and hold a conference. Then they would shout the name of the street they had decided to go down, and wave their arms in that direction. Everybody repeated it and waved their arms to those behind. Still there were no police. Not a sight or sound of anybody as we went down Broad Street, where all the insurance offices and lawyers were. It was quite dark after the shops. At last we came out into the wide junction immediately below the Town Hall, where the fire station was. Then I sensed something in the ranks in front of me—a kind of shiver—and looked up to the rising ground which led up to the Town Hall. For the first time in that evening I was really afraid. It was not a vague chilling shiver at the unknown now, but horrible, desperate fear.

The slope was packed with men facing us. They were silent and motionless. Those in front were on horseback. They were police. Now we knew why we had met none on the way.

We halted. Stanford, Gregory and the boy Stanley Rivven advanced a little and then stopped too. This was stalemate. Nobody seemed to know quite what to do. Then the chief of the mounted police urged his horse forward quite gently.

"Are you Stanford?" he asked, ignoring the others.

"You know perfectly well I am."

"Well, the game's up, Stanford. I'm going to take you in with me. And twenty others."

"What's the charge?"

"Assaulting Superintendent Jones and other police officers in the performance of their duty."

"They started it, the bloody swine. This would have been a peaceful demonstration if they hadn't provoked us."

"You know as well as I do that even if that were true it is no excuse."

"And you expect me and twenty others to give ourselves up to be tortured in there"—flinging an arm in the direction of the Town Hall—"just so's you can revenge yourself for what you say we've done to your chaps when they deliberately brought it on themselves?"

"You know I can't arrest the lot of you. But I can and must make an example of some of you. You'll be treated perfectly well until you're brought to justice."

Rivven broke in jeeringly:

"Oh yes, I know what the inside of your blasted police station is like. Feather-beds and a cup o' tea to help you to sleep. Oh, we'd love to come."

The chief ignored him and addressed himself to Stanford again.

"I'm not going to waste any time on you. Either you come quietly or——"

"Well, or what, Superintendent?" said Gregory, speaking for the first time.

The chief jerked his thumb over his shoulder.

"I don't want to do it, but I shall take them, sir. I shall order my men to charge you."

"Let us see the Mayor and the Council," demanded Stanford.

"That's impossible. They went home an hour ago, in any case."

"Bloody liar."

"Bad language won't help." He shot his cuff, looked at his watch. "I'll give you exactly two minutes." He backed his horse away.

Stanton and Gregory and the other leaders gathered in a group. Those nearest them milled around, shouting and cursing:

"Let's charge them before they charge us." "That's right, get at them." "Give it 'em hot." "Burn the Town Hall."

The rest of us just stood there waiting. Round me they had gone quiet, staring ahead, leaning forward to hear what was said in front.

I thought this must be the way armies waited for the word "go" in the old days. I looked round, panic-stricken, utterly miserable. I might as well have been locked in a room. The whole mass of the procession had tightened up. It was just as it had been when they were facing the speakers in Stocks Square. What a fool, I said to myself, what a silly, futile idiot I was not to escape while I had a chance. I must get away. Shout for Gregory. He'll help me. I tried to cry out, but my voice was cracked and it would not carry. I'm going to be trampled on. I'm going to be killed. Hemmed in as I was, sweating, I suddenly felt myself going quite cold. It was like getting into a cold bath. Round me they were breathing hard again. One thin man with hectic cheeks and haggard eyes retched, then was sick on the back of the man in front of him. The man in front took not the slightest notice. The stench reached me, made me retch too. A woman beside the man who was sick caught him by the arm as he swayed, and threw her shawl, all she had over her thin dress, round his shoulders.

A man behind me dug me in the back. " 'Ere, take this, pass it up." Something short and hard was pressed into my hand. It was a piece of lead piping. I looked at it stupidly. "Pass it on, lass, pass it up," said the man hoarsely. I did so. Some instinct made me pass on my truncheon too. I had forgotten I was holding it. Now I had nothing to defend myself. I saw other weapons being passed up to the front. I felt wound up tight inside. My heart hammered faster and faster. All at once Stanford swung round, held up his arms.

"Do you want me and twenty comrades to spend the night in there at their mercy?" The crowd roared back. "No, let's give it 'em, Willy. Let 'em have it good and proper."

"Is that your final answer, comrades?"

They roared assent.

"Then follow me to the Town Hall. Let's take the Town Hall."

They ran forward. We all followed. It was like a dam released. One moment we were still, the next shuffling, stumbling, then running. The noise seemed to split my ears. Dimly I saw Stanford jump up at the chief, try to pull him off his horse. The policeman drove his stick at Stanford's eyes and yelled to the riders behind him to come on. With incredible swiftness they came in line together, their arms raised and fell on the front rows of the marchers. Again and again they struck, on heads, shoulders, bodies. The horses reared and kicked. The place was a shambles in a minute.

Madly I scratched and elbowed and hacked my way sideways to a wall and flattened myself against it. I saw a group of the unemployed drag the chief from his horse with a yell of triumph. One of them jumped on the horse, pulled it roughly round, tried to force it against the police. I caught sight of Gregory. He was not fighting, but he urged the others on. His face was radiant. Yet it seemed to me to be the face of a madman. Then I lost sight of him and they were fighting all round me. There were curses; red, glaring eyes, grunts and groans. There was a dreadful crack as wood came down on a skull. I heard the soft thud of falling bodies. A helmet scudded along the ground in front of me. I saw one big, hefty marcher wrestling on the ground with a policeman as tall and burly as he. They were absorbed in their private fight, oblivious of everybody else. Over and over they rolled, clawing at each other's faces. Then a horse trod on both of them and passed on. Where the marcher's face had been was a hole.

The policeman got up, looked round, plunged into another fray. A woman was wielding a piece of piping like a flail. Three policemen went for her, tore the dress off her back, clubbed her. Then, as she was down, one stooped to push her out of the range of the horses' hoofs and a marcher heaved him on top of her with a terrific kick at his behind.

A boy not five yards away from me stood irresolutely for a full minute watching the fight eddy around him. Then he looked at a stone he held in his hand. It was not much bigger than a bird's egg. He seemed dazed, and as if he did not know what to do with it. Then he threw it quickly into the police, as if it had been a ball in a game. He grinned, turned and ran. But not fast enough. A mounted police saw him, made for him, split his skull with a tremendous blow. He sank on the ground sideways with a surprised look on his face.

I heard a long blast on a whistle, and to my amazement the police all turned and ran. The marchers shouted in glee and swept after them. But as soon as they got level with the gates of the fire station, which were open, half a dozen jets of water shot out. I had never known how powerful water could be. The marchers went down, squirming on the ground like great, ungainly fishes. The street began to run like a river. The water lapped round my ankles. A dozen firemen, two to a hose, advanced out of the station and across the road, sweeping their nozzles from side to side. Nobody could break through those hissing streams. It was as if the gods of old had come down to fight beside the men they favoured. A thousand times stronger than the fury of man was the cold power of this element, harnessed to the forces of the law.

The unemployed made tentative rushes in groups, but each time they had to break and run. Nearer and nearer came the hoses, while I seemed to have lost the use of my legs. There was room now, in the rout of the marchers, for me to run to safety. But I could not run.

I sank to my knees and began to crawl away through

267

the slush. Painfully I made my way to the entrance of an alleyway and down it. I found some steps and lay back on them to recover myself.

It must have been a long time. I looked up to see two policemen standing over me.

"Now then," said one sharply, in the meaningless way they have.

"I want to go home," I said stupidly. It was the only idea left in my brain. His manner changed a little when he heard my voice.

"Where do you live?"

"Chestnut Gardens, Higher Bronton."

"What are you doing in all this?"

I thought it over dully and said, "I wanted to catch a tram."

They looked at me in silence, then at each other. One said, "I should think the best thing for you is to go home and we'll say no more about it."

They helped me to my feet.

"There aren't any trams now," remarked one.

"I could get a taxi." My brain was clearing now. "There's a garage somewhere, isn't there?"

"Down to the bottom of the alley and first turn to the left, Miss," said the younger one briskly, as if I had asked him in the broad light of blessed everyday. Without a word I turned and walked unsteadily away. Every bone in my body seemed to ache, and my head throbbed as if a piston were driving up and down inside it. It took some time to make the garage-men understand what I wanted. They seemed extraordinarily stupid.

CHAPTER XIV

FOR THE whole of Saturday and Sunday I lay in bed. Enid and Daphne were very good-natured and missed their usual Sunday outing to stay in and wait on me. On Monday morning I got up painfully, still very stiff and looking wonderingly at the blue bruises all over my body as I dressed. Lower Bronton seemed unusually subdued. There were few people about in the streets. The very children seemed scared and eagerly obedient as they marched into school. Simpson had a plaster on her cheek and limped badly. Dennis Rivven was bubbling over with something and boasting in a whisper to his neighbour.

At lunch-time in the staff-room Thornby was gossiping about the riot. I looked up and caught Freda's eye. We looked at each other and neither of us said a word. I went back to my classroom as soon as I had eaten my sandwiches and got on with some work.

I avoided everybody for a few days. I felt tired and depressed. I was continually finding new bruises and having aches where I had thought no bruises were. I scarcely read the paper. I tried to absorb myself in work and forget it all.

Then one day, at the end of the week, my Arithmetic lesson was disturbed by distant cheering. The children looked up and then looked at each other knowingly. I sharply checked an outbreak of whispering. As I went through the hall to drill the milkman came in with his daily container. He stood aside to let us pass, and as I went by him he said, "They've restored the dole cut, Miss."

Outside the school fence one or two little groups of men were talking excitedly to each other. When the milkman had gone I sent a child to tell the caretaker to lock the school gate. I did not want any of those men, delirious at their one-and-sixpenny victory, swarming over my breathing exercises and arms bending.

Simpson went about looking as if she had been transported into Elysium. When she met me in the corridor she seized my hand and shook it. I was extremely embarrassed. At lunch-time Thornby sent out for a paper. It was at pains to point out that the restoration of the cut had no connection with the outbreak of hooliganism of last week. The two things, it seemed, were just one of those strange coincidences that almost prove the existence of the occult. In fact, the *Bronton Evening Post*, midday edition, thought that it would be a good idea if only the men who had been patriotic enough not to join in the riot were awarded this magnificent prize for good conduct. I daresay it would have been a good idea, and cheaper too.

However, it seemed as if the unemployed of Lower Bronton could not be among the registered readers of the *Bronton Evening Post*, for they went about boasting of their glorious victory. Mr. Gregory's name was uttered in reverent accents, as though he had been some latter-day Messiah. Some of the townsfolk even went so far as to patronise his church, and the following Sunday saw the strangest sight that the ugly old church by the tram terminus had ever witnessed in its centuries of silent watching—a queue of ragged men, women and children lined up in the flagged pathway leading to the porch, only afraid that there would not be seats for them all.

The spirit of the whole town changed. There was laughter and chattering in the shopping streets as though they had been in an ordinary suburb. The children were high-spirited and unruly. They were always trying to tell us something about Mr. Gregory— that they had seen him in the street, or that he had spoken to Dad when he met him at the parish hall. We all hoped fervently that Gregory would not come down to the school during his wave of embarrassing popularity or it would have been as bad as trying to keep order at the yearly entrance of Santa Claus.

Worst of all were the unemployed girls. Nothing but my own knowledge of a happy release in sight at the end of term made me stick to the job. I thanked heaven three times a week that there was no night-school during the summer term.

I let the discipline of the night-school class—such as it was—slide now and then for the sake of peace. I ceased, for one thing, to wage my long struggle against their dabbing powder on their dirty little noses, and cheap red wax on their lips during class. I had thought from the first that it would be unfortunate if an inspector happened to look through the panel while half a dozen of them were thus engaged. But it had been a struggle. So far as they had any passion in life it seemed to be this. It was like the nervous monotony of a chain-smoker, this everlasting fidgeting with their appearance. Sometimes I thought, in my more charit-able moments, that it was the visible sign of that sense of insecurity which hung over their lives. Starvation for ever crouched next door to them. Well might they feverishly watch their looks—the only goods they could realise money on—as one watches one's last coin when there is no more to come. Other times I thought they were just a lot of dreary little Yahoos, with all their horrible habits natural to them.

However, during the earlier part of the night-school season I had made a tremendous effort to stop the face-dabbing until the bell rang, when there would be a flutter of dirty powder-puffs and a sudden flashing of thirty little mirrors. I used to confiscate them if they appeared earlier, but there would be such temper, such impertinence, and so much difficulty for the rest of the hour, that I was glad to let the matter slide towards the end of term.

But one night, a week or two before we closed, Maggie Hunt shook me out of my *laisser-faire*. She sat with her paper in front of her for the first half-hour, spending the time in taking out a tube of face-cream, all burst and dripping over her bag and the desk, spitting on it to moisten it and then spreading it all over her face, then producing a powder-case and spilling powder over her paper. I looked at her, but she grinned at me and went on. She took out a little tin of rouge and smeared it on her cheeks, then unscrewed a lip-stick and put a different shade of red all round her mouth. Finally, she took up her mirror and carefully scrutinised the effect. She evidently came to the conclusion, with some reason, that she had made her cheeks too red and got out her powder-case again. But I thought things had gone far enough and left my desk, walked down the gangway to her, and took the powder-case from her. She made a snatch at it, but I was prepared. I said as I went back:

"I shall keep this till the end of the class, and if you haven't finished your work by then I shall keep it altogether."

"That's stealing," she called out.

"Very well. You can complain to the police if you wish."

I had wished to remind her that last time we had a set-to it had ended up with her and her young man being hauled off by the police. I thought the hint might have a salutary effect. But I was not prepared for the sudden shout of laughter that went up at the word "police." All the girls joined in, in their high, shrill giggle, and some of them shrieked with delight. Maggie herself sat smirking and looking round her, very pleased with herself.

When the noise had died down a little I looked at the clock and said that I should keep the class fifteen minutes extra if they did not settle down to work. At this some of them languidly took up their pens and there was comparative quiet.

I went on marking papers and watching them for the more blatant outbreaks of cheating. The powder-case lay on the desk in front of me. It was red, with a silly little picture of a man and a girl dancing on the lid. It caught my eye whenever I put a paper on the finished pile, and something about it seemed vaguely familiar. I thought I must have seen one exactly like it somewhere. I turned it over and looked at the snap. It was not a good one. It did not fit well enough to keep the lid closed. But I knew what you had to do with it. You had to press the lid on very firmly and push the clasp a little way along and then it would go right over lid and base. I tried it, and it worked. I could not remember how I knew that.

I marked another paper and it came to me that I had seen Jenny's hands, with scarlet nails, manipulating the little snap so often that it had imprinted itself half-consciously on my mind. I looked at it again. Yes, it was Jenny's all right. It was not likely that two would have the same fault. I thought I would enquire into this.

When the bell rang Maggie said:

"Miss, I want my flap-jack now."

I told her to wait until the others had gone. Then I called her up to the desk.

"Where did you get this powder-case from, Maggie?"

"That's my business."

"I'm afraid not. You see, I recognise it as one that used to belong to Miss Lambert."

"Well, it doesn't belong to her now."

"Then how did you get it?"

"Find out."

"Very well." I put the case away in my bag. "But I shall have to go and put it in the lost-property office at the police station and tell them how I came across it."

She glared at me. Her little pointed face was an odd mixture of babyishness and vice. Her eyelashes and eyebrows were stiff with sticky lacquer.

"All right. You do. And you can ask Miss Lambert's gentleman friend where it came from, and find out some dirt about that Miss Lambert that sets up to be so much better than anyone else, and such a good girl, I don't think. She thought she'd got him nailed proper—didn't she? with her smart clothes and her swanky voice. But she's nothing but an old school-marm like all the rest of you and I'll bet she can't keep a man for all her schooling."

I got up. "Well, Maggie, I'm going to call at the station on the way home unless you can give me a better explanation of where this came from. It will be a pity if you have the police round at your house again, just when your father's got a good job at last, and there's some money in the house for once, won't it?"

I was putting on my jacket. She stood hugging her vanity-bag and staring at me. At last she burst out.

"Well, I will tell you, then, if you'll promise not to go sneaking round to the police. It was given to me."

"Did Miss Lambert give it to you?"

"Not she. Dick Hannaford gave it me, and told me to keep quiet about it."

"The policeman? I don't think that's a very likely story, Maggie."

"Oh, isn't it?" said Maggie, quietly and triumphantly, so that I began to think she must be telling some measure of truth. "Well, I'll just put you right about that. Dick Hannaford's being going with me ever since that night when he came in here 'cos you'd kept me in. And you can just tell Miss Lambert where he's been the nights he wasn't with her, and I'll bet he had more fun than with a stuffy old school-marm like her. He likes a girl with some fun in her—he told me so. And he gave me the powder-box for doing of him a favour, so there."

"You can go now, Maggie," I put in. I could see the superintendent coming round to put out the lights.

"I'm going to give this case back to Miss Lambert."
She hesitated, and then the superintendent came in,
and she went out unwillingly. She was a little in awe of
him, since he was a man.

I was amused at the situation. I thought it was like
a modern version of *Othello*. I did not think Jenny's
heart would be broken, and I was glad to be proved
in the right about the policeman. Of course, romanc-
ing came more easily than telling the truth to the Hunt
family, but I hardly thought Maggie would make up a
story that could be so promptly disproved by the police.
So the next morning I called for Jenny on the way to
school, and on the tram asked her if she had lost her
flap-jack. She looked bewildered and said she did
not think so. I produced it, and she pocketed it un-
concernedly.

"Oh, thank you. Where did you find it?"

"Maggie Hunt had it in night-school and swore that
it was a gift to her from your Dick."

"What an imagination those Hunts have got. I wish
it showed in Betty's compositions."

"She said she had been going out with Dick Hannaford."

"Going up to the station with him when he's caught
her out at her job, I should think."

"Well, I should ask him," I suggested. I was curious
to know the truth.

I think he must have been on night-duty for the next
week, because I did not notice any difference in Jenny
till about ten days after, when she turned up at school
looking like a thunder-cloud. I saw her first thumping
out the *Soldiers' Chorus* as if she had a spite against
every note on the piano. She would not look at me,

and at break she kept in her own room. During the morning Miss Thornby came round with pencil and paper and said she wanted to take down particulars about anything we had missed from our rooms lately. I asked her if she knew why. She pursed up her mouth and whispered, "It seems that Hunt has been taking things home, and Miss Harford wants to get a complete list to give to the police."

I had lost an Eversharp pencil, but had concluded that one of the children must have taken it, and that it was my own fault for leaving it about. Miss Thornby entered it on her list and went on into the next room. I watched her round the hall and noticed that she missed Jenny's.

At twelve o'clock I went over to Jenny's room and asked her if she had come to the conclusion that the flap-jack I had found had been stolen by Hunt.

"Yes, I have, you inquisitive female," she answered crossly.

"Then your lover's name is cleared?" I suggested.

"Thank you, but the policeman isn't my lover. And what's more, he isn't my gentleman friend any longer. Maggie Hunt can have him to herself now."

"Oh—so it was true?" I was just going out when Jenny said:

"By the way, Madge, I said you had told me you had seen them together when you were coming home from night-school. He accused you of plotting to part us because you were jealous of him and of me, but I don't suppose that will worry you. You see, I had to say that because he said she'd been making it up at first, and I had to invent a lot of evidence before he'd admit it. But in the end he positively boasted about

it, though he swears he never took my powder-case and
gave it to her. I thought myself that that didn't sound
likely and that I'd left it under some books in my desk.
Still, it's served its purpose of getting him cut out of
my young life once and for all."

"I can't think how he could bring himself to touch
that little tart," I commented.

"Oh, he explained it all to me most plausibly, a little
too plausibly. Gave me to understand that a great big
lady-killer like him must have one woman to satisfy
his immediate needs and one for his permanent mate.
I told him that if he thought I was going to be number
two wife in a harem he'd misjudged my yielding
feminine nature. Then he offered, very handsomely,
to promise not to see her again as I took such a conventional view of the situation. I said he could collect
the entire Hunt family as far as I was concerned,
because it was lover's farewell for us, and no touching
scene of forgiveness was going to take place in my flat
nor anywhere else."

"So you've really finished with him."

"I have."

Here, to my hideous embarrassment, the hard-boiled
Jenny suddenly burst into tears. I looked round nervously to make sure that the children had all gone
home, and then said:

"Here, this is too painful. I'm going out till you've
recovered."

She dried her eyes and sat down at the desk. She
murmured in an unsteady voice:

"It's so damned humiliating, Madge, to think that I
come in the same category with a little animal who
earns her money—oh, my God, I feel so absolutely

sick when I think of him being welcomed by us both. I've never been jealous, and it isn't that. It's just that it makes me feel so—unclean. I never imagined such disgust—that I don't like to think about, but it won't go out of my mind. He told me all about how it happened—how it excited him the night he arrested her—and knocked her about—and I'll bet she enjoyed it. You see, in a way, I'm not much better. I liked his brutality, until now it looks—different, and absolutely disgusting."

"I don't see that you're so much better than she is that you need take up such a superior attitude," I could not help remarking.

"Don't exaggerate, Madge," said Jenny, drying her tears and sitting up again.

"Well—maybe you are a bit better. But you asked for it, didn't you?"

"Don't improve the occasion, Madge."

"It's professional. I can't help it. But what I can't understand is how you came to take up with him."

"Oh, I suppose I wanted an antidote to Ronnie and Judith and their high-falutin' vice, and to that ridiculous curate wanting to rescue the sinner—and I thought Dick was just a healthy animal and very suitable. But this has shown me the logical conclusion of that, and I don't much like it."

I agreed with her, and went away to have my lunch. I was sorry for Jenny in a way, but it was very interesting to find out where she would stop. I thought that probably promiscuity looked quite different on oneself and in other people. Apparently one could stand just so much and no more, like getting a little bit drunk and then meeting a sot on the way home. I also

279

wondered, for the fiftieth time, why it was that everyone pitied women like me so much for missing this experience of sex, when at its most violent it consisted in Dick Hannaford's being unable to keep away from the unpleasant little Hunt. If that was the peak, the initial stages could hardly be so marvellous that life was wasted without them. Anyway, I felt neither regret nor hankerings and I began to make up my Progress Register and add up my own monthly budget quite contentedly.

Hunt, of course, was dismissed. They found a tremendous collection of our old possessions in his house. All sorts of things that I had never missed turned up again and were given back to me by the police—though not by Constable Dick. He kept away from the school. It was bad luck on Mr. Hunt. If one must be a thief, it was best to be like him, we all agreed, just cheerfully appropriating whatever he thought his family would like, and saying afterwards that it was because we were all so untidy that he never knew what we meant to be thrown away and what was just left about by accident. It seemed almost a shame to deprive the Hunts of the small possessions they had come to look upon as their own—red and blue pencils for scribbling on the walls of their house, and coloured blackboard chalk for inscribing their opinions of the neighbours all over the neighbourhood, and books which they could raise money on when they were in bad straits, and an incredible number of handkerchiefs. I should think these were the first they had ever owned, and I wonder if they knew what to do with them. However, the authorities took a narrow view of the matter and Hunt again joined the ranks of the unemployed.

There was, of course, no question of reinstating Cook. He had been certified insane and would probably not emerge again into the world until he was carried out feet first, as they say in Bronton. We got a tidy, priggish young man as caretaker, who was always saying disparagingly that the neighbourhood was not what he had been used to. We all took this as a reflection upon ourselves and agreed to take it out of his Christmas-box next year. We quite missed Hunt, and his children went back to their former bedraggled state.

For the next week or two I had rather a gay time. Jenny had nothing to do with her evenings, now that she had parted from the policeman, and she insisted on my going out with her whenever she was free. She said that she could not possibly go to the pictures by herself and that it was up to me to treat her tenderly on account of her unhappy love-affair. I thought, though, that she was not really feeling as flippant and indifferent about it as she pretended. For one thing, she did not trouble about her appearance as much as usual, and she bought a dress that was brown instead of red, and not so tight as hers usually were. It would be funny, I reflected, if the disclosure of the police constable's coarseness should lead to her reform. I hoped not. I liked Jenny best as she was.

So we went to the pictures. I scarcely ever went, in the usual way, and I did not like to confess to Jenny how much one or two that we saw embarrassed me. Sometimes there would be quite a lot of children in the audience, too, and I thought it was dreadful. It was one thing to see little harlots like Maggie Hunt scamper off towards the badly-lighted side-streets, after evening school, and know that she was going to make money in the only way she could. But it was quite another to see some highly-paid creature with a husky voice being embraced by various manly figures twelve feet high, and then explaining that she was really extremely pure at heart and was consumed by a burning passion for One Man. It exasperated me, and it disgusted me very much, though I knew it was only because I was prudish and did not go to the pictures enough.

One night, when we were having coffee and biscuits in the cinema restaurant before going home, and Jenny insisted on discussing the picture we had just seen, I could not help saying to her that I did not want to spend any more evenings seeing plays about Pure Prostitutes.

"If there's a very funny comedy I'll come with you," I said. "But no more of the Harlots of History, no matter how correct the costumes are, nor how much they've spent on research of the period."

"I like seeing the same thing in a different setting," argued Jenny.

"It's your hobby," I told her. "It's not mine."

"No," answered Jenny, considering me. "But hasn't the most primitive passion of mankind enough interest for you to make you spend a shilling now and then?"

"I'm more interested in other passions."

"Such as?"

"Well, there are others. Think of that unemployed riot. I got a heap more excited over that than I ever could over witnessing anybody's love affair. I mean anything that can drive a whole mass of people to violence they'd never commit in cold blood must be a bit more inspiriting than anyone's tuppeny-halfpenny mating instincts. And that had nothing to do with sex."

"No. It was about money. So you think that's the grandest human passion?"

"Not entirely about money. Don't you think it was more a fear of being pushed out of the living community and becoming outcasts, with no rights for themselves or their dependents?"

"There you are then. Their women and children. You see, you always have to come back to sex, however hard you try to pretend it doesn't exist, Madge."

"I don't, Jenny. Don't be silly. But according to these films you're so impressed by, it doesn't seem to have much to do with marriage after about a fortnight. It irritates me the way they insist on terming physical attraction 'love' with a capital 'L.'"

"The censor makes them," said Jenny absently.

"Well, I think it's ridiculous."

"Don't you think perhaps—" Jenny hesitated and looked almost shy, "don't you think perhaps that you might begin by admiring a person not because they had any physical attractiveness, but because they had the things you'd always admired, like education, or a cultured background, and you might end up by feeling as fond of them for that as you might feel of someone for being an absolute Adonis?"

"Not on the pictures," I said firmly.

"Well, but in real life?"

"It sounds to me just like another commercialised version of sex—'Love,' if you and the censor prefer it."

"You've got to love a person for *some* reason," argued Jenny.

"I haven't got to."

"Well, other people haven't your strong-minded detachment. I believe you'd be happy on a desert island, provided you had a stack of registers to add up."

"That reminds me—I've got to be home early. Hi, waitress!"

We divided the bill. As we went down the orange-and-purple stairs, with Jenny stopping to look at the pictures of handsome young morons, an idea suddenly came to me and I turned back to speak to her.

"I know!" I exclaimed.

"What?" asked Jenny, looking round for the cause of my excitement. A man and a girl came down the stairs arm in arm. I hesitated, and we went out into the air. It felt good after that cinema.

"Honestly, Jenny, I think it's a bit shameless, even for you, breaking off with one man one week and then wanting to start up on another straight away."

"How do you know it is straight away?"

"Oh—pooh to that. Don't pose, Jenny. I know you think of men as fish to be hooked and I don't despise you for it as long as you're honest about it. We all have our hobbies. But if you start hinting at hidden flames of love, as though there were any more to this sex business than buying and selling for either short periods or else ninety-nine year leases—that's the sort of sentimental hypocrisy that makes me absolutely sick. Better be honest about it, like Maggie Hunt, than that."

"I suppose a person who had lofty ideas might look upon Maggie Hunt as a girl forced into it by circumstances and me as—beneath contempt."

I was struck absolutely dumb with surprise. We had

been waiting for a tram, and I was so much taken aback that I did not notice one had come up. Jenny leapt deftly into the one vacant space on its platform. She waved apologetically to me as the tram bore her away.

CHAPTER XV

W E H A D the impression that there was a lull in the town. It came to us in various ways. There were fewer missed attendances among the children, which always means that the district is in the flow of its usual routine. The men hung about talking intermittently to each other instead of gathering in groups and having fierce discussions. There was a general sense of a storm being over, though not the flatness there had been in the winter.

Freda Simpson said that it was simply because Gregory was working up to the peak point of his campaign. This was to be a petition to Parliament to put the factories on their feet again. A little band of men were to walk with it to London and be sponsored by their local member when they got there. He and Gregory were hand in glove. Freda said that if she had her way the factories would be taken from the man who owned them and given over to the workers without any compensation to the capitalist.

"Why not just hang him from one of the lamp-posts and settle the whole question?" suggested Jenny sarcastically.

Freda said she would like to.

"It amazes me how your humane feelings extend to dogs and cats and rats and stop dead at a harmless old man just because he happens to have some money," I remarked. It really did amaze me, when I came to think about it. But Miss Simpson just looked black and went out of the room. She was getting more and more difficult lately. I thought that the way Gregory's plots were looking up should have made her more cheerful, but it seemed to work the other way.

Even the *Bronton Echo* ceased its outcries against Gregory at this time. Instead of headlines about "Red Curate's Amazing Sermon," we had almost approving discussion of "Local Curate's Amazing Scheme." As soon as there seemed to be a chance, however remote, of his being the means of bringing some money into the town, they ceased to prefix his name by "Red." I thought it extremely sensible of them.

All the children whose fathers were going up with the petition used to tell us about it every day, and give themselves airs in consequence. On the day that the deputation started Mr. Gregory held a service to bless the marchers. I remember that it was the first warm, still day of the spring, and that the children, for some reason, were behaving themselves very nicely. They were doing an examination paper, and I was standing at the window with half an eye fixed on them and half an eye dreamily fixed on nothingness. The sill was faintly warm, and I was idly leaning my arms and elbows on it, enjoying the feeling of the warmth penetrating my sleeve.

The church bell began to toll. The children glanced up from their papers. I listened, enjoying the unaccustomed sound. It was a good bell, deep and clear, and it seemed to hang over that silent, rotting town like a benediction. It struck me that if we heard it more it would be like a deep, wise, comforting voice in that dreadful silence. After a while I saw a little group come from the direction of the church and wend their way towards the by-pass. A few straggling friends and companions walked by their side for a little way, and then stood waving good-bye. Up the broad, wide road, battleground of last winter, they walked, seeming, from so far away, to be progressing slowly though steadily. I watched them until they were a group of midgets on the narrowing ribbon, and then they went round a bend and out of sight. I turned back to collect the papers. I was glad I had not missed it. Whatever happened to that pitiful little army of messengers, I thought I should remember this morning for its feeling of hope and benediction after so many months of dark despair.

Next morning, as I read my paper on the way down, I learnt that the Prime Minister had agreed to meet the deputation and that the paper now called Mr. Gregory an "enterprising young social worker" instead of an agent of Moscow. And the next day we learned that the Prime Minister had seen them, listened to all they had to say and promised that something should be done.

Miss Simpson said this proved it was a failure.

"But why?" asked Thornby. "You see it says he was very nice to them."

"Only to keep them quiet while he shelved their petition."

"Dear, aren't you just a little bit pessimistic?" Mrs. Lee reprimanded her sweetly. Simpson gave a short, rude laugh.

Mr. McCarthy came down to the school one day the next week to see the children who were getting free milk and to ask us if we had any more cases of real malnutrition that we would like to put up to him. He was in his best Santa Claus mood, and seemed to have something up his sleeve. He dropped hints about the children's troubles soon being over, and when we asked him what he meant he wagged a finger at us and said he did not want to be put into prison under the Official Secrets Act and that we must just have patience a little longer. I should have liked him all right if he had not been so full of brightness and jollity that talking to him was like trying to support a bad music-hall turn and extremely exhausting.

One evening soon afterwards I thought I would go out and have a high tea at the local café before night-school. My lunch-time egg had been bad, and I was feeling very empty. So I told Nellie that I should not want any tea made, and walked down the road and had ham and eggs at the shabby little restaurant where the tram drivers sometimes had a hasty meal between journeys. On my way back I heard a boy shouting "Paper," and recognised the voice of one of my old pupils, who now eked out his father's relief-money by selling papers after school. I thought I would wait for him at the church gate, which I knew he passed, and buy a paper.

The churchyard was the only bit of grass in the district and it was very yellow. The church was blackened by the smoke of long ago. It seemed strange that the dirty breath of those lifeless chimneys should still linger on the stained stone, while they had been still and derelict for so long.

I noticed a man sitting on the flat grave-stone, which everybody used as a seat, halfway up the path to the porch. It was not his dejected attitude that made me look twice. That was perfectly normal. But something was familiar about him. I saw that it was Mr. Gregory.

I opened the iron gate and went it. He did not look up at its grating sound. I thought he might be ill.

"Mr. Gregory," I called to him as I went up the path. He looked up at that, and his face gleamed dull white in the darkened churchyard. But he did not answer and I went up to him and sat down beside him.

"What's the matter? Are you ill?" I asked.

"Oh no." His voice was flat and hoarse. I hesitated, wishing I had not come. I decided to go away. He was staring at the ground again. I thought he was behaving in a most peculiar manner and being rather rude.

"Well, I mustn't stay then. Only I thought you might need help."

He was silent.

"Oh—do tell me what's the matter!" I cried, between impatience and curiosity.

"The matter is that I'm a fool who's been rewarded with the most laughable failure disguised as success."

"Oh dear, please don't talk like a person in a Shakespeare play. It's so irritating."

"All right. Read my paper if you want it in plain terms."

I picked up the paper from the ground. It had got dirty from the damp pathway. On the back were the usual pictures of children's mutilated bodies, legless or armless or faceless, in Spain or China or somewhere. I turned it over. The headline on the front page was "Munition Factory for Lower Bronton."

I read the column as well as I could in the fading light. It announced that the biggest factory in Lower Bronton—the one that had been the last to close down —was to be converted into an armament factory. There would be well-paid employment for a thousand men to start with, and the smaller factories were to follow suit as soon as possible. Prosperity had turned in its headlong flight and would come back to Bronton by leaps and bounds, announced the *Bronton Evening Post*, getting its metaphors a little mixed in its excitement. It seemed that Mr. McCarthy had put down the money for converting the first factory and would negotiate with the Government for contracts which should, in time, reinstate a large proportion of the factory workers who had fallen into unemployment during the last few years. I read it twice before it occurred to me what it was had thrown Mr. Gregory into such depression.

"I suppose you don't like them making munitions here because you must be a pacifist?" I said to him.

He gave a short laugh. I nearly got up and left him. But I was sorry for him because he did look miserable. So I stayed and said:

"Well, of course I understand that it isn't the industry you would have chosen, but it's surely better that they should be doing that than have nothing at all to do?"

He opened his mouth, and I thought I was going to be treated to one of his speeches, and glanced at the church clock to see how long there was before nightschool. But he flopped down again, as if he had not the heart to make a speech, and said quietly and without much expression:

"Miss Brigson, let me put it in a way you'll understand. It's been very painful to watch your class going hungry and cold, hasn't it? Not just because they are the children you know, but because it offends one's sense of justice that they should have to pay for older people's foolishness. Now they are to be fed and clothed, and their food and clothes are to be earned by their parents preparing implements to tear other children limb from limb, to put bullets in their lungs, to burn them alive with liquid fire, to suffocate them with poisonous gas, and to mutilate them so that their own father and mother cannot identify them. This is the end of my campaign to bring better times to this particular town. I feel to-night as if every word I have spoken in the last few months has succeeded in so far that some other child will finish its life prematurely, in frightful agony, in some other town, some day. There's my triumph for you. Do you expect me to rejoice over it?"

"Munitions aren't only meant to kill children," I argued. "They're for soldiers in the first place."

"No. But, as you know, the children have a knack of getting in the way."

"Well, one can't be expected to take responsibility for that."

"Quite. Nor for them getting in the way of cars. If a few hundred children finish up like that little girl Moira Watson, we can't be responsible for that, can we?"

"I must go to night-school," I said, getting up. That subject was still too sore for me to be able to talk about it. I don't know if he said it to hurt me. But I left him there, and thought he would probably get pneumonia if he sat in the damp churchyard for much longer. I felt chilly myself.

The girls were quite impossible that evening. They all told me, when I reproved them, that they wouldn't be coming to night-school much longer, Miss, because they would all be getting jobs. I replied sincerely that no one would be more pleased than I should, but that, until they got them, they had got to go on learning how to write decipherable English. Maggie Hunt seemed slightly subdued, I thought, and when I went through the gate afterwards I saw her walking off up the road arm-in-arm with her original young man. I had a kind idea that I would call in and tell Jenny that the policeman had evidently had enough sense of shame to drop Maggie, as I knew that she had previously jilted her young man for him.

Jenny did not seem particularly interested. I told her about seeing Gregory in despair in the churchyard.

"Poor man. How awful it must be to be so earnest," she commented.

"He did look bad," I said.

Jenny stood thinking. Then she went into her bedroom and came back carrying her coat.

"Where on earth are you going?"

"Never mind."

"I believe you're going to console Gregory."

"Don't be silly."

"Jenny, you can't go out at this time of night."

"You're out yourself."

"But I'm on my way home."

"So shall I be in about half an hour."

"Jenny, you can't, you simply can't go and force yourself on a man like that. It isn't decent. It's so—so forward. I shouldn't have even thought it was good technique, of the kind you usually employ."

"All this dirty-minded Grundyism," said Jenny mockingly, and ran out, leaving me wondering where I had heard the phrase before.

The next Sunday Mr. Gregory annoyed everybody

intensely, and the *Bronton Echo* most of all, by preach-
ing a sermon advising the citizens, in no measured
terms, to refuse what he called the "Hangman's Job."
The *Bronton Echo*, which I read clinging to a strap
in the tram going down on Monday morning, observed
with dignified reproof that Mr. Gregory did not seem
to be able to distinguish between what he called paid
murder and the defence of our glorious Empire. The
paper recounted, with sympathetic approval shining
beneath their condemnation of "Hooliganism outside
Church," how some of the local people had made a
demonstration after the service. There had been scorn-
ful laughter mixed with genuine indignation, and some
stones had been thrown. The bare idea of anyone
trying to deprive them of their long-awaited chance to
work had terrified the unemployed into immediate
violence. The Stop Press column announced that Mr.
Gregory had been attacked on his way home after
evening service, when he had, undaunted, preached a
sermon about "Judas in Modern Dress," and had been
badly hurt and taken to hospital. I could not help
hoping, for everyone's sake, that that would keep him
quiet for a bit, and that he would not go on trying to
achieve the impossible after he came out.

It was astonishing to find, during the next few days,
how quickly the popularity that he had gained over
so many months seemed to have been killed stone-dead
in a day. The papers all called him "Red" again, and
the unemployed decided that he was a traitor to the
working-class movement, and that they should have
distrusted his cloth from the first.

I sent him some books to read, and received a note
from my nurse friend saying that he had been con-

cussed and was not allowed to do anything but lie flat in a darkened room. I thought that his reflections throughout the long, dull twenty-four hours could hardly be likely to help his recovery.

On the last day of the spring term Mr. McCarthy came down to give an end-of-term address and to give away such small prizes for good conduct as we usually awarded in the middle of the year. He also took the end-of-term service, when we sang "Lord, dismiss us with Thy blessing." Afterwards he told the children that they must thank God that better times were at last coming to their town, and they would all soon have enough food and clothes, and perhaps better houses too, and jobs when they grew up. He started an extempore prayer, thanking God for these blessings upon them. They were all kneeling, with bent heads and their hands folded, but glancing at each other and giggling a little, because it was so near holiday-time and they were feeling excited, when there was the sound of someone getting up at the back. They all peeped round, thinking that some child had been sick, and Miss Harford looked up and frowned. But it was Miss Simpson rising noisily to her feet. She walked straight out, not looking at anybody, and went into her classroom, swinging the door instead of closing it quietly. Inside her classroom, she began putting books away, without troubling to prevent paper rustling or walking on tiptoe. The children's heads were turned, like six rows of identical toy soldiers, towards her door, watching her in thrilled amazement. Miss Harford turned absolutely crimson. The children forgot to say "Amen," and never even noticed when Mr. McCarthy had finished his prayer and Miss Harford had signalled them to get up. We had to tap them on the shoulder and pull several of them to their feet before it registered with them, and then they stood gaping at Miss Simpson's classroom, in spite of being told loudly by Miss Harford to turn round. It was a relief when we got them into the playground at last and term was over.

Miss Harford summoned Miss Simpson into her room, and we could hear a long argument going on, with Mr. McCarthy's voice trying to shout down Miss Simpson's, and Miss Harford failing to get a word in between them. Some of the others hung about waiting to hear what had happened, but as soon as I had finished locking up I went home. I was not going to spend one single hour of my holiday prolonging the controversies of term-time.

The last few days of the holiday I went down to stay with Miss Jones—Mrs. Owen, that is. I still could not get used to her name being changed. It seemed so absurd at her age. She and the captain had a cottage by the sea, and it sounded ideal. It was one of those little towns on the south coast where sailors and soldiers all seem to spend their declining years.

The old fellow met me at the station. I wished he had not, because before we got a hundred yards from the station I gathered that it had meant his missing his morning walk by the sea, and that he had had to wait twenty minutes, because he always was ten minutes early for trains and this one had arrived ten minutes late. But when we got to the house, which was a little villa just outside the town, I forgot about it in the pleasure of seeing old Jones on the doorstep. She was simply bursting with enthusiastic welcome, and was fairly gabbling with delight, when an ominous smell of burning filled the house. Old Owen said, "Sara, you've let the dinner boil over *again*," and went off in a pained way to turn off the gas, while poor old Miss Jones trotted beside him, apologising and explaining that she had been so excited that she was afraid she had left it just a minute too long. It was the potatoes that had caught in the saucepan, and they did taste rather unpleasant burnt, but I did not think the old sailor need have spent the whole of dinner saying how sorry he was that my meal should be completely ruined.

In the afternoon he went to sleep in his chair with the *Daily Telegraph* and Miss Jones showed me all round the place. There was a little bit of garden, and they kept chickens at the bottom of it, and were hoping to keep themselves supplied with eggs, as well as making a little money out of the corpses later on. She said that it was difficult to remember all the care they needed when they were small, and that in the spring she had accidentally killed an incubator-full through leaving the light too low on a cold night. She said she still felt like a murderess, and that she had cried herself to sleep about it for a fortnight afterwards.

The house was quite nice in a fussy way. I suppose that her generation likes tassels on the bed-covers, and two sets of curtains—one net and one plush—in every window. I did not like it much myself, but still, I admired everything enthusiastically enough to please her. We were so much occupied in examining bedspreads and colour schemes that the clock struck four before we knew it and she dashed downstairs to get the tea ready, because John liked it at four o'clock prompt. He did not say a word about its being late, but she spent the whole of tea-time apologising, and I found myself chiming in at regular intervals, like an opera chorus, explaining that it was all my fault.

We spent the evening playing cards. He was teaching her bridge. It should have been idealistic, but it is exasperating, really, teaching other people bridge. You cannot get away from the idea that they are being stupid on purpose.

The next day was Sunday. I should have liked to stay at home and help Jones to cook the joint. But the old man insisted on my going to church with him and leaving her to it. He said playfully that she was such a very raw beginner in the culinary line that we should get no dinner at all if there was anything to distract her. I gave a polite giggle, but I was beginning to get a little tired of that kind of joke.

The fact was that he was "picking on her" all the time, in the kindest, most playful way possible, but still, definitely picking on her. It was brought home to me sharply that when you have been a teacher all your life this complicated business of hot meals and clean sheets and managing gas-cookers does not come naturally to you at all. But he could not understand it. I suppose he was used to say Go, and he goeth, and Do this, and he doeth it, and was completely baffled by poor old Jones' inabilities.

I think he imagined that all women were born with domestic abilities all ready-made and packed up with their feminine instincts. On our way home from church we passed a girl walking on the promenade in shorts. He made some scathing remarks about her, and in the course of the argument that followed I began to understand him better. I had no real convictions about shorts either way, but I thought it was time someone contradicted him. He maintained that such things were "unfeminine" and gave me to understand that a woman who wore shorts would automatically be a bad cook and bed-maker, while one who was "feminine" and gave way to male opinion would automatically have a light hand with pastry. I believe you get into that categorical way of thought when you have been captain of a boat for as long as he had.

But it was not only the question of housekeeping that worried him about old Jones. He told her two or three times that day, quite pleasantly, that she was chattering too much, or getting too excited over trifles, and she subsided like a child.

However, he went out in the evening to see what he called a "crony," and we were left to ourselves over the fire. The wind whistled outside, and there was the faint sound of the sea roaring on the beach. It felt safe and cosy in their fussy little sitting-room. I said to Jones:

"Isn't it wonderful to have a refuge like this, and to know it is yours, and that you need never be afraid of a lonely old age any more?"

She said it was, and then, without a pause, began talking about old times at school, and the children, and how touching it had been the way they appreciated anything you did for them, poor neglected little creatures that most of them were. She asked me about the syllabuses we were using now, and how Ernie Brown was getting on with his writing, and whether the Howard child had got the scholarship she needed so badly. The old man came in before we had half finished talking shop.

At ten-thirty prompt he got up, locked all the doors and windows and raked the fire out, and off we went to bed. I lay awake for a long time. I like the sound of the sea. But it makes you feel sad. I could not get it out of my head that Miss Jones, at the bottom of her heart, wished she was back at school. There she had been adequate, and had been able to bask in the satisfaction of doing the thing she had been trained for and had spent so many years in perfecting. I wondered whether, secure in her little married villa, she thought longingly, as she wrestled with an egg-timer in the mornings, of the whistle blowing and her squad of well-behaved children marching past her with anxious looks upward for her approving smile. I wondered whether, in the little sitting-room that she could not keep properly cleaned and dusted, she thought of the classroom with its highly-coloured nature-drawings that the inspector had praised. And I wished with all my heart that that fussy old creature, whose only recommendation was that he wore trousers, had never come into her life at all.

CHAPTER XVI

W H E N W E came back for the summer term we found,
somewhat to our surprise, that Miss Simpson was still
there. She said that the Education Committee were
still disputing over her case and that she could not
be dismissed until they had come to some agreement.

Miss Harford was absolutely freezing to her. She
spoke to Freda only when she had to, and that in the
most distant and impersonal manner. Freda herself
was more amenable than we had ever known her. She
was quiet and sensible, and seemed perfectly happy
and not at all worried about the future. Jenny said
that it was because she was an exhibitionist and that
once she was the centre of attraction she was perfectly
happy and did not need to make any more abortive
efforts to get herself into the public eye. But I thought
this explanation was too easy, and, anyway, she was
not really getting any extra attention at the moment.
We were all far too busy, in the heat of getting the
term's work prepared, to bother about whether she
had walked out of prayers or not.

The curate was out of hospital and was getting no
more brickbats thrown at him because nobody took
any more notice of him. Miss Thornby said that his
congregations had dwindled down to two or three
people of the old guard, her sister among them. Before
the end of the first month of term one of the factories
had re-engaged its staff, and some of the children had

new clothes. They were completely unpractical—the girls' being mostly frilly "Shirley Temple" frocks, and the boys' thin, bright-coloured imitation-wool jersey suits that looked as if they would not wash. However, since nobody was likely to try to wash them, it did not matter much.

"Oh, well. I've got what was coming to me," Miss Simpson announced one morning, about this time, as I came into the staff-room. She showed me a letter on the official paper of the Education Office. It was a formal note requesting her resignation on account of the breach of discipline previously discussed.

"What will you do?" I asked, when I had expressed the necessary commiseration.

"I don't know. No use trying to get another elementary-school job anywhere. The first thing they'd ask for would be my reference from here, and that would finish me before I began. I shall just have to starve."

She seemed extremely light-hearted about it. I did not think it was a pose. She accepted the sympathetic indignation of the others as they came in quite nicely and naturally, and went about for the rest of the day looking as if she had been offered a new job instead of having been thrown out of work altogether.

"You might get a job as governess somewhere," I suggested at dinner-time, trying to be helpful. I did think it was a monstrous piece of injustice that she should have her career completely wrecked because she had acted a little over-dramatically in a matter of conscience, however silly.

"The type of people who employ governesses wouldn't absolutely jump at an elementary school-teacher," she objected. "I haven't been brought up in the right society."

"You'd better try and get a post teaching the children of some Bolshevik peer. There are some."

"My disapproval of his peerage would outweigh my approval of his Bolshevism, I'm afraid."

"You'd better ask Gregory if there are any paid jobs for women agitators, then." I got up to take my boiled egg off the gas-ring. She bent over the table to get on with the books she was marking. Thornby came in and began to fuss round her with offers of attention, as if she had been ill instead of sacked. Freda replied very pleasantly. She certainly had something on her mind.

I had a kind of idea what it was, but I was not sure until one day, shortly afterwards, when her month's notice was nearly up and we were discussing what we should give her for a leaving-present. We were determined that she should have a full ceremony and a presentation just as if she was leaving to be married. We wanted to make this gesture, partly to show the authorities how unjust we thought it was to sack a teacher on such trivial grounds and partly to annoy Miss Harford, who was behaving abominably to her, though you would have thought that, since she had won, she could afford to be generous. Miss Thornby said:

"Listen, do you think we could possibly give her the cheque instead of buying something with it? It would be so much more use to her now she may be really in difficulties about money."

Mrs. Lee said she really didn't see how we could do that. It would be so indelicate.

"Surely she'll be able to get some sort of job—if it's only in a little country school."

"I think—and I told her so too—that I thought the curate ought to use his influence to get her into a church school, since he was the real cause of her losing this job," Miss Thornby remarked.

"What did she say to that?"

"Oh, something about her having acted of her own free will and nobody else being to blame. But I said I had a very good mind to speak to him about it."

"Then what did she say?"

"She just laughed."

"She wasn't indignant?"

"Oh no. Why should she be? I was only trying to help her," said Miss Thornby innocently. Mrs. Lee chimed in to say that she thought it was a very good idea and only right. I thought Thornby was quite capable of doing it.

So she was, too. The curate came up one morning, two or three days later, and had a row with Miss Harford. I heard them arguing hammer and tongs when I went past her door taking my children out to drill. At midday they came out, both looking self-conscious and freezing, as people do when they have been losing their tempers with each other. She said good-morning to him in dismissive fashion, but he answered that he was going to stay behind to speak to Miss Simpson. She pursed up her lips and looked as if she would have liked to have thrown him out, but he was a difficult subject to browbeat. He just glared back at her and stayed where he was. Then he saw me across the hall and came to speak to me. I murmured:

"Have you been up on the mat? And don't you pity

the children who are sent to her for bad behaviour now?"

"Oh, I do. I'm thinking of starting a movement among them to unite against tyranny and overthrow it."

"They do pretty well without you," I said, scowling at the Hunt child who was spitting on his finger and drawing pictures on the glass panel in defiance of rules.

"In the Hunts I acknowledge my superiors," he admitted. "Their technique is perfect. Where I fling myself against the law, and get bruised in vain, they calmly ignore its existence and go on their way without it."

When I had asked after his injuries I said:

"Have you come up to see what you can do for Freda?"

"Yes. The little one—Thornby—wrote to me. I had no idea she'd been in trouble with the Office. I think it's absolutely scandalous."

We moved slowly across the hall to Freda's classroom. The last few children were drifting out to the playground. Freda looked up and smiled at us through the panel. I left him and went to have my lunch.

There were only Miss Thornby and Mrs. Lee and I at lunch. I wondered what had happened to Jenny. I was just going to tell her that her egg had been in the water for twenty minutes when Miss Thornby stopped me.

"I think she'll come when she's ready, Madge."

"Why? Of course she won't. She's forgotten the time."

"I think she's busy." Thornby was looking absolutely full of cunning and self-importance. I stared at her.

"Thornby, what are you trying to get at?"

"Nothing. Only I think Miss Lambert would rather not be interrupted."

I was incredulous. But when Jenny came in at last for lunch, singing to herself, I remarked:

"You always do that when you're pleased with yourself."

"Nonsense. I was only practising the song I'm going to teach my class to-day."

Thornby very obviously changed the subject from Jenny, and began to talk about the big party Mr. McCarthy was giving to celebrate the opening of the new factory. He also had an idea about raising the standard of living in the district and was collaborating with the *Bronton Echo* to award a prize for good housewifery.

"Isn't it a nice idea?" said Miss Thornby. "It's to be given to someone quite poor, and the committee is going round to judge all the houses during the week before, and then they'll give the prize at the factory-opening ceremony."

"Poor old Freda will be gone by then," said Jenny. "I asked her if she would stay with me for a week or two until she finds something, but she seems to want to get out of the place as quickly as she can."

We were all being as nice as we could to Freda. I had never liked her so much before. When you feel that someone is being unjustly treated I think you naturally incline towards them, and if they behave, as Freda was doing, extremely well under the injustice, you get more indignant still, and they get more congenial still. Freda's present was mounting up to quite a handsome sum, and we had decided, after all, to give her the cheque.

But after that day she began to go back a little to her old manner. We thought that the strain of not knowing what was to become of her was telling on her nerves and redoubled our efforts. On her last afternoon we made up our minds to give a little party for her in the staff-room after the children had gone home. We asked Miss Harford to it, but she refused and said that she thought it was very unsuitable of us to have arranged it.

However, we were feeling so defiant—and, after all, they could not dismiss a whole staff, whatever we did— that we all let our classes out early so that we could get the tea ready. Miss Harford swept out of the school without even saying good-bye to Freda, and we all laughed very heartily about that. I have never known the staff-room so united as it was that afternoon. Two little girls stayed behind to help with the tea. Miss Thornby and I had planned it and we had had great fun making the arrangements.

When Freda came into the staff-room, with her belongings in an untidy pile tied up with string, everything was ready. She stopped in the doorway in amazement. The tablecloth was a banner—borrowed from Gregory's club—with "Down with Tyranny and Fascism" across it in huge letters. There was a cake in the middle of the table with "Religious Toleration for Atheists" inscribed shakily on it in red icing and a red flag stuck on top of it. As she came in Jenny began to thump out the *Internationale* on the school piano. Freda was a little confused at first and then she began to laugh and say that if her activities hadn't been brought to an untimely close it would have been easy enough for her to convert us all to Bolshevism.

We all sat down, and I handed Freda a hammer and sickle to cut the cake. We had borrowed the hammer from the caretaker, and my class had made the sickle in Handwork lesson out of a sheet of tin. It was a good thing that no inspector had come in, though I had a story ready that we were illustrating the parable of the wheat and the tares. Freda cut the cake with the sickle and hammered it in while we all clapped. Miss Thornby poured out the tea while Freda handed the cake round. It was a merry party for us. "It must not be good-bye, Miss Simpson," Mrs. Lee was saying, as she cut her cake into ladylike slices. "You must be sure and come to stay with us as soon as ever my husband comes back from abroad and we have moved into our new house."

Freda said she would love to.

"And with us—me, I mean," cried Jenny. She had been as nice as she possibly could be to Freda lately. I wondered if she only found her congenial because she was going.

"No, thank you," said Freda.

It was a jarring note. There was an uneasy silence, and I tried to restore the spirit of harmony by saying that perhaps she had better come and stay with each of us in turn. But it was not successful. Jenny stared at her, looking hurt and bewildered. "What's the matter, Freda? Have I said something to annoy you?"

"No," answered Freda indifferently.

We broke into conversation to cover it up. But Jenny and Freda sat looking at each other steadily, like a couple of dogs who are working up to a fight.

"What reason have you to be so chilly to me?" asked Jenny, as if none of the rest of us were there.

"It's not intentional. I haven't any quarrel with you. You just don't come into my life at all."

"Then why do you speak to me like that? Why do you say so pointedly that you wouldn't come and stay with me?"

"It's just that your charm doesn't happen to work with me—that's all. I wouldn't trouble to dislike you. I'm quite indifferent."

"Oh no, you're not. Something's the matter, and it's no use pretending it's not," cried Jenny fiercely.

"Couldn't you forget the quarrels you've had this afternoon?" Mrs. Lee was beginning officiously, when Jenny broke in:

"Oh, all right, all right. Let it pass. It's an innocent enough remark to begin such a storm."

"Have you made any plans, Freda?" I asked quickly, anxious to change the subject. She answered composedly that she was going to share a house with a friend.

"Where?"

"Earlham."

"In Earlham? Anywhere near the college? I forgot you were there. Is it anyone I know?" said Jenny, trying to hold out the olive-branch.

"I don't know who you do know."

"Oh, good God," cried Jenny impatiently. "I think I'd better go home. I'm obviously spoiling the party for Freda, though what I've done to annoy her so I've no idea."

"That's a point that you've never given much consideration to, isn't it?" remarked Freda sweetly. She was beginning to flush up, from the bit of skin I could see at the neck of her blouse upwards. She was obviously spoiling for a fight.

"It seems that the fact of my existence annoys you, but I can't be expected to lie awake at night over that."

"If you never had existed, or, alternatively, were a little less of a hard-boiled gold-digger, two or three people would not have had their lives spoiled."

Jenny ceased to be angry and began to giggle.

"You make me sound like a *femme fatale* instead of a respectable school-teacher. Don't be silly, Freda. You know that the only ruined life to my credit is the policeman who twisted your wrist, and you ought to be jolly glad about that, though he's recovered himself with a speed that is downright insulting."

"Of course, you think only in terms of men."

"Well, I don't have any passionate love-affairs with women, so what would you?" said Jenny lightly. She made the statement flippantly and without hidden meaning, I think, but Freda rose to her feet and said:

"How dare you? Just because I have a very good friend who your promiscuous immorality has ruined you insinuate filthy things like that?"

"Who—what?" gasped Jenny, staring at her as if she had broken into a foreign tongue.

"Your precious paramour—who his wife loved as you can't visualise anyone really loving—was taken away from her by you first—just because you couldn't wait until you had a man of your own to seduce. You do these things and forget them. But people not quite as shallow as you can't go from man to man quite as easily."

"Oh—the professor," I said involuntarily. It had

suddenly dawned on me what it was all about. Miss Thornby and Mrs. Lee sat there, with their half-eaten cake on their plates, looking from one of us to another as if they thought we had all suddenly gone crazy.

"You side with her, of course," cried Freda, turning on me. "You would. You think she can't do anything wrong, don't you? Just because she's got a pretty face. You never think what damage she may do someone who is really faithful and unselfish—too much so to employ her methods."

"If you mean Judith," I said. "I don't think——"

"What do you know about Judith?" Jenny broke in.

"I know a great deal. She happens to have been a friend of mine for years—since college."

"Was that what you thought I meant when I said something about love-affairs with women? Because I assure you—this is the first I've heard of it."

"I don't care what you meant or what you think. But your fancy lover liked so much the taste of promiscuity that he learned under your expert tuition that now he's settled down to it altogether, and she's heart-broken, though I know that expression is just a joke to you, since you've never had any feeling stronger than dashed vanity because you've let a man slip through your fingers—and fear that you'll be caught out, you beastly little coward."

"You sent me that anonymous letter," said Jenny slowly, more in surprise than anger.

"How could she have done? No one knew what was happening beside yourself and me," I said to her irritably.

"Don't you see? Judith knew about us all the time and just pretended not to, in case he should think she was spying on him. I remember I wondered when she said something about being at the sea when we were on the moors."

"Lying among the heather sun-bathing, I don't think," muttered Freda vindictively. But it was she who blushed, not Jenny.

"Were you spying on us?"

"You think that stings," remarked Freda calmly, though still red in the face. "But where it's a question between someone like you and someone like Judith I'd do more than that."

"Ugh," said Jenny. "You ought to have been a policewoman. You've got just the kind of gifts."

"But look here," I put in, because my head was reeling and I wanted to get things straightened out. "You got that letter just at such an appropriate time——"

"A lucky guess," said Freda calmly.

"But the circular?"

"That frightened you, didn't it?" Freda sat down at the table and looked triumphantly up at Jenny. "Do you think I didn't see you were worried? and having seen you at Wilton I could guess why all right. I thought you'd have the guts to get out of it some way yourself—marry another of your fancy men and then you'd be out of Judith's way. But you went whining to him with your troubles. I misjudged you. I thought even you would be too proud to do that. But you needn't think you've got away with everything. There are some things you don't know about men—even you. And you'll find out that what you've done will wreck your marriage though your own memory is so conveniently short. Other people's aren't."

"Whose marriage?" I turned to Jenny, completely perplexed.

"I was going to wait till Freda had gone. I thought she might be a bit upset about it——"

Freda began to laugh. Her shoulders shook and her voice rose. Miss Thornby got up quickly, took a jug and ran out to the tap for cold water. But when she came back she stood hesitating, doubtful whether or not to use it, for Freda was only crying now, and saying through her tears:

"You thought I might be upset! Oh—God—the little harlot begins to suspect that other women may have feelings! What a miracle—wonders will never cease! You thought I might be upset."

"Let's get this straight," I said. I was beginning to have a headache. "Who's marrying who?"

But Jenny picked up her bag, took her cap from the peg, and saying, "I'm going home. Sorry the party's been upset. Good-bye, Freda," slipped out of the door. We were left looking foolish and uncomfortable. We all looked anywhere but at each other. At last Miss Thornby rose too, saying:

"Well, I must go. My sister will be expecting me. Good-bye, Freda dear, and good luck." Mrs. Lee got up with her and leaned over Freda, patted her shoulder, and murmuring:

"I know so well how you feel. Women like that—I've suffered it too," marched out with a tragic air. Freda and I were left alone. I was only staying because I had the cheque in my jersey-coat pocket, with the envelope inscribed with facetious messages. They did seem foolish now when I remembered them. I wished I had not been left to do the dirty work of getting rid of them.

At last I said:

"Shall I tell the children they can come and clear up?"

"Not for a minute." Freda sat up and began to dab her eyes.

"Have another cup of tea?"

"No, thank you. It's cold and stewed."

I remembered that I had some cigarettes in my bag. We were not allowed to smoke on school premises, but I thought it would be a good idea for calming Freda down. She took one and puffed at it uncertainly. I do not think she often smoked.

I remarked conversationally, "I expect it would do us much more good if we used cigarettes as dope instead of all this tea-drinking and aspirin-swallowing."

"I daresay. We ought not to need either really."

"Cook used to say it was along of the life we led."

"Everyone thinks that—that we must be raging masses of nerves because we aren't married."

"Yes," I said encouragingly. We were getting on towards the point I had meant to lead up to.

"You think I've made an awful fool of myself, Madge."

"Oh no," I murmured insincerely.

"It was idiotic of me. But it's all been boiling up for such ages that it had to come out sometime. I must say I feel better in a way now that it has, though a bit limp. It's that woman's magnificent unconsciousness that got me down—her complete inability to comprehend that even if she feels nothing other people may. I could have borne it if she'd boasted of her achievements. I could have borne it if she'd been unhappy. But to turn up here day by day, cheerful, unconcerned and unconscious—I couldn't stand it. My God, it must be magnificent to have a hide as thick as hers and no heart whatever underneath—no capacity either to suffer or be very happy—just a dead level of animal spirits. Asking me—*me*—if I'd go and stay with them when they were married."

"I suppose you mean she's marrying Gregory?"

"Didn't you know?"

"No."

"Marvellous. I suppose she was so indifferent about it that she didn't even bother to tell you."

"I suppose it was you who first put him on her track?"

"Yes. I thought, knowing her, that a good-looking young parson might be able to head her off getting Ronnie to divorce Judith. That's what I was terribly afraid of—in a way. But now it's happened. And I've done all the things I did, and was glad to do for for Judith's sake, however beastly they were at the time—all for nothing. And to crown it all I've got the satisfaction of knowing that I first introduced Jenny to Bill—to Gregory."

"Freda, I don't want to pry into your feelings" (but I did), "but are you very fond of that ridiculous—of him?"

"I can't tell you how fond."

I considered her. During my brief set of visits to the cinema I had made acquaintance with Greta Garbo. Jenny had told me she was marvellous because she managed to hide such seas of feeling. I thought that it would be easy enough to be a great actress if you only had to tell people that you were seething underneath and then look just a little worried so that everyone

315

said how self-controlled you were. I wondered if Freda
was a little in that line.

"Of course you have the same views," I remembered.

"We feel exactly the same about everything that
matters. We have both been proud to suffer for what
we believed in. When I was sacked—he had told me
that even if you were an atheist you could still be horrified at the blasphemy of religious people—and I didn't
tell him about my dismissal notice because I'd done
that. I thought that when he did find out his—his sym-
pathy would be all the nicer. And then he falls for a
pretty face without a brain behind it—without a
capacity for sharing his feelings—without a single idea
in common with him. It's—it's disastrous."

"It's very bad luck indeed for you," I said soberly.
However much she felt, or thought she felt, I did see
that. I supposed that she had built up a wonderful
imaginary happy ending with his marrying her because
she had given up everything for the principles they
shared. But it was a plan that was too like Freda herself—on too rarefied a plane for everyday use. I
thought that she would have to come abruptly down to
earth now that she was out of work and penniless. That
reminded me.

"Freda, we were going to give you a leaving-present
and then we thought it would be better if you bought
something for yourself, as you're moving and so on,
and don't want to be cluttered up with ornamental
clocks and things. Here it is." I thrust it into her hand
and waited, bracing myself for another embarrassing
scene. But Freda took it, looked at it carelessly and
put it in her pocket.

"Oh—thanks. I suppose they think money can comfort one in any misery," she said, and got up to collect her things. I felt a little dashed.

"I hope you find a new job soon."

"I'm going to live with Judith. She and I are going to start a modern, co-educational, self-governing school."

"You'll be in your element," I said, as nicely as I could. But to myself I said, Poor children. They'll educate them into such a state of idealism that they'll be no more fit to cope with ordinary life than either of themselves. And I was extremely thankful that my job stopped at teaching children Arithmetic and Writing and did not include Laughing and Grief, Ambition, Distraction and Derision.

It was a glorious summer. There was one blazing hot day after another. We used to draw the blinds in the classroom so that the pale shadow fell in patterns across the rows of children and divided their little white faces —now beginning to take on a faint tinge of brown— into light and dark. A girl straight from college came to take Freda's place. She was very ignorant and amateurish and we all had to spend spare time helping her with her syllabuses and register. But I did not dislike having her about. She was a pleasant reminder that, however else I might have wasted the last ten years, I had at least acquired some sense and some confidence at my work.

The factories merrily recruited men and the town began to hum with the prelude to activity. The opening day of the big factory—Mr. McCarthy's pet model factory—was to be the great festival of the summer. All the children were to march in procession, wearing white frocks and carrying paper flowers (I don't know why), and then there was to be a free tea for them in the factory garden and games afterwards. McCarthy had great ideas about being an enlightened employer, and had taken the waste ground near the factory to make into a kind of garden for the workers to wander about in during their lunch-hour. I wondered if he knew that the public-houses were open at that period. It is funny how people who do not drink themselves always imagine that the smallest counter-distraction will tempt the ones who do away from it. However, he undoubtedly meant well.

On the day of the ceremony I called for Jenny an hour early and suggested we should lunch in Higher Bronton on the way down. I was feeling stupid and sentimental about how much I should miss her when she left at the end of term, and wanted to see as much of her as possible. But I found her wearing an old overall and with her room littered with silk and paper patterns. In the middle of the chaos sat Jenny, with furrowed brow, carefully making up the Progress Register for next term that she would never use again.,

"I must get it properly done or the next person will get all the work into the most frightful mess," she explained.

"Isn't it funny to think you'll never use it again?" I asked her curiously.

Jenny said that it was not in the least funny to think of someone like Mrs. Lee wrecking all the work she had done and then saying it was the last teacher's fault. "But I'm in the middle of making some cami-knickers to wear under my new dress this afternoon and I shall never finish them in time," she mourned.

"I'll fill in your book and you can finish your gar-ment," I suggested weakly, knowing very well that it was the suggestion she had been leading up to. Jenny gladly got up and settled down on the floor to fitting lace and measuring ribbons.

"I shan't have any time to do sewing in the holi-days," she observed, with her mouth full of pins. "What are you going to do?"

I told her that I was going to stay with the Dermotts. Mrs. Dermott had written to ask me, and added, in an excited postscript, that Marian was going to be married. I was afraid that I should have to spend my holiday in the same trousseau atmosphere that seemed to have been dogging me for months.

"I'm taking my mother to the seaside for a month," said Jenny. "After that, when I'm married, I'm going to try to blot her out of my life again. She's never taken much notice of me, but now she's dying for me to take Bill home and drag him all round the neighbourhood so that she can boast about her daughter who's married a clergyman. Bill wants to go, too. He likes the lower classes, you know."

"You are a snobbish little beast," I said, ruling off the columns in her Progress book.

"Yes," answered Jenny complacently.

"I can't imagine what Gregory sees in you. You're the absolute antithesis of everything he believes in. You're a horrid little middle-class snob, you're a petty bourgeois reactionary, you're promiscuous and im-moral, you're far too fond of money and the flesh-pots, and you accept everything and give out nothing. How in the world you managed to get off with him beats me, unless he means to spend his life reforming you, and is marrying you as a painful duty he owes to his cloth."

"I expect so," said Jenny, sucking her cotton and hunting about for a needle.

"Another thing I can't understand," I went on, beginning to copy out the syllabus for next term, "is why you're marrying him. You've always referred to him as a tiresome little parson. You'll never be able to live up to either his social or his professional position. You'll get off with his churchwardens and make a public scandal, and I don't suppose you'll even succeed in being monogamous until the end of your honeymoon. Do you imagine you're going to reform?"

"Now there you have hit upon an important point," observed Jenny, holding up the rose-pink cami-knickers and looking earnestly to see if she had got the lace on straight. "In fact, I brought it up some time ago on the very occasion when I told the Rev. that I would like to take up the option on his proposal of last autumn. But he said no, he thought my reforming was too dangerous an experiment and that I had better go on as I was."

"Do you fancy yourself as a clergyman's wife?" I asked thoughtfully.

"You bet I do. It's the answer to my maidenly dream of respectability. You know how I hate the thought of the squalor I was brought up in."

"But clergymen are always terribly poor."

"But very respectable. They get asked to dinner with the bishop."

"If they do, it's the only square meal they get in the year."

"Are you trying to put me off so that you can hook the curate for yourself, Madge? By the way, he's going to spend a week with old Wolfe who used to be curate-in-charge here. You'll only be a few miles away, won't you? So don't go trying to seduce him away from me while I'm doing my duty by my mother."

"It would be only poetic justice if someone did after your goings-on with Simpson," I said. Jenny looked bewildered and got up to machine a seam. I added, because she was so pleased with herself that her happiness was almost irritating: "Anyway, I wouldn't if I could. I don't think he's very attractive to the average woman."

"I daresay," answered Jenny absently. She finished her seam, then pulled off her overall, revealing herself naked underneath. I looked at her critically, but, as usual, her beauty completely disarmed me. In that untidy little room her long, ivory-brown limbs and dark, ruffled hair shone like a gleaming statue forgotten in a dingy store-room. I helped her to pull the pink silk garment over her head, and immediately she seemed to change from the timeless beauty of early womanhood into a pretty little chorus-girl in a state of undress. She fetched an emerald-green frock with a broad white sash from her bedroom and turned into a perfect imitation of a nice girl going out to a garden-party.

We met Thornby on the way down. In her linen costume and gloves she looked dowdy and genteel beside Jenny. There was a crowd trailing up to the factory. Some of the local fathers were there, and they made the usual remarks to Jenny about wishing they were back at school and in her class. She commanded scarcely any respect among the parents. The wives glared at her angrily.

The square before the factory entrance was almost filled before we got there. Miss Harford was on the steps, which were to form a platform for the speakers, and so was the night-school superintendent and the head of the Senior school. Nearby, waiting to go up and join them when the ceremony began, was the local M.P., and a fat old party who was someone from the War Office, and a tall, thin man whom Thornby said was a famous doctor scientist.

"What's his name?" I asked.

Thornby said she thought it was Adams. Then I remembered that he was the one who was always writing to the papers complaining that English women did not have nearly enough children, and that if they went on being so selfish and pleasure-loving there would be practically no British Empire at all in about a thousand years or so. Thornby said he was an acquaintance of McCarthy's and had come down out of compliment to him. A shabby reporter and a shabbier photographer from the *Bronton Echo* were buzzing around him like flies, and he was trying to brush them away.

The children arrived, rather hot and sticky, but very pleased with themselves and the notice they had attracted walking through Bronton in their best clothes. Teddie Hunt had seized the opportunity to be sick, but he was quite unconcerned about it and was looking round for something to cram down his throat in place of what had come up. One of the Sunday-school teachers, who were hanging about looking helpful, provided him with a stick of chocolate. I reflected grimly on the probable consequences. It was very pleasant to see someone else in our place of responsibility for the three hundred.

Presently we were all asked to sing *Jerusalem*. I could not help wondering, when we came to the verse about "dark Satanic mills," whether it was intended to refer to the arms factories or whether they were supposed to be the new Jerusalem. However, the children, who had been forced to learn it during the last week, had not the remotest idea what it was about, so there was no harm done.

The fat old gentleman with Mr. McCarthy then panted up the steps and was delivered a steel key. They had decided, Miss Thornby informed me in a whisper, that a steel key would be more appropriate than a golden one. I muttered back that dynamite to blow the lock open would have been more appropriate still. Jenny giggled and several people murmured "Sh."

The old thing opened the door, looking very pleased with himself, and everybody applauded. Then he made a speech about prosperity, which I could not hear, as I was too far away, and did not much want to, anyway. Then he announced above the summer breeze that carried his words away over the by-pass road, that he would now have the great pleasure to introduce Dr. Adams.

Dr. Adams stood up and started a long preamble about how pleased he was to be there. I began to wish with all my heart that Mr. McCarthy's factory amenities extended to providing seats in the courtyard.

The breeze dropped for a moment and his words came to us, tossed and broken out of their sentences, as if the wind had thrown them into the air and flung them together again like a jig-saw puzzle. He was talking about a great nation and a great heritage. He instanced the things that great women had done for England, from Boadicea to Queen Victoria and Lady Astor. Jenny said aloud that she thought Boadicea was an anti-imperialist and several of the people around us looked so shocked that it was quite evident they thought the term meant something indecent. I yawned, and moved from one foot to another, and wished there was going to be something more than tea to drink. Then I pricked up my ears as I caught something about the *Bronton Echo* and their housewife's prize. I had an idea that whoever had done the judging must have been puzzled to discover anything approaching a perfect housewife in the district.

However, it seemed that he had been one of the judges. It had been a great privilege, he said solemnly, and then something about its being a difficult and delicate matter to choose between so many claimants, which he apparently intended to be humorous, since he stopped and smirked around, and the people on the platform with him tittered dutifully. He began to quote the old bromide about a woman's noblest task being the carrying on of the race, and I knew we were in for ten minutes of his hobby-horse. I nudged the other two, and we drew out of the crowd and went to the back of the courtyard to sit on the brick wall that supported a new iron fence. We whispered to each other about Miss Harford's costume, and hardly noticed what he was saying until he ended up, in a sudden bellow that overpowered the wind so that it seemed to slink away, ashamed and beaten, by saying

"Motherhood!" in capital letters, so to speak, and sitting down.

He got up immediately, however, in response to nudges from his neighbours, and said that he would now have the very great honour to award the housewife's prize—the Woman Citizen's Prize, as he now suggested it should be called, since he and the rest of the judging committee had decided that its original purpose should be slightly amended, and the award given for the encouragement of woman's highest duty to the Empire, rather than the secondary, though also important one. With that, he looked vaguely round him and discovered Mrs. Hunt trudging up the steps towards him, wearing a brand-new violet silk dress and in the family way again. Behind her trailed all the previous little Hunts, now increased to eight. Stanley was carrying the baby who owed its life to Thornby, and Betty, the latest one, who owed its life to the chemist who would not give goods on credit. At the end of the procession, with a modest air of having had nothing much to do with it all, was our erstwhile caretaker, looking absolutely hideous in a striped suit and brown boots.

The applause drowned our laughter. The old party handed Mrs. Hunt a purse and a gilt medal and said something to her, which she appeared to answer in a vein that embarrassed him, for he drew back and looked extremely shocked. The eight little Hunts looked all around them grinning and not in the least shy, acknowledging the noisy appreciation of the fact that they existed as if it had long been their due. Teddie seized the opportunity to be sick again and was hurried off the platform.

We spent the afternoon in a dazed state. I congratulated Mrs. Hunt when I met her in the crowd, and she made a remark to the effect that if it was as easy as that——! I suggested that it would perhaps be unwise always to expect one's efforts to result in a proportionate reward, to which she replied that she did not expect old maids to be able to understand how it was, if I would excuse her saying so, Miss. This piece of courtesy on her part surprised me more than anything that had gone before.

Towards six, very weary and full of indigestible food, I suggested to Jenny and Thornby that we should go home. We left the noisy swarm of human beings and walked down the road to catch a tram. Jenny said she was going to call on her young man.

"Oh—of course. He wasn't there," I remembered.

"Wasn't he asked?" Miss Thornby wanted to know.

"Oh yes. But he wouldn't go. He doesn't approve of it or something. I said I'd bring him a meringue in my pocket if it wouldn't prejudice him to accept the profits of murder and usury."

"What did he say?"

"That he hated meringues."

I could not help wondering what he and Jenny talked about when they were alone together.

"Are you glad you're marrying him, Jenny?" I asked seriously.

"Don't be romantic, Madge. As a matter of fact I'm only doing it because I fancy myself as depriving Mrs. Hunt of her trophy."

Thornby, who had bought an evening paper, was looking critically at the photograph of the Hunt parents and offspring grinning on the front page.

"Just fancy anyone being rewarded with a medal for producing those seven little mischief-makers. The trouble they've caused in the last year——" I remembered something. "By the way, Jenny, are you going to tell Gregory all about you and the policeman and Maggie, or do you think the past should bury its dead?"

"He knows," said Jenny indifferently. "Freda told him just before she left."

"How vindictive of her."

"Oh, I don't know. I suppose I annoyed her. Anyway, it doesn't matter," said Jenny carelessly.

She left us. We watched her out of sight as we waited for a tram. I could understand Miss Simpson's exasperation. To forgive might be one thing. But not even to bleed when wounded, I thought, was quite another, and quite the most irritating characteristic of all, in friend or enemy.

CHAPTER XVII

THE SCHOOL year ended at last. I was so tired that I could not imagine myself ever having any energy again. When the children were at last dismissed and ran off, yelling and whooping, into the smelly streets with their blazing pavements, and I was free to lock up my cupboards and go, I felt too weary even to be glad. I dragged my case down to the tram, hauled it aboard somehow—the conductors never helped me as they did Jenny—and leaned back on the uncomfortable seat, wishing that I need never move again.

The train was hot and crowded. There were sweating children, on their way to the seaside, in the carriage, and I had barely room to open the magazine I had brought to read and no energy to read it. When at last I reached Bellby I was damp and crumpled and suspected that I had a dirty face. I climbed wearily out of the carriage and looked up and down the platform, hoping that they had sent to meet me.

Marian was leaning on the doorpost of the waiting-room, her hands in the pockets of her linen coat. She was dressed in pale-blue and white, and looked cool and detached, as if she was living in a different temperature from everyone else. She came a few steps towards me, called a porter to take my bag, and by her uninterested glance made me feel twice as grubby, sticky and lower-middle-class as before.

"How awfully nice of you to come and meet me," I exclaimed, more gushingly than I had meant to.

"Why?" she asked coolly, opening the car door for me and shutting me in competently.

"Now that you're getting ready to be married and everything, I thought you'd be too busy."

She smiled faintly, let in the gear and swung out of the station yard with that absorbed concentration she bent only on animals and mechanical things. With all my heart I wished I had been her, unconcerned with the everlasting weariness of dealing with unsatisfactory, unresponsive human beings. I felt that if she would only offer me a job as her kennel-maid I would take it gratefully and never hanker after my own work.

We sped along the lanes. The corn was coming to an early, dried-up maturity. I had forgotten the coloured procession of the seasons in my long exile in the town. Through my hot, weary body there seemed to rise a trembling stir of life. Looking back on that day now, I feel as if I must have known that something was going to happen. I don't suppose really that I did. I hardly remember.

There were long, glowing days when only the woods were cool and I used to wander in them by myself. The ground was too hard to ride, and Marian was busy with her red-faced young man. I took novels out, which I never read, but lay looking up through the complicated leaf designs at the burning sky above. There were the cornfields, burning gold, with poppies like splashes of blood scattered among them. Once I found a dead seagull lying on the narrow grass pathway between corn and hedge. I wondered all day long how it had come to stray so far from its own world of cold green sea and end its life amid the alien glory of an inland cornfield.

One day I walked over to Mr. Wolfe's village to see Jenny's Bill Gregory. I found him lying on the burned lawn in front of the rectory writing letters. He seemed glad to see me and said that my coming had saved him from becoming mentally unhinged.

"I feel like Alice," he said, as I sat down on the grass beside him. "You know, 'A dog's not mad, is he? But I growl when I'm pleased and wag my tail when I'm angry. Therefore I'm mad.' Everybody here regards the animals as being so clever for not doing the things I do that I'm slowly coming round to the conviction that I must be the insane one."

"It has rather that effect on me," I admitted. "Only I still spend my time debating as to whether I'm the sane one in an asylum or the crazy one in a sane environment."

"Honestly," he said, "I can't bear it much longer. I'm not allowed to eat anything that the cats might want, nor kick them off my bed if they fancy the eider-down. And to crown it all, Mr. Wolfe assures me that, after a few years in Bronton I too shall turn and live with the animals, they are so placid and self-contained."

"Poor old thing. The stink of humanity was too much for him, wasn't it?"

"And for me," he added despondently.

"You're not beaten?" I said, surprised. I had never seen him humble before.

"Yes, I am. It wasn't when they threw half-bricks and things at me because I told them to turn down the munitions contracts. There was a kind of exhilaration

in that. It was violence and it was action, and you
don't feel beaten while you're alive and suffering. But
it was when I was in the hospital so long with the blinds
drawn down—horrid oily green blinds they were—I
used to lie in bed and debate as to whether it would
be better to rip them into ribbons or throw them on to
an enormous bonfire—and I had nothing to do the
whole twenty-four hours but think what an idealistic
fool I'd been and how laughably I'd failed. Then I
came to my senses and gave up."

"So what are you going to do?"

"I'm going to go on with the comfortable round of
services that are archaic survivals of a social period
when the Church was the life-blood of its people, and
spend hours and hours debating with the Parochial
Church Council as to whether Choral Eucharist smacks
of Popery or is plain Protestant enough for Lower
Bronton. And I shall go out to tea-parties with the
parish tabbies and make mild curatorial jokes which
they'll all titter at very heartily. But at home I shall
have Jenny, and so I shall survive it. And I shall tell
everybody that I don't approve of churchmen interfering in politics."

"Well, I think it's a pity," I said.

"You don't really."

"Yes, I do. You'd be like a bowdlerized version of
Shakespeare."

He sat up and looked at me. "His people were
beaten dreamers, weren't they?"

"Yes. But they either fell on their swords—it must
be difficult, you know, I've often thought, to keep the
thing steady enough while you parked on it—or else
went on facing the insanity of human beings that they

331

couldn't alter. I mean, none of them went off into monasteries or convents or anything, did they?"

There was a long silence while the midges circled endlessly, only stopping now and then to begin a new and agonising attack upon us in a spot they had hitherto overlooked. Presently we saw the old rector looking dazedly at us from the top of the lawn, as if he suspected that we were his guests, but could not place us.

I stayed for lunch with them in the dining-room with its perpetually doggy smell. The animals sat beside us, watching every bite with a savage concentration, so that it was enough to spoil your appetite. The rector kept on giving them bits and pieces of his food. We ignored them as best we could.

Afterwards Gregory walked back with me through the woods. He asked me idly about the rest of the staff, and I told him stories of the staff-room and of their peculiar private lives. He was amused, and began to tell me about his father, who was a fashionable preacher.

"He has a swagger church at St. Jude's-on-Sea," he said. "He has a queue outside his church every Sunday night, and when they get inside he tells them, in his musical, sonorous voice, that God put that view of the bay, with fishing-fleet attached, outside the door for them to enjoy. Service, as you might say. And he tells them that it's up to them to do the polite thing and enjoy it. I've seen them gaping at it when they came out. So, you see, he has his influence, as he says. He wanted me to be his curate. I rather think he fancies me coming back as a prodigal after this dénouement."

"You could always do that."

"No, thank you. Bronton's squalor for me any day."

" 'There was a poore parson, of a town—' " I stopped still, trying to remember it. "Let me see—'He ran not to London, to Saint Paul's, Nor with a brotherhood to been withholde, But dwelt at home and kepte well his folde. But if were any person obstinate, What so he were, of high or low estate, Him would he snybben sharply for the nonys. For first he wrought and afterward he taught.' My father taught it me when I was in the top standard at his school. I hadn't known that I remembered it after so long."

"I'd give something to be in your class, Miss," he said, and turned to look at me in the dusky shade of the trees. "You have a knack of fastening on the one thing in the world that can stimulate a person into tearing up what's done and starting again. I used to read that description a long, long time ago, when I thought that they had only to make me dictator for a day and I'd have the world put to rights before the whistle blew for lunch."

"I wonder why people like you—and I suppose I'm as bad about the children—have this awful passion for trying to rearrange the mental make-up of people that don't want to be rearranged?"

"I don't know. It's like lying ill in an untidy room, isn't it? You feel you'll go stark, raving mad if you don't hop out of bed and pull the tablecloth straight."

"But it's so tiresome of us. When I'm introduced to people—ordinary people like Marian's young man, for instance—I always try to keep my profession a dark secret, because I know that the minute the word 'teacher' is sounded any slight flicker of interest goes flat out of their eyes and they start muttering painfully

that it must be interesting work. Then I can't help
pretending feebly that I'm awfully bad at it really, and
can't keep the little ones in order at all—you know, *so*
madcap and attractive of me. I don't know why people
should think it's so creditable for a teacher to be bad
at her job."

"My friends all seem to think they've offered me the
final compliment when they say I'm not in the least like
a parson. Why does everyone laugh at curates?"

"They think they're in earnest."

"But is that funny?"

"Oh yes. It's a terribly easy target. You can always
get up a feeble giggle about earnestness. People immediately see themselves as dashing cynics beside you."

"Mm. I suppose so. Mind your dress on that
bramble."

"The thing to be, you see, is awfully detached and
fatalistic, like a Greek philosopher, having exclusive
information that the world is rushing to ruin and that
the human race is not worth saving, anyway, even if
anyone could do anything about it, which they can't."

"Is that my only alternative to going on as I was?"

"I should think so."

"Here's your gate, isn't it? I remember old Wolfe
told me, when I said I was thinking of coming to see
you if you weren't too involved with your friends, that
I could get through by the orchard entrance here and
save half a mile."

I left him. I was rather pleased to think that he had
suggested coming to see me. It had been a pleasant
day. For the first week of the holiday I thought it had
been wonderful to be alone. But now, when I was not
so tired, it was fun to talk to someone of my own age.

Marian was so occupied with her wedding arrangements that she did not seem to have any time for me at all.

As I passed by her bedroom door I saw that she was having a review of all her clothes. They were spread over the bed and chairs and hanging in festoons on the door. I stopped and asked her if I could help her to spring-clean.

"I'm just deciding what to take with me and what to throw away," she said. She looked round. "I shall keep all my old riding things, I think. You never know when they'll be useful. But cotton frocks—I can't take them all. I was wondering if you knew of any deserving person in Bronton that I could send them to. Or what about a hospital or somewhere?" she added vaguely.

My eye fell on an apple-green dress with a ruffled white organdie collar and cuffs. It was lying limply over the window-ledge, its belt swinging over the late white roses that hung beneath. Marian followed my glance and said, "That, for instance."

"It's pretty," I said. She looked surprised.

"You can have it if it will be any use to you."

I took it back to my room and tried it on. There was a dark, scratched old mirror. From its smudgy shadows a different person looked back at me—not Madge Brigson at all, but a girl, young, sunburned, eager, in the colours of spring, and the white ruffle hanging down between breasts that were clearly visible as I seemed never to have seen them before.

Gregory called to ask me to go for a long walk with him two days later. Mrs. Dermott had some lunch packed up for us. I think she was rather relieved to

335

be rid of me for a day, because Marian's future-in-laws were coming over and she was involved in preparations for large meals. We set out along the high road and then turned off up a hill path that led to a grey little village high above the valley. He said, as I carefully negotiated the stepping-stones over a stream:

"You know, you do look nice. Like a maiden in an old song-book I've got at home. I used to think she was the most charming woman I'd ever imagined when I was a boy and sang the songs in a squeakly little treble voice."

"It confuses me, you know," I couldn't help saying, stopping on the middle stone to explain myself. "Things like that—being told I look nice—are foreign to me. I'm so green that I don't know what to answer."

He laughed and began to sing:

"Early one mo-orning, just as the sun was ri-ising,
I heard a maiden singing in the va-alley below."

He slipped on the stone and went ankle-deep in the water. I held out my hand to haul him up on to the stone. His hand was dry and warm and hard. When we got to the bank he took off his socks and shoes and left them to dry in the sun. We had our lunch and lay watching the shadow creep across the stones.

"We must look disreputable," I yawned at last, sitting up and beginning to smooth out the green dress.

"Only me. Anyway, what of it? We're on holiday, aren't we?"

"You'll have another holiday, won't you? Your honeymoon."

"Only a week. In London. Jenny wants to spend it among the bright lights."

"Do you?"

"I'm always damped by the fact that they all adver-tise laxatives. They're enough to upset your stomach for a week. But I shall enjoy it."

"I expect so. Were you very surprised to find your-self engaged to Jenny?"

"Simply stunned. I never imagined that I, drab, black-coated worker that I am, should become trans-formed into the husband of anyone on Jenny's plane. She's so beautiful that I'm always expecting to wake up and find that I'm really in a museum, just gaping dreamily at some ancient goddess and wishing I could take it home with me. And everything she does is on the same scale. I mean—it's her careless lavishing of affection on any person who might like it that has landed her in all her difficulties. I couldn't love a per-son who was virtuous only through having their heart tightly locked up in case it should take cold—could you?"

"I can't follow your similes. But I know what you mean about Jenny. It was funny that Simpson's griev-ance against her was that she couldn't feel."

"Was it? Miss Simpson felt strongly about different things, didn't she? You can't help thinking people are chilly if their passions are different ones from yours."

"We must go home," I said. "They will think we're feeble products of city life when they hear that we only got as far as this."

"And when I tell them that I fell in the water."

"That's the joke they like best of all except some-body falling off a horse. That's the funniest thing that ever happened. But the best of all is when somebody falls off a horse into the water. That's ecstasy."

The Dermotts asked him to stay to dinner. He made a good impression, I thought. It seemed that he knew something about rowing. Listening to him being technical and argumentative with Marian's young man, I sympathised a little with Jenny's snobbishness. It seemed to matter that he could become part of their world for the duration of the dinner-hour. I don't know why it should have mattered to me, anyway.

After that he used to call quite often. The Dermotts began to tease me about my "young man." It was silly, but I did not exactly dislike it. After so long of the irritated consciousness that society despised me for my spinsterhood it was pleasant to be temporarily one of the elect.

One night I stayed late at Mr. Wolfe's house and Gregory walked back with me. Our feet rustled loudly through the leaves that had fallen too soon. I said, "It's going to rain before morning." The summer clouds were low and the swallows swooping almost to our feet.

I remember everything about it—how there were a few red blackberries on the brambles and the bracken trembled because some small animal was concealed in it. I remember how there was dust on my shoes and that it gradually rubbed off in the grass. I remember that I was saying to myself all the way: "This is what you have missed. Hold on to it, drink it in, because it will never happen again."

"Oh, listen!" he cried suddenly. "The rain."

We heard it among the leaves before we felt it. Then it came through them, seeming to dodge them wickedly, so that it could pierce, in a hundred tiny, cold spearpoints, on to our arms and necks and through our thin clothes.

"We must run for it," he said, and took hold of my arm.

We ran, gasping and laughing and stumbling in the half-dark. Halfway through the wood there was a little shed, once used by the keeper, but now empty. He drew me in there and said, panting:

"Let's wait till the worst is over."

I stood in the entrance, trying to see the dark sky through the trees. The green dress was dripping wet and clinging to me.

"We shall catch our deaths," he remarked.

"I don't mind."

Suddenly he was close beside me in the darkness. I could feel his breath on my neck. He seized my soaking wet arm in a warm hand.

"Why do you say that?" he asked quietly, but with a kind of breathless eagerness under his tone.

I had not a word to say. I had said it unthinkingly because I had been so happy and excited and felt that the fates could not harm me now.

"Madge, tell me, are you happy with me? Do you love me?"

"I've been very happy," I said. It did not seem to be a moment for considering and giving a reasoned statement.

"Then do you? Because I do, you know. I can't think how I didn't realise it before."

"I think I must," I said slowly, trying to get my head above water in this dream-like sea of unaccustomed feelings. It was not what I had imagined love to be like. It was more like knowing that a very old friend was going away to a far country and never coming back again. Then I felt his arms close round me and

339

was surprised at the hard resistance of a man's chest and the hardness of his lips.

I seemed to be wandering, bewildered, through a whole lifetime of strange sensations. I was Maggie, scampering off to the dark streets, and Jenny, singing gaily to herself as she tidied up her classroom, and Freda, with a burning flame under her sulkiness. All the things that had sickened me in the smoke-darkened town seemed to be burned away and rise transformed from the flames. That dark, hidden menace that evaded me and conquered me in whatever I did had suddenly come out into the daylight and revealed itself, fearful no more. It was as if I had met a river—the same river that stenched under black city archways, flowing clean and sparkling among the green fields, or tumbling over a rocky hillside—caught by the sun so that you could not look upon it.

This was love—this quiet, comforting friendship, making all other ties seem like the casual acquaintance of an hour beside it. This justified the murky vice that sickened me at every meeting, as an eager, affectionate child justifies the dark agony and the blood and pain that carry its existence before them.

"We must get married," he said, and his voice startled me in the gloom.

"But what about Jenny?"

"I'll have to tell her. It seems criminal that she should have to suffer for my idiotic short-sightedness before. But when everything seemed to fall around my ears last spring she seemed the one thing left to me out of the wreck. It was wonderful, but unreal. Now I know that it wasn't a wreck at all, and that this is what I'd always planned and hoped for—a wise friend who turned into a lover. Then I know that it can last for always. You're a familiar dream that's gradually materialised into reality. I always wanted someone like you—strong and honest and gentle. I feel as if I deserved to be lynched for finding out when I'd already started out in the wrong direction. But only started, Madge. Jenny will forgive us when she knows. She knows already what a blundering fool I can be when I set my mind to it. Tell me, what are you feeling? Is this anything like what you'd planned for yourself?"

"It's a thunderbolt," I said. "Look, the rain has stopped."

We went back slowly through the woods. He said he would go to Jenny next day. When we got into the Dermotts', and Marian's young man had offered to drive him home, Mrs. Dermott sent me upstairs to have a hot bath. I was surprised that they were dull enough to be under the impression that it was Margery Brigson, spinster, school-teacher, aged thirty, who had come in again. It was somebody quite different—a woman who I scarcely knew, a woman who was going to be married and have children of her own, and go shopping every day with a basket on her arm—a stranger, with whom my childhood and youth and my ten years' teaching had nothing at all to do. I was surprised, in a dazed way, that I was not more excited.

But it was afterwards, when I was lying in bed, wide awake as if I should never sleep again, that I felt it. Now a hundred hot, burning rivers of excitement were running up and down all over my body and round and round my head. Now I was living every second of the day over and over again and tossing from side to side of the big bed as though I was ill. Now I was trembling and hot and cold at once, and tired and full of energy and thirsty and sick, as if every single feeling of which my body was capable had arranged to meet and romp in the one long moment of that night.

I could not bear it. I got up at last and walked about the corridor and staircase. Behind those closed dark doors were the sleeping bodies of the ones that were the commonplace bodies of my friends in the daytime, now mysteriously suspended in the eternity of unconsciousness. "I can't bear it," I murmured aloud, and laid my head on the cold window-pane, beyond which the rain was beating in ceaseless rhythm.

But I must face it, I thought. Somehow I must pull myself up out of these ecstatic dream-waters and get my feet on the firm ground to which I was accustomed. What use was so much heady delight if my mind was working so vaguely that I could not appreciate it calmly? With what seemed almost a physical effort I summoned all the calm of mind that I had learned to bring to my aid in the last ten years when I was weary and exasperated over the human material that was intangible as quicksilver. I fought down this new, strange dizzy irresponsibility. I closed the door of my senses firmly against the gleaming, dazzling intrusion that had taken possession there. I dwindled down gradually to being myself.

Then came sense. Was it possible that I should accept this incredible thing that had happened to me? Was it possible that I should fall in love, get married, take Jenny's place? With a chill conviction I knew it was not possible.

It was not for Jenny's sake. I was not fond enough of her to sacrifice myself, even if I believed that kind of sacrifice could ever be kept up over years. But it was because the metamorphosis that had overtaken me was not real. The person I had been the last fortnight was not me at all. It was a woman of my imagination—and probably of his, too. I could no more turn into a wife than—than old Jones could.

I thought about Miss Jones. If I rushed into this extraordinary marriage I should be doing exactly as she had done—believing that the old, tinsel-trimmed fairy-tale could come true. And I should find myself left, as she had been, with the shoddy wreck of it left on my hands in the grey light of day.

If I got married because I wanted to remove my reproach among women I should be like Miss Thornby —building up a pitiful façade of romance to impress the gossipers. I had fallen, like Simpson, for the old, unpractical ideal of principles shared. You could not live on that. You could not continue for a lifetime to be a girl in love who had only come to life five or ten years too late in the last few weeks.

For I was a woman now, mature, fixed in my ways, trained from my childhood in the school house for this one job. Mrs. Hunt might be honoured among women before me. Idle, thieving, uncontrolled, a murderess but for want of a shilling, a grateful State gave her gold medals for the one thing she could do. But I, if I did not grasp at illusion, could go on steadily with my task and know that, however the world mocked, I was doing the part that I could do to heal the sickness of the world. This was reality—that I should go on day by day, hour by hour, controlling the weariness of the flesh in order that some child whom I should never see come to maturity might be a little better, a little stronger, a little clearer of mind, a little more fitted to cope with the world that should not beat me into accepting its values.

I had wished to come down to earth. Now I was there, and it was just as dreary as it ever had been in its flat familiarity.

I went back to my room, switched on the light, and found my fountain-pen. I sat down at the table and began to write. "Dear, Now I am wide awake, and not confused any more with the astonishing happiness of knowing you loved me. And now I know that it is impossible for us to get married. When I say that I'm not the marrying kind I mean that I have grown up now into someone who can't change their outlook because of one happy fortnight. Please don't try to persuade me out of it. I shall not change, and it will only mean that we quarrel and spoil the memory of what we have had. I'm determined not to let that happen, and by the time you get this I shall have gone away, without leaving an address, and shall not write to you or see you again until you are married to Jenny. You must do as you think best about telling her. I shall never speak of it. I think it would be foolish to spoil the possibility of her own life-happiness as well as yours by ill-timed heroics. She will not alter towards you because of what has happened. I know her and I know that. She came to you in your worst failure, as you came to her in hers. Neither of you will be marrying an imaginary paragon. If you break off with her because of this I think you'll deserve, not only to be unhappy yourself, but to see her unhappy too, through your fault. I'm not, of course, being tiresome and self-sacrificing about this. I don't want to get married. You must believe me. I hope you won't repent too much about me. You have done so much for me. You've opened my eyes so that I feel as if I could look at the world steadily now and be wise where I was foolish before. Yours, Madge."

I looked at the time. It was four o'clock. I remembered that at five o'clock the cowman got up. I sat by the window and waited. When I heard him stirring I put a coat over my dressing-gown and went out into the yard. He grinned stupidly when he saw me and it took seven minutes' explanation and seven and sixpence in cash before he gathered that he was to take the note over to Mr. Wolfe's as soon as he had had his breakfast—neither sooner nor later.

I went back to bed and slept soundly. When I heard the breakfast gong through my dreams I was afraid to wake because I thought I should be left with the dreary ruins of yesterday's coloured hours to face in the daylight.

But it was not so bad. The rain had ceased and the sweet smell of the wet garden filled the room. I was going back to school next week. And now I could settle down to the life I had chosen, perfectly content with the secret knowledge that I had been offered this thing that all women pitied me for missing and had refused it. I would be myself, but stronger now that the weak link in my self-knowledge had been replaced by a new strength. I felt humbler, less arrogant, and yet I knew that I should not again make the mistakes I had made in ignorance. The world I thought I knew had shifted round so that I saw it whole.

I made my apologies to Mrs. Dermott, caught an early train to the south, and took a small room in a cottage near old Jones, so that in the afternoons, when she was free of her exacting duties, we could go for walks by the sea together.

September. There are new faces in my class, new faces in the staff-room, new babies in the infant-class. The whistle blows, they march in orderly rows and line up for prayers. Registers are marked in identical red strokes, with black noughts added half an hour later—neither more nor less. Books are given out, taken up, we march into the yard for drill, have singing in the hall and tea in the staff-room at break. And beyond our little island of order and quietness, where the three hundred voices hum with the steady monotony of bees in a hive, is the maze of mean streets and dark yards swarming up to the green-painted fence like the jungle round an outpost of civilisation. Day by day we take them one more tentative step on the difficult and dangerous path to maturity. There may be an Adolf Hitler or a Joseph Stalin staring at me from those orderly rows. There may be a poet who will never be forgotten while men still use human speech. There may be a scientist who will draw stars from their courses and make a suburbia of the mysterious universe. But long before then I shall have forgotten their faces, lost the sense of their personalities, and even their names in the register will have vanished as though they had been written in sand.

THE END